T0367539

For All Time

Third book in The Sweet Ever After Series

Elaine E. Sherwood

FOR ALL TIME
THIRD BOOK IN THE SWEET EVER AFTER SERIES

This is a work of fiction. All of the characters, names, incidents, organizations, and dialogue in this novel are either the products of the author's imagination or are used fictitiously.

iUniverse books may be ordered through booksellers or by contacting:

iUniverse
1663 Liberty Drive
Bloomington, IN 47403
www.iuniverse.com
1-800-Authors (1-800-288-4677)

ISBN: 978-1-4917-8372-6 (sc)
ISBN: 978-1-4917-8373-3 (e)

Print information available on the last page.

iUniverse rev. date: 12/07/2015

Dedication

I want to dedicate this book to my Golden Retriever, Olyvia. Some of you may say that's a stupid thing to do. It won't matter to her, she won't even know.

The "Olyvia" in this book is based on the real deal; the real Olyvia. Let me tell you a little story about her.

We were at an event in Wisner Park in downtown Elmira. There were lots of people milling around and Olyvia, being a very social dog, was in her glory. A man walked toward us and Olyvia's tail immediately went into high gear. The man was ragged and filthy; probably homeless. Olyvia dragged me up to him. I had to breathe through my mouth just to stand next to him.

He dropped to his knees in the middle of the street and put his arms around her. She licked his face and tried to sit on his lap. It wasn't long before she was on her back with her feet in the air so he could give her a belly rub, which he did enthusiastically. I wish you could have seen the look on that man's face...

This is called *unconditional love*. There are a lot of people out there who call themselves "Christians" who could learn a lot from my dog.

Oh, and by the way, when I told her I had dedicated the new book to her she was so happy she rolled on her back so I could give her a belly rub.

Olyvia with a nursing home resident.

Acknowledgements

T hanks to all my friends and family who keep reading my books and encouraging me to keep writing.

Adam Sherwood, Linda Burroughs, Brenda Weigel and Linda Bennett; thanks for your in-put.

David Ripley and everyone from Studio 1262 Dance Academy; you're the best.

And Jack Tidlow, my dance partner and friend, thank you so much.

Thanks to my dog, Olyvia. She's the best dog ever to walk on four legs.

Prologue

Luke Peterson, K-9 officer for the Cedarville Police Department and head of security for Peterson Enterprise, sat in his office with his feet up on the desk. It was a month before the wedding. He had never been prone to day dreaming, but the thought of the honeymoon with his soon-to-be wife, Theresa "Tess" O'Shay, made his body tingle and his mind wander.

The loud ringing of his phone jerked him out of his revelry. It was Bruce Watson, fellow officer and good friend.

"Get Butch and meet me at 124 Spring St. We have a homicide and a missing, injured three-year-old little girl. Luke, it's a bad one."

Chapter 1

Emma Page was the only child of a very conservative preacher. In her house, the rules were laid down and her father, Reverend Thurmond Page, expected obedience without question or discussion.

No movies, no dancing, no smoking, no male friends, no shorts... No fun in Emma's mind. She chaffed under all the rules and the harsh discipline that followed if she didn't comply. As time went by, and Emma got older, she resented her parents more and more.

Thurmond Page was a bully; albeit a well-dressed, well-spoken bully. Her mother was weak, fearful and submissive, just the way Thurmond demanded she be. He knew where to slap and pinch so that no marks showed. Belittling and degrading worked with his wife, but only made Emma more and more angry as time went on. On the outside, they appeared to be a lovely family. It was all a charade.

Emma's only goal in life became to get out from under her father's thumb. She didn't want someone telling her what she could and could not do all the time. Rebellion blossomed.

At fourteen she began sneaking out of the house on Friday nights to meet some of her friends from church - who were also sneaking out. She hid clothes in the shed out back: skinny jeans, a crop top, flip-flops and a short denim jacket.

After all, she didn't want to look like a geek when she went out. It hadn't been hard to take clothes from the boxes of things people brought in to send to the "pagans in Africa," no matter how inappropriate the clothes were for people living in Africa.

What hypocrites, Emma thought disgustedly. *They don't care anything at all about people in Africa. They just want to get a break on their income tax for charitable giving. And, oh, how pious and spiritual they look.*

Her own father couldn't stand black people, although you would never know it by listening to his sermons. Poor people, dirty people, illiterate people, Hispanics, Asians, drug addicts, hookers, gays... all the same in his book. Worthless. But God loves them so fortunately, he didn't have to. He never said those words outside his own house, however, the attitude was there if anybody bothered to notice.

Chapter 2

They were basically good kids who got together on Friday nights. Nothing was stolen. Property wasn't destroyed. Most of the kids were like her; tired of over bearing parents and church. They all went to Sunday School, church and youth group together so these escapades weren't really wrong, or that's what Emma told herself. It was like an extension of youth group, wasn't it?

A good share of their time together was spent discussing what they hated about their very strict, non-responsive parents and the church in general.

"I don't see what's wrong with going to the movies. I know my dad watches them in his study. What does he think, I'm deaf or something?" Emma complained.

A chorus of agreement followed.

"And clothes. What the heck is wrong with the ones we're wearing right now?" Emma's friend Janice stated emphatically.

"I think all you ladies look hot," Brian interjected.

And on the discussion went. Each person present got to state his or her grievances and received support from the group.

A few cigarettes were passed around; it made them feel very grown up. Some heavy petting went on; the boys were always very accommodating. No one had gone "all the way," at least not yet. As they experimented and talked, they made decisions about what they thought life was like in the real world.

When she turned sixteen, Emma's father allowed her to take a part-time job working at the local grocery store. She was not allowed to work at any time when the church doors were open, a rule that was made very clear to her boss by her father.

If something was going on at church, she was to be in her appointed spot sitting beside her mother on the front row of the New Community Christian Church in Cedarville, VT. The name of the church had been changed with the advent of the new pastor, Reverend Page.

Now at age seventeen Emma felt very grown up and ready to go off to college in the fall, a religious one of course. It hadn't been her choice. She would go where she was told. Besides, her father was paying for it and at least she would be out of the house! She was excited about making new friends and not having to sneak around so much to have a little fun.

All the money she earned, except for the ten percent owed to the church, went into a savings account. She had opened the account in one of the local banks; not the one where her father did business. It was one of the little secrets she kept from her parents. She had amassed a fortune. Four hundred and sixteen dollars and twenty-seven cents.

Chapter 3

Emma had met Otis at the grocery store. He was handsome, charming, charismatic...and black. Picking out a ripe melon seemed to be a challenge for him so when he asked Emma for help, she was flattered.

Over the ensuing weeks, Otis came in a lot. Emma was positive he came just to see her. She suspected he was older than she, but that didn't matter. A plan began to take shape in her mind. A plan that was sure to cause her father to blow a gasket. Getting even. That's what it was all about.

Thurmond Page wasn't the only actor in the family. Emma could put on her "innocent, good girl" persona when she needed to. *I learned from the best*, she thought as she put her plan into motion.

Emma asked her parents if she could bring her new friend to church, then to dinner with the family. With much huffing, hawing, theatrics, lectures and posturing, her father finally agreed.

When she and Otis walked into the church foyer, amid whispers and stares from other church-goers, her father's back was toward them. His booming, albeit fake, laughter could be heard throughout the church as he vigorously shook hands with his head usher.

She justified her actions by focusing on what her father always said from the pulpit about loving your neighbors. "God loves everyone no matter what race or color. Should we do any less? We are all equal in God's sight." and blah, blah, blah...

Knowing how he really felt, she wasn't at all surprised by her father's reaction when she introduced him to Otis. Inside, she was doing her happy dance. Outside, she slipped seamlessly into her naive, innocent act.

"Dad," she said uncertainly. "This is my friend, Otis Williams. Otis, this is my father."

With barely concealed loathing on his now beet red face and with the vein in his forehead pulsing, he stared at Otis.

All conversation around them stopped. People quietly backed away from the scene playing out before their eyes. Emma watched her father closely. *Perfect*, she thought. *This is perfect. He's ready to explode! And in front of his adoring congregation.*

Hesitantly, Otis stuck out his hand.

"It's a pleasure to meet you, Reverend Page, Sir."

Quickly regaining his composure, after all he had an image to maintain, Thurmond shook the pre offered hand. It was plain to see he desperately wanted to wipe his hand on his suit jacket afterward, but...his image...

Chapter 4

Without saying a word, the good reverend turned on his heel and strode down the aisle toward the pulpit at the front of the church. The choir began swaying and singing as if nothing out of the ordinary had happened, although everyone was acutely aware of the tension in the building.

Emma sat next to her mother, as usual, with Otis on her other side. He was the only black face in the church. It was uncomfortable to say the least. The perfunctory hymns were sung, the offering collected, the prayers...recited. The official meet and greet time was strained. No one greeted Otis.

The sermon that followed offered nothing to alleviate the situation. Pacing back and forth in front of the choir box, waving his Bible like the sword he claimed to believe it was, Thurmond Page offered up a true "fire and brimstone," ear-singeing sermon. Sinners would burn in the fires of hell. There was no escape except through repentance and on and on, punctuated by glares at Emma and Otis.

After the closing prayer, Reverend Page headed straight for his daughter. All eyes were discretely turned away as the congregation hurried toward the exit. But it was impossible not to hear what was being said.

"Take your...friend...and leave this minute through the side door. You have embarrassed me enough. I will deal with you at home. And you!" he said as he jabbed his finger at Otis. "Get out of my church and out of my sight."

With that said, the good reverend stomped toward the church foyer and into the waiting arms of his concerned and consoling parishioners. His wife followed a few steps behind, torn between being loyal to her husband or supporting her daughter.

Otis quickly turned away and headed for his car, leaving Emma standing by herself. *I guess dinner's off,* he muttered to himself.

On cue, tears filled Emma's eyes. This part was sticky. Her reaction to what her father said had to be believable. As she started out the side door, Mrs. Rimsky caught her arm. How the old lady had gotten from the back pew to the side door so quickly surprised Emma. She hadn't anticipated anyone taking her side.

Mrs. Rimsky was a pillar of the church having been there long before the instillation of Reverend Page. She was old, very old, as evidenced by her face that resembled a road map. Tufts of steel gray hair stuck out from under the hat she always wore to church.

Her liver-spotted, wrinkled hand shook as she tenderly cupped Emma's cheek.

"God is not like your father, my child," she whispered just loud enough for Emma to hear.

Emma saw great compassion in the washed out blue eyes. Mrs. Rimsky turned and hobbled away leaving Emma feeling a little guilty about what she had done.

There had never been any love lost between Reverend Page and Mrs. Rimsky. She had seen the arrogance and the fake humility at his first interview with the church board. *I never did like that man, God forgive me, and now I know why,* she thought as she left the church, avoiding the obligatory conversation at the door with the pastor. Besides, several members of the church board were hovering around him in fervent conversation. He certainly wouldn't miss her.

Chapter 5

"How could you do this to me, Emma? He's black for God's sake! You march him into my church like it's okay for a white girl to be with a black man. What is the matter with you?" her father screamed in her face.

"But, but, but, Daddy." Emma stuttered. "You have always said we're all equal in His sight. We are, aren't we, Daddy?"

"That's for church!" he shrieked. "This is MY house and I make the rules for my family."

The tirade went on and on until Emma finally bolted for the bathroom upstairs. Her mother could hear her gagging and retching. Facing her father's wrath had been worse than she had expected.

Winifred Page, Emma's mother, busied herself in the kitchen getting lunch ready. She wanted no part of what her husband was putting her daughter through. Silent tears ran down her cheeks.

I should do something; stand up for my daughter. But I'm a coward. Thurmond would make me pay later... What kind of mother am I? Her hands trembled as she set the table.

Emma never reappeared for the rest of the day.

Chapter 6

E mma tossed and turned all night. Guilt was a foreign emotion to her. She certainly didn't know what to believe any more. The church was full of hypocrites, her father being the biggest of all. Maybe it would help if she could talk to Mrs. Rimsky.

As the sunshine crept through her window, her final prayer to God was that he send Mrs. Rimsky to her; somehow, some way. He was God after all. Able to accomplish anything.

Days turned into weeks and Mrs. Rimsky never came. Emma sank lower and lower into despair. Her father didn't speak to her at all. Her mother drifted through the house like an uneasy spirit and the people from church pointedly ignored her. Her eighteenth birthday passed without acknowledgement of any kind.

All this rejection was definitely not part of the plan. She was supposed to be eliciting sympathy as the injured party in all this.

Otis was the only bright spot in her now desolate life. He came into the grocery store on a regular basis and did his best to cheer her up.

One day he appeared with a bouquet of roses, a ring and a proposal.

"Hey, Baby," he said.

That's what he always called her, Baby. And right there over the fresh produce, he asked her to marry him.

"Let's run away to Vegas and get married. I have money for a nice honeymoon. You can move in with me until we find a house. It'll be great! What do ya say?"

He put the ring on her finger and waited expectantly for her answer.

Why not, she thought. *Apparently God has abandoned me along with my family. I have a right to be happy, don't I? And Otis is a nice enough guy...*

Knowing when her father would be "working" in his church office, she crept into the house. In her bedroom, she flung some clothes in her backpack. Writing a quick note to her mother saying not to worry about her, she left the house, never to return.

Chapter 7

Otis worked hard as the manager of the men's department in a local department store. He was a snappy dresser and drove a nice car. The airplane tickets to Vegas were paid for in cash. Emma decided she had made a wise choice.

They were married in a drive-thru chapel by a minister who attempted to look like Elvis. Oh well, they were married and that's all that mattered. Her father couldn't rule over her anymore. She could control Otis. He was black. He should be grateful an attractive white girl had married him.

The honeymoon was everything Otis had promised. He was kind and attentive to her and in bed, on their first night together, he was gentle and patient. They went to shows, drank fine wine and ate good food. Otis played poker far into the night and seemed to know what he was doing, because he frequently won.

After two weeks of sex, fun and sun, Otis said he had to get back to work, as he had used up all his vacation time. Emma protested. She was a little surprised when he didn't immediately acquiesce. They flew back into Dixon airport and drove to Cedarville in his fancy little sports car.

He'll pay for this, Emma decided on the ride home. She liked the Vegas lifestyle and the partying. How he could afford it never crossed her mind and frankly, she didn't care where the money came from. She wanted what she wanted.

"Can't wait for you to see the apartment, Baby," Otis told her during the drive home. "I spent a wad of cash getting it fixed up for you. I hope you like it."

With her husband's hand on her thigh and the wind blowing her hair, her hopes rose. This wouldn't be so bad.

The apartment was in one of the better sections of town. It was clean and well furnished. She wondered if he would expect her to do all those "wifely things" like cleaning and cooking. She certainly hoped not.

One day Otis came home with a box of her favorite candy. He grabbed her and kissed her soundly.

"I don't want you to work at the grocery store any more. I don't like the way the men look at you. You're mine. All mine. I want you here taking care of me and our home."

She protested, saying she enjoyed a little time out of the house, talking to people and having a little spending money of her own. But no amount of sulking and pouting changed his mine. She finally agreed to give her notice at work and stay home.

Crap, crap, crap, she thought. *This is not how this was supposed to go.*

"I know you're disappointed about your job and all, but we don't really need the money," he said after passionate love-making. "If we're frugal, the money I make will be enough to provide for us. You'll see. This will be great."

If we're frugal? I don't want to be frugal, she screamed inside her head. *I want to go out. I want to have fun! Frugal? No, no, NO!*

There was only so much cleaning and cooking to be done for two people in a small apartment. Emma was soon bored and lonely during the day. When Otis came home at night and on the weekends, things were better.

Several times during her first months of married life, Emma tried calling her mother. She knew when her father was likely to be out of the house; when it would be safe to talk. If she miscalculated and he answered, she promptly hung up. But her mother was so nervous about being caught talking to her daughter that it was more stress than it was worth. Emma stopped trying.

For a time, things went along smoothly for Emma and Otis. Otis came home at night and spent quality time with his young wife. He took her to the movies, out to eat; he did everything he could think of to make her happy. He loved her.

He would nuzzle her neck and caress her body until she was breathless.

"I'm so happy to have you all to myself," he would whisper in her ear.

Emma groaned inside. This was almost as bad as being controlled by her father. The great sex was a plus though.

When Emma discovered she was pregnant, Otis was thrilled. With his wife curled up against his side, her head on his shoulder, he talked about the future long into the night. Emma listened, her mind whirling in an entirely different direction. Maybe she could use the baby against her husband to get what she wanted.

Chapter 8

Jamal Williams slid from the birth canal screaming. The nurses said it was normal and he would settle down once they got him home and into a routine of eating and sleeping. He was a beautiful little boy and Emma was shocked when she realized she loved him beyond belief.

The breast feeding went well, but little Jamal wanted to eat every hour on the hour or sometimes sooner. Emma got almost no sleep at night and she was soon exhausted and cranky. Jamal slept in short spurts and woke up screaming. Nerves began to fray. Tempers flared. Suddenly, Otis wasn't the center of his wife's universe anymore and he didn't like it.

He never helped with anything around the house, preferring to sit and watch TV as he slurped down a couple of beers. On those rare occasions when Jamal was quiet and smiling, Otis would hold him. That was the extent of his involvement with his son.

Emma couldn't remember exactly when the actual, outright, fighting started. She started yelling one day and never let up. Otis yelled back and Jamal screamed louder. Things went from bad to worse.

Never losing an opportunity to belittle and berate Otis, Emma finally succeeded in driving him away from the apartment. He began spending more and more time at work, or out with his friends, leaving Emma to deal with the baby, the wash, the meals, the cleaning; everything by herself. She became more angry and resentful as the days passed. And Jamal continued to cry.

Emma had called her parents from the hospital the day the baby was born. She thought they should know they were grandparents. She also hoped by-gones could be by-gones and once they saw little Jamal their hearts would soften toward her. No one answered the phone, so she left a short message. She never received a response. Her parents never came. No help could be expected from that corner.

Chapter 9

The constant crying had to stop. Emma was at the end of her rope. Otis was almost never home anymore. She took Jamal to the doctor, thinking something had to be wrong with him.

Linda, the nurse practitioner, held Jamal over her shoulder and patted his back.

"No, nothing seems to be wrong. He's just a fussy baby. Things should improve as he gets older," she said with a reassuring smile.

Easy for you to say, Emma thought.

On the way home, Emma stopped at the grocery store. She needed a few things and she hoped a different environment might distract Jamal long enough for her to do some shopping.

Former co-workers crowded around her to get a look at the baby. For once, he smiled and cooed for a few seconds before he began to work himself up to a full blown tantrum.

One of the older ladies pulled Emma aside when everyone else went back to work.

"I think he's hungry," she said. "I know the doctors don't recommend it, but if it was me, I'd try some formula and some rice cereal. You don't have to give him very much and you'll know right away if he can't handle it."

Before leaving the store, Emma bought a box of baby rice cereal and a container of pre-mixed formula. She would try literally anything at this point.

When she got home, she immediately offered Jamal her breast. He latched on and sucked like he hadn't eaten in a week. When he had taken all she had to give, she opened the can of formula and poured two ounces in a bottle. He drank it all, falling asleep with a little droplet running down his chin.

Oh, the bliss! He slept for three solid hours! Emma checked on him several times to make sure he was still breathing. He hadn't slept that long at a stretch since she brought him home from the hospital.

She actually had time to take a short nap herself before getting supper started. *Could it be this simple? Maybe my milk just isn't nutritious enough for him. I hate to give up nursing though. It's the only time he's quiet and I get to snuggle with him. Maybe I'll just keep doing both.*

From then on, Emma nursed her beautiful baby, then gave him a bottle. At night she added a teaspoon of the rice cereal. The difference in the child was amazing. He began sleeping for longer periods at night and he took a nap in the middle of the day.

Even Otis noticed a difference. He began coming home for supper and spent time playing with Jamal. It became obvious that the little boy loved his father. No one could get him to giggle and babble like Otis could.

For a while, things evened out for the Williams family. Jamal grew like a weed. Otis started taking the boy to the park and the zoo, played games with him and read him stories before bed. The little boy would squeal with delight whenever he saw his father.

Emma wasn't so sure she liked this new relationship between Otis and Jamal. She worried that Jamal loved his father more than her! She was the one who had suffered through the first months of his crying constantly. She was the one who did all the work to keep him clean and comfortable. She was the one he should love more!

Chapter 10

Jamal was two years old when Emma became pregnant again. This pregnancy wasn't easy like the first one had been. Every morning without fail, Emma spent time hanging her head over the toilet vomiting. She did everything the books said to do. Nothing helped. The vomiting continued on and off throughout the day.

Otis was beside himself. The frustration level was through the roof, prompting comments he would later regret.

"Why did you let yourself get pregnant again anyway?" he yelled at her one evening after a particularly difficult day. "I didn't want the first kid, but he turned out okay...finally. Now I have to go through this again?"

"So, the truth comes out," Emma sneered.

Now she felt justified in turning her full wrath on her husband. She made his life hell. She nagged, yelled, complained... Nothing he did was right.

Well along in her second trimester, the doctor finally gave her some medication for the vomiting. Emma was worried how it would affect her unborn child, but the doctor told her she wouldn't carry the baby to term if she didn't take care of herself.

Things improved somewhat after that and two weeks before her due date, Emma delivered a healthy baby girl. Otis wanted her named, Keysha. Emma was so completely enamored with her daughter that she accepted the name, and the spelling, even though it wasn't one she would have chosen.

She called her parents and left a message.

Again, Emma went the breast feeding route, mostly because she needed to bond with her baby and she enjoyed the closeness. After every feeding came a bottle of formula. It worked perfectly.

Now with a three-year-old and a newborn, Emma had her hands full. Otis began disappearing again, at times staying out all night. She just didn't have the time, the energy, or the motivation to baby-sit a grown man so she just accepted what she didn't seem to know how to change.

Chapter 11

It was a cold winter morning that Emma got up to find an envelope with her name on it lying on the kitchen table.

"Emma,

I can't take it anymore. You win. Here is a few hundred dollars. Make it last.

Otis"

And just like that, he was gone. Emma stood in the kitchen holding the note and the money for a long time. Her hands trembled and tears streamed down her face. *What am I going to do now,* she wondered.

She had to pull herself together. Jamal would be awake soon and wanting breakfast. Then there was Keysha to feed. She had to think! The apartment was too expensive. She would have to move to a cheaper place. And three hundred dollars wouldn't last long to buy food, diapers, pay utilities...so the first order of business was to go to the Department of Social Services. The very idea of asking for assistance made her inwardly cringe.

Her father's church had a food pantry and the good reverend was very proud of the fact that his church was always ready to "help those less fortunate." The local TV stations even came to the church and interviewed Rev. Page.

"Showing the love of Jesus is what we're all about here at New Community Christian Church," he said as he wiped tears from his eyes. "We will help anyone in need; that's what the scriptures command us to do. We love our neighbors no matter who they are."

What a crock, Emma had thought at the time. He had given a performance worthy of Broadway. At home he would talk disparagingly about the lazy people who showed up to get their hand-outs.

Mrs. Rimsky ran the program and Emma knew she really cared about the people who came. But that's as far as the "caring" went. The other parishioners, the ones with money and position, the "spiritual ones," didn't have a good thing to say about the "dredges of society." They helped, grudgingly, because Mrs. Rimsky made them feel guilty.

Just one of the unwashed masses. That's how Emma now saw herself. Determined not to beg from her father or his church, she made an appointment with Ms. Caruthers for later that afternoon. Time to put on her down-trodden, victimized wife act.

Chapter 12

It was no small task to get Jamal and Keysha ready to go out. Emma didn't have a car and she didn't want to spend any of her precious cash-stash on a taxi, so she strapped Keysha on her back, took Jamal by the hand and prepared to walk downtown to the Human Resources Building. Despite her obvious faults and failures, Emma loved her children. She would do anything it took to take care of them.

By the time Emma arrived at her destination, her back and feet were killing her. Jamal was whining that he was tired and Keysha was winding up to let everyone know she was unhappy, hungry and probably wet.

The little match-box cars and trucks Emma always carried in her oversized purse, along with a peanut butter and jelly sandwich, were enough to keep Jamal occupied. A bottle was all Keysha wanted. With her tummy full, and a good burp, she was soon asleep on her mother's shoulder. The diaper change would have to wait.

They didn't have to wait long, thank God, before a short, stout woman stepped into the waiting room and called Emma's name.

"I'm Beatrice Caruthers and you must be Emma," she said, offering her hand to help Emma to her feet. "Follow me right this way. My office is in the back."

She stooped down and looked into Jamal's little round face.

"Those are really great cars," she said, with a smile in her voice. "Would you like to see my big desk? I think I have some graham crackers in one of the drawers."

The little boy scooped up his cars and trucks, took Ms. Caruthers' hand and skipped beside her down the hall. Emma was grateful. She liked her social worker already.

Chapter 13

"**B**ea" Caruthers had been a social worker her entire working career. With all that experience under her belt, she thought she could spot a free-loader with her eyes closed. She didn't think Emma was one of that breed.

"I'm so sorry I have to ask for help. If it was just me, I would make ends meet somehow. But Jamal and Keysha deserve better," Emma tried to explain.

That was probably the first adult, selfless statement Emma had ever made. It was the first time she had put someone else ahead of herself.

"Why don't you just start from the beginning and tell me what happened to bring you to my office," Bea said kindly.

Emma's whole demeanor was apologetic and it wasn't part of her act. She couldn't quite meet Bea's eyes when she began her story. She pulled herself up in her chair and straightened her shoulders. Beginning at the beginning, with her parents, the church, the hypocrisy, the bigotry, the lies...it was extremely hard for her to spill her guts to a complete stranger.

For the first time in her life, Emma told the truth, the whole truth and nothing but the truth.

She retrieved the note Otis had left her from her purse and handed it over to Ms. Caruthers. Tears threatened, but were held in check.

"I admit it. I'm the reason my husband left. I was terrible to him. It's all my fault."

Bea picked Jamal up off the floor and held him on her lap. She showed him how to make a bridge for his cars out of the books and folders she had on her desk. It gave her a minute to collect her thoughts without having to say something before she got her own emotions under control.

This poor girl, she thought. *Hardly anything more than a child herself. I know Rev. Page. His church is on the list I give to clients as a place to go and get food. I will need to revise my list! And maybe it would be worth my while to have a chat with Mrs. Rimsky. I think that's her name; the elderly woman who runs the program...*

Sitting on her lap, munching on graham crackers, the little boy was content. Keysha continued to sleep. For several minutes, no one spoke. Both women were lost in their own thoughts.

The realization of her culpability in her situation rolled through Emma like a tidal wave. *What have I done? How can I fix this? I've been so selfish. I have no idea how to even contact Otis, and even if I found him, what would I say?*

How can I help this poor little family? Emma needs so much more than just money and a place to live. I'm approaching the end of my career, Bea thought. *I'm tired and I don't know if I have anything left in me to give, but I have to try!*

Chapter 14

ᴏ⧸ᴑ

"**H**ow long can you stay at your current address?" Bea began. "I would recommend staying where you are as long as the rent is paid. Any apartment I find for you will not be as nice or as large."

"Three months. I checked and Otis paid the rent for three months before he left," Emma replied, tears threatening again.

"Okay, that's good. I'll start making inquiries right away for another place. In the meantime, I'll give you a voucher for emergency food, we'll get you and the kids enrolled in the WIC program, and here is a list of the food pantries in the area. I completely understand if you don't want to go to your father's church."

Jamal started to get antsy. The cars and trucks had lost their appeal. The peanut butter and jelly sandwich was long gone. He began whining and pulling at his mother's pant leg.

"We'll need to get an application started for public assistance and Medicaid. I'll need a fair amount of information from you. It might be easier for you if you take these forms home and do the best you can completing them, then I'll help you with the rest at the next appointment. How does that sound?"

Bea handed Emma an appointment card for the following week. She watched as the young woman gathered her belongings and got her children ready for the walk home.

"Thank you so much, Ms. Caruthers," Emma murmured. "Thank you for being so understanding."

When Emma finally made it home, she was exhausted. Jamal was whining. Keysha was fussy and wanted to eat. Emma dropped to the couch and finally let the tears come. Still holding the baby on her shoulder, sobs shuddered through her body.

Never having seen his mother like this, Jamal ran to her and threw himself into her lap. Emma hugged her children close and the three drew comfort from each other. Even Keysha seems to understand the seriousness of the moment.

I have to pull myself together! I only have three months to make some kind of life for my kids. Time is wasting...

Emma never cried again. Crying was for the weak.

Chapter 15

All the paperwork had been filed and Emma was approved for services. Working wasn't an option as child care would eat up everything she earned working at the grocery store. Ms. Caruthers had told her she was better off to just stay home and take care of her children herself.

True to her word, Ms. Caruthers had found an apartment. It was on the fourth floor of a rundown apartment building on Spring Street, lower east side. The "poor section" of town.

It only had one bedroom, the kitchen/living room was small, the bathroom was miniscule. The paper thin walls did nothing to block out the noise from the other people living on that floor. No bugs that Emma could see when she looked at the place, so that was a plus. With some paint and curtains it would work. Beggars couldn't be choosers. It was a roof over their heads.

Emma had stripped their belongings down to a bare minimum. She couldn't take all her nice furniture, which saddened her. She had sold everything except a loveseat and chair, a kitchen table and four chairs, one double bed, three small dressers, Jamal's toy box and the TV. A few dishes, cups and silverware, a frying pan and a soup pot would have to suffice. Two sets of sheets and blankets for the bed, some curtains and a few towels should be enough. It was all so depressing.

She had done her best to explain what was happening, but how much did a three-year-old, soon to be four, understand. Keysha, now a sturdy one year old, was happy playing with a cardboard box.

They each had a back pack stuffed full of clothes and personal items. Jamal was extremely upset that he couldn't take all his toys. Emma told him to pick out his favorites. That was it. He had screamed and cried to no avail. *He'll get over it,* Emma thought. *He'll have to.*

Chapter 16

The day before the welfare-sanctioned movers were to arrive, Emma made one last attempt to call her mother. She let the phone ring several times.

"Hello?"

"Mom! Is that you? Is it really you?" Emma whispered into the phone.

"Yes. Yes, it's me. Your father has been away all week at his church conference. I don't expect him home until Saturday. How...how are you, Emma? I'm so sorry for everything..." Her voice trailed off.

"Could you meet us in the park this afternoon, Mom? I want you to meet your grandchildren and...I miss you so much. I want...I need to see you," Emma pleaded.

A long silence followed. Emma had almost given up.

When she spoke, Winifred's voice shook. She was terribly afraid of what would happen if her husband found out. But how could he find out? She wouldn't stay long. She could always say she just happened to run into them. For once, she had to do the right thing by her daughter. For once...

"I'll be at the playground at one," she said, hanging up quickly before she had a chance to change her mind.

Chapter 17

⁓⧜⧜⧜⧜⧜⁓

E mma and the kids were at the appointed spot long before one o'clock. They ate sandwiches and fruit at one of the picnic tables. It was a sunny, warm afternoon. The sounds of happy children laughing and playing filled the air. It was the kind of day that made you glad to be alive. Emma was learning to be thankful for the small things.

She watched her mother walk toward them from the parking lot. It had only been about five years since Emma had run away with Otis. It was a shock to see how much her mother had aged during that time. Her dark brown hair was streaked with gray. There were wrinkles around her eyes and mouth. Emotional strain and pain were evident on her face.

Emma hid the shock she felt as she hugged her mother tight. It felt so good; safe somehow. When she stepped back there were tears in her mother's eyes.

"Here, Mom. Sit down. Have you eaten? We have some fruit left."

"No, I...I'm not hungry. Emma...I don't know what to say. I'm so sorry I never came to your defense. Your father...he can be difficult..."

"I know, Mom. I don't blame you. You were just trying to get along; not make waves," Emma said, even though resentment still simmered just below the surface.

Jamal was watching this interaction with interest. He leaned against his mother's leg.

"This is your grandson, Jamal," Emma said as she encouraged the little boy toward his grandmother.

"Jamal, this is your Grandma."

Winifred held out her hand, beckoning him forward.

Finally, seeming to make up his mind, he threw himself into his grandmother's open arms. Tears pricked behind Emma's eyelids. She bounced Keysha on her knee to give herself something to do.

Emma finally held the baby out to her mother.

"And this is Keysha, your granddaughter."

Having no fear at all about being passed off to a total stranger, Keysha's chubby little hands grabbed her grandmother's sparkly necklace.

For over an hour, Winifred got to know her grandchildren. She loved them instantly.

Jamal was small and thin for his age and reminded her of a cinnamon stick. That was the color of his skin and his cap of fuzzy, coarse hair. His eyes were hazel with flecks of green. He was a vivacious little boy and he rattled on about bugs and snakes; his favorite things.

Keysha dark brown eyes remained focused on her grandmother's face as she continued to play with the necklace. She was a chubby little angel of a girl with skin the color of cafe-o-lait. Emma had tied a red bow in her soft, black ringlets.

Both of my grandchildren are absolutely beautiful, Winifred thought. *Thurmond is missing so much. It's such a shame.*

Chapter 18

Winifred and Emma were consumed with re-establishing their broken relationship and didn't notice that church board member, Cecelia Rutherford, and her family was picnicking at a nearby table.

"Bernard, do you see what I see? Isn't that Winifred Page with Emma and two black children? Oh, my Lord. I wonder if the Pastor knows about this."

"Cecelia, why don't you mind your own business?" a disgusted Bernard responded, wiping mustard off his chin.

He didn't much care for Reverend Page and he only went to church because his wife nagged him. His opinion was that the good pastor was a pompous ass, but then, what did he know.

Winifred reluctantly handed Keysha back to her mother.

"I have to get going, Emma. I've probably stayed too long as it is. I'm so afraid your father will find out somehow."

"Okay, Mom. I understand. Jamal, give your Grandma a kiss and a hug. She has to go home and so do we. We have a big day tomorrow."

"Your children are beautiful Emma. You can be very proud of them."

On impulse, Winifred released the clasp that held her necklace in place. She handed it to Emma.

"When Keysha is older, please give this to her. I want her to have something from me."

There were tears in her eyes when she turned to walk away.

Emma watched her mother until she drove away. Jamal leaned against her, his eyes searching her face.

"Will we ever see her again, Mommy?" the little boy asked.

"I don't know, Jamal. I really don't know."

Chapter 19

⁓

Thurmond Page didn't get home until late Saturday night. He was tired and went to bed early, completely ignoring his wife. After all, he had to preach in the morning and he needed his rest.

Church went on as usual the next day. Thurmond was "hopped up" from his week-long conference and went fifteen minutes over "quitting time." He finally said the benediction and proceeded to the foyer.

Winifred noticed a huddled conversation between her husband, Mrs. Rutherford and a couple of the other women. She began to feel more and more uncomfortable when she realized they glanced her way several times.

Thurmond didn't say a word as they drove home. His face was set in a hard line and the vein in his forehead throbbed; always a bad sign.

The door to the house was barely closed when he turned on his wife.

"You were seen with Emma and her black bastards! You have disgraced me and your disobedience will not be tolerated!" he said in a quiet, deceptively calm voice.

Winifred swallowed hard. Her heart thudded in her chest until she was afraid it would explode. Her breath came in short, shallow gasps and her palms began to sweat. She had seen him mad before, but never like this. She almost preferred the yelling and ranting to this cold, calculated rage.

"You'll have to be taught a lesson. You. Are. Never. To. See. Them. Again. Do you understand?"

She could only nod her head, not trusting herself to speak. She began to tremble. *He's going to hit me*, she thought. Afterward, she wished that was all he had done.

He grabbed the back of her neck and forced her to her knees in front of him. Shock shot through her when he unzipped his pants.

He humiliated and degraded her for the next half hour. She was powerless to stop him. When he was finished, he grabbed a fistful of her hair and yanked her to her feet. He shoved her toward the kitchen.

"I expect lunch in fifteen minutes."

Chapter 20

Winifred stood in front of the sink. The water splashed over her hands. She didn't remember turning on the faucet. Cupping water into her mouth, she tried in vain to wash away the vile taste.

Her mind was numb as she moved around the kitchen on auto-pilot. The table was set and the food appeared on the plates. Thurmond ate and talked about the conference as if nothing had happened. She watched him through dead eyes.

When he was finished eating, he threw his napkin on his plate.

"That was nothing short of pig-slop," he said viciously. "You'd better improve or you'll get another 'treatment,' only the next time it will last longer. Maybe I'll even have a friend join me."

The stairs creaked as he stomped up to his study. The door slammed. Winifred jumped reflexively at the sound. She stood in the kitchen for a long time. Her mind blank. Her eyes staring at nothing. She continued to stand there even after she heard the bedroom door close.

Hours later, butcher knife in hand, Winifred climbed the stairs. Snoring emanated from the bedroom indicating the sleep of the innocent. She quietly pushed the door open.

Standing over him for only a minute, she held the knife with both hands and raised it slowly over her head. Without any conscious thought, she drove it into his chest up to the hilt.

The knife made a sucking sound as she pulled it out. His eyes flew open and he looked at her for only a few seconds before he sank into...hell. She kept stabbing him over and over. Blood flew everywhere, immediately soaking his pajama top and seeping into the sheets and blankets. It splashed on the headboard and the wall behind the bed. Even the ceiling was the recipient of cast-off blood spatter. It covered the front of Winifred's dress and ran down her arms.

Finally, too tired to continue, she sank to the floor beside the bed. Her hand found the phone on the bedside table of its own volition. In a red haze, she dialed 911.

When the operator answered, she responded in a flat, mechanical voice.

"I've killed my husband."

The blood-covered phone dropped into her lap.

Chapter 21

Officer Luke Peterson and his partner Officer Bruce Watson were on patrol that night and took the call.

"Bruce, you and Luke please respond to a 911 call at 1496 Upton Ave. A woman says she has killed her husband. I'll send backup. She may be dangerous."

Luke made a tire-screeching "U" turn and flipped on the lights and siren.

"Here we go!" he hollered to Bruce, adrenaline already pumping.

Arriving on the scene within five minutes, Luke swung the cruiser across the street about one hundred yards from the house. Backup pulled in within seconds and blocked the other end of the street.

It looked like every light in the house was on, including the porch light. The front door was unlocked when Bruce turned the knob. Another black-and-white pulled in and now six officers prepared to enter the house.

Luke went in low and to the right. Bruce followed low and to the left. The other officers poured silently through the door and the first floor was quickly cleared.

"She must be upstairs," Luke whispered to Bruce.

On opposite sides of the staircase, Luke and Bruce crept up to the second floor. The doors to three rooms were closed. Light was spilling out into the hallway from the last room on the left.

The other officers cleared the closed rooms as Luke and Bruce approached the open door to the fourth room. A quick look around the doorjamb revealed a lot of blood and a woman holding a large knife sitting on the floor next to the bed.

Very cautiously, first Bruce, then Luke, entered the room, guns aimed at the woman on the floor. They could hear the 911 operator as she continued to try and engage the caller.

"Ma'am, can you put the knife down for me?" Bruce asked in a low, soothing voice. "We're here to help you, but we can't do that until you put the knife down."

No response. Winifred continued to hold the knife limply in her lap where the telephone receiver also rested. She stared straight ahead, without moving, without making a sound.

Bruce inched his way forward until he was able to take the knife and toss it back and out of reach.

"Get the paramedics up here," Bruce said, without taking his eyes off the woman. "I'm pretty sure the guy on the bed is dead by the way his guts are spilling out all over the place, so no hurry with him. But the woman may be injured. It's hard to tell with all the blood. My guess is that most of the blood came from the victim."

Things happened fast after that. The house was soon swarming with the paramedics and the the coroner, followed by the crime scene investigators. Somehow the media had gotten wind of what was happening. A truck from Channel Nine news was set up just outside the police barricade.

Chapter 22

C hief Franklin Stevens pulled out his handkerchief and mopped his face. He was getting too old for this. The media people were waiting like vultures for him to make a statement. *Why can't they have some common decency,* he thought disgustedly.

Everyone in town knew who lived at this address. Reverend Page made sure his face was splashed all over the TV and in the newspaper every time he could finagle it. You either loved him or hated him. Most of the people in town attended his church and were enamored by his charismatic personality and fiery sermons.

What had happened would be on the early morning news whether he talked to the press or not. If he didn't give them something, they would just speculate and spin their own story. The chief knew the daughter had been estranged from her parents for several years and, as far as he knew, she was the only family. She would have to be notified.

The sleepy little town of Cedarville, VT had always been a very safe, quiet, pleasant place to live. That is until Dr. Lauren Ann Reynolds-Peterson and her husband, multimillionaire M. Bryce Peterson had taken up residence just down the road on a one hundred acre estate. They had set up headquarters for Peterson Enterprise and the chief's life had never been the same.

Since their arrival, a human trafficking and prostitution ring had been exposed. Then there was the pack of derelict teenagers with drugs and weapons that had surfaced when Ann Peterson, Officer Luke Peterson's mother, had been kidnapped. Now this!

The town had also benefited greatly from the arrival of the Petersons. They were law-abiding, philanthropic minded people, well-liked by everyone. When they had become the owners of the Vincenzo Restaurant and Ballroom, the town flourished like never before. People came from all over Vermont to eat the best lasagna and dance to the best music in the whole state.

Almost everyone in town followed the competitive dance team that represented Vincenzo's. Ann and Bryce Peterson, known affectionately as the King and Queen of Romance, were so popular their admirers came to town just to see them!

Everywhere they went, a huge German Sheppard dog named Gunner, followed. He had been instrumental in rescuing Ann from the wannabe mobster, Tony Marco. Gunner had become a celebrity in his own right.

Visitors to Cedarville wanted pictures and autographs. Tee shirts with Gunner's picture on the front had become a best seller. Every kid in town wanted to pet the dog. It was mind-blowing! The Chief thought of it as the "Peterson Phenomenon."

He had had numerous conversations with Ann and Bryce and he liked them very much. He also had a standing reservation at Vincenzo's with a waistline to prove it. Luke Peterson was one of his finest officers.

Luke and his friend Bruce Watson were putting together the plans for Peterson Search and Rescue, which would be a huge benefit to Cedarville and the surrounding towns. Their dog, Butch, had gained a reputation as one of the best tracking dogs in the northeast.

More personnel had to be added to the department just to keep up with the demand from other police agencies wanting to "borrow" his officers and their dogs.

The Chief sighed as he trudged toward the line of reporters. *I guess you have to take the bitter with the sweet,* he thought. *Damn! This is going to be messy.*

Chapter 23

It was Monday morning and Jamal sat at the table eating his breakfast. Earlier, he had tried to talk his mother into letting him stay home from Pre-K. He didn't like school very much. The kids made fun of him because he was "half" and because he didn't have a father. He slurped his cereal as he sulked and watched his cartoon on TV.

"We interrupt this programming to bring you a breaking news story. Early this morning, police were called to 1496 Upton Ave. An anonymous source has told this reporter that a woman believed to be Mrs. Thurmond Page called 911 claiming she had killed her husband. Stay tuned to Channel Nine News where we will keep you updated on this story as developments unfold."

Emma had been gazing out the window, absent mindedly washing some dishes left over from supper the night before. She spun around upon hearing the news bulletin. She ran to the TV and turned up the sound.

Oh my God! What has Mother done? Should I go to the police station? Keysha is still asleep...I'll have to get her up. Jamal has school... he can stay home... What could he possibly have done to push her over the edge like this?

In thirty minutes, Keysha was dressed and fed. She sat on the couch sucking her thumb and fondling her favorite blanket, which she called her "chi-chi." Jamal, ecstatic about missing school, sat beside her watching TV. He didn't care what the reason for the reprieve was, he was just happy not to have to go to school.

Emma was in the bedroom putting the finishing touches on her makeup when there was a loud knock at the door. Emma jerked. *What now? I don't need any more problems today. I bet it's Mrs. Thomas from across the hall wanting to have coffee and chat about nothing.* She threw the door open. Two police officers blocked the view of the hall.

"Ma'am, I'm afraid we have some bad news. Can we please come in?" Bruce asked politely.

For an instant, Emma didn't move or speak. They made an imposing pair. One black. One white. Both huge. Emma could only stare up at them.

"Please, Ma'am. We need to come in and speak with you," Bruce repeated.

Bruce and Luke filled the tiny living room. Emma suddenly felt like there wasn't enough oxygen to go around and sank to the couch beside her children.

Bruce squatted down so that he was at eye level with this little, frightened family. Luke stood by the door.

"Hello, little man," he said to Jamal. "Why don't you take your sister to the other room and play for a minute so we can talk to your Mommy. Can you do that for me?"

Jamal openly stared at Bruce. He had never seen anybody as big, as black or as ugly in his life. The scar that ran from the corner of his eye to the corner of his mouth gave Bruce a sinister look that would have frightened a lesser child. Jamal was just curious.

"What happened to your face, Mr. Policeman?"

"Well," Bruce began. "I was a soldier before I became a policeman and in a fight with the enemy, I was hurt."

"Wow!" Jamal said, admiration in his eyes. "It doesn't look so bad. Does it hurt still?"

Bruce chuckled.

"Nope. It doesn't hurt any more. The doctors fixed me up just fine. Now take your sister and go play."

Jamal slid off the couch and took his sister's hand, pulling her to her feet.

"Okay. Come on, Keysha. I'll play restaurant with you."

Keysha's big brown eyes lingered on Bruce's face for just a minute before she trailed after her brother, dragging her chi-chi with her.

Bruce took the children's place on the couch beside Emma.

Emma licked her lips and fiddled nervously with the buttons on her shirt. She had never had any interaction with the police and frankly, this cop scared the daylights out of her.

"It's my parents isn't it? I saw it on the television. What...what happened? My mother would never do anything to my father. She's too afraid of him. Is...is my mother all right?"

"She was checked by the paramedics at the house and she seems to be okay physically. Mentally, we're not so sure. Of course we will be conducting an investigation, but from the look of things at the scene, your mother stabbed your father to death. She hasn't said a word since the 911 call. Right now she's in custody and being examined by a psychiatrist. Under the circumstances, I doubt the judge will set bail."

Tears began their slow crawl down Emma's cheeks. She angrily wiped them away. She refused to be weak and pathetic. Right now, she just felt numb and confused.

"What do I do now? Should I come down to the station? I don't know what to do!"

"It would be better if you waited until this afternoon to come to the station. By that time we may know more about what happened, that is, if your mother will talk to us. We will also have some questions for you."

"Okay...okay. I...I'll come down after lunch. I'll ask my neighbor to watch the kids. I don't know what I can possibly tell you that will help. I just saw my mother the other day for the first time in over five years. My father is...well...he can be...unreasonable. I haven't seen him at all."

Bruce stood and stepped to the door beside Luke. They dwarfed Emma when she rose to see them out.

"Well, give it some thought. Anything you can tell us, no matter how inconsequential you think it is, might help us piece together what happened."

Luke tipped his hat respectfully.

"We're very sorry for your loss, Mrs. Williams."

After they were gone, Emma dropped back onto the couch. Her mind raced. *What the hell? I just saw Mom the other day. She was fine.*

Chapter 24

M rs. Thomas agreed to watch the kids so Emma could go down to the police station. She had seen the news. Her heart went out to Emma. Watching the kids wasn't a big deal for her. She loved them as if they were her own and to Jamal and Keysha, she was the grandma they had never had. Cookies were always readily available; the big, soft sugar cookies that were Jamal's favorite.

Emma told Officers Watson and Peterson everything she knew about her parent's relationship, which wasn't much. Her father was domineering, sometimes cruel, and her mother was a mouse of a woman who had never stood up to him in her life.

"Maybe he found out that Mom came to visit me and the kids," Emma speculated. "That would have set him off; he hates me. Mom was worried about him finding out, but he was away at his church conference. How could he have known?"

Luke paced around the small interview room, lines of concentration on his face.

"So far, your mother hasn't said a word. She hasn't even moved on her own...nothing. One of the female officers has had to direct her; actually take her hand and lead her around. The doc says she is in a catatonic stupor. Unless she snaps out of it, we may never know exactly what happened. She has been read her rights and booked, but I'm not entirely sure she understood any of it."

"Can I see her?"

Bruce motioned for Emma to follow him.

"Sure, just for a few minutes. Maybe it will wake her up."

Back in the bowels of the police station were the holding cells. Winifred was the only prisoner. Sitting on the cot behind the bars, she looked shrunken and frail.

Emma sat down on the cot next to her mother and grasped her hand.

"Oh, Mom. What have you done? And why?"

Winifred continued to stare straight ahead. There was nothing to indicate she even heard her daughter.

"Won't you talk to me, Mom? Tell me what happened?" Emma begged. "At least look at me."

Nothing. Not of flicker of recognition. Not a twitch. Nothing.

After several minutes, Emma stood and nodded to Bruce. He opened the cell door.

"I'm sorry I couldn't help. You have my number. Please call if you find out anything. I'll do whatever I can..."

"After arraignment, she's going to be transported to the mental hospital in Dixon for further evaluation. We will certainly let you know if anything changes. Thanks for coming in, Emma."

She walked home in a daze. Mrs. Thomas tried to pry information out of her when she picked up the kids. Emma just wasn't up to it and hurried Jamal and Keysha out the door and across the hall. She shrugged out of her jacket and hung it in the closet. *This is a hell of a situation.*

Chapter 25

E mma was surprised when a committee from the church contacted her about her father's funeral service. *Now they can talk to me? What a bunch of hypocrites. I don't want anything to do with any of it.*

The representative from the committee was shocked when Emma told her to go pound salt.

"Well I never... You have a responsibility to your father, young lady. I expect you to honor him as a decent daughter should."

"Why should I? He wasn't a decent father. I don't care what you do with him."

With that said, Emma slammed down the phone. She didn't attend the service or the burial.

There was a huge funeral at the church. It was splashed all over the front page of the newspaper. All the gory details of the murder were there for all to read, making her mother out to be some kind of demon. But her father had been presented as such a Godly man who had obviously endured so much in his personal life and on and on. It made Emma slightly sick to her stomach.

Her mother's public defender plead Winifred Page not guilty by reason of mental defect. She was sentenced to a mental hospital until such time as she was able to stand trial. That day would never come.

Life would go on as usual for Emma and her children. Her father had gotten exactly what he deserved in her opinion. Her mother was...well...just gone. None of this would affect Emma's life in the least.

Chapter 26

⌐◦⌐

The dance team representing Vincenzo's Ballroom had been hard at work preparing for their biggest competition to date. All the couples were now consistently scoring in the top five at the local events. Bobby was enthusiastically proud.

"Hey! I told you guys our team would eventually be the best. But you doubted. You didn't trust old Bobby to know about dancing stuff. Now look at us. Ready to compete in the big-time."

"Oh, please," Victor responded. "It only because of teaching you get from me and Anika that you can even walk in straight line. You're ugly and you don't have any natural talent."

Bickering was a part of everyday conversation among the young people of the Peterson clan. The fact was, they were all very close and more like brothers and sisters. Their backgrounds were varied and their personalities different, but they all had one thing in common.

Each one had found a family. Something they thought they would never have. They were grateful and appreciated each other. They loved each other. When adversity reared its ugly head, they circled the wagons and stood together. Unified. That's what family was all about.

Victor and Anika Petrov, co-leaders and choreographers for the team, were Russian born and raised. Their start in America had been a rough one until they had met the Vincenzo's and the Peterson's.

Not only were they a stunningly handsome couple, they were serious competition in any style of dance.

Their talent was immediately recognized by Georgio and Rosa. Experience was all they needed. As they learned English, their confidence grew. Surrounded by the love of this unorthodox family, they blossomed.

Victor's mother, Helena, a widow still living in Russia, had been brought to the United States by Ann and Bryce to be reunited with her son and daughter-in-law.

Helena and her late husband had been professional dancers in Russia and had actually competed in Europe against Italians, Georgio and Rosa Vincenzo.

She had brought more attention to the ballroom by offering dance lessons. A studio had been added to the complex to accommodate all her students from the surrounding communities.

"It's a small, small world isn't it, Mama?" Georgio was fond of saying. "We find Helena after all these years and now we are friends."

The darlings of the dance team, and by far the most popular, were Ann and Bryce Peterson. Their chemistry, the romance they portrayed so beautifully and their love for each other was evident to even the non-dance crowd.

When they danced together, it was breathtaking. It left the audience with a sigh of pure pleasure and a renewed belief that true love did, in fact, still exist.

The Latin dances were Bobby and Maria's specialty. The Hispanic duo was also the most charismatic couple on the team. All the teenage girls were in love with the handsome and charming, Bobby Rodriguez. All the boys were mesmerized by his hot and spicy wife, Maria.

"Maria and I are the ones to beat," Bobby arrogantly boasted. "Just look at us. We have it all. Great looks, sexy dance moves..."

"Oh, get over yourself," Luke, a non-dancer, chided his old friend. "Remember what the Good Book says. Pride goeth before a fall."

"And don't forget, I made you, I can break you," Victor added very seriously before breaking into laughter.

Georgio stroked his ample mustache and interjected.

"All this is amusing, but who are the real champions among us? None of you were even born yet when Mama and I were winning first place all over Europe."

Georgio and Rosa Vincenzo, even in their sixties, had excellent technique, stamina and vast experience in the world of dance competition. They were invaluable to the success of the team.

Chapter 27

Now the team was facing their biggest challenge yet; a dance competition in Burlington, Vermont. All the best teams in the state would be competing. It would require them to stay in the city for several days, leaving their own restaurant and ballroom in the capable hands of John and Carla Benson.

The first few years of John and Carla's marriage had been hard. Dealing with the emotional aftermath of the accident that had put him in a wheelchair often made John morose, depressed and snappy at his young wife.

Rehab had been slow and frustrating to say the least. No good jobs were forthcoming for a black man who just happened to be a paraplegic no matter how educated he was.

Bryce had seen the potential and offered him a job. With a master's degree in business administration under his belt, he was in charge of everything related to finances for Peterson Enterprise.

It was an extremely important position and he was very capable of maintaining financial stability for each branch of Peterson Enterprise, which included: Stratton Industry, a large manufacturing company in Dixon, Vincenzo's Restaurant and Ballroom, the Goodwin-Schwartz free clinic, the one hundred acre Peterson Estate where Ann and Bryce lived and Peterson Village, a small housing development.

Peterson Village was the name Bobby had given the cul d' sac owned by Peterson Enterprise where Bobby and Maria, and John and Carla had built homes. There was plenty of room for future houses to be built should Anika and Victor and Asia Kim and Bruce want to move there.

For now, these two couples preferred to live in the apartments attached to the Vincenzo Restaurant and Ballroom.

John was conscientious and he did an excellent job. They had two children, John Bryce or "JB" as he was called and newborn, Melissa Ann.

John was not usually involved in the day to day running of the restaurant and ballroom, but Bryce trusted him implicitly and felt confident he could handle anything that came along. Weekly family meetings kept everyone updated on what was going on in general, so the specifics wouldn't be hard for John to pick up.

The restaurant would continue to be open its usual hours and the dinner buffet would run smoothly under Carla's supervision.

The "house band," under the direction of good friend, Jimmy O'Brien, would be on hand so that after dinner, people could dance. It was one of the main attractions for people who wanted the whole dinner-dance experience. They came from far and wide for the great Italian food and wonderful music.

Luke would be on hand to open the dancing with an explanation to their guests as to why the dance team was unavailable to perform for them.

He and his fiancé, Tess O'Shay would help in any area that needed an extra pair of hands. The staff had been informed in advance what was going on and who to talk to with any problem that arose.

The ancillary staff in all areas of Peterson Enterprise was like none other. Turn-over was minimal to non-existent. Every employee was considered part of the team. Every person was important to the success of the whole enterprise.

The salaries were higher than any other business around. All opinions and concerns were taken seriously and addressed. Any employee felt entirely comfortable talking to any one of the leadership team. No gossip was tolerated and everyone was expected to do their job to the best of their ability. The result was happy, loyal employees.

Bruce and Asia Kim Watson would be traveling with the dance team. Asia Kim was responsible for hair, make-up and costume requirements. Bruce drove the limo and provided security.

Helena and her new husband, Dr. Mark Goodwin, went along for moral support. Dr. Goodwin had known Ann since she was sixteen years old when she had been a regular patient of his in the ER. Her first husband abused her horribly and her injuries were often severe. Dr. Goodwin had been her "white knight."

Never having married, he fell in love with Helena Petrov upon being introduced to her at the Vincenzo ballroom. And the rest was history. She had even gotten him to dance...a little.

Of course, Gunner would accompany Ann and Bryce. Since the kidnapping of Ann, Gunner never left her side and neither did Bryce. It had been a very traumatic time for the whole family. Thanks to Gunner, she had been found and returned to her family relatively unharmed.

Butch would stay at home to assist Luke and John with any security problems.

Chapter 28

❦

Spirits were high as the limo pulled up in front of the hotel where they had made reservations weeks in advance. It was within a block of the competition venue. Many of the other dance teams were also staying at this hotel, not only because of its five star rating, but also because of its proximity to the arena.

The conference rooms in the hotel were set up so that teams could practice. The restaurants were open 24/7 for the duration of the competition. It was a perfect arrangement.

Gunner was accepted with some reluctance by the hotel management. They had little recourse, since he had all the appropriate documentation needed for a K-9/service dog. Assurances were given that he wouldn't make any "messes" or cause any trouble.

Once everyone was settled in their assigned room, it was decided that exploring the city was in order. Competition didn't start until the next day and the girls wanted to check out the shopping. The guys tagged along hoping to find a spot where they could sit and drink coffee.

Victor stayed behind to complete the many forms and pay the fees required to compete. His team was prepared and they were here to win. He wanted to see the dance floor, the waiting areas, the judges tables, the audience seating; anything that would give them even the slightest advantage.

When he was satisfied with his inspection, he headed back to the hotel. Music was pouring out of one of the practice rooms and he briefly glanced in the open door.

What he saw turned his blood to ice and bile rose in his throat. On shaking legs, he barely made it back to the room he and Anika shared. Dropping to the couch, he covered his face with trembling hands. That's how Anika found him.

"Honey! What is wrong? Are you sick?" she gasped in rapid Russian, rushing to wrap her arms around her distraught husband.

Under the stress caused by seeing Victor so shaken, Anika had fallen back into her native tongue.

"I get others. They know help. Wait, Victor."

Chapter 29

Everyone responded immediately. Even Gunner sensed something was wrong.

Georgio sat down next to Victor and put his arm around the young man's shoulders.

"Victor, my boy. What happened?"

Victor rattled off the explanation in Russian. The others picked up a word here and there. The words they all recognized were "Natalia and Vladimir."

Natalia and Vladimir were the Russian dance couple who had brought Anika and Victor to the United States under the guise of providing teaching and mentoring in regards to the professional dance world. No mentoring or teaching of any kind was forthcoming.

They had abused the two young people and used them like servants. Anika was terrified of Vladimir and Victor was afraid he couldn't protect his young wife against the older, bigger, stronger man.

When Natalia and Vladimir auditioned for a spot on the Vincenzo dance team, the family met Anika and Victor. After Vladimir's attack on Anika, Luke had tossed them out with explicit instructions as to what would happen to them should they ever re-appear in the area. No one had seen them since.

"They here. They compete, maybe against us," Victor continued, his voice just above a whisper. "What we do? Vladimir, he lose weight. More fit. Natalia, hair different. Better. They look...pretty good."

Bobby punched Victor's arm.

"What the heck, Bro. You know we're better than they are! We've seen them dance! We compete and beat the pants off them. What do ya think we do?" was Bobby's profound reply. "We'll get revenge on the dance floor. It'll be awesome. I can't wait to see their faces when they lose!"

Bobby's little rant was just what was needed to shake Victor out of his panic. His head snapped up and a spark returned to his eyes.

"You and Anika are absolutely beautiful dancers. Your technique is superb. I should know, I taught you both myself," Helena assured them. "You go out and dance brilliantly; the way we all know you can. They took my money. They made promises. They need to be taught a lesson."

Victor stood, pulling Anika up beside him. Their faces filled with determination.

"Game on! Woot, woot," became the mantra of the whole team. "GAME ON!"

Georgio pursed his lips. He got a look on his face that told the rest of the group that he was formulating a plan.

"They don't know we're here. That gives us the element of surprise. Victor. Anika. We need to keep you out of sight until you step onto the dance floor. And you two, act like you don't even see them. Keep your heads up and smile. Anika, you look like an angel," Georgio said as he cupped her cheeks in his hands. "And Victor, you are her handsome prince charming."

Georgio looked around the room.

"And that goes for the rest of you too. Win over the crowd. It's not likely to affect the judges scores, but it will make them take notice of you. Don't allow other couples to get between you and the judges and make as many passes by the judges as you can without looking like you're hogging the floor. The other couples will be trying to do the same things so you will have to be on your toes... literally."

"I don't know these people, but if they threaten you in any way or cause trouble for our team, Gunner and I will handle it," Bruce added. "And don't let them intimidate you. As soon as they see you, that will likely be their way of dealing with the situation. Georgio's right. Don't speak to them, don't look at them. Just beat them fair and square."

Georgio suddenly clapped his hands and jumped up, startling everyone.

"Let's go find a room and get some practice time in before we go to bed. Then I want everyone to get plenty of sleep tonight, that means you too, Bobby...and Maria. No fooling around half the night, and you know what I mean," he said with a grin. "We want to be in top notch shape tomorrow."

Practice was horrible. Steps were fumbled. Routines got mixed up. The longer they worked the worse they got.

Finally, Bryce spoke up.

"You know, we're all tired from the trip and the shopping and certainly we're stressed by the current situation. Why don't we just forget all this for tonight. We know our dances. We've done them a million times. Let's get some rest, think about something else, have a snack... Tomorrow we'll be fine."

The response was unanimous.

"Agreed!"

Ann gave Victor a hug.

"We're your family now. We love you and we'll support you no matter what. Have faith in what your mother taught you. You've worked hard. You're ready. You can do this."

Chapter 30

A light breakfast was ordered from room service. Everyone congregated in Georgio and Rosa's room to eat. Victor passed out copies of the schedule for what dancing would take place that day.

"Most of the Latin dances are today," Victor instructed, back in control. "That means Bobby and Maria, you're up for Samba, Cha Cha and Meringue. Ann, you and Bryce are in for the Rumba and Bolero so, all of you...work it! Anika and I will watch from the balcony and try to stay out of sight. All of our dances are tomorrow, as are yours, Georgio and Mama. The rest of you also have dances tomorrow. Our schedule is full, guys! Any questions?"

No one had any. They all knew exactly what they had to do and they were determined to do it.

All of them could dance any one of the Latin and Ballroom dances, but for this competition, Victor had decided to keep everyone in their specialty. He wasn't taking any chances. This was their first major, state-wide event. He wanted his team to make the best of this opportunity.

The winners from today's and tomorrow's rounds would then compete head to head for the overall title of grand champion dance team and individual champion couple. That would mean if everyone won their dance, they would be competing against each other, but that was okay. Their ultimate goal was to beat Chadwick's Ballroom, where Natalia and Vladimir danced.

"Okay, let's go get this!"

Victor and Anika, Georgio and Rosa, Helena and Mark, Bruce and Asia Kim all headed for the balcony up the back stairway. They got front row seats so they could see the entire dance floor clearly.

They were pretty sure as soon as the Rusinko's saw any one of them, they would know the Vincenzo team was competing. They wouldn't necessarily know that Victor and Anika were part of the team.

Bobby was the perfect person to make that initial contact. He and Maria were dancing Samba and it was up for the first dance of the day.

Chapter 31

The minute Bobby and Maria stepped onto the floor, Bobby started working the crowd. He waved, bowed, a big grin on his handsome face. Maria was the best "spinner" of the group and as they walked across the floor, throwing in their original dance steps, Bobby sent her into a spin right in front of the judges.

Bobby saw Vladimir and Natalia out of the corner of his eye. They were on the other side of the dance floor; perfect. He would keep track of them until just the right moment.

The music started and Bobby and Maria threw everything they had into their dance. Victor had given them the foundations of good dancing. Helena had given them polish and had helped create a spectacular Samba routine.

At times, actually, most of the time, they tended to get too enthusiastic. Control and technique suffered as a result. Not today. Every step was perfectly controlled, while at the same time representing the fun, "party dance" for which the Samba is known.

"Georgio! Look at Bobby! I've never seen him more in control of the dance," Victor whispered, his voice full of excitement. "I can't believe my eyes!"

They were also doing exactly what Georgio had instructed. He was right. The other couples were aware of the same strategy for getting and keeping the attention of the judges. *But they have never competed against me,* Bobby thought as he and Maria whizzed past the judges, doing a technically perfect step while pretending to ignore the four seated at the table.

Bobby waited until Vladimir and Natalia were moving in their direction. When the couples passed, Bobby made direct eye-contact with Vladimir. For a split second, Vladimir hesitated, a shocked look on his face. It was just enough to throw them off a couple of beats. And the judges saw it. They recovered nicely, but that wouldn't be enough to save them.

The group watching from the balcony also saw it.

"Perfect!" Georgio exclaimed. "Bobby's face never changed. He continued to smile just like I told him. I wish I could have seen the look in his eyes though. I bet he gave them his best gangster-stare. This could be enough to throw them off for the rest of the competition. They won't know when we will pop up again."

The rest of the dances were completed and the winners would be announced during the evening session. Excitement was running high.

The day's events were finished around eight thirty. At nine, all the couples filed onto the floor.

"Ladies and gentleman," the announcer began. "Here are the judge's top three couples in the Samba."

Two other couples were announced for third, and then second place. You could hear a pin drop as the contestants, as well as the audience, waited for the winners to be announced.

"First place in the Samba goes to...Roberto and Maria Rodriguez representing the Vincenzo Ballroom in Cedarville, VT."

The spectators went wild. Bobby graciously accepted the first place award, grinning from ear to ear. He and Maria danced their victory lap around the arena.

"Oh, gosh," Victor moaned. "I never hear end of this."

That being said, he shouted and clapped harder than anyone else. He was ecstatic for his friend and his confidence in his team was bolstered. *We could do this*, he thought. *We could really do this!*

They placed, but didn't win, any of the other dances they performed. However, one win was enough to get Bobby and Maria into the finals.

This was not the case for Ann and Bryce. The sensual Rumba and the equally sexy Bolero were the perfect dances for them. Every graceful movement, every extension, every caress was...WOW. Vertical sex. Their passion for each other was unmistakable. Every man in the room was hot and bothered, just watching. Every woman wished she was Ann.

"First place in the Rumba...goes to Lauren Ann and Bryce Peterson representing the Vincenzo Ballroom in Cedarville, VT."

"First place in the Bolero...goes to Lauren Ann and Bryce Peterson representing the Vincenzo Ballroom in Cedarville, VT."

Georgio was afraid Victor was going to have a seizure or something. The usually stoic young man was jumping around hugging everyone, even strangers. Anika was usually the excitable one and the one prone to jumping around. Today, even if they themselves didn't win anything, their dreams had come true.

A smile crossed Mama's lips. *It's so good to see Victor and Anika so happy. They have worked so hard and overcome so much. They deserved this.*

Chapter 32

I t was late by the time all the winners were announced. Victor wanted to stay to the bitter end just to see if Natalia and Vladimir placed. The mistake they had made when Vladimir had seen Bobby had cost them dearly. They had been off their game for the rest of the day.

The Peterson wins had hit them hard and they had not placed in any of their dances. They were furious. As they left the arena with their teammates, Vladimir made a vow to Natalia.

"We will get even. We will make them pay. Somehow we will make them pay."

The atmosphere in the Vincenzo camp was entirely different.

Bobby was over the top in his excitement.

"Yo, can you guys believe our Samba? It felt great! And when I gave Vladimir my 'stink-eye,' I thought he was going to fall over. Oh, man. I wish you all could have been close enough to see the look on his face. It was priceless!"

He clapped Bryce on the back after he hugged Ann tight.

"And you two were...beyond words. Wonderful. I doubt if any of the others even came close in the scoring."

Victor finally interrupted; the only way he was going to get a word in.

"I've been keeping track of the totals. We have three wins so we're tied for second with the Bellaire Ballroom. For the moment,

Chadwick's Ballroom is on top. Tomorrow we really have to bring it home."

"Okay, okay everybody," Georgio interjected. "As you all know, we have a full day tomorrow. We need to get some rest so we'll be fresh in the morning. Then Mama and I will show you what a winning Fox Trot looks like."

With a wave and a bow, he took Mama's hand and they headed for their room. The rest followed, reluctant to put an end to their self-congratulations.

"We can't celebrate until the first place trophy is in our hands," Helena reminded the young people. "Don't count chickens, before hatch."

Chapter 33

V ladimir and Natalia spent most of their night trying to come up with a plan to sabotage the Vincenzo team. At this point, they had not seen Victor and Anika.

"I wonder if those brats are with them," Natalia mused. "Maybe there is some way we can, shall I say, incapacitate one of them. Vladi, why don't you go down to the lobby and check the schedule for tomorrow. See if their names are on it."

Vladimir protested, but he knew better than to cross Natalia. She could make his life hell on earth if she was mad at him.

There were only a few people in the lobby this late at night. Vladimir skulked around until no one else was near the board where the schedules were posted for the next day's dancing. Sure enough. Anika and Victor Petrov's names were there.

Sauntering up to the desk clerk, a young, pretty little thing, Vladimir put on his most charming smile.

"Hi there beautiful. I wonder if you could do me a little favor? Tell me which room belongs to the Petrov's, Anika and Victor? They are old friends of mine from Russia and I'd like to send then a basket of fruit tomorrow as a surprise."

"Of course," she replied, batting her eyelashes and giving him a slow, seductive smile. "They are in room 220; the second floor."

"Thank you, aaahhhh, Judy," he said, reading her name from the tag on her blouse. "I'll catch you tomorrow. Maybe we can have a drink or something."

He walked away, trying to come up with a plan of action. He drew his lips back in a snarl. *You little bastards. You'll be sorry you ever crossed us. I promise you that.*

Chapter 34

The Vincenzo team was rested and ready for the last day of competition. Anika and Victor were up for the first dance, the Tango. They would also be dancing the Quick Step, Jive and the Viennese Waltz.

Anika was a bundle of nerves as they waited at the gate to make their entrance onto the floor. Victor drew his wife close and pressed his forehead against hers.

"You look amazing, my love," he whispered in Russian. "We have danced the Tango a million times. Don't worry so much. Forget everything else and just be with me in the dance."

The dance was announced and the couples began to file in. Vladimir and Natalia stepped in front of Anika and Victor. The young couple never flinched or betrayed any emotion at all.

"You better watch yourselves. Bad things can happen," Vladimir said quietly in Anika's ear.

He figured she was the weakest link and if anyone screwed up, she would. She had always been a flighty, emotionally fragile little girl, easy to intimidate. The defiant look on her face gave him pause.

About a minute into the dance, Vladimir and Natalia, having worked themselves into close proximity to Victor And Anika, did a fast series of steps, and seemingly by accident, plowed into them. Vladimir made sure he accidentally, on purpose, came down hard on Anika's ankle.

He knew they would forfeit this dance for causing the collision. It would be worth it. He didn't care.

Victor was thrown off balance and wasn't quick enough to catch Anika before she fell. A gasp went up from the crowd. The music did not stop and the rest of the dancers avoided the little drama playing out in the middle of the floor.

Outwardly, no one could tell there was any animosity between the two couples. Vladimir apologized profusely as he offered Anika his hand. She tried to stand. Pain rippled across her face.

Without a word, Victor picked her up and carried her to the gate where the rest of his team had gathered.

"She need doctor. Ankle maybe broken. They did on purpose!"

Georgio had never seen Victor so angry. He was seething. Anika was weeping softly.

Outside the arena, an area had been set up for medical emergencies. This was not the first time during a competition something like this had happened. It was always unfortunate, but it did happen. An ambulance was parked outside. After a cursory evaluation by the EMT on duty, Anika was whisked off to the hospital for an x-ray.

Victor went with Anika in the ambulance. Helena and Mark followed the ambulance to the hospital while the others got ready for their dances. Bruce and Asia Kim stayed behind in case they were needed. Everyone was badly shaken.

Bryce gathered the group together.

"I know you're all upset by what happened. But now, more than ever, we have to pull ourselves together, go out there and win this thing. Their next dance isn't for a little while yet, maybe they will be able to continue."

"Yes," Georgio agreed. "We have a job to do and Victor would be the first one to tell us to go ahead and dance our best."

The doctor advised against any more dancing for at least two weeks. Anika would have none of that.

"You say ankle not broken. Only bruised and sprained. That good. Wrap it up tight. I will dance," Anika told the doctor.

"Are you sure, Anika," Victor asked, concern written on his face. "The doctor say could cause permanent damage if continue to dance."

"If we drop out of Jive, that will give us more time for foot up and ice. Then we only have two more. I can do this, Victor. We have to do this! We have to show Natalia and Vladimir they did not beat us."

When the announcer told the audience that the Petrov's had withdrawn from the Jive there was a murmur of sympathy for the young Russians. Vladimir and Natalia gave the appearance of sympathy, while giving each other a congratulatory smile.

Chapter 35

When the Quick Step was called. Victor and Anika stepped in line behind Vladimir and Natalia.

"We not stoop to your level. We will beat you fair and square," Victor said with a deceivingly pleasant smile on his face.

A cheer went up from the crowd when Victor and Anika stepped onto the floor. They smiled and waved as if nothing had happened. Anika's ankle was wrapped and she had on different shoes to accommodate the bulk. Otherwise, she appeared fine. No limp, no stress lines on her face. Only Victor knew she was in pain.

As soon as their dance was finished, Anika leaned heavily on Victor's shoulder and limped to a chair in the hall where an ice bag was waiting for her. Her face was pale and there were tears threatening.

Victor stroked her hair as he sat beside her, his other arm around her shoulders.

"That's my brave girl. I'm so proud of you. Are you sure you want to do the other dances? No one will be upset if you can't do it."

Just as she was about to answer, an official from the dance competition approached them.

"Mr. and Mrs. Petrov, I'm Barry Cabot. The judges have asked me to talk to you about what occurred during the Tango. The tapes of the dance have been reviewed and we believe the collision was intentional. The judges are ready to ban the Rusinko's from the rest of the competition for unsportsmanlike conduct. Their previously won awards will be taken away and you have the option of filing assault charges. As a curtsey, they would like to know how you feel about it."

Victor looked at Anika. She shook her head no.

"Thank you so much for consider our opinion, Mr. Cabot, but we would like the Rusinko's to be allowed to continue and to keep their awards. We not wish to file any charges. We want compete against them...beat them," Victor stated with a ghost of a smile on this face."

"So be it," replied Mr. Cabot. "I'll let the judges know your wishes. It will be up to them to make the final decision."

The Viennese Waltz was called. Anika stood up, winced, then quickly put on her game face. She took Victor's arm and they headed through the gate.

Natalia and Vladimir had been allowed to continue. However, it had been made perfectly clear to them that this consideration was being given at the request of the Petrov's. The judges had been ready to bounce them.

When the music began, Victor swept Anika away. They became one with the music and Anika's pain vanished from her conscious thought. The spectators were mesmerized.

Natalia and Vladimir were also competing in this dance. They stayed as far away from Victor and Anika as they could possibly get and still be on the floor. The judges had allowed them to dance, but had laid down the rules specific to them in no uncertain terms.

Word had gotten around, somehow, that the Chadwick couple were only allowed to continue because of the generosity of the Petrov's. It made for a wonderful, romantic story surrounding the young Russian couple.

When the television crews and reporters got wind of this story, they were waiting at the gate when Anika and Victor stepped off the floor.

Chapter 36

Arena security was completely inadequate to handle what was happening at the gate. The media was out of control without any consideration for the safety of the contestants. Bruce saw the danger to an already injured Anika. Panic was written on her face as she and Victor were being jostled by the gathering crowd. Microphones were thrust in their faces. Questions were being yelled out.

Victor picked up Anika and she buried her face in his neck. They were quickly surrounded and nearly toppled over by the press of so many bodies pushing and shoving.

Gunner gave one sharp bark. In the silence that immediately followed, Bruce began elbowing his way toward Victor and Anika.

"Step. Back!" he bellowed. "And this is why I came along," Bruce muttered to Georgio who was following right behind him. "I hate the media. I hope one of them gives me a good reason to throw a punch."

The reporters parted like the Red Sea in front of the huge, black, scar-faced, ex-Marine. Under his tight black tee shirt, huge muscles rippled, biceps bulged. The look on his face was enough to strike terror in even the bravest heart.

Bruce stood in front of the terrified young couple.

"We will take a few questions if you can all act like civilized adults."

Everyone started shouting at once. Gunner gave another loud bark. Silence again ensued.

"Okay. If that's the way you people want to act, you lost your chance for questions. Get out of our way. Now!"

No one said a word or tried to stop them as Bruce lead the way out into the hall and through the door to their waiting limousine. He had anticipated something like this might happen when Victor and Anika were determined to dance. The limo had been brought around as a safety precaution before the dance had ended.

Once back in the hotel room, Ann unwrapped Anika's ankle. It was already black and blue. The swelling had only been kept down because of the wrap. Ann gently poked and prodded, finally determining that no further damage had been done.

Ann re-wrapped the ankle. Bruce picked Anika up like she was weightless and deposited her on the bed. The ice bag was put in place. Tylenol was dispensed. She looked deflated and fragile. But she had grit. Nobody could deny that.

As Anika's heart rate returned to a somewhat more normal beat, she looked up at Bruce with tears in her eyes.

"Thank you so much for save us! I thought we die, crush to death!"

Victor stood, offering his hand to his friend.

"I owe you, my friend. You did save us."

"No," Bruce interrupted, his face serious as a heart attack. "Remember what the little punk, Bobby, says? There is no debt between friends."

Laughter broke the tension. Bobby clapped Bruce on the back.

"That's right, bro," Bobby chuckled. "I'm glad to see you remember my words of wisdom."

Bruce looked heavenward.

"Oh, please. Spare me."

Back in the arena, the judges had decided to call a short delay so that order could be restored. There were still dances to be performed and they wanted the competitors and the crowd to calm down before dancing continued. The announcer stepped to the middle of the arena.

"Dancing will resume in one hour. We are sorry for any inconvenience this may cause. Please take this time to get something to drink, use the restrooms, whatever you need to do. Thank you for your cooperation."

There was plenty of mumbling and grumbling, but most saw the wisdom in this decision.

Chapter 37

The competition had been covered from the beginning by the local Cedarville TV station, Channel Nine. And why wouldn't they? The hometown team was dancing! Those who had stayed behind in Cedarville to keep the home-fires burning had been glued to the big screen in the ballroom from the pre-dance interviews to the melee that had just occurred. No one left unless their job responsibilities called.

They were all very surprised to see Vladimir and Natalia. Their last encounter with these two had not been pleasant. They never expected to see them again. When Vladimir rammed Victor and Anika, hurting Anika, eyes popped in disbelief.

"I can't believe that just happened. I should have been there," Luke groaned. "Maybe I could have prevented it."

John's voice of reason prevailed.

"Hey, man. It happened on the dance floor. What could you have done? Dance around behind them as their body guard? We'll just have to wait and see what happens."

When Bruce stepped in, everyone relaxed a little. They knew things would be handled, one way or another.

Last year, it had been decided to convert the wall behind the band into a TV screen. From a computer in the security office, anything could be projected onto the screen.

During the Christmas dance, when outside it was bone dry, inside the snow was falling and it was a beautiful Christmas scene. They used the screen a lot as a background for the, now eighteen piece, band.

Tonight the grand champion team and individual couple would be decided. Nobody wanted to miss that!

Luke made the executive decision.

"I think we should put the competition from Burlington on the big screen tonight so our guests can see what's happening. And so we don't miss anything," he added. "What do the rest of you think?"

Even though it was a little bit self-serving, agreement was unanimous. Everyone would get to see the Vincenzo team in the final rounds of dancing.

When the guests began to arrive, they were treated to watching the hometown team dance. Everyone was excited. They got to see Bryce and Ann dance the waltz. Bobby and Maria did a fast and furious swing. But the biggest dance of all was Georgio and Mama's Fox Trot.

Fox Trot was the only dance in which Georgio and Rosa were competing. All of the other dancers were thirty-five to forty years younger than the Vincenzo's. No one was disqualified because of age, however, Georgio was smart enough to recognize their weaknesses and strengths.

In the costumes the dancers wore, Georgio wouldn't have a problem; pants and shirts or tuxedos. But Rosa adamantly refused to wear the skimpy, slinky, skin-tight outfits the girls wore.

"Oh, my Lord," she had gasped with her hand covering her heart. "Can you just imagine how I would look in one of those get-ups?"

Georgio stroked his mustache, a twinkle gleaming in his eyes.

"Mama, I sure would like to see you in one, in private, of course! In fact, I would love to see you model something like that for me, say tonight?"

Rosa had smacked his arm.

"In your dreams, you old fool. In your dreams."

"Ah, yes, yes." Georgio had sighed, a wistful look on his face.

On the Q-T, they had been working with Helena to bring back some of the old Fox Trot steps they had used in competition in Europe when they were young. So much had changed, no one ever saw the old steps any more. It was a risk they were willing to take. The steps were complicated and beautiful.

Georgio was very smug and secretive when the rest of the team wanted to see their dance.

"You'll just have to wait and see like everybody else," was always his reply.

Chapter 38

Finally the announcer called for the Fox Trot; the last dance of the competition before the "dance-off," which would decide the grand champion couple.

Ann got a lump in her throat as she watched Georgio and Rosa take the floor. They looked amazing. Both with white hair, both dressed in black; Mama in a sequined, evening gown, Papa in a black cut-away tuxedo. They drew attention from the crowd if only by virtue of their age!

The Vincenzo's filled the role of Mom and Dad for Ann, who had lost her parents as a child. Bryce looked on them as dear friends who had seen him through an extremely difficult time in his life. The rest of the "Peterson Clan" loved them like grandparents.

The rest of the team watched from the balcony. None of them had entered this dance, knowing it was meant for just Mama and Georgio.

"Don't they look wonderful, Honey?" Ann whispered to Bryce. "I'm so proud of them."

Bryce hugged her close. He knew exactly what she was feeling. With his finger under her chin, he tipped her head up and kissed her lips, then tucked her under his arm against his side. Her arms came automatically around his waist.

Georgio led Mama to the middle of the floor right in front of the judges table. He bowed formally from the waist to Mama. She, in turn, gave him a deep curtsy. Then they turned and gave the same respect to the judges. Old-school all the way. Gracefully, they moved along so that others could walk in front of the judges. It was only common courtesy.

When the music began, Papa swept Mama away in a beautiful series of spirals followed by, what they called, the "skippy step," for lack of a better name. It was a difficult step because of the timing that was required.

They continued with long-forgotten steps that surprised and amazed the watching members of their own team. Even the more current steps were performed with a definite "Vincenzo twist."

Some of the younger dancers may have thought the steps were "simple." The judges knew otherwise. The whole dance was performed perfectly, with great presence and graceful flow. It was outstanding. The sophisticated, polished presentation would be remembered long after the dance was over.

"So that's what they've been so secretive about!" Bobby breathed. "It's really quite... I can't think of the right word...great."

When the dance ended, the couples took their bows. The crowd stood as one as Georgio and Rosa accepted the applause. Mama's cheeks were pink and Georgio's lips were curved in a huge grin.

Georgio squeezed Mama tight and twirled her around, her feet not touching the floor.

"What do you think, Mama? Did we win it?"

"Put me down. Put me down," Mama laughed. "People will think we're tetched in the head."

Chapter 39

It was finally time to announce the winners of the day's dances. At nine o'clock, the dance-off between all the first place winners across the two days of competition would take place. It would be a late night.

Anika, now on crutches, stood beside Victor and the rest of the days dancers to hear the winners announced. When they were named the winners of both their dances, they were shocked. Sure enough. They won the Quick Step and the Viennese Waltz, beating Natalia and Vladimir.

The older Russian pair had won a couple of the other dances qualifying them for the dance-off where they would compete against everyone on the Vincenzo team, except Victor and Anika.

Victor had decided not to take the chance of further injury to Anika's ankle. They were more than satisfied with their wins over Natalia and Vladimir in the individual dances.

"We not have anything else to prove," Victor explained to the group during the intermission. "We win our dances, fair and square. We happy."

"I'm very proud of you two," Georgio told the young couple. "You're making a very wise choice. Of course, we would like to see you win the whole thing, but we certainly understand your decision and we support you."

Bobby hugged Anika and pounded Victor on the back.

"We kicked some serious ass...oops, sorry, Mama."

Everyone laughed, including Rosa. Ann and Bryce passed around glasses of Champagne.

"I would like to propose a little toast to the best family anyone ever had, not to mention the best dancers!" Bryce said.

"Hear, hear," they all shouted as they clinked glasses and drank.

Chapter 40

There had been much controversy in the past over how the final dance of the competition would be chosen for the dance-off. In previous years, the judges had made that determination. Some felt the judges picked a dance to give their favorite dancers an advantage.

This year six random people from the spectators were asked to write the names of all the dances on separate slips of paper: Waltz, Rumba, Fox Trot, Jive etc. Then the announcer would pull a slip out of a hat. This method had never been tried before, but it seemed a fair way to handle things.

Tension ran high as the winners over the past two days gathered in the arena. This dance would decide the grand champion couple.

Victor and Anika, Bruce and Asia Kim, Helena and Mark watched these final proceedings from their spot in the balcony.

"Who knew dancing could be so cut-throat," Bruce said, shaking his head in amazement.

He had the limo waiting at a side exit at Georgio's recommendation.

"You have seen the behavior of the media," he said. "They will be all over this after the trophies are handed out. We don't want to get caught up in any of that."

Silence descended over the arena as the announcer made a grand show of reaching into the hat and withdrawing a small slip of paper.

"The final dance of this year's state-wide competition will be..." A long dramatic pause followed as he slowly unfolded the paper. "The Fox Trot!"

"We all dance," was Bobby's excited response. "I sure wish Victor and Anika could be with us. Let's one of us go bring home the trophy!"

When the music began the Vincenzo team swung into action. Bobby and Maria would give it their best shot even though the Fox Trot wasn't their best dance. Ann and Bryce could dance a wonderful Fox, but the undisputed champs were Georgio and Rosa. If anyone had a chance at winning, they did.

The last notes of the music died away. Everyone had done their absolute best. Now it was in the hands of the judges. There was much whispered, heated discussion at the judges table. Georgio was pretty sure their old style dance was being discussed. It seemed to take forever for them to come to a decision. Finally...

"The winners of the final dance of this season's state-wide completion are Georgio and Rosa Vincenzo of the Vincenzo Ballroom in Cedarville, Vermont."

The crowd went wild! Victor jumped into Bruce's arms and raised his fist in victory. Anika jumped up and down as much as her crutches would allow. Helena an Mark clapped wildly. Tiny, little Asia Kim tried to keep everyone from falling over the balcony rail in their excitement.

Down on the arena floor, Georgio held Rosa tight, surrounded by Ann and Bryce, Bobby and Maria. There were tears streaming down Rosa's face. She cupped Georgio's face in her hands and kissed him soundly.

"We did it, Georgio. I can't believe it."

Georgio accepted the huge trophy with a gracious bow. He and Mama held it high as the crowd stood, giving them a long ovation.

The announcer stepped away from the celebrating couples, back to the middle of the arena.

"We still have one more trophy to award," he hollered above the din.

Things settled down enough for him to continue as Anika and Victor made their way slowly onto the dance floor to stand with their team.

"As you know, the scores of all the winning dances over these last two days have been tabulated to come up with the team winner. The team with the overall highest score is...The Vincenzo Ballroom team from Cedarville, Vermont!"

Confetti and balloons fell from the ceiling as the crowd once again went into a frenzy of clapping and yelling.

As team leaders, Victor and Anika accepted the trophy that was almost as tall as Victor. They all held hands and bowed in unison. Long hours of practice, with all the minor injuries and frustrations that went along with it, had been spent in preparation for this event. Victory was indeed sweet.

In the balcony, Helena sobbed in Mark's arms.

"Victor's father would be so proud. I wish he could have lived to see this."

On the floor, the Vincenzo team received congratulations and good wishes from the other teams. There didn't seem to be any hard feelings, at least not tonight.

Back at the ballroom in Cedarville, the crowd was no less raucous. Each table had a bottle of champagne and the staff, as well as the guests, joined together to toast their team's win.

Vladimir and Natalia skulked out the backdoor and left without saying a word to anyone.

"This is all your fault, Vlad," Natalia snarled. "We will go back to Russia where our talent is recognized and appreciated."

Chapter 41

Georgio had been right. The media people were everywhere with their cameras and microphones. To say they were pushy and obnoxious was an understatement.

The Vincenzo team moved slowly through the mass of people, finally making it to the side door where Bruce was waiting in the limo. They all managed to pile in, thus escaping the crowd.

The reporters surrounded the limo, shouting out questions, cameras rolling. Bruce gave a long blast on the horn and yelled out the window.

"If you people don't move, I'll run over you."

They moved.

Back at home, Carla had long since hustled little JB and Melissa off to bed. The guests had left and the restaurant was closed for the evening.

Tess, Luke and John stayed to the bitter end in front of the big screen. They knew Channel Nine would stay with the competition to the end. It was worth the wait just to watch Bruce deal with the situation.

As the limo had pulled safely away from the curb without any loss of life, there was much high-fiving and loud whistling from the three gathered in the ballroom.

"You get 'um Bruce!" Luke yelled at the screen. "I guess it's a good thing he went along."

Much laughter followed as they raised their bottles of beer in toast. The real celebration would take place when the team got back home. Channel Nine had already called to set up an interview.

Chapter 42

Emma had worked hard to carve out a life for herself and her children. Jamal was good in school, even though he hated it. Keysha would be going to Head Start next year. They were both good kids. Oh, they had their moments, but overall, they were good kids.

One day Jamal was brought home from school early by one of the school administrators. His eye was swollen, he had a scrape on his cheek and his shirt was torn.

"What happened?" Emma gasped when she opened the door.

"We don't really know," Mr. Clarkson said. "Jamal isn't talking. So he's been suspended for three days for fighting. Here's a list of his homework assignments and his books. If you can pry out of him what happened, we would appreciate hearing about it."

Jamal walked to the couch, his head held high, and sat down. The little boy's face was hard except for the slight trembling of his lower lip.

Mr. Clarkson finally left after being assured that Emma would have a serious discussion with Jamal about fighting.

As soon as the door closed, Jamal broke and the tears came.

Emma sat next to him on the couch and drew his trembling little body into her arms.

"Honey, what's going on? You're not a fighter, you're a good boy. What happened?"

Keysha heard the commotion and came to stand in front of her mother and brother, her thumb in her mouth and her chi-chi dragging on the floor. Huge brown eyes stared at her brother's swollen eye. Her little face crinkled up as she let out a loud wail in sympathy for Jamal.

"Ssshhh, little one," Emma whispered, drawing Keysha in with her other arm. "Our neighbors will be calling the cops with all this racket."

With much sup, supping and hiccupping, both children finally calmed down.

"Talk to me, Jamal. I want to know what happened today at school."

Jamal's shoulders slumped and with a huge sigh he began his story.

"It was Trevor. He's the bully at my school. We were at recess when he started pushing and shoving me, calling me dickhead and half n' half. My friends couldn't help me because they're afraid of him too. The teachers don't do anything about it..."

His voice trailed off.

"I'm going into that school tomorrow and have a talk with the principal..."

"No, Mom," Jamal interrupted. "You can't. It will just make everything worse. Besides, I handled it myself."

The little boys head snapped up. He looked his mother in the eye.

"I couldn't take it anymore. The thought of this happening every day for the rest of my life made me so mad! I just hauled off and punched him as hard as I could right in the face."

Jamal demonstrated the punch for his mother and sister. Keysha's thumb popped out of her mouth. She just stared at her brother.

"After that, there was some more punching and rolling around in the dirt until the recess monitor came running over and separated us. He got the worst of it though, Mom. Sorry about my shirt. But I'm not sorry for hitting him!"

"Oh, Jamal," Emma sighed. "I'm so sorry this happened and I don't condone fighting. But I'm proud of you, Honey, for standing up for yourself. Sometimes that's all you can do because the only person you can depend on is you. It's a hard lesson to have to learn, especially at your age."

Emma hugged him close, then swatting his bottom she gave him a push toward the bedroom.

"Now go change your shirt and wash you face and hands. We'll put an ice bag on your eye. And I made cookies this morning. How does that sound?"

When Jamal was out of sight, Keysha crawled up into her mother's lap.

"Wow, Mom. Does this mean Jamal is a man now?"

Emma laughed softly.

"No, Sweetie, he's still just a little boy. He's growing up fast though and so are you," she said as she tickled Keysha's tummy. "I suppose you want cookies too."

"Yes!" the little girl shrieked, jumping down and running round the living room.

The love Emma had for her children often made her heart ache. She knew they weren't going to have an easy time of it in life. Her only hope was that they had learned from this little experience that is was okay to defend yourself. And accepting the consequences for those actions was part of it. Jamal would be helping her around the house for the next three days and doing homework, not playing with his toys.

Chapter 43

D ennis Lodge had seen Emma around the neighborhood. He thought she was hot. He fantasized about her all the time and the things he would like to do to her. Never giving him the time of day, Emma would just turn her head and walk away every time she saw him.

It was a cool spring evening and Dennis had been drinking beer and smoking weed all afternoon with his friends. The only reason he had friends was because his parents were wealthy. In his own right, he was obnoxious.

His father had made a lot of money in the stock market. His mother was an interior designer. They had moved to Cedarville from New York City looking for a quieter life in a small town. They coddled and pampered their only child giving him anything he wanted no matter how outrageous.

Discipline was thought to inhibit his natural curiosity and creativity. At seventeen, he was a spoiled brat with a fancy car and money to burn.

"The Den-Miester" was always good for buying beer, cigarettes, drugs; anything the guys wanted, so they put up with him. Today they had been egging him on and razzing him about Emma Williams.

"Hey, man. You be needing a little bit of extra courage to make your move?" one of the boys said loud enough for everyone to hear.

"I got me some of the good stuff right here, man. It'll cost you though. You got any cash?"

"Yeah, of course I got some. How much?"

"Twenty-five will get you two uppers. Fifty will get you five. I'm givin' you a price break 'cause we're tight, man."

Dennis pulled a fist full of rumpled bills out of his pocket.

"Give me the five, Bro. These ain't gonna kill me is they?"

"Hell, no. Make you feel like superman is all."

Dennis washed down all five pills with the rest of his beer. When he left an hour later, his friends, all high, giggled until they fell over. He was such a pig. They were glad to be rid of him, hopefully for the rest of the day.

Having followed Emma home on numerous occasions, Dennis knew where she lived. Getting up the stairs all the way to the third floor was a challenge. He kept seeing flashing lights and the steps looked warped making it hard to navigate.

By the time he got to her floor, the sweat was pouring down his face and he was panting like a horse with the heaves. The long climb had royally pissed him off. He pounded on the door.

Jamal was sitting on the floor with his homework spread out on the coffee table.

"What on earth is that?" Emma said, getting up and hurrying to the door.

When she saw who it was and what shape he was in, she tried to push the door shut. *Not this time*, he thought as he threw his considerable weight against the door knocking Emma backward. She stumbled and fell hitting the back of her head on the coffee table.

Blood immediately began to seep into the threadbare carpet. She didn't move. Jamal was petrified. Dennis threw himself on top of Emma and began pounding her in the face with his fists.

"Wake up, you bitch! Get up. Ole Dennis got sompin for you," he yelled, eyes wild, spit flying.

All he could think about was the telephone pole sized hard-on he had; the biggest in his sorry life. The flashing lights, the roar in his ears and the mosquitoes buzzing and stinging in his brain made it hard for him to stay focused.

It took only seconds for Jamal to fly into action. He threw himself on the fat guy's back and tried to gouge his face; anything to make him stop hitting his mother.

Dennis stopped long enough to reach back and grab Jamal by the arm. With more strength than he had ever had before, he flung the little boy against the wall. The bone in Jamal's arm snapped. The pain was all-consuming. Consciousness faded.

When Keysha heard the ruckus, she came running from the bedroom, dragging her chi-chi.

"Mama!" the little girl screamed.

Jamal came to just in time to see a now enraged Dennis lumber toward his sister.

"Well now. Here's a tasty little morsel?" he slurred as he grabbed the little girl.

She was only three. He ripped her clothes off and raped her as she continued to scream. More blood. Too much blood. Dennis dropped Keysha on the floor and ran out the door.

Jamal pulled himself to his feet. The pain in his arm was excruciating, but he knew he had to act fast. The guy might come back! He might have bad friends! Shaking his mother's shoulder, Jamal tried to wake her up. Down deep he realized she was dead. Now his only thought was to get his sister out of danger.

He half dragged, half carried Keysha down the back stairs and out into the street. He headed for the woods behind the apartment building. Playing in the woods was one of his favorite pastimes. Maybe he could hide his sister there, then go and get help.

Keysha was heavy for Jamal to carry with only one good arm. She was in shock, bleeding and mostly naked with the exception of her chi-chi, which was still clutched in her hand.

There was a hole in the side of the hill where some animal had made a nest. Jamal had played there in the past. Strength was fading. Finding the hole became a matter of life or death.

"If I can just find that hole," Jamal muttered to himself. "I can push her in there and go find help. I know I can do this. I have to do this."

They slowly shuffled along together in the gathering darkness until the hole came into view. Jamal carefully pushed his sister backwards into the hole as far as he could, then stuffed her chi-chi under her head.

Tripping on an exposed tree root, he fell and rolled down the hill all the way to the bottom. For a few seconds, unconsciousness numbed his brain.

Not knowing just how long he had laid there, Jamal jumped to his feet, only to fall back to the ground as a fresh wave of pain washed over him. Using his good arm and his elbow he crawled out of the woods and onto the sidewalk. Forcing himself to his feet, the little boy began to stumble down the street.

Chapter 44

The dance team had gotten home the day before yesterday and Bruce was back on the job. *No rest for the weary*, he thought. It was the end of his shift and he was making his last pass through the eastside. He was bone tired and couldn't wait to get home to a hot shower and crawl into bed beside his sweet Asia Kim.

His mind had drifted back to his warm, cozy bedroom, where he intended to be in just over an hour, when he spotted a little kid limping down the sidewalk.

Bruce pulled slowly to the curb and got out of his patrol car.

That looks like Jamal Williams. What's he doing out at this time of night? Oh, my God. I think he's hurt!

Jamal had stopped when he saw the police car pull over. He collapsed into a little heap from pain and exhaustion as Bruce ran over to him.

A call for an ambulance and backup went out immediately. Bruce lifted the little boy's head.

"Jamal. It's Officer Watson. Hey, little man. Can you tell me what happened?"

Jamal opened his eyes and relief spread over his face before the pain again clouded his vision.

"It's Mommy. I think she's dead. I hid Keysha in the woods. We gotta find her. She's bleeding somethin' awful. The man did a bad thing to her," he tried to explain.

Approaching sirens could be heard in the distance.

"Okay, Jamal. Don't try to talk anymore. I'll find Keysha, I promise. The ambulance is almost here," Bruce said calmly and quietly to the terrified boy. "Hang in there just a little longer."

The EMT's quickly assessed Jamal's injuries and the ambulance sped away to the hospital.

"Let's head over to Spring St." Bruce directed the responding officers. "I think we might have a homicide on our hands."

In the meantime, the station's 911 operator had gotten a call from a hysterical woman saying something about a murder in an apartment house on Spring Street.

Chapter 45

On the way to Spring Street, Bruce called for another ambulance to meet him there.

Taking the stairs three at a time, Bruce quickly made it to the floor where the Williams family lived. He was met by the hysterical neighbor, who could only point in the direction of the open door to the apartment across the hall.

Bruce had seen enough dead bodies to know at a glance that Emma was gone. He felt for a pulse anyway and finding none he started looking around the apartment. The paramedics were coming up the steps; he motioned them in. They would take care of the body. He had to find Keysha.

Following the trail of blood to the back stairway, he pulled out his radio and called Luke.

"Get Butch and meet me at 124 Spring Street. We have a homicide and a missing, injured three-year-old little girl. Luke, it's a bad one."

Luke flew out of his chair and whistled for Butch.

"Roger that. On my way."

By the time Luke and Butch arrived at the apartment building, the coroner's wagon was out front. Time of death was estimated to be only a couple of hours ago. The trail would be fresh and Butch shouldn't have any trouble following it.

There was blood leading to the back stairway. Butch was on it in a heartbeat. Bruce and Luke had to trot to keep up with the big dog as he made his way down the stairs and toward the woods.

Through the woods it was a little slower going. The officers had to put their big flashlights on to keep from tripping over fallen branches and rocks. It took Butch a little longer, but he soon picked up the scent in the leaves and moved along at a brisk pace.

Finding the hole in the side of the hill, Butch began barking until the officers caught up. Luke signaled Butch away while Bruce got down on his hands and knees and flashed his light into the hole.

He could just make out the top of Keysha's head. She was so still, Bruce was afraid she might be dead too. He called her name.

"Keysha. It's Officer Watson. I'm going to get you out of there. Just hang on."

She had wiggled backwards in the hole and was too far back for Bruce to reach her. Even extending his arm all the way and forcing his shoulder into the dirt at the mouth of the little hole wasn't enough.

"Keysha. Can you talk to me? I can't reach you. Can you put your hand out, Honey?"

No response.

Bruce and Luke began carefully digging with their hands. They didn't want the roof of the hole to cave in on the little girl so it was slow going. Finally they had removed enough dirt for Bruce to touch her head.

Very gently he worked his hand under her shoulder and began to slowly, slowly, draw her out of the hole inch by inch. She still hadn't made a sound.

By the time Bruce had pulled her all the way out, the paramedics were on scene and waiting with a stretcher and their other necessary equipment.

Keysha turned her dirty little face to Bruce. Her hair was matted with debris and her eyes were dull. Relief washed over the big man. She was alive; for now at least.

"Atta girl, Keysha. I got you. You're gonna be fine."

With great tenderness, Bruce very gently cradled her tiny body to his chest for a second before handing her over to the paramedics. He picked up her blanket. It was caked with dirt and blood. He brought it along. Maybe the lab people could get some trace evidence from it.

He was pretty sure the blood was all hers, but maybe they would get lucky and find something that would point them to the scumbag who did this. Now it was up to the paramedics to get her to the hospital alive.

With a blast of his siren, Bruce pulled out ahead of the ambulance. There would be no delays getting this baby to the hospital. He also wanted to talk with Jamal; try to get more details about what had happened, that is, if the kid was up to talking. His anger grew as he sped downtown toward Cedarville General Hospital.

He had seen so much death and suffering as a Marine fighting in the middle east, he thought he was hardened to it. This was different. This was personal. He knew this kid and her brother.

"These are children, for God sakes," he ground out through clenched teeth. "What the hell."

Chapter 46

Jamal was resting comfortably in a bed in Pediatrics when Bruce and Luke arrived. His arm was in a cast and he had been given pain medication. He was groggy, but brightened when Bruce sat down on the side of his bed.

"Hey, Buddy," Bruce began. "How's the arm? That's quite the cast. Red. Nice touch."

"It's my favorite color," Jamal mumbled. "My arm ain't hurtin none since they gave me that pill." After a few minutes when he seemed to doze, he continued. "Is my mama alive? Did you find my sister?"

Luke stayed back. Bruce seemed to have a relationship of some sort with the boy already. He would probably get more information out of him than anybody else.

"Jamal, your Mama didn't make it. I'm sorry, Son. We found Keysha and the doctors are working on her now. Officer Peterson and I need to know what happened. Do you feel up to telling us about it?"

Jamal shook his head, yes. He closed his eyes and tears began pushing out from under his lashes. Bruce's heart broke for the little boy.

"A man came and banged on our door. Mama opened the door and the man gave the door a really hard shove. It knocked Mama over and she fell backwards. She hit her head on the coffee table.

There was a lotta blood. When she was on the floor, the man sat on her and kept hitting her face with his fists. I tried to stop him," Jamal wailed. "He threw me against the wall." His voice escalated. "Then Keysha came out of the bedroom. He grabbed her and ripped her clothes. And he did the bad thing to her!"

The nurse, hearing the yelling, came running in.

"Officers, I think he's had enough for now. He needs to rest."

"Just one more question, Ma'am, if I may," Bruce said politely and calmly to the nurse.

"Jamal, do you know the name of the man who did this?"

"No," Jamal answered. "I seen him around though. Sometimes he follows us. Mama always told us to ignore him and he would go away.

Jamal's agitation began to increase again.

"He didn't go away!"

"Okay, Officers. That's it. You'll have to go. Why don't you come back tomorrow. He may be able to remember more when he's had some rest."

As they were leaving, Bruce looked back. Jamal had turned his back to the door and was sobbing into his pillow.

"Poor little guy. I'm going to catch the son-of-a-bitch who did this, Luke, if it's the last thing I do. The only family the boy's got is his sister. Father's in the wind and grandmother's in the loony bin awaiting trial for killing her husband. These kids got nobody."

They stopped in the emergency room on the way out to see how Keysha was doing.

"It's not looking good," the ER doctor told them. "She's torn up pretty bad. It'll be quite a while before we know anything. The surgery will likely take hours."

"Thanks, Doc," Bruce said, shaking the doctor's hand. "We'll check back tomorrow."

The crime scene people were at the house gathering any evidence they could find. After their reports were written there was nothing more they could do tonight so Bruce and Luke headed back to the restaurant in Luke's car.

Bruce had called Asia Kim to let her know he would be late; that he had caught a case involving a couple of kids. Most people didn't know he was such a softy when it came to children. She would understand how this affected him.

"We can all pitch in and help these kids," Luke assured his friend.

"I know. I know," Bruce sighed.

Chapter 47

The Peterson Clan had gathered, as Bruce knew they would, to support him and the children.

"If there's anything at all we can do, Bruce," Bryce said, his hand on the big man's shoulder, "just let us know. You know you can count of us."

"I know, Bryce. Thanks."

After his shift the next day, Bruce headed for the hospital. He asked his wife to go with him. He had a plan swirling around in his head and it would involve them both. He had presented his idea to Asia Kim last night as they laid in bed. He wanted her to meet Jamal and also be aware of Keysha's situation, that is, if the little girl had survived the surgery.

He hadn't been able to sleep until the wee hours of the morning. Tossing and turning, he considered all their options. Asia couldn't have children as the result of the damage done to her during the years she had been forced into prostitution. They both wanted children. This seemed like the answer.

Jamal and Keysha needed a family. It was that simple. Asia Kim readily agreed. She had kissed Bruce gently.

"You good man, Bruce Watson. Asia love you so much."

Ann had offered to go along to talk with the doctors about the condition of the children. She had privileges at the hospital and often admitted patients from her clinic should their condition warrant.

She knew all the physicians on staff. Bruce accepted her offer. He knew she would understand all the technical medical stuff better than he.

They had checked at the information desk and Keysha was in the intensive care unit. She had made it through surgery, but just barely. Jamal was still on Pediatrics.

Of course, where Ann went, so went Bryce and Gunner. While Asia and Bruce went to talk with Jamal, Ann and her entourage headed toward ICU where they hoped to find the doctor who had done the surgery on Keysha.

Chapter 48

Jamal was propped up in bed eating toast with peanut butter when Bruce pushed the door open.

The boy's eyes lit up when he saw Bruce.

"Officer Watson! You came back. Did you find the guy who hurt Mommy and Keysha?"

"No, not yet. But you can help me by telling me what the guy looked like. Do you think you can do that for me?"

"I'll try. Who's that?" he asked, pointing at Asia.

Asia had waited by the door giving her husband time to reconnect with the little boy. She was all too familiar with what trauma could do to a child. She had experienced it herself. The Petersons had saved her. Bruce had loved her and helped her heal. Now she was ready to give back.

Bruce beckoned Asia toward the bed. She came to stand beside him and his arm immediately encircled her tiny waist.

"This is my wife, Asia Kim. Honey, this is my friend, Jamal. He and his family have been through a really rough time."

Asia bowed from the waist.

"It is honor to meet friend of husband's."

"She's awful little, ain't she?" was Jamal's first comment. "And she talks funny."

Bruce chuckled.

"Yep, she's pretty little and she does talk kinda funny. She's from China. That's a long ways away from here; a different country."

"I know about China," the little boy said indignantly, carefully pulling himself up in the bed using his good arm. "I heard about it in school. And my mommy says every damn thing on the rack comes from China."

Bruce did his best to hide a smile at the boy's comment. He would have to talk to him about the swearing though.

"That wonderful," Asia said, glancing up at Bruce. "You smart boy. Do you think we be friends?"

Jamal looked from Asia to Bruce and back to Asia. Obviously, studying her and this new development.

Finally, making his decision, he said, "Yep. We can be friends if Officer Watson says it's okay."

"Of course it's okay. I want you to be friends. Bruce hesitated a minute, dreading having to bring up the subject of the attack. "Now, Jamal, can you tell me everything you remember about what the bad man looked like? Anything about him at all will help me catch him."

Jamal's chin began to quiver. Tears gathered. Details began spilling out.

"I think he hangs out at the bar across from the laundromat. We always saw him when me and mommy lugged our clothes down there to wash them. He's white and really fat. He has these funny eyes; one looks straight ahead and the other one looks up at the sky." Jamal wrinkled his nose. "And he smells real bad."

Asia made her way to the other side of the bed. Gathering the little boy in her arms, she rocked him back and forth while the sobs came. Tears ran down her own cheeks as she remembered another time. Another place. Pain. Humiliation. Panic...

The telling of it seemed to be cathartic for the boy, because he soon fell asleep in Asia's arms. She laid him gently back down on the bed and covered him with the blankets.

She looked over at Bruce.

"We take. We be family."

Quietly leaving the room, they headed for the nurses' station. Bruce knew a social worker would likely be involved with these children and they needed to talk to her, sooner rather than later.

There were not an abundance of foster parents available in Cedarville. He was pretty sure the kids could be placed with Asia and him, at least temporarily. They were given an appointment for later in the day. Oscar Schwartz, the family attorney, could probably help them with the adoption procedure.

Bruce called the station and gave the new information to the detective on the case.

"This should help you nail the bastard. If I get anything more, I'll let you know."

Chapter 49

Meanwhile, Ann and Bryce had found Dr. Barneski coming out of the intensive care unit.

"Ann. How are you?" he said shaking her hand. "Bryce, nice to see you again." He gingerly patted the big dog's head. "Gunner. Always a pleasure. I take it you're here to talk about the Williams girl. Why don't we go down to the conference room."

Confidentiality and the HIPPA regulations were in place, however, this situation was unique. Dr. Barneski had been updated on the status of this family. There simply wasn't anyone else except the child's five year old brother.

Mother, dead. Father's whereabouts unknown. Brother, also in the hospital after sustaining injuries from the attack that had killed their mother. Grandfather, murdered. Grandmother, in the psychiatric center in Dixon. No other known relatives.

Of course, social work had been called in, but Ann was a colleague. She and Bryce were well known in this small town. If anyone could help these children the Peterson's could...and would. God knows where they would find anyone else to take on this responsibility.

After Ann poured coffee all around, she and Bryce sat down with Dr. Barneski.

"This is the worst case I've ever seen," Dr. Barneski began, pushing his fingers through his abundant dark hair. "This girl will never be the same. She will never have children, that's for sure. I had to remove all her female organs. They were literally ripped to shreds. I had to do extensive repair of her bladder. She's got a urostomy tube with a drainage bag. Same with the colon. Colostomy with a bag. Hopefully, down the line after healing takes place, we can reverse all this so that she can eliminate normally again."

He shook his head.

"The next twenty-four to forty-eight hours are critical. Of course, we'll be monitoring her closely. She's intubated right now, hopefully tomorrow or the next day she'll be breathing on her own. No other injuries to speak of. Some bumps and bruises, I presume from hitting the floor. She'll need extensive home care if she makes it out of the hospital."

Taking a sip of his coffee, he continued.

"My hope is that she will recover physically. Kids are resilient. Mentally will be another story entirely. She's going to have a long, hard road ahead of her. Whoever takes her in will have to be prepared to devote considerable time to caring for her. Plus they will need to be able to accept and deal with her emotional and psychological damage. I really don't know where we will find a family like that. Oh, one more thing. They did a rape kit in the ER. The lab has it now."

Bryce watched Ann's face throughout this discussion. He knew her so well. She was agonizing over this child.

Reconnecting with Bruce and Asia Kim, they decided to have lunch at a diner in town.

"How's Keysha? was the first question Bruce asked. "Is she going to be okay?"

"Well..." Ann began, "the next day or two will be crucial. If she makes it, she's going to need almost constant care. It will take time and money. Whoever takes her will also need training on how to care for the medical issues that will be involved. Bryce and I have talked about it briefly and we have some ideas..."

Bruce interrupted.

"Asia and I want to adopt both kids," he blurted out. "We know it will be hard. That's okay. We'll learn whatever we have to learn and I make good money. We can do this. We WANT to do this."

A smile spread across Ann's face. Bryce squeezed her hand.

"That's wonderful. You know you can count on the rest of the family to pitch in. Oh, one more thing about Keysha. Dr. Barneski said they did a rape kit in the ER. It's in the lab as we speak."

"How about Jamal? How's he doing?" Bryce asked.

"He's a little trooper. Tough. Smart. With the information he gave me I think we can find this guy. Detective Morrow has been assigned the case. I know him pretty well; he's good. He'll probably want Jamal to pick the guy out of a line up after they bring him in. I think the kid's up for it."

Their food finally came; not as good as Mama's, but not too bad. Bruce didn't care. He was ravenous and the appointment with Miss Barnes, the social worker, was looming. No time to be choosey. He had to admit, he was a little nervous, an unusual feeling for him.

Chapter 50

The meeting with the social worker went well. Bruce and Asia Kim were considered solid citizens in Cedarville. Both had good jobs. Asia's work hours were flexible enough to be able to spend time taking care of the children.

Down the line, when more was known about what Keysha would need, she would arrange whatever teaching was necessary to care for the little girl. And of course there would be piles of paperwork to be completed.

Bea Caruthers at the Dept. of Social Services had already been contacted and had provided information on this family. She had been shocked and dismayed to hear about Emma and the children.

"Jamal will be discharged to a family who is willing to take both children. Keysha will be with us for a while yet. I'll be sending you all the paperwork as they will both eventually be under your purview since you already have an open case."

"If there is anything at all I can do to help, just let me know," a shaken Ms. Caruthers told Miss Barnes.

The social worker breathed a sigh of relief. She was pleased with this placement. The Watson's were a lovely couple, once she got past how odd they looked together.

Another positive in this situation, Dr. Lauren Ann Reynolds-Peterson was a respected member of the medical staff at the hospital. She was known to be an excellent, caring physician. Miss Barnes was sure she would be willing to supervise the medical needs of both children.

Jamal could be released to the Watson's that evening. Medically, he was stable. When the nurse asked him if he wanted to go with Officer Watson, Bruce could hear him hollering all the way down the hall.

"Can I really go home with Officer Watson? Really? When can I go? Can Keysha go with me? What about my toys? What about my clothes? Can I go right now?"

Bruce was laughing when he and Asia entered Jamal's room.

"Yes, you can come home now, little man," Bruce chuckled as he picked the little boy up and lifted him high. "Check out the bag. Asia and I got you a few things until you're up to going shopping."

It was like Christmas. The clothes were...clothes. The toys, on the other hand, were outstanding. Electronics and games. Trucks and cars. Books and paper supplies.

"Oh, gosh," Jamal gasped. "This is so great! Thanks!"

He immediately slapped the Chicago Bulls cap on his head and shoved his feet into the Jordan Spizike basketball shoes.

He jumped into Bruce's arms nearly clocking the big man with his red cast

"Wow!" was all he could say.

Asia helped Jamal get dressed in his new clothes and packed all his new things back in the bag.

"Ready to go home, Buddy?" Bruce asked, a huge smile on his face.

Jamal got very serious.

"What about Keysha? Can she go too?"

Bruce hugged the child tight.

"No, Jamal. She has to stay in the hospital a while longer. We'll bring you to see her whenever you want to come. How's that? Then when she's better, she can come home too."

Satisfied, the little boy wrapped his arms around Bruce's neck.

"Okay. I'm ready. Let's go home. Officer Watson? Does this mean I can I call you Dad?"

Bruce felt like someone had reached in his chest and squeezed his heart.

"I'd be proud to have you call me Dad, Jamal."

Chapter 51

The wedding was a week away. Preparations were in full swing and the women of the Peterson Clan were frantically decorating, cooking and cleaning. Luke and Tess were having the private ceremony in the large back yard behind the ballroom.

A canopy would be set up under the huge, old oak tree where Tess's parent's parish priest would be performing the nuptials. It was a beautiful, romantic setting. The reception would be in the ballroom.

Practically everyone in town had been invited to the reception. Mama Rosa and Carla were already fretting over whether there would be enough food. Ann was more worried about the weather than the food. It wasn't supposed to rain, but you could never quite trust the weatherman.

Maria, Anika and Asia Kim were all standing up with Tess. Her best friend from childhood, Gretchen McLaughlin, was her maid of honor. They had all been to Claire's dress shop in Dixon numerous times for fittings and re-fittings. Excitement was running almost out of control.

Luke, on the other hand, was being razzed incessantly by the guys about the honeymoon. Bobby, who was Luke's friend from their teenage years, was his best man.

"Yo, Bro! You couldn't have made a better choice. I AM the best man," Bobby never failed to remind Luke. "Are you up for the honeymoon? I know you are!"

The kidding was non-stop. Georgio just shook his head.

"Oh, to be young again, Mama. Remember when we were married? It was the best thing that has ever happened to me. You were the most beautiful bride ever."

"You old fool," Mama Rosa replied with sentimental tears glistening in her eyes.

Bruce, Victor and John were Luke's groomsmen. With Bobby in charge, they were taking Luke into Dixon for a bachelor party. The details had been sketchy and Luke had wondered briefly what was in store for him. But being focused on the two week cruise he had planned for Tess was all he could really think about.

The log cabin on the other side of the lake from his parents house on the Peterson Estate was finished. Tess had been busy with decorating and furniture while Luke worked with the contractor building a barn with a large correl.

They could have had a house built on the cul 'd sac where Bobby and Maria lived across the street from John and Carla, however, they had opted for the log cabin in the woods. It was no ordinary little log cabin. It had every modern convenience and security second to none.

Doug Hagan, the contractor who had designed and built Ann's first house in Dixon before she married Bryce, had been kept busy over the last couple of years just building for Peterson Enterprise. He was almost like one of the family.

The house was just what Tess and Luke had dreamed it would be. From the wrap-around porch to the balcony off the master bedroom on the second floor, it was perfect. Enough bedrooms had been incorporated on the third floor to accommodate the children they planned to start having in a year or so.

Tess and Luke loved all things involving nature, so the house in the woods was just what they wanted. A big garden was planned, using the fresh produce at the restaurant. They were interested in the whole "going green" thing. A couple of milk cows and a couple of horses would be added in time. Bobby had already started calling Luke, Farmer Brown.

An added benefit to building another house on the one hundred acre Peterson Estate was having a way to patrol the land to the north of the main house where Bryce and Ann lived. Tony Marco, Ann's kidnapper, had used a tree on that side of the estate to do surveillance on the house.

At the weekly Wednesday family meeting they had discussed adding to the existing fence that ran along the property line that separated the Peterson Estate from the Cedarville park.

The fence currently ran about a mile along the line. It was decided that putting a fence around the whole one hundred acres was not cost effective. It would also be hard to maintain and would inhibit the free movement of the wild life that lived in the area at the foot of the Green Mountain range.

Since Luke and Tess wanted to be out in the woods anyway, the responsibility for patrolling that section of the estate would be theirs.

After the fervor of the kidnapping died down, Frank (Biggy) Bigelow had gotten restless and had disappeared for long periods, reappearing occasionally to get caught up on the current news and pick up supplies. He was an ex-Marine buddy of Bruce's who had been hired for extra security. Now he didn't seem to have anything to do.

It seems he had also taken to the woods and had asked permission to build a cabin on the Peterson Estate at the foot of the mountain. He wanted to build it himself even though Bryce offered to have it done for him. Patrolling across the back of the estate would be up to him.

"I'm getting older, you know. It's time to settle down," he had told the family. "Maybe I'll even find a good woman somewhere to live in the woods with me."

"And where exactly are you going to find a woman that desperate?" Bobby laughed.

Biggy scowled at Bobby and struck a manly pose.

"Oh, I have my considerable charms when I want to use them. The ladies love it."

Even Georgio laughed at that one. Biggy wasn't offended, he just sauntered away.

After their marriage, Mark and Helena had bought a house in Cedarville. Helena continued to work with Victor and Anika teaching dance at the ballroom and helping with the choreography for the dance team. Mark was on staff at the hospital.

Victor and Anika continued to live in one of the apartments attached to the Vincenzo establishment across the hall from the apartment occupied by Bruce and Asia Kim.

Everyone worked, in one capacity or another, for Peterson Enterprise. Bruce and Luke remained officers for the Cedarville Police Department along with running security for Peterson Enterprise.

Chapter 52

When Asia and Bruce brought Jamal home for the first time, most of the family was there to welcome him. Initially, he was shy and clung to Bruce's hand. He had never seen such a big, unusual family. Everyone was talking at once.

When Butch trotted over and started licking Jamal's face, the boy was terrified of the big, ugly dog.

"It's okay, Jamal. This is Butch. He's a tracking dog. He's the one who found Keysha. He won't hurt you and he won't let anyone else hurt you either," Bruce explained.

Peeking out from behind Bruce, Jamal stared at the dog. Butch whined and laid down on the floor at the little boy's feet. That was all it took. Jamal threw his arms around the big dog's neck and buried his face in his thick fur. Butch looked rather embarrassed, but he didn't move until Jamal was ready to let go.

Mama saved the day with a tray of cookies and milk.

"Let's everybody sit down. I've just taken cookies out of the oven. Come on, Jamal. Here's a place for you right beside me. I won't let any of these yahoos bother you."

She hugged the little boy and pulled out a chair for him. He smiled gratefully up at her.

Mmmmm, she sure smells good, he thought. *Like cookies. She looks like a grandma. I wonder what that white stuff is on her apron. The* only cookies he'd ever had came out of a bag from the grocery store. Jamal decided he liked her.

Once every one was seated and munching on cookies, Jamal felt better. He looked around the table. This was his new family. He could hardly take it all in.

Just then the Benson's arrived with JB and Melissa.

"Sorry we're late. We were almost ready to leave when Melissa spit up all over her clothes."

JB's eye sparkled. He had been told Jamal was his age and he was anticipating having a playmate his size. Melissa was no fun at all.

"Hey, ya wanna come and play with me? I brought some cool toys. Can he play, Uncle Bruce? Please?"

"Do you want to go play with JB, Jamal?" Bruce asked.

Jamal stared at JB, seeming to check him out.

"Yep. I wanna play," the little boy responded before sliding out of his chair and stuffing the rest of his cookie in his mouth.

"Geeezzzz. That's a really great cast," they heard JB comment as the boys raced off.

Once the boys were safely out of ear shot, the coffee came out and Bruce related Keysha's condition and what all had happened that day at the hospital.

"So Asia and I are going to try and adopt the kids. Ann, do you think Oscar will help us?"

Ann looked at Bryce.

"Oh, I'm sure he will, don't you, Honey?"

Bryce brushed her lips with his.

"No doubt about it. Bruce. Asia. After the wedding we'll ask him and his wife to dinner and explain the situation over some of Mama's fine lasagna."

Chapter 53

Otis Williams hadn't seen or heard from his wife in over three years. He had never bothered to get a divorce, not sure if he ever wanted to try marriage again. Apparently she hadn't either since papers were never served.

Once in a while, he wondered briefly how she was doing. *She's like a cat,* he thought. *Always lands on her feet. No worries. I do wonder about Jamal sometimes though. He must be five years old or so by now. Never did know Keysha...*

Wandering around until his money ran out had Otis coasting into Las Vegas on fumes. He had loved the glitz and excitement of the city when he and Emma had been there on their honeymoon. He decided to stay.

Being a good looking, personable guy he soon had a job in one of the big hotels as a waiter in the hotel restaurant. His goal was to obtain his croupier's license and work in the hotel's casino.

There were girls galore. Pretty, voluptuous girls. Finding a willing partner wasn't a problem. Never one to let the grass grow under his feet, Otis was soon wooing a pretty little chorus line girl named Kitty Katrel. He wondered if the name was legit, but she was good in bed so he didn't care what she called herself.

Neither of them had any interest in marriage, so a purely sexual relationship suited them both. Eventually, they moved in together to share expenses.

Unfortunately, Kitty had some not-so-nice friends and a gambling problem, hence the need to share expenses. Otis didn't learn about any of this until about three months into their co-habiting. He got a rude awakening when a big, burly guy named Tiny showed up at the door demanding the money Kitty owed his boss, Vito Patrelli.

Kitty promised Otis she would stop gambling away all her money if he would help her out just this one time. She insisted that Vito Patrelli was a horrible, brutal man who wouldn't think twice about having Tiny cause her considerable physical pain. She had a week to come up with the money.

Being basically a nice guy, Otis agreed to help her. He drained his bank account and still had to take out a loan to come up with the ten thousand dollars to pay off the gambling debt. Knowing how people gambled in this town, he was surprised the amount wasn't higher.

Otis decided Kitty was just too expensive, no matter how good the sex. Looking for a new apartment, this time by himself, was going to be harder now since he didn't have the money for a security deposit.

Every week he began building his savings back up with the hopes of being able to move out in a few months. This aggravation was something he didn't need. Most people didn't just stop gambling after it had become an addiction. This would happen again. She was not his responsibility and he was done paying. Kitty would be upset, but, oh well.

Chapter 54

Wedding day dawned clear and sunny.

"See, Sweetheart? I told you everything would be fine," Bryce said as he zipped Ann's dress.

Ann turned into his arms.

"I know you did. I just want everything to be perfect for them. I don't think I've ever seen Luke this excited."

Bryce chuckled.

"He's probably anticipating the cruise. Remember our first night together, Ann? You were so timid, afraid the scar on your back would somehow repulse me, as if that could ever happen. And I was so unsure of my...abilities..."

"Yes, and we were both fine as I remember," Ann replied, nibbling on his ear.

With last night's activities still fresh in his mind, Bryce kissed her deeply, drawing in the feel of her, the scent of her, the taste. He loved her so much.

More amazing was her love for him, even after she had been kidnapped right out from under his nose. He had promised her she would always be safe with him. That broken promise would haunt him always.

She insisted it was not his fault, but sometimes a shadow passed over his heart when he thought about what had happened; what could have happened. He would rather die than live without her.

Ann could always tell when those thoughts were lurking behind his eyes. The whole horrific experience had changed them both. Unless they were in their own home, she was never out of his sight; never wanted to be out of his sight. He even stood outside the bathroom door if she had to use the powder room.

Gunner was their constant companion. Everywhere they went, he went. The injuries he had received during Ann's rescue had been severe enough to retire him from active K-9 duties for the police department, but he was still their guard dog. Nothing could change his devotion to Ann. Even with a permanent disability, he was a force to be reckoned with. Now he waited patiently for them at the door.

They stood together in a close embrace for a minute longer before Ann pulled away.

"We better stop this or we'll be late," Ann chided, a tender smile on her up-turned face. "I'll make it up to you later tonight, my love."

Chapter 55

The family and close friends had gathered under the oak tree behind the restaurant. The sky was blue, the white clouds big and fluffy. The gentle breeze made it almost chilly being early spring. Nobody minded. It was the perfect day for a wedding.

The list of people invited to the reception was a long one. The whole Cedarville police department would be in attendance. Most of the business owners in the area had responded positively to the reception invitation. Ann's colleagues from the hospital were coming and Bryce had invited several people from Stratton Industry.

And then there was Tess's family and friends. *I hope there really will be enough food*, Ann thought.

All the people Ann loved the most would be there. Even a few people she hadn't seen in quite some time. Pete McHenry and Walter Ackerman were elderly now and retired, but they had both said they wouldn't miss Luke's big day for the world. Bryce had sent the limo to pick up both men.

Walt had been head of maintenance at Stratton's. Seeing the potential in an awkward fifteen year old kid who was sullen and defensive, Walt had given Luke his first job.

Pete had been the Chief of Police in Dixon who had helped Luke get into the police academy. Even the lawyer who had facilitated Luke's adoption by Bryce had said he would be there.

There were also those who would be missed. Lillian Hamilton, retired teacher who had loved Luke like her own and tutored him all the way to his GED high school diploma was one of those people.

In later years, she had come to stay at Vincenzo's and had been invaluable taking care of odds and ends that no one else had time to do. She was buried in the private cemetery on the Peterson Estate.

Ann's beloved Harriet Lewis was buried beside "Lil." She had been a mother-figure to a terrified, fifteen year old run-away and had been the only positive influence in a young Kathy Martin's life.

Before the life on the streets of Boston, the disastrous marriage, the abuse, the trials and finally witness protection where Kathy became Lauren Ann Reynolds, Harriet's "just in case" philosophy had been ingrained in Ann. It helped to direct her life to this day. Hope for the best, but plan for the worst...just in case.

She and Ann had been reunited just shortly before her death, giving Ann a chance to say good-bye. Tears ran down Ann's cheeks as her heart still ached for the loss of her friend.

All these thoughts were running through Ann's mind as she and Bryce took their place with Luke and Tess.

The ceremony was beautiful in its simplicity. The look on Luke's face as he said his vows and placed the plain gold band on Tess's finger was reminiscent of how Bryce had looked when Ann first met him; hopeful and somehow vulnerable.

"You may kiss your bride," Father Madigan said with a smile.

Luke cupped Tess's face between his hands and kissed her with such gentleness, it was obvious how much he cared. The sweet smile he got in return expressed everything Tess was feeling. They would be happy together...always.

"May I present to you Mr. and Mrs. Luke Peterson."

Bobby, not able to hold it much longer, finally let loose with a rousing cheer. When everyone joined in, the look on his face was priceless.

Luke and Tess snuck out of the reception early as they had a plane to catch, then off to Florida where they would board the ship for a ten day cruise in the Caribbean.

The reception went on until the wee hours. A good time was had by all.

Chapter 56

J amal had been enrolled in private school in the same class as his now best friend JB. The class size was small, the teachers, excellent.

The two boys couldn't be more different. JB was an all rough and tumble boy. Good in sports, class clown, always with a sparkle in his eyes. The teachers loved him in spite of his sometimes raucous, too social behavior.

Jamal, on the other hand, was quiet and studious. "A's" were all he ever got. He loved learning about animals. Asia had to be careful when she washed his clothes. More than once she had found some kind of bug or small creepy, crawly in one of his pants pockets.

If JB was having trouble with homework, it wasn't unusual for Jamal to essentially be his tutor. At five years old, Jamal was a miniature grown-up.

Both boys benefitted from this friendship. Jamal became more out-going and adventurous. JB got better grades and developed some interests other than sports.

Bruce was the center of Jamal's world. He adored his "father." When Bruce was home, Jamal was on his heels every minute. Asia had to work a little harder to win him over.

Visiting Keysha in the hospital became a daily event for Asia. Even though the little girl was breathing on her own, she had yet to open her eyes. The doctors told Asia and Bruce they didn't think there was a physiological reason for this behavior, it was more psychological; a way to hide, so to speak.

Not willing to give up on the little girl, Asia came every day. Sitting on the edge of the bed, she read stories, sang little songs and talked to Keysha as if she were awake.

Being an excellent seamstress, Asia had made Keysha a rag doll. The doll had exactly the same skin tone as the little girl. She had brown button eyes and a head full of shiny black ringlets. The clothes were sown on so they wouldn't come off. Asia had a problem with nakedness; even with dolls.

The doll was tucked under Keysha's arm along with her chi chi. Asia had washed the little blanket thoroughly before giving it back, knowing it had some special meaning. The nurses told Asia the two items were moved around in the bed in the morning leading them to believe Keysha was doing something with them during the night.

Bruce brought Jamal to see his sister about once a week. It always upset the little boy that his sister wouldn't open her eyes and talk to him.

"You have to remember she's been through an awful lot, Son," Bruce would say. "Give her time. She'll wake up when she's ready."

Chapter 57

And she finally did wake up. Asia Kim was at her usual spot on the side of the bed looking down at the book she was reading out loud. When she glanced up, Keysha was staring at her with huge, somber eyes.

Asia gently stroked the little girl's cheek.

"Well hello, Keysha," she said softly. "You finally decide wake up. It make Asia so happy. My name Asia Kim and I want be your friend."

No response was forthcoming, but Keysha's eyes never left Asia's face. Her little arms tightened around the doll and the blanket as if she were afraid they would be taken away.

"Asia make doll for you, hope you like. Maybe you want give name. Wash blanket. Know it special to you."

Asia busied herself tucking the blankets around Keysha. Adjusting the pillow and straightening the bed gave her something to do as she continued talking quietly in her sing-song voice.

"You remember Officer Watson? He my husband. Jamal live with us now. When better, you come too."

Keysha just stared at Asia. Asia and Ann were the only ones who completely understood what the little girl was going through; coping with. Terrified and unsure of what would happen next, it would take time for Keysha to trust anyone.

Being satisfied with Keysha's comfort, Asia picked up the book and began reading again until the little girl's eyes closed in peaceful sleep.

Asia hurried to the nurse's station to report the newest development. Then she called Bruce.

"Bruce, she wake up. Say nothing, but look at me. Asia so happy!"

It was the beginning of a close relationship between the young woman, who had been through so much herself, and the traumatized little girl.

From that point on, Keysha healed rapidly...physically. Asia learned how to take care of the child's special needs, staying at her bedside for hours at a time. Asia encouraged her to play, but Keysha never participated in the puzzles or games.

If Asia asked her to move, she moved. If she was asked to eat, she opened her mouth and ate. Cradling the doll, fondling the chi chi and sucking her thumb, the little girl stayed in a silent world of her own.

Keysha's private room looked like a toy store. As the rest of the family came to meet her, they couldn't resist bringing some small gift. The little girl sat in bed clutching her chi chi, which Jamal had informed them was the correct term for the worn blanket, and the doll Asia had made for her. She solemnly watched everything, her eyes frequently turning to Asia.

Without some kind of communication, there wasn't much the counselor could do. The family was told they were doing everything right; just keep at it. The only time Keysha seemed to brighten a bit was when Jamal visited. He would jump on the bed, tug on her chi chi and talk to her as if nothing was the matter. He chattered away about his room at their new home, his toys, school, which subjects he liked and his teacher.

One day he asked if JB could come with him. Keysha stared at JB and a very reticent JB stared back. Bruce found a tight-lipped JB something of an anomaly. Once outside the hospital, he was back to his exuberant self. He was reluctant to visit again.

Chapter 58

The day finally came when Keysha was discharged from the hospital. Asia had become an expert at changing the bags and caring for the ostomy sites. The doctors were sure that the initial surgeries could be reversed later in the summer.

It was frustrating that Keysha remained so disconnected from everyone. She was compliant when asked to do something, but she remained indifferent and withdrawn. Asia continued to fuss over her, dressing her in pretty dresses and fixing her hair with bows and barrettes. Socially, no progress was being made.

Most of the time, unless someone was holding her, she sat huddled in a corner, under a table or behind a chair holding her prize possessions tight to her chest and sucking her thumb. Something had to be done. Bruce had an idea if the rest of the family was willing to give it a try.

There was a well known Golden Retriever kennel in northern Vermont. Their dogs were the best in the northeast; beautiful, healthy with pedigrees beyond reproach. Bruce knew the owners. He gave them a call.

One puppy was left; a little red female. The people who had wanted her had fallen onto hard times and could no longer afford her. Bruce would have paid any price if it meant Keysha would respond.

It was time to go pick up Olyvia. She was a little ball of red fur with sharp little teeth and seemingly limitless energy. The constant whining from the cage in the back seat had Bruce wondering if this was such a good idea.

If Keysha would somehow bond with the puppy and begin to come out from behind the emotional walls she had built around herself, it would be worth the gigantic headache he was developing on the long ride home.

Chapter 59

Otis had finally saved enough money for the security deposit on a very small efficiency apartment. Kitty had not contacted him since he had moved out. That was fine with him. There were lots of girls to be had.

Good money was coming in now. A croupier's license had finally been obtained. He worked the late shift at the hotel's casino. The new apartment was within walking distance of the hotel. Life was good.

Early one morning as he was walking home after his shift, he was grabbed from behind. Something hard was shoved into his ribs.

"Just keep walking."

The voice sounded familiar. Then the light dawned. It was Tiny. Fear crawled up his spine. Bile hovered at the back of his throat. *Oh, God. Oh, God. Oh, God.*

At this hour of the morning, no one was out and about. One or two cars passed. No one paid any attention to two men walking casually down the street.

How Tiny knew where he lived was a mystery to Otis, but that's where they went. With trembling fingers Otis unlocked the door. Tiny shoved him inside where he crumpled to the floor. Tiny locked the door.

The first, unexpected kick went to his ribs and completely knocked the breath out of him. As he curled up in a ball, Otis knew he would probably die today and briefly wondered why.

The next kick landed to his left kidney. Pain shot through his body. His brain exploded. He vomited on the floor and his bladder emptied.

Tiny grabbed him by the back of his coat and threw him into a kitchen chair.

"Now listen up, ass-wad," Tiny breathed into his ear. "Your girlfriend, Kitty, has run up a considerable debt and Vito wants his money. You're going to get it for him. Kitty has other uses so her pretty face is still intact."

For emphasis, he hit Otis in the face. Blood poured from a broken nose. He tasted blood and spit out a front tooth.

"One hundred thousand dollars. Get it. Interest will be added daily so I wouldn't take too long. We'll be in touch. If you talk to the cops, you're a dead man."

One more punch to the side of his head sent Otis reeling into unconsciousness. How long he laid on the floor, he didn't know. Crawling to the phone was an excruciatingly slow and painful process. He dialed 911.

Chapter 60

When Bruce was almost home, he called ahead to let Asia know he would arrive in about twenty minutes. He wanted to make sure the rest of the family was present at the ballroom. They all knew the plan.

Bruce stepped through the door with Olyvia under his arm. For a moment, there was silence. The grown-ups were sitting around the table drinking coffee. Keysha was sitting under the table.

JB and Jamal stopped running and jumping as soon as they caught sight of the puppy. They had not been told about Olyvia. Bruce wanted the excitement he knew would follow.

Olyvia began wiggling and squirming. Bruce sat her on the floor where she immediately peed.

"Oh, gross!" JB shouted. "Somebody get some paper towels," he instructed.

Mama Rosa complied, shaking her head. *Here we go again,* she thought as she mopped up the little puddle. Hiding the smile on her face wasn't easy, but necessary. After all, she had an image to maintain.

The boys ran across the ballroom floor encouraging the puppy to follow. Not able to get good traction on the slippery, hardwood floor, Olyvia ran in place before finally taking off after the two little boys. She skidded and slid as she tried to keep up. Round and round they went until Olyvia stopped and flopped on her side, her little pink tongue sticking out in exhaustion.

Bruce kept his eyes on Keysha, waiting for some reaction; any indication that she was aware of what was happening.

Ever so slowly, she turned her head toward the boys now lying on the floor petting the puppy. Bruce held his breath.

Olyvia dragged herself to her feet and began wobbling toward the little girl under the table. The boys reached out to pull her back.

"No, leave her be," Bruce whispered. "Let her go."

Keysha solemnly watched the puppy's approach. All eyes in the room were focused on the little scenario as it played out. Everyone knew how much Bruce and Asia wanted this to work.

Finally arriving under the table, Olyvia pushed her cold nose against Keysha's bare arm. The little girl pulled back. The puppy was not dissuaded in the least. She grabbed one of the dolls arms and began tugging.

When Keysha realized that her doll was slipping away, she grabbed the other arm and for a few seconds there was a little tug-of-war between the puppy and Keysha. Olyvia let go and Keysha hugged her doll.

Worn out by all the day's activities, Olyvia crawled onto her lap and promptly went to sleep. The little girl stared down at the puppy.

Bruce got down on his hands and knees and crawled under the table to sit beside Keysha. He slowly reached for the puppy and began petting her head. The dog snored on.

Hesitantly Keysha raised her sad brown eyes to meet Bruce's. She stared intently at his face.

"Asia Kim and I got this puppy for you," he said quietly, continuing to stroke the dogs head. "Her name is Olyvia. You can talk to her; tell her all your secrets. She will never tell. She can be your best friend."

For several minutes all was quiet. Even the boys seemed to understand something important was happening under the table.

"Wibbywa?" Keysha whispered to Bruce.

In that moment, the sun came out for the big man. Tears came to his eyes. Apparently, that's the only way she could pronounce

Olyvia's name. And it was okay. It was the first word she had spoken since this whole mess began.

"Yes, Baby. Wibbywa."

Keysha gathered the puppy up in her arms and began to rock slowly back and forth. Bruce could see her lips moving close to the puppy's ear.

Chapter 61

Otis stayed in the hospital a month. He was slowly recovering from surgery for a ruptured spleen and facial surgery to put his nose back in the middle of his face. Kidney function was slowly returning to normal; thank God for that. The doctors had told him he could live with only one kidney, fortunately he would not have to find out if that was really true or not.

The police had visited several times as soon as he was stable enough to talk to them. No matter what they said, he kept his mouth shut.

"Listen, Mr. Williams, it's obvious someone did a number on you. Tell us who it was and we will protect you. We'll put him away, you can be sure of that."

Yeah right, Otis thought. *You can't protect me. Nobody can. They would track me down and kill me no matter where you tried to hide me. I'm not stupid.*

"I can't remember anything," was Otis's standard answer.

The doctors told the police it was probably true. The concussion had quite possibly caused him to have amnesia relative to this event; he really couldn't remember. Maybe in time...

Officer Schoonover didn't believe the amnesia crap for one hot second. He was a seasoned detective. It wasn't hard to see the fear that exuded from Otis. The guy was terrified.

This looked like the work of Alvin "Tiny" Granger and his boss, Vito Petrelli. These two, along with several of their associates, had been on the radar of the Las Vegas police department for several years. There had never been enough evidence on any of them to get a conviction.

Evidence got lost and witnesses suddenly disappeared. Others, like Otis, ended up being beaten to within an inch of their lives. Talking to the cops was not an option if they wanted to survive.

Since Otis had been left alive, odds were, Vito wanted something from him. All Schoonover had to do was find out what that something was.

He had reams of investigative paperwork on both Granger and Petrelli. He decided his best course of action was to dig into the past of one Otis Williams; see where their paths crossed.

Chapter 62

Luke and Tess had planned to come back from their honeymoon several days early so they could spend that time in their new home before they both had to go back to work.

Bryce and Ann had been told mainly so they wouldn't call the police if they saw lights in the house across the lake. Ann smiled to herself. She remembered that first night with Bryce in their new home. It had been spectacular...and she wasn't just talking about the house. She was glad Luke and Tess understood the importance of spending "alone time" together.

All the chicken feed was ready to be scattered. The loft in the barn was full of hay. The bins were full of grain. Everything was ready for the arrival of the animals. Two chestnut geldings complete with tack were on the way. Four milk cows and a couple of goats would soon be residing in the barn.

The plot where the garden would be planted had been plowed. The flower boxes along the deck on the front of the house were filled with dirt and ready for the flowers Tess wanted to plant.

All this for two people who knew absolutely nothing at all about caring for horses, cows, chickens, goats, crops or flowers.

Luke had been considering this problem all day. They were in way over their heads with this farming, living-off-the-land business. The idea of it was great. The implementation of it was another story.

"I think we should hire someone to oversee the farm. Someone with experience. Someone reliable and trustworthy. What do you think, Tess? We don't know how to do any of this stuff!"

Tess giggled.

"Are you just thinking about all this now?"

"Well you have to admit, I've had other things on my mind of late."

To prove his point, Luke drew her close and nuzzled her neck at that extra soft spot just below her ear that always smelled so good. His hands were soon busy with the buttons on her blouse.

"We can discuss the farm later. Right now I have something else in mind."

He scooped Tess up and headed for the bedroom upstairs.

Chapter 63

Tess was a planner. An organizer. She always had a plan, A, B, C and D ready to put into action. All too often, she had seen friends and colleagues end up in a bad situation when a little forethought could have prevented the problems.

Having thought about this issue weeks ago, she had put out some feelers. Several responses had been received from people who were interested, and who had the expertise, to run a small farm.

Luke had been so busy right up until the wedding with the Williams case, he hadn't had time to consider what operating a farm would entail. He had been glad Tess was on the ball.

Molly and Horace Reidy was one of the couples who had answered her query. They were her choice to be interviewed in person. Luke had read through the other responses and he agreed the Reidy's were the best of the bunch.

Horace had been a forest ranger for twenty-five years. They had lived on a five acre section of land provided by the forest service as part of his pay. Having both grown up on farms, he and his wife had plenty of experience living off the land.

The five acres was soon their own little patch of heaven. Horace covered his areas of responsibility for the forest service with enough time left to work on his own small farm. They had raised and educated three children who now lived in other towns close by. Six grandchildren made their lives rich and full. But they were bored to death.

When Horace retired they had to vacate the property. Making the adjustment to living in a small cottage in town with a little postage stamp size piece of grass in front had been hard. They missed the open spaces, the animals; the whole routine of farming.

Both in their late forties and not ready for the sedentary life just yet, they were eager to come to Cedarville for the face-to-face interview.

Since they would be, in reality, working for Peterson Enterprise, they were invited to come for several days so the rest of the family could meet them. If all parties were in agreement, a small house would be built for them back up in the woods behind Luke and Tess. It would be close enough for them to be able to perform their duties, but far enough to afford privacy for both families.

Since Bryce and Ann had a spare bedroom, the Reidy's would stay with them for the duration of their visit.

Horace was tall and lanky. Molly was short and plump. They reminded Luke of Jack Sprat and his wife. He had checked out their references, which were very complementary. They appeared to be a perfect fit for the Peterson Clan.

By the time their visit was over, they had been hired and had worked with Doug Hagan, the contractor, on plans for their house. It would be a small cabin looking rustic on the outside. The inside was a different story. It would have every convenience including the same security system that ran throughout all the other buildings that made up Peterson Enterprise.

Horace was given the same wrist communication unit that all the other men wore.

"Wow, this is all really high-tech! Me and the missus are just plain folks. Hope we can figure out how to use all this equipment." Horace chuckled. "I guess we can ask the grandkids. They'll know."

"Yeah, we'll help you," JB chimed in. "Me and Jamal know how to use all this stuff...well, almost all."

When the laughter died down, Bryce spoke up.

"Don't worry. It's all pretty easy once you get use to it. We'll walk you through everything before you assume your duties. And there is always someone available to help if you get stuck on something."

When they were ready to leave, Luke shook Horace's hand.

"Glad to have you on board. I'm looking forward to working with you."

Not to be left out of any conversation, Bobby interjected.

"So do you think you can teach this city boy how to become Farmer Brown?"

"No sweat," Horace replied good naturedly. "I'll have him whipped into shape in no time. Just let us know when you want us to move in. We can be ready any time."

As they watched the Reidy's car pull out of the driveway and head south, Luke draped his arm around his wife's shoulders.

"Whew! That's a relief. Now I can put my mind to more important business."

He grabbed Tess's hand and pulled her into a tight embrace.

Guess I know what we'll be doing for the next few hours, Tess thought with a contented smile curving her lips. *We only have one more day left of our honeymoon. Guess we should make it count.*

Chapter 64

Oscar had been working diligently on all the required paperwork necessary for Bruce and Asia Kim to adopt the two Williams children. There was only one hitch. The father. Yes, he had abandoned them years ago, but if he was still alive, he would have parental rights.

Otis Williams would have to be tracked down and asked if he would be willing to give up his rights to Jamal and Keysha in order for them to be adopted. Oscar had a bad feeling about it. He knew it would break Bruce's heart if something happened and the adoption couldn't go through.

Just the right man was needed for this task and Oscar knew the person he wanted. Back in the day, Harold Tweaks had been the investigator who had worked the case involving Kathy Ann Martin Madison, now Lauren Ann Reynolds-Peterson. He was meticulous. Oscar trusted him.

Harold would be in his late sixties now. Probably retired. Oscar wondered if he would be willing to come out of retirement and work this case. It shouldn't be a dangerous or lengthy job. It might require travel, motels and whatever else Harold needed. All expenses would be paid. Remuneration for his efforts would be generous.

Oscar gave him a call.

"Hey, Harold. Oscar Schwartz here. How the hell are you?"

"Good. Retired and living the high life," Harold responded with a chuckle.

After pleasantries were exchanged, Oscar got down to business and the reason he was calling after such a long time.

Retirement was getting on Harold's nerves, high life or not. He jumped at the chance to do something useful.

Chapter 65

Since the advent of the puppy, Keysha had come a long way in a short time. She still didn't talk except to the dog, but she was more involved in what was going on around her. She didn't purposely isolate herself anymore. Only rarely did she hide behind a chair or sit under the table. And once in a while she smiled.

Olyvia was her constant companion and confidant. This didn't mean that the now four month old puppy didn't find the time to get into trouble on her own. She chewed on absolutely everything. No one's belongings were safe if left unattended and within reach. Dirty underwear was a favorite; especially Anika's. No clothes hamper was impenetrable.

Food was swiped off the table or snatched from an unsuspecting person's hand. How she managed to do that was a mystery. Sometimes her sharp little teeth would find purchase on a finger along with the food. No one ever saw her until the deed was done.

Towels, rugs, blankets, pillows were all ragged around the edges. Shoes came up missing. Chair legs showed tiny chew marks. She would eat anything and acted like she was always starving.

Even Georgio wasn't happy with the current situation.

"I have to repair and refinish several of the chairs in the dining room," he sputtered. "We can't have our guests sitting on chewed-up chairs. This is supposed to be a classy place. Our reputation is at stake!"

Mama thought that statement was a little over the top, but she kept quiet. Her favorite slippers had gone missing.

If her name was called, she immediately ran in the opposite direction. When someone came in the door, she was all over them; jumping, yipping, rolling. In general, she was a nuisance. And she could be very rough, but never with Keysha.

The bond between the little girl and the puppy was nothing short of miraculous. It made Olyvia's less attractive qualities a little more bearable.

One afternoon Olyvia came flying down the hall with Bobby hot on her heels. She was dragging one of his good ties. She didn't know the meaning of the words "drop it;" or she knew and ignored them.

"Somebody stop her," he yelled. "If I catch her, I'm going to ring her neck!"

She skidded to a stop in front of Keysha and dropped the tie on her lap. With innocent brown eyes, Olyvia looked up at Bobby. She loved this chasing game!

"I swear, she's laughing at me," a usually good natured Bobby fumed.

It was decided something had to be done.

Chapter 66

The restaurant was closed on Mondays so Bruce decided this was a good day to have a lesson on dog obedience. All family members were expected to attend, even the kids; especially the kids.

JB, Jamal and Keysha sat on the floor. Olyvia wiggled her way between Jamal and his sister. She seemed to know she was in trouble.

"Olyvia is out of control," Bruce began.

"You got that right," Bobby grumbled.

Bruce had everyone's undivided attention.

"From now on it is everyone's job to train this dog," he began in his no-nonsense voice usually reserved for the criminal element. "Consistency is the key. Luke and I aren't always here to see that she behaves so the rest of you will have to carry through with what I'm going to tell you today."

Nods of agreement all around.

"Georgio. No more sneaking her table food just because she looks at you with her beggar-face.

Georgio glanced in Mama's direction and looked chagrined. She had told him that exact thing several times.

"Okay. Okay. Guilty as charged. I'll restrain myself."

"From now on, she only gets her dog food at feeding time. Keysha. She's your dog so you will be responsible for feeding her in the morning and at night. I'll show you how to do it, Baby. And don't worry. If you need help Jamal or JB will help you. Right boys?"

"Yes, sir," both boys responded in unison.

"No more chasing her around all over the place when she won't drop something you want. Understood?"

"But it's so fun," Jamal piped up.

"I don't care how fun it is," Bruce thundered. "It stops today. We'll get her some toys specifically for play. The only time you chase after her is when she's running with those toys."

"I guess that'll be okay," JB whispered to Jamal.

"Every one of you who picks her up and cuddles her, and you know who you are, stop it. She'll never learn to stay down if you keep doing that and it won't be so nice when she weighs sixty pounds!"

There was some fidgeting and embarrassed looks from everyone except Luke. Even he had been temped on occasion to pick her up. She was so darn cute it was hard to resist.

Then Bruce went over the rudiments of using the commands: no, sit, down, stay, drop it, heel and off. He gave a handful of tiny puppy-sized doggy treats to everyone.

"As we all know, she's highly motivated by food. The treats are a reward given for responding to a command correctly. They aren't for just handing out because she begs and looks cute," Bruce continued, looking pointedly at Georgio.

"When you call her, say 'Olyvia, here' one time. When she finally gets around to coming, give her a treat and praise her. When you want her to drop something, show her the treat and say 'drop it.' She will drop whatever she has in her mouth to get the treat. Then praise her. Don't forget to praise her, it's a very important part of training."

Bobby couldn't help himself. He started laughing.

"Okay, Bruce. I think we've all got the praise part."

The big man scowled in his direction before continuing.

"If she's jumping, turn your back and completely ignore her until she is sitting quietly. She's a people pleasing dog and she will turn herself wrong-side-out if you pet her and tell her what a good puppy she is."

"Enough with the praise thing," Bobby repeated.

Now everyone was laughing. Bruce just shook his head. Finally, not able to resist he joined in.

Once everyone had regained their composure, Bruce looked around the room. He had really come to love these people. At the oddest times, that emotion would surface. It was a little overwhelming. He pulled himself together.

"Any questions?"

When there weren't any, he continued.

"This will be very frustrating at first. However, Olyvia is a very smart little pup and she will learn quickly as long as everyone sticks to the rules.

Olyvia seemed to understand that the lesson was over, or so she thought. She grabbed Keysha's rag doll and ran. All eyes turned to Bruce.

"No one move," he commanded. "Olyvia. Here."

When the puppy realized no one was chasing after her, she stopped, a puzzled look on her face. It took several seconds for her to trot back to Bruce dragging the doll.

Bruce let her get a good whiff of the treat he held out to her and said "drop it."

She immediately dropped the doll and wolfed down the treat. Bruce handed the doll back to Keysha.

Bruce ruffled the pup's ears and ran his hand down her back.

"What a good girl you are," he told her in a soft, high, sing-song voice.

At that, everyone was laughing again.

"Gosh, Bruce. Is that your feminine side showing?" Bobby chortled.

"No. That's just how it's supposed to be done," he said with satisfaction. "And as you can see, it works."

Chapter 67

Surprisingly, the one who excelled at training Olyvia was JB. He was firm, but gentle. Always lavish with the praise when a task was completed correctly. Bruce was impressed. *I think I'll talk to John and Carla about JB working with Luke and me with the other dogs. Might as well start training the next generation to take over,* he mused.

John had high hopes for JB. A lawyer in the family would be nice. Carla argued that there was lots of time for JB to decide on a career path; he was only six after all. This would teach him responsibility and Bruce had said he and Luke could really use the help.

JB was thrilled. Jamal was not. His friend was now spending a lot of his free time learning "dog stuff," as Jamal put it. It wasn't much fun to play "galactic battle" by himself.

John knew how it felt to be left out. *The kid has a head for numbers and math. Maybe he would like to learn about money and accounting. I'll talk to Bruce and Asia Kim.*

Both boys were now gainfully "employed." Bruce would make the "boy swap" in the morning before his shift. JB went to Vincenzo's and Jamal went to John's home office.

Among other things, Jamal learned to add columns of numbers using the calculator. When all the columns added up to the same number, John said they "balanced."

He was taught the basics of budgeting. John would give him a dollar amount and a list of things to "buy" every day. Then ask him to figure out how much he could spend each day without going over the "budget" for the week.

John would ask Jamal to "inventory" the supplies in his office. He was shown how to count everything and mark it off on a check list. When a particular item was down to one or two, more were ordered.

It wasn't long before Jamal could be seen walking around with a pencil behind his ear and a clipboard in his hands.

"Can I inventory your cupboards, Grandma Rosa?" he would ask.

Rosa would give him a hug and opened the cupboards.

"Have a ball," she would say with a grin.

JB was taught exactly how much food to give Butch and Angel. Gunner lived with Grandma Ann and Grandpa Bryce so he didn't have to be concerned about him. Bryce did show him what Gunner required, just in case.

He learned how to brush the dogs and check their nails and coats for signs of anything amiss. Angel was the only dog in the kennel up behind the maintenance building. He was shown how to keep her run free of poop, not his favorite job, but necessary none the less. Her dish had to be kept full of fresh water and her bedding clean and dry.

Angel was the only Peterson dog without a specific talent. She was obedient and followed commands, but she had never excelled in any one task. Bruce or Luke took her on their rounds in their cruisers, but she didn't really bond with anyone. *I'll have to spend some time thinking about what to do with Angel,* Bruce thought.

JB tried to teach Butch some tricks, but the big ugly dog just wasn't interested in learning anything new. He would flop down on his side and promptly go to sleep, drool making a puddle on the floor.

Bobby patted JB on the shoulder.

"You can't teach an old dog new tricks."

JB persevered, not willing to believe the old adage. Bobby was surprised when Butch obediently "shook his hand" one day.

Jamal soaked up the financial aspect of John's job like a sponge. JB couldn't get enough of the dogs. Limits had to be put on the amount of time each child could spend on their new learning experiences. Then it was off to play.

"All work and no play makes Jack a dull boy," John had said.

JB and Jamal looked at each other.

"Huh? Who's, Jack," Jamal asked.

"Never mind," John said as he shooed the boys outside. "Go play."

Chapter 68

Harold Tweaks was soon residing in one of the guest rooms at Vincenzo's. He couldn't complain. The accommodations were far better than any hotel he'd ever stayed in and the food from Rosa's table was...well, he'd have to make another hole in his belt.

It was nice to reconnect with Ann, previously known as Kathy Martin before witness protection. He remembered her case vividly. Life with her first husband, Donny Madison, had been horrific, the abuse extensive. He didn't know how she had managed to survive.

It gave him a great sense of satisfaction to know that he had helped to change her life for the good. She had grown up to be a beautiful, gracious, delightful woman. It was obvious she was very happy and her current husband seemed to worship the ground she walked on.

Bruce helped Harold get a copy of Otis's last driver's license. The picture wasn't the best, but it would have to do. There wasn't a record of the guy having a current license so he was either dead, had not renewed when he moved or had gotten a new identity; the latter would have cost him a lot of money.

The fact that Otis had only been gone three years helped with the investigation. People who knew him should be able to remember something about him. It's not like he'd been gone for twenty years.

Harold was hopeful he could uncover useful information in a short amount of time.

Checking with the two banks in Cedarville revealed that Otis paid his bills by check and had a small savings account. Both accounts had been closed on the same day giving Harold an approximate date when he left town.

Some time was spent scouring city records going back ten years. Nothing of use popped. It was time consuming but every business in town was checked out until he finally found the last place Otis had worked.

The owner was forthcoming with tax and employment information. Several of the employees who had worked there when Otis was there were willing to talk to Harold. One of them remembered Otis talking a lot about Las Vegas where he had taken Emma on their honeymoon. *Okay. Here's my starting point,* Harold decided as he read over all the information he had collected. *It's a shot in the dark, but it's all I've got.*

Chapter 69

Every morning for the last several weeks, Tess had been sick. As soon as her feet hit the floor, she ran for the bathroom. Luke was extremely worried about her.

One morning, when the vomiting never seemed to stop, Luke insisted she talk to his mother.

"Honey, I know Mom will know what to do," he pleaded. "Just talk to her today, okay? Promise?"

Tess leaned over the bathroom sink and splashed cold water on her face. Standing up straight brought on a new wave of nausea.

"I will, Luke. Really I will," she promised. "I need to go lie down right now. Could you please bring me some crackers and Ginger Ale?"

Glad to have something to do, Luke hurried off to the kitchen.

By mid-morning, Tess was feeling better. She called Ann. When the symptoms were discussed, Ann thought she knew the cause of this particular malady.

The home pregnancy test Ann suggested turned up positive. *Wow,* Tess thought. *I must have conceived on our honeymoon!*

That night when Luke got home he found his favorite meal on the table, the candles were lit and he could hear soft romantic music coming from the sound system.

"Well, well, well. What's all this about?"

"What do you think about becoming a father?" Tess replied.

"What? Well, I haven't really given it much thought," Luke responded. "We've got lots of time for that...haven't we?"

Tess couldn't keep the smile off her face.

"You'd better give it some thought real soon because the time is in about eight months."

Luke was ecstatic! They decided to keep their little secret to themselves until Tess was further along. The possibility of a miscarriage wasn't far from their minds. Tess's mom had miscarried her first baby.

Chapter 70

Otis had recovered enough to go back to work. Smiling wasn't an option since he didn't have enough money to replace his missing front tooth. The colorful bruising around his eyes and nose had mostly subsided; the swelling was gone. He decided he finally looked half-way human.

Every morning after his shift, he made sure he walked with a group of people until he was close to his building. It didn't even matter if he knew them. *Safety in numbers,* he thought as he punched the elevator button.

When the door opened for the second floor, he was shocked and immediately terrified as Tiny entered the car. Tiny hit the button to stop between floors.

"Vito wants his money. When can he expect it?"

"Are you kidding, man. I just got back to work. Cut me some slack," Otis whined.

Tiny lounged against the wall of the elevator examining his fingernails.

"Time's a-wasting and interest is a-mounting. Ca-ching, ca-ching," he said, raising his eyes to look at Otis.

Tiny took one long stride forward and grabbed Otis by the neck, lifting him until he was balancing on his tip-toes.

"Get it. Soon. Or else."

Otis didn't have to ask what "or else" meant.

When the doors opened again, Tiny got off. He looked back over his shoulder and pointed at Otis with a manual imitation of a gun. The meaning was unmistakable.

By the time Otis got to his door his hands were trembling so bad he dropped his keys several times before managing to turn the locks. Finally entering his apartment he leaned against the closed and triple locked door.

Not for the first time, Otis wondered *what am I going to do? I don't know where to get that kind of money short of robbing a bank.*

Chapter 71

Luke and Bruce had gained a reputation with police departments across the state as a top notch search and rescue team. They were getting more and more calls from neighboring counties and even the State Police when someone went missing. Peterson Search & Rescue had been formed to handle this new demand.

Bobby and John had worked out the financial and logistics issues and they were satisfied they could make this thing work.

Much time and energy had been spent putting together all the documentation and completing the forms necessary to get this endeavor up and running. And they wanted a helicopter. It would be a huge financial undertaking, but how could extreme rescue situations be handled without one?

The police department wasn't the only organization that wanted the expertise Luke and Bruce had to offer. With the right contacts, Bobby and John were sure they could hire out to hospitals, private individuals or industries that needed air transportation outside of using public air travel options. It would take a while, but they felt Peterson Enterprise could re-coup their investment and begin to make a profit.

Bryce and Georgio had had many questions and required projections based on facts before they, being the senior partners, would sign off on borrowing that kind of money. In the world of business the reputation of Bryce Peterson went a long way in getting a bank willing to lend that much money.

Bruce and Biggy had chopper experience in the Marines. It had been only a matter of refresher classes, recertification as civilian pilots and flight hours with a qualified instructor for them to be able to put a chopper in the air. It hadn't taken long for them to be licensed.

Luke would have to go away for several months training before he was qualified to operate the big bird. Now was not the time. He was a newlywed and soon to be dad. The training could wait. There were certainly other things he could do in a rescue situation that didn't require a pilot's license.

The plan was for Bruce and Luke to eventually leave the police force and run the search and rescue operation full time. Of course, they would still work in conjunction with local law enforcement when their special skills were required. Both men were only part time with the Cedarville Police Department right now and there weren't enough hours in a day.

The time had finally come. Biggy had radioed Luke with his ETA. Bruce was in the co-pilot seat. The whole family had gathered at the end of the newly constructed landing pad to await the arrival of the most recent acquisition to the Search and Rescue branch of Peterson Enterprise.

The thump, thump, thump of the rotors could be heard a few minutes before the chopper came into view. It was a Eurocopter EC175 mid-size helicopter outfitted for rescue situations and medical transport. The price had been staggering even by Peterson Enterprise standards.

JB was the first to spot the approaching aircraft.

"There it is. There it is. See it, Daddy? Can ya see it?" he yelled excitedly.

"Yes, son. I can see it," John laughed. "You better calm down, JB. You can't be hopping around like a kangaroo if you expect Uncle Bruce to give you a ride in that thing."

"Me too. Me too," Jamal piped up. "I wanna ride too."

Georgio put his arm around Bryce's shoulder.

"Well, looks like we've got ourselves a helicopter. I hope the boys know what they're doing with this venture. Otherwise, we may all end up in the poorhouse."

Bryce chuckled.

"I have to admit, in the beginning I was skeptical. But the guys have put together a solid plan. If everything works out the way they expect, we should be very successful. Besides, it will certainly be possible to help a lot of people in trouble and that's the bottom line."

Chapter 72

ne topic of discussion at a Wednesday family meeting was the breeding and training of dogs for police work, rescue situations, special needs dogs like Olyvia, as well as dogs for drug and bomb work. It seemed to be an obvious outgrowth of Peterson Search and Rescue.

Bobby had done his research and he knew there was a demand for well trained dogs to meet these needs. Buying other dogs from Germany was unprofitable and any agency with the money could buy a foreign bred and trained dog. "With the money" being the operative words. The goal for Peterson Enterprise would be to breed and train their own dogs and make them more affordable. For that to happen, they needed puppies.

Over the ensuing weeks, the pros and cons were debated. Sometimes heatedly and not always at family meetings.

Finally, it was time to make a decision one way or the other. Time was a-wasting as Biggy was fond of saying. Funny, coming from a man who was known for his procrastination techniques.

At the end of that week's family meeting a decision would be made. Georgio stoked his mustache.

"This isn't something that's going to happen overnight," he mused. "It would have to be more of a long term goal for us. Mama and I are in if the rest of you want to do it."

Everyone agreed to participate to a more of lesser degree.

It had never ceased to amaze Bruce how willing this family was to pitch in and support each other, no matter how harebrained the scheme was sometimes.

"Thanks, you guys. You could all help in the puppy stage of training. Especially JB. He's got real potential. The puppies need to be socialized. They need to learn basic obedience and commands; all those kinds of things."

"Anika and I, we not know about training dog. We can pet and help make friendly though," was Victor's offer.

"Yes," Maria excitedly agreed. "We can all help with that part. It'll be fun!"

"Luke, Biggy and I will handle the more advanced training, so you don't have to worry about that," Bruce promised.

It was decided that the next time Angel came into heat, she and Gunner would have a play-day. Both dogs had impeccable pedigrees, excellent health backgrounds and were all-around solid dogs.

Luke had made a strong case for "mutts" citing Butch as an example.

"There will be agencies or even private individuals out there who don't have the capitol to afford a registered dog," he stated earnestly. "That doesn't mean the need isn't there. We should be on the look-out at the local shelters for possible candidates. We can't just keep breeding Gunner and Angel."

"Are you sure you guys won't be spreading yourselves too thin? Bryce commented. "I don't know much about training dogs, but it would seem to me that it would take a lot of time."

Biggy spoke up. Unusual for him.

"I had a friend in the corp. Retired the same time I did. He was good with the dogs. I could track him down. See if he would be interested in coming on board with us."

"That's a great suggestion, Big," Luke said. "See if you can find him. In the meantime, I'll make regular rounds of the area shelters. See what turns up.

"Okay. It seems we're all on board with this new project," Bryce said at the conclusion of the discussion. "Let's make it happen!"

Chapter 73

With everything else that had been going on Bruce and Asia Kim had almost forgotten about the investigation into the death of Keysha and Jamal's mother, Emma Williams.

Finding Dennis Lodge hadn't been difficult. The description Jamal had given was spot-on. It had given Detective Morrow great pleasure when he had found the guy right where Jamal said he would be.

Of course Dennis had cried lawyer as soon as the handcuffs came out. The kid's parents came to the station immediately, flanked by their legal team.

With the evidence the police had gathered, the State's Attorney in Dixon had brought several charges against Dennis as a result of Emma's death. The list of charges related to Keysha was a long one.

Dennis had been transported to Dixon where the trial would take place. The Cedarville Police Department only had a holding cell used for drunks and perpetrators of petty crimes. It wasn't meant to house prisoners for an extended period of time. The town was too small to support its own court system other than the local magistrate, so this case was transferred much to the relief of the police chief.

Lawyers for the defense had buried the State's Attorney's office with motions, several for inconsequential things, just to delay the proceedings. The parents could afford it so the lawyers pulled out all the stops. The kid would have the best defense money could buy. It didn't matter that he was guilty as sin.

The lead attorney had assured his parents he would not be convicted. The only eye witnesses were a five-year-old and a three-year-old. They would be easy to intimidate. Evidence could be lost, compromised. Money could buy anything.

If they had to, they could always fall back on the "not guilty by reason of mental disease or defect" defense. Dennis had been high after all, and obviously out of control.

Chapter 74

 ✧

Harold had never been to Las Vegas. It was the Peterson's dime so why not go do some sleuthing in person. Besides, there was only so much that could be done over the telephone.

Upon his arrival, Harold checked in with the local police. It was common courtesy since he was going to be poking around and asking questions on their turf. It was also possible they might have information that would help him find his guy.

The driver's license photo was a few years old, but the vice cop Harold contacted recognized Otis immediately.

Detective Billy Stokes leaned back in his chair and studied the picture.

"Hey. Yeah. I know this guy. He got beat up pretty bad here a few months ago. Wouldn't give up the guy who put the hurt on him though. We're looking at a thug nick-named Tiny. It's his MO sure enough. Works for Vito Petrelli, small time mobster into racketeering, prostitution, gambling, drugs, you name it. Tiny is his enforcer."

"Do you have any idea what this Tiny wants from Otis Williams?" was Harold's first question.

"Not a clue. My suspicion is that it involves money, and a substantial amount. Vito doesn't send in Tiny for chump change. We investigated Otis. He doesn't gamble, in fact he's a croupier at one of the casinos. Makes good money. Seems like a decent fellow. No outstanding large debts that we could find. We've been unable so far to find a connection."

Stokes scribbled something on a scrap of paper and handed it to Harold.

"Here's his current home address. He works the night shift at Treasure Island. Go talk to him. Maybe you can get something out of him that we couldn't."

"Okay, Stokes. Thanks for the information. If I turn up anything I'll let you know. Here's my card if you need to contact me. I'll probably be in town for a week or so staying at the MGM Grand."

The men shook hands and Harold walked out into the busy street. He headed toward his hotel. Over a dinner of prime rib he mulled over the information provided by Detective Stokes.

After polishing off his steak washed down by a couple of beers, he decided to visit Otis at his job. He waited until after midnight, then took a cab to Treasure Island. A few hundred dollars worth of chips should be enough to get him a spot at Otis's Blackjack table.

Otis was an excellent dealer. Harold watched him as he played several hands. The only thing of note was that Otis was watching the room as much as he was watching his cards. His eyes darted around every few minutes.

Hum. He's nervous about something that's for sure, Harold thought. Just when he had decided he had seen enough and was ready to cash in his chips, a very big man with a shaved head elbowed his way into the game. He looked and acted like any street thug Harold had ever seen, only dressed better.

Well, well, well. I'm betting this is Tiny.

The response from Otis was enough to lead Harold to believe his assumption was correct. To the untrained eye, nothing out of the ordinary was happening. The cards were dealt, bets were made and chips thrown down. Curses erupted from losers. Winners celebrated.

No one was paying attention to the dealer's face, only to the hands that dealt the cards. Harold noticed how the fingers trembled slightly. A wordless message was sent and received. Tiny stayed only long enough to make sure Otis was sufficiently intimidated.

Otis had turned white as a sheet. Something Harold didn't think was possible for a black man. His eyes were wide, nostrils flared. Breathing came in short, rapid gasps. Perspiration beaded on Otis's forehead.

After a few seconds passed, Harold followed the guy out into the lobby. Anyone watching would have thought he was reading a message on his cell phone, when in reality he was taking a picture.

A black SUV pulled up in front and the bloke hopped in. The windows were dark so Harold couldn't see who was driving or whether there was a passenger already in the vehicle. He took a picture of the back of the SUV as it drove away. The license plate number was good and clear.

In the morning, Harold called Stokes.

"Hey. Can you run a plate number for me?"

"Sure. What's up?"

"I spent a little time playing Blackjack last night. A fellow player sure had a certain dealers attention. And I'm sending you a couple of photos."

"That's Tiny sure enough. Stop by the station in an hour or so. I'll have the information for you."

While he waited, Harold ordered breakfast from room service and placed a call to Oscar.

"Oscar. I found your guy. Here's his address," he said and gave Oscar the information Stokes had provided. "There's something going on with our man, Otis. Don't have any details yet so I need to stay around a little longer."

A deep sigh could be heard on the other end of the phone line, whether from relief or frustration Harold couldn't tell.

"Okay. Thanks, Harold. Good work. Keep me posted."

Oscar hadn't dreaded anything quite so much in a long time as he did having to make this call to Bruce and Asia Kim.

"We found him, Bruce. He's living in Las Vegas. I'll have to send him notification of your petition to adopt the kids. All we can do is pray he doesn't want them."

Bruce felt like someone had punched him in the stomach.

Chapter 75

As if Bruce and Asia Kim weren't already dealing with enough stress, they got a subpoena for Jamal AND Keysha to appear...for the defense at the rape/murder trial of Dennis Lodge.

Bruce immediately called Oscar.

"What the hell, Oscar. Testify for the defense? That's just crazy. And Keysha! What could they possibly want with her. She can't testify. She's barely communicating verbally at all! She's made so much progress. This could send her back to the beginning! Isn't there any way you can stop this from happening? She's going in for surgery to reverse the urostomy and colostomy in another month. I can't have her traumatized again by having to see the guy who raped her!"

"The first thing we have to do is petition the court to appoint me as Keysha and Jamal's attorney or guardian ad litem. In that position I can legally speak for what is in their best interest. The State's Attorney will be the one prosecuting the actual case against Dennis Lodge. I'll do everything I can, Bruce. I think the defense is counting on using the children's testimony of Lodge's erratic behavior to bolster their 'the drugs made me do it' defense strategy. It's rotten and underhanded, but not illegal."

Oscar began scribbling notes on a legal pad.

"The fact that Keysha is scheduled for surgery should help. I'll also need to get access to her medical records from the hospital and the doctors who treated her. I think we have a good chance of stopping Keysha's participation in the trial. Jamal can testify if you think he's up to it and he wants to. It might give him a feeling of closure and satisfaction that he helped put away his mother's killer and the person who hurt his sister. From what I've seen, the kid's a tough little guy. I don't think they'll be able to get him confused about what happened. What the defense is trying may very well backfire!

After gathering his thoughts, Oscar continued.

"The defense lawyers must have gotten their list of witnesses submitted ahead of the prosecution. Hard to believe that could have happened. I've never heard of such a tactic being tried, but anything is possible. I'm sure there will be motions flying from the State's Attorney's office. To clarify for you, different states and jurisdictions have different names for the person prosecuting a case. In Massachusetts when I had my practice in Boston, we called it the District Attorney's office. It's essentially the same thing just different terminology."

"Okay, Oscar. We'll do whatever you say. I can't thank you enough for your help."

"You and Asia, try not to worry. I know. Easier said than done! I'll be in touch, Bruce."

After a long discussion with the State's Attorney, Sidney Hoffman, a plan was put into action. Oscar knew Sidney well. They had worked together before on a couple of cases. After graduating from Harvard Law School at the top of the class and passing the bar exam Sid Hoffman came up through the ranks quickly. Her reputation for fairness and perseverance had gotten her reelected three times. She was a powerful and fearless black woman.

All of the documentation from Cedarville Hospital, as well as records from the doctors who treated Keysha and Jamal, were subpoenaed. All parties were more than willing to provide any information the State's Attorney's office wanted.

A request for Oscar to assume the role of attorney/guardian ad litem for the Williams children was submitted. Because of the unique circumstances; the fact that the children were in foster care,

Oscar felt certain he would be granted permission to act in this capacity.

He used the information in the medical records and the police report to put together the presentation he would make to the judge should that be required. It sickened him to read about what had happened that day.

Bruce and Asia Kim were summoned to Judge Jason Bailey's chambers at the courthouse in Dixon. He would be presiding over the Lodge trial. They were to bring Keysha and Jamal. The judge wanted to see for himself if the children were qualified to testify. Oscar had received his own notification to appear with the family.

Oscar called Bruce.

"This is a positive thing, Bruce. This means the judge will probably allow me to represent the kids. If he sees Keysha's condition for himself, the ruling will probably go our way for her. Jamal. I don't know. It's a toss-up."

Bruce explained to Jamal and Keysha in terms he hoped they understood, what was going to happen. Keysha just stared at him with sad, brown eyes. Jamal was ready for a fight with the judge. Bruce had to smile. *This kid has guts, that's for sure.*

On the appointed day Bruce, Asia Kim, Jamal, Keysha and Oscar presented themselves as requested.

The little girl was terrified the minute they stepped into the judge's chambers. She hid her face in Bruce's neck. As usual, her doll and chi-chi were clutched to her chest. Everyone sat down.

Bruce tried to pry Keysha off his shoulder and get her to sit on his lap. She would have none of it. She hung on tighter and began crying softly. He was livid. He hung on to his temper by a thread and only because he didn't want to frighten Keysha further.

The judge was patient and kind.

"Keysha," he said. "How pretty you look today. I would sure like you to talk to me for a minute. Can you talk to me?"

Bruce did his best to try and persuade her.

"Baby, it's okay. Nobody is going to hurt you. Can you turn around and talk to the nice man?"

No response from Keysha. She continued to whimper against Bruce's neck.

Jamal got off his chair and came over to stand next to the judge.

"I need to tell you something in your ear," he said very seriously.

The judge leaned over. Jamal cupped his hand around his mouth and whispered.

"My sister don't talk hardly at all since that man did the bad thing to her. She's scared of everything except us. And Olyvia," he added.

"And who is Olyvia?" the judge whispered back.

"Oh, she's the puppy my Daddy-Bruce got for Keysha. He said my sister could tell Olyvia anything. So Keysha only talks to her."

"Thank you, son, for clearing that up for me. How about if we let Atty. Schwartz talk for her?"

Jamal climbed back up onto his chair.

"That would be lots better," he said looking at Oscar for confirmation.

"Well," the judge murmured quietly. "Trying to get anything out of Keysha looks like a lost cause to me. Atty. Schwartz, I have decided to allow you to represent the best interests of these children so please present the information I'm sure you have collected."

Sometimes Judge Bailey hated his job. It was obvious to him that the child wasn't going to be able to testify. The lawyers for the defense were idiots, a thought the judge dared not express out loud.

Oscar concisely presented all the information he had obtained. The judge listened intently. A couple of questions were asked and answered.

"Your honor, Keysha barely speaks at all and then only to the dog. Since the arrival of the puppy she has begun to make progress. I'm afraid appearing at trial would set her back immeasurably and quite possibly emotionally destroy her. She is facing more surgery soon and I respectfully ask that she not be made to testify."

"I tend to agree, Atty. Schwartz. It's clear to me that this child is in no condition to provide the court with any substantive testimony. In my opinion, it would be cruel and serve no purpose whatsoever. I won't allow Keysha to be called as a witness."

Bruce breathed a sigh of relief. He gently patted Keysha's back. "It's okay, Baby. The judge says you don't have to talk to anybody if you don't want to."

The little girl laid her head on the big man's shoulder. With her thumb firmly in her mouth, she closed her eyes and relaxed.

"What about me?" Jamal piped up. "I want to say what that man did to my Mom and my sister. I can do it. I'm not afraid."

"Do you remember exactly what happened?" the judge asked.

"I'll never forget it. I see it in my head almost every night when I close my eyes," he responded quietly.

"Can you tell me about it now?"

Jamal nodded and began to relate the events of that day. Even for a person who had been sitting on the bench for decades, it was hard to hear. The little boy calmly stated the facts. At times his chin trembled and tears ran down his cheeks, but he didn't break.

"Okay, Jamal. You'll get your say. How's that?"

With that said, the judge stood, nodded to Oscar and left the room.

After this trial, I'm going to retire he thought as he tore off his robe and flung it on the back of the door to his private office. *These lawyers with their thousand dollar suits and fancy cars have no compassion at all; no concept of right and wrong. They don't care about justice being served. All they care about is collecting their extravagant fees. I know everyone deserves fair representation, but what about the victim for God sake. It seems the defense has changed its plea. They couldn't get past the physical evidence so the dirt-bag is pleading not guilty by reason of mental disease or defect. In other words, the drugs made me do it. What bullshit.*

After he finished his mental rant, he collapsed into the chair behind his desk. There was a bottle of White Label Dewar's blended scotch locked in the desk drawer along with a box of Cuban cigars. He poured himself a liberal double shot, then put his feet up and lit a cigar. With the whiskey warming his belly and smoke curling around his head, he started to feel a little better. Drinking and smoking weren't allowed in the court house, but at this moment, with the sounds of the little girl's anguish and Jamal stoic rendition of what happened still fresh in his mind, he didn't give a damn.

The defense team would have a fit and probably inundate his office with more crap.

Screw them all. I've made my ruling. They'll just have to live with it.

Chapter 76

Tess and Luke had invited Ann and Bryce over for dinner one evening. For dessert Tess had made a big chocolate cake with Grandma and Grandpa written in frosting across the top.

It took several seconds for realization to set in.

"Oh, my gosh," Bryce exclaimed. "You're having a baby? Ann, we're going to be grandparents!"

Ann wrapped her arms around her husband's neck. They both laughed and cried.

Luke was beaming from ear to ear. He reached for Tess's hand.

"We wanted you guys to be the first to know. The baby is due sometime in January. And before you ask, no, we haven't decided on names yet." He waited a heartbeat. "We're thinking maybe Clyde or Myrtle."

"Oh...that's ah, that's nice," Ann stammered, trying her best to look pleased with those choices.

Luke and Tess couldn't help laughing at the look Ann was trying desperately to hide. She loved these two so much. Hurting their feelings wasn't an option. *Whatever name they pick, I will love it,* she told herself.

"Don't worry, Mom. We'll try to come up with something better than that," Luke assured his parents.

The announcement was made to the rest of the family at their weekly meeting. Everyone was overjoyed. Especially Georgio.

"See what I say, Mama. I try to tell you there would soon be babies!"

"So, Luke, you're going to name a boy after me, right? Roberto Peterson. That has a nice ring to it if you ask me."

No. Not really, Bobby," Victor piped up. "He will be dancer so he should be name after me."

"Wait a minute. Wait a minute," Luke interrupted. "you both might want to use those names for your own kids someday. And who said anything about him being a dancer? He's going to be a cop like his old man."

Ann looked around the table.

"And who said it's going to be a boy? It might be a girl and she's going to be a doctor just like her Grandma."

It was a happy afternoon. Thoughts of trials and foiled adoptions were put aside for a few hours. There would be plenty of time to worry about all that tomorrow. Right now, Georgio opened a bottle of Champaign even though it was only early afternoon.

He raised his glass with the others.

"Too a healthy baby."

They all joined in the toast.

"Hear. Hear!"

Chapter 77

A s the hot, muggy days of summer passed, Tess got bigger and bigger. It soon became apparent this was not a normal pregnancy.

"I'm going to set you up for an ultrasound at the hospital," Ann told Tess after a cursory examination. "I only hear one heartbeat, but one baby could be behind the other. You're too big too early for it to be only one baby."

The ultrasound revealed twins. Luke was dumbfounded.

"How...how did that happen?" he asked his mother.

Ann gave him the textbook explanation then laughed as she added, "as to exactly how this happened, I guess you would be the best judge of that."

Luke grinned.

"Well...yeah, there's that..."

He squeezed Tess's hand. Finally a look of complete amazement crossed his face.

"Wow, Honey. We're having two babies."

His joy was tainted a bit when the doctor seemed concerned and encouraged Tess to have an amniocentesis.

"I just want to make sure both babies are healthy," he said to the young parents. "The nurse will get things set up and we can do the procedure right now."

Dr. Horton took Ann's arm, leaving the nurse to her preparations including drawing blood and collecting a urine specimen from Tess.

"Walk with me, Ann," he said with a grim expression on his face. "No use worrying them until we know for sure, but I think something is wrong with one of the babies."

By the time all the tests had been run, Tess and Luke were both exhausted. They waited in the hospital room for most of the afternoon before the doctor finally came in with the results.

"I'm afraid I have good news and bad news," he began, looking at them over the top of his glasses. "You are having fraternal twins; a boy and a girl. The little boy appears to be fine. That's the good news. The bad news is that I'm fairly certain the little girl has Down Syndrome.

Ann had been stunned when Dr. Horton had told her. There had been only a few minutes for her to come to grips with the situation before Tess and Luke got the news. When Luke nearly collapsed, she guided him to a chair beside Tess's bed.

At first there was denial. Then realization of the truth. Then acceptance. In a matter of minutes their world came crashing down.

"So...what do we do now?" a devastated Luke asked.

"Well," Dr. Horton began. "There are options. We can terminate the female fetus," he began.

Tess came up out of the bed so quickly if Luke hadn't grabbed her, she would have fallen.

"What? Absolutely not. You're telling me I can kill one of my children? How could you even suggest that," she raged as she dissolved into tears.

Luke looked stricken as he held his sobbing wife.

"Mom...what...we can't do that! She's our daughter. We can't kill her..." his voice trailed off as tears ran down his cheeks.

Dr. Horton spoke calmly.

"We aren't 'killing the baby.' We would be terminating the defective fetus. It would be the humane thing to do. She will never have a normal life and she may suffer from a myriad of health problems..."

Luke grabbed the doctor by the front of his white lab coat.

"She would be dead wouldn't she? And you would have caused it," he yelled into the doctor's face. "I'm a cop. I know all about killing and death. It's called murder. I put people in jail for doing it. Terminating the defective fetus, as you so nicely phrase it, is murder."

The doctor was familiar with any number of reactions from distraught parents upon receiving this kind of news. He held up his hands in surrender. Luke let go of his coat and stepped back.

"Okay, okay. You have other options. Tess, you can certainly carry both children to term and put the girl up for adoption or put her in an institution. There are very nice facilities for children like her..."

"Children like her?" Luke made another grab for the doctor. "Are you freaking kidding me? She's our daughter! Get out of here. We'll have our babies. We'll love them and raise them both the same. Get. Out. Now."

Luke and Tess went home. It took a few days, but they finally came to terms with what the future would hold. Of course, the rest of the family gathered around to offer comfort and support.

When Georgio and Mama Rosa got the news, Georgio wiped his eyes with the big, white hankie he always carried in his back pocket.

"Mama, we'll just handle this like we do every other crisis we face," he firmly stated. "We will love this child no matter what and everything will be all right."

Yes, Mama thought. *Everything will be all right. As long as we have each other and the family is together, we can come through anything. I'll pray our little girl is not as serious as we have been led to believe. Miracles do happen sometimes...*

Chapter 78

❧

Since Tiny had appeared at his job, Otis had been out of his mind with fear. He couldn't eat or sleep. Nausea was always a swallow away. It was beginning to effect his work and his boss had called him in for a chat.

"Listen, Otis. I like you. You're a good worker, always on time, always efficient and responsible. What the hell is going on? Your table has been short the last few nights. Whatever is happening in your personal life, it cannot spill over into your job. Do we understand each other?"

"Yes. Yes, of course. Yes, Sir. I understand completely," Otis stammered.

He walked home as fast as his shaky legs could carry him. He didn't know how long he sat on his couch staring off into space when his doorbell rang. It jerked him back into the real world and sent his heart racing. Sweat began pouring down his face. The bell rang again.

Looking out the peep hole revealed...the postman. *Maybe it's a trap. Maybe Tiny is waiting out there around the corner to get me. What should I do?* The bell rang a third time. Otis reluctantly opened the door.

"Mr. Williams? I've got a letter here for you. You need to sign for it, please," the young man said politely.

He handed Otis a clip board and an official looking envelope with a return address of a lawyer's office in Dixon, VT.

Otis sat back down on the couch and stared at the envelope. *What could this possibly be about. I try to mind my own business, do a good job, why can't I catch a stinking break?*

The letter was from an Attorney Oscar Schwartz. It explained that upon the death of his wife, Emma Williams, his two children, Jamal and Keysha Williams, had been placed in foster care. The foster parents, Bruce and Asia Kim Watson, wanted to adopt both children.

In order for this to happen, he would need to sign over his parental rights. The letter went on to explain in detail the legal in's and out's of the whole process. He could be assured that the Watson's were good people, had good jobs and would give the children a loving home.

It went on to disclose that Keysha had some serious health issues which would require close monitoring, extensive home care and surgery. A form was enclosed for his notarized signature. If he had any questions, a phone number was included.

What? Emma is dead? I wonder what happened. Oh, my God. What kind of health issues? Expensive, I'm sure. I don't need this right now! I can't take care of two little kids, especially a sick one! I wonder if Emma's parents were contacted? Her father hated me. They sure aren't going to take in my kids. Maybe I should just sign the paper. What other choice do I have?

Otis sat there, unmoving, well into the evening. The letter had slipped from his fingers and fell to the floor between his feet.

Then a light bulb came on and a preposterous plan began to take shape in his mind.

Chapter 79

Oscar couldn't imagine the trial of Dennis Lodge taking very long. The evidence proved he was the perpetrator of this crime. The tough part would by trying to figure out how the defense was going to spin the mental disease or defect argument, then staying ahead of it; proving it was nonsense.

One scared little boy was all that stood between a "guilty on all charges" verdict or evading punishment with the trumped up insanity plea. Oscar had thoroughly coached Jamal to only answer the questions that were asked, tell the truth and don't focus on the people sitting at defense table.

"Just look at the person asking you the questions. Don't look at anybody else, okay, Jamal?"

The little boy vigorously shook his head, yes.

Oscar also explained that none of the family could be in the courtroom when he testified. The judge makes the rules and this is the rule for the Lodge trial. Bruce and Asia would be waiting in the hall. They could see him before and after he took the stand. Bruce and Luke would also have to testify all by themselves.

"But I'll be there right in the front row. You'll have to trust me to look out for you, Buddy," Oscar said. "Do you think you can do that?"

Jamal pondered Oscar's statement for a few minutes.

"If my Dad and Uncle Luke can do it alone, so can I," he answered with confidence. "As long as you're going to be right there."

A trip to the court house had been arranged so Jamal could sit in the witness chair and meet one of the bailiffs as well as Atty. Hoffman. Oscar explained what was going to happen. Jamal listened intently to everything Oscar said.

Jamal looked around the room. He hadn't said anything and Oscar was beginning to wonder if this was going work. Maybe he should have tried to get Jamal disqualified as a witness along with Keysha.

"What's that over there?" Jamal asked, pointing to the judge's robe.

Oscar had been given permission to let Jamal see and do anything he wanted short of destroying property in order to make the child feel less apprehensive when he took the stand. He wondered where this was going, but he answered the boy's question.

"That's the judge's robe. Remember when we talked to Judge Bailey? He'll wear it during the trial."

"Why? Doesn't he have enough clothes?"

"Yes, he has lots of clothes. He'll wear his regular clothes under the robe."

"Why? Will it be cold in here? Will I need to wear a jacket?"

Oscar was getting a little frustrated with all the questions.

"No, it won't be cold and no, you shouldn't need a jacket. The judge just likes to wear the robe so everyone will know who he is and that he's in charge."

"Okay," Jamal responded. "Can I try it on?"

Oscar sighed.

"Okay. Sure, why not."

Of course the robe engulfed the small boy and dragged on the floor.

"Now can I sit up there in the judge's seat?"

Oscar picked him up and helped him onto the chair.

"This is where the judge will say if that man did it or not?" Jamal asked so softly Oscar had to strain to hear him.

"The jurors will make the decision after they hear what everybody has to say. They will write what they decide on a piece of paper. The judge will read what they decide from this chair."

A hard look of determination came over Jamal's face. He picked up the gavel and banged it down.

"Guilty," he shouted with finality.

The little boy slid off the chair and shrugged out of the robe.

"Okay. I'm done now. Let's go home. Can we stop for ice cream?"

Chapter 80

Tess and Luke had decided on names for their twins. The boy would be Charles Luke and his sister would be Galva Grace. Charley and Gracie. Tess talked to her children all the time, calling them by their names.

She also read stories and played music. One of the books she had gotten from the library said this was essential in establishing a bond with the child even before birth. Luke felt ridicules reading "The Three Little Pigs" to Tess's belly, but he was willing to do anything she asked. If it would put a smile on her face, he would read it while standing on his head.

Luke had insisted she stop working. She didn't feel this was necessary, however as the pregnancy progressed and she got so big she couldn't see her feet, she was happy to be able to sit down and put those now oversized feet up on a stool.

Puttering around the house, weeding the flowers and scattering feed for the chickens gave her something to do. Keeping busy, not thinking too much. That was the key. Dwelling on the obvious problems didn't benefit anybody or change anything.

Molly Reidy was a huge help. Doing the Peterson housework and cooking wasn't something she had been hired to do, but seeing a non-complaining Tess lumbering around trying to keep up with everything had touched her heart.

"You just sit down right here," Molly said as she plumped up a pillow and put it behind Tess's back. "I'll throw together a chicken pot pie. It'll be done when Luke comes home."

Tess put her hand on the older woman's arm.

"Molly. How can I ever thank you. Luke is so busy he doesn't have time to do much around the house. He would if he could. And he worries constantly about me and the babies..."

"I know, I know. I enjoy helping you. It's no trouble at all. Just remember me when you need a baby-sitter for those little ones."

As her hands busily peeled potatoes, Molly let her mind wander. She smiled to herself. *There won't be much need for a baby-sitter. I'll probably have to stand in line just to hold them. This is one amazing family to be sure. Not a day goes by that someone isn't here checking in, bringing some little gift for Tess or the babies. Both these children will be well loved. Sweet little Galva Grace will certainly be born into the right family.*

Chapter 81

L uke now worked only as a K-9 officer at the police department when they needed the dogs for some reason. It had freed up a little more time for him to work at getting Peterson Search and Rescue established.

Gunner and Angel's "play-day" had been a success and Angel was going to have her first litter of puppies. JB was so excited. That's all he talked about. Luke had asked his parents if JB could keep one of the puppies. The kid worked hard and didn't even complain too much about the dog poop. He had earned a puppy. It would be his birthday surprise.

Olyvia's current good behavior was due mostly to JB's efforts. Of course, everyone had helped when they had time. However, no one was more dedicated than JB to making the pup do what she was supposed to do.

She continued to be Keysha's link to recovery. Olyvia's loving, outgoing personality, which was essential for Keysha, had remained. Her enthusiasm was just more directed and contained. Commands were obeyed and nobody had lost an article of clothing in a week.

Relapses were expected and handled appropriately. JB's patience astounded his parents. They knew him to be a boy who couldn't stick to anything for very long if it got tedious or "boring." They were very proud of him.

On one of Luke's visits to the local animal shelter a certain medium sized, mixed breed dog caught his eye. "Rex" had lived a horrible life before being found running loose in an alley behind the grocery store in town.

There were several scars from physical abuse. One ear would never be the same. The dog was nothing but skin and bones. It wasn't a problem to catch him. All they did was offer him food and he willingly hopped up into the cage in the back of the animal rescue van.

Once he had been fed on a regular basis, had antibiotics administered for the infection that had developed in his torn ear and had the fleas eliminated, he had been neutered. His physical recovery was now complete and his personality had surfaced.

Distrustful, snappy, scrappy; a real handful so Luke was told. There was just something about the look in the dog's eyes that drew Luke. Yes, he was frightened and distrustful. What animal, or person for that matter, wouldn't exhibit this behavior after being kicked around.

I was kicked around myself as a kid. Probably acted much like Rex, Luke thought as he considered the dog. *If not for Dad...but that's in the past. I think I'll take a chance. He'll go into the kennel though, not with the rest of the family. I'll tell JB hands off at least for the time being. Bruce will think I've lost my mind!*

That's exactly what Bruce did think.

"Hey, Man. What were you thinking? We don't have time to work with a dog like this one. It will take intensive, constant attention and JB's not ready to take on something like this..."

"I know," Luke interrupted. "I just want to give him a chance. See what develops."

Chapter 82

Justice Parker sat morosely in a jail cell in Silver Springs, Maryland. There was dried blood on his swollen knuckles and a knot the size of a small country on the back of his head. How it got there, he couldn't remember. Several shots of something-or-other had dulled his already foggy mind enough to erase the past several hours from his memory.

Fortunately, his opponent in this most recent brawl was also sleeping off a drunk in the adjoining cell. The arresting officer didn't know who-did-what-to-whom first, so no charges would be filed... this time. "Tinker" Parker was a frequent flyer, always drunk, always fighting, always ending up as a guest of the county. It was only a matter of time before he killed somebody.

He had grown up in this town. The fourth generation to carry the name Justice Parker into the Marine Corp. His family was proud of their long, distinguished military history. *How the mighty have fallen*, his father thought as he arrived to bail his son out for the umpteenth time in the last year.

Justice IV had picked up the nickname "Tinker" during his fourth tour of duty in the middle east. Gathering odd and ends of metal, sticks, irregular shaped stones, anything he could find, he made little toys for the Iraqi children who hung around the American camp. A good chunk of his pay was spent buying candy for the kids. He was a decorated, hardened, ruthless fighter who absolutely loved children.

In the field, if his platoon was embarking on a tough mission, Tinker Parker turned into a fearless, killing machine. He was cool, calm and collected under fire. Places nobody else wanted to go, he went. Situations nobody else wanted to handle, he handled. No task was insurmountable for him. No enemy, too fierce.

Up until this last tour, he had been able to control his PTSD symptoms. He just kept going and pushing and firing his weapon. Sleep was never restful. The nightmares kept getting worse. There were always children being blown apart. Children he couldn't save. At times, the commotion in his head was so great he thought he might be going crazy. Still he fought on.

His commanding officer had begun to notice some behavior that concerned him. Talking to Tinker about it was pointless. Taking him out of the field wasn't an option the captain wanted to consider. The unit depended on soldiers like Justice Parker.

The politicians back in Washington who ran the war from their cushy offices didn't have a clue, nor did they care, about the mental trauma some of these soldiers endured. Tinker was scheduled for leave in a few months and he had assured his captain he would see a doctor in the states.

He had seen a doctor in the states all right, but not for his PTSD. The loss of his right leg as a result of an IED had finished his military career. He had come home to a hero's welcome.

Everything went downhill from there. Fighting was the only thing he knew how to do, so that's what he continued to do. In bars, on the street, in back alleys; it was all the sun-baked desert to Tinker. He would flashback to battles he had fought. They seemed so real. Sometimes he fought enemies he couldn't even see. Those were the worst.

In the beginning, the veteran's administration had promised the best in prosthetic limbs. The best rehabilitation. Nothing but the best for a war hero, they said. It was all talk. Tinker was still waiting for his artificial leg. He hopped around using crutches, his empty pant leg pinned up. His PTSD was still incapacitating and he had to move back in with his elderly parents because he didn't have a decent place to live.

More and more of his time was spent wandering the streets, often being gone for days; even weeks. He usually reappeared in the drunk tank at the county jail. People in town felt sorry for him, but turned away rather than deal with his poor hygiene, rambling conversation and often incoherent babbling.

Chapter 83

Biggy had spoken to every contact he still had in the military about the whereabouts of Justice "Tinker" Parker. Even the people in the veteran's bureau who were supposed to know, didn't seem to know anything about him.

What a crock, Biggy snorted as he left the office in Dixon. *But par for a stinking government agency. It's no wonder the country's in the shape it's in. A bunch of idiots are running the show.*

As a last resort, he had left a message for an acquaintance from back in the day who was now working in the private sector as the head of a security firm out in Nebraska. The next day his cell phone rang.

"Big! It's been a long time. How's it hanging?"

"Good, Zeke. Real good. Got me a sweet job working security for a big outfit in Vermont. No worries."

"I know you ain't calling just to pass the time of day, so what can I do for you?"

"Looking for Tinker Parker. You know anything about him; where he's staying or working?"

"Gosh. Last I knew he came home without his leg. Couldn't deal with it too good. Screwed up in the head, you know how it goes. Might try his parents. I think they live in Silver Springs, Maryland. Sorry I can't give you more."

"No sweat, Zeke. It's more than I had on him this morning. Thanks, man."

Two weeks later, a letter arrived at the home of Justice Parker III for his son.

"Tinker. There's a letter for you on the kitchen counter from a Frank Bigilow. Maybe it's something important."

"Yeah. Sure, Dad. Because God knows I get a lot of important mail these days. I don't know the guy."

The letter sat unopened for a month.

Chapter 84

J amal was dressed in his suit and tie. Bruce told him he didn't really have to dress up quite that much to go to court, but the little boy was adamant.

"This is important. My Mama would want me to dress up; look my best. She always said appearances were important. So...I miss my Mom sometimes," he concluded with tears in his eyes."

Asia Kim straightened his tie.

"Asia know you miss Mama. She very proud looking down from heaven. You fine boy. Look handsome."

Jamal stepped into her open arms. He had grown very fond of Asia Kim. She was quiet as a mouse most of the time, but she was always there for him. He hugged her tight.

"You're gonna be there, right? In the hall like Uncle Oscar said?"

"Of course. Asia be there. No matter what happen, Asia be there."

With a sigh of relief, the little boy pulled back his shoulders, gave his suit jacket a hitch and headed for the car.

Keysha and Olyvia were staying with Bobby and Maria. Bruce would drop them off on the way into Dixon. He had done his best to explain to her that he and Jamal were going to go tell what had happened to her Mommy and to her. They were going to tell what the bad man did so he would have to go to jail and not hurt any other little girls or their mommies. He didn't know if she understood or not.

Sometimes he felt completely inadequate to deal with this silent, damaged child. Those sad eyes touched a place in him that he never knew existed. It tore him up to think about what had been done to her.

"We'll be back late this afternoon, Baby," he promised.

When those little arms went around his neck, Bruce knew in his heart he would kill anyone who tried to hurt her again. From the moment, several months ago, when he had lifted her out of that hole and held her broken body to his chest, she had captured his heart in a way that had amazed...and terrified him.

"You be a good girl for Uncle Bobby, okay Baby?"

Maria took her hand and shooed Bruce out the door.

"She'll be fine. Don't worry. Go get the son-of-a...well, you know."

Chapter 85

As Biggy drove into Dixon to meet Tinker's flight, he had mixed emotions. He hadn't heard about the man's injury or his mental state until talking to his friend in Nebraska. Maybe this job would be too much. But like Luke had said about the mangy mutt he brought home from the shelter, he deserved a chance. He was a decorated veteran after all!

Tinker obviously wasn't the man Biggy had bid farewell to back in the desert. The man who hopped on crutches toward him in the airport didn't resemble the proud soldier he had known at all.

Long, stringy, gray hair framed a pale, haggard face. Sunken dark eyes peered out from under bushy brows. What once had been a muscled, beefy physique was now frail and rail-thin.

The shock he felt didn't show on Biggy's face as he stuck out his hand and clapped his friend on the shoulder.

Always a man of few words, Biggy got right to the point.

"Hey, Man. Ya got a bag or something? My car's at the curb. Can't park there for long you know."

"No bag. Everything I got's here in my backpack. Is there any place I can get a drink? It was a long trip and they ain't got no amenities on flights these days."

Biggy stopped at a little sports bar off the beaten path. After gulping down a straight shot of bourbon, Tinker finally looked his friend in the eyes.

"So, Big. What's this about? I ain't seen nor heard from you since we were discharged, then I get this letter saying you've got a job for me. What makes you think I want a job?"

"You're here ain't you?"

The waitress appeared just in time saving Biggy for commenting further.

"I ain't got much of an appetite these days. Maybe I'll just have some soup. And another shot."

Seriously lacking in social skills, Biggy didn't know what to do or say. He ordered a burger and fries for himself and the soup-of-the-day for Tinker. They ate in silence.

On the drive back to Cedarville, Biggy attempted to tell Tinker about the Peterson Search and Rescue operation and the need for another man to help with handling and training the dogs.

The man's disinterest was undeniable. When Biggy glanced over at him, drool was dripping out of the side of his open mouth. His head bobbed back and forth with the motion of the car and his eyes were closed.

Biggy sped through traffic toward home. *I ain't nobody's nursemaid*, he thought, shaking his head. *He's going to have to snap out of it if he's going to work for us. The job's too critical. Screw-ups are unacceptable and won't be tolerated.*

Chapter 86

A tty. Pontus Preston was a weasel of the highest caliber and the attorney for the defense of Dennis Lodge. Notorious for getting the guilty set free on technicalities and underhanded theatrics, he had made a fortune defending the worst of the worst. His fees were astronomical.

The State's Attorney was asking for life without parole. The Lodge's could afford Atty. Preston and were willing to spend the money to save their son. This wasn't the first time they had had to spend large sums of money to extricate him from some unsavory situation. This was, however, the most serious. They had Pontus Preston on speed dial.

The list of charges against their son was a lengthy one. Preston assured them Dennis couldn't be charged with the premeditated murder of Emma Williams because he hadn't gone to her home with the intention of killing her; she had fallen and hit her head. Certainly, his actions had caused her death, but Preston felt sure he could get around that.

The rape of Keysha Williams was another matter. The physical evidence was insurmountable. The brother had witnessed it, the medical records substantiated it and the forensic evidence contained DNA verification. Dennis had done it, no question. He had even admitted as much to his lawyer. He was proud of "doing a little girl."

Causing reasonable doubt in the minds of the jurors and intimidating witnesses on the stand were two of the honed skills in Preston's tool box. He desperately wanted a crack at Keysha Williams. That she was only three years old was of no consequence to him. He was completely devoid of compassion or any moral code.

Even the great Pontus Preston had to admit the options for defending Dennis were few. He had made promises to the parents upon accepting this case, assuring them that their son wouldn't be convicted. A guilty verdict was unacceptable.

His team of underlings had worked hard at trying to get evidence excluded by attacking procedures and policies of the local police, the lab, the hospital and physicians; the case was solid. The State's Attorney's Office had been flooded with motions without success.

The only chance Dennis had was to plead not guilty by reason of mental disease or defect. He would serve his sentence in a mental ward, but that was better than going to prison with hardened criminals.

The chances of him surviving prison were non-existent. Even convicted killers didn't take kindly to men who raped children. Dennis would be an easy mark.

It had galled Preston to have to resort to using this defense strategy. Try as he did to find another way, this was the only viable choice. The parents had finally agreed. Dennis didn't seem to care. He was so accustomed to having his parents fix his mistakes, he acted like this trial was no big deal.

Preston was sure he had blind-sided Sidney Hoffman when he had put the Williams children on his witness list. It would be easy enough to lead their testimonies around to admitting Dennis had "acted crazy" when he came to their home.

Damn that Oscar Schwartz! He had managed to get Judge Bailey to rule that the girl would not be allowed to testify. Maybe I underestimated this whole situation. I didn't think this back-water town would have anyone with enough smarts to compete with me, he thought as he sat in his plush New York City office readjusting his defense plan.

Plan "B" was to use the boy to prove that Dennis was not in control of his actions when the rape occurred. That shouldn't be too hard. The day he couldn't manipulate a kid was the day he would hang up his license to practice.

Chapter 87

The previous days in court had been consumed with the presentation of the prosecution's case. Bruce and Luke had testified as to their roles in what had transpired at the scene of the crime and the subsequent search for Keysha. Detective Morrow had spoken to the investigation that had led to the arrest of Dennis Lodge. The forensic evidence was presented, the coroner verified Emma's cause of death.

The defense threw in some questions on cross examination related to the possibility of cross-contamination of lab evidence and/or the mishandling of trace evidence.

He had even hinted at police incompetence and corruption during the investigation. The object of the questions, of course, was to raise reasonable doubt with the jury as to the police department's efficiency.

Keysha's medical records were introduced into evidence. A representative from Cedarville General Hospital and the treating physicians explained hospital policies and deciphered the information in the records in laymen's terms for the jury.

Pictures of the children's injuries had been blown up and presented to the jury. Preston had done his best to get them excluded. No such luck. Judge Bailey had seen Keysha. He had spoken with

Jamal. This slimy New York lawyer wasn't going to down-play their injuries.

After three days, the prosecution rested. It had been a powerful and draining few days for the jurors. They didn't expect the next few would be any easier.

Chapter 88

Finding the Watson's and Jamal waiting in the hall outside the courtroom, Oscar gave Jamal a few last minute words of encouragement.

"I'll be sitting right behind Atty. Hoffman. You remember her don't you, Jamal? If you get scared look at me. Okay, Buddy? Are you ready to do this?"

"Yep. I'm ready," Jamal responded without hesitation.

"Good man. You wait right here and the bailiff will come out and get you when it's your turn."

Oscar's eyes met Bruce's before he headed through the door and into the courtroom. He took his seat on the front row behind Atty. Hoffman. The judge was seated, preliminary remarks were made and the jury marched to their chairs.

Several of the defendant's friends were called to testify to the fact that he had attended a party where he drank and smoked weed. The jury also heard about the pills he took before he left the party. One of the boys admitted to teasing him about Emma Williams.

"I told him, you're not man enough to take her. Do you need our help to get it up? We all said stuff like that. He got crazy when we brought up his failures with girls. He even grabbed Sharon and tried to do her just to prove he could. Everybody just laughed. You're pathetic, we said. He bought a handful of pills from one of the guys and tossed them back. He was pretty high when he left."

Each of the kids who were called to testify repeated similar stories.

Atty. Hoffman had her own questions for each witness.

"Remember you are under oath," she began with each cross. "What did you yourself do at this party?"

The first boy remained silent.

"Answer the question," Judge Bailey instructed.

The boy squirmed in his seat. Atty. Hoffman repeated the question.

"What. Did. You. Do. At the party. Besides watch and tease your friend?"

"I drank beer and got wasted. Had some monkey sex with a couple of the hot girls just like the other guys."

When each of the other attendees at the party answered in a similar manner, Atty. Preston ground his teeth in anger and frustration. The pencil he was holding snapped in two.

He knew exactly where Hoffman was going with this line of questioning. She would save the "punch" for closing statements. He also knew there would probably be an investigation launched into who provided the booze and the drugs for this party.

Jamal Williams was Preston's star witness. He would lead the boy, question his word, question his memory of the events, try to confuse him and stare him down; do whatever it took to get him to say his client was crazy when he entered the apartment. It shouldn't be all that hard. He was a little kid.

Judge Bailey called a recess for lunch. Court would resume at two o'clock. Jamal would be the last witness called to the stand by the defense. After that, depending on how long it took, court would be adjourned for the day. Closing statements would take place first thing in the morning and the case would then go to the jury.

Preston had dragged out his other witnesses testimonies as long as he dared, hoping for the lunch break. A couple of times he had been reminded by the judge to move things along. He had contritely apologized.

He wanted the kid to cool his heels in the hall all morning. Hopefully, he would get more tired and cranky as the hours went by making him easier to intimidate and manipulate.

Chapter 89

The night before his court appearance, Jamal hadn't slept at all. He wasn't afraid to tell what had happened to his mother and sister, he was nervous he would say something wrong. Everyone had told him to just tell the truth and he would do fine.

By the time they arrived at the courthouse, his eyes were getting heavy. As soon as they were seated on the benches in the hall outside the courtroom, Jamal crawled up onto Bruce's lap and promptly fell asleep.

He woke up in time to go to lunch. Oscar took them to Andre's. Jamal had never eaten in such a fancy place. He would have preferred Burger King, but he didn't want to hurt Uncle Oscar's feelings.

When Oscar had made the reservation, he had given Andre a brief synopsis of what was going on that day.

Andre had pulled out all the stops to make the little boy feel at home. He had never served a burger in his restaurant in his life. He made an exception for Jamal.

After a visit to the local Burger King, Andre had duplicated the kid's meal right down to the toy. His toy wasn't some cheap plastic thing though. The burger presented to Jamal looked just like what he always ordered, however it was made of ground prime rib, seasoned and cooked to perfection.

Being a bachelor all his life, Andre didn't have any children. That didn't mean he didn't have a soft spot for Jamal. His own childhood had been rough. Identifying with Jamal wasn't a reach.

The upcoming trial had been in the newspaper all week so he was familiar with what was transpiring. His heart ached for the little boy and his sister. *They couldn't have found a better family than the Peterson's,* he thought as he prepared the food himself.

The meal was a great success. The tip Andre got for his efforts made the unsavory trip to Burger King worth the effort. Even without the tip, it would have been worth it just to see the boy's face when he bit into that burger. Andre smiled. *He'll never want to eat at Burger King again, that's for sure!*

"Mr. Andre," Jamal had said as they were leaving. "Thank you for the great toy."

Andre sighed as he watched Jamal skip out to the car pretending the airplane was a real one. The remote control was still in the box.

Chapter 90

The bailiff he had met during his visit to the courthouse poked his head out the door.

"Okay, Buddy. You're up."

Jamal marched up the aisle. He stopped beside the defense table and openly stared at Dennis Lodge. A hair cut, some glasses and an expensive suit didn't change his looks as much as Atty. Preston had hoped. Jamal wasn't fooled for a minute.

"Son? Right up here in the chair," Judge Bailey encouraged, bringing Jamal's attention back to the front.

Jamal hopped up on the chair and looked around. He saw Oscar right away and waved.

"Hi, Uncle Oscar."

The people in the gallery chuckled. Oscar waved back with a smile on his face.

The bailiff held out the Bible and Jamal immediately put his hand on it.

"Do you swear to tell the truth, the whole truth and nothing but the truth so help you God?"

"Yes, I do. Uncle Oscar and Daddy Bruce, Grandpa Georgio; everybody at home told me I had to," was the little boy's serious response.

"State you name for the record."

"Jamal Troy Williams."

Jamal sat back in the chair and began swinging his feet back and forth. He appeared cool, calm and collected.

Show time Atty. Preston thought as he stood up and strolled toward the witness box. He slicked back his thinning brown hair before putting both hands in his pockets.

He began jingling his change as he walked back and forth in front of the box, appearing to ponder what was going to happen next. He gave Jamal a couple of sinister glances before he actually stopped and stared directly at the little boy. Jamal stared back.

Uncle Oscar had told him to expect something like this. He thought it was pretty funny actually. The attorney was tall and skinny. He reminded Jamal of the scarecrow in Uncle Luke's cornfield.

Suddenly, the unexpected happened. It started out as a giggle. Jamal tried to stop by putting his hands over his mouth. In a matter of seconds he was full on belly-laughing.

He pointed at Atty. Preston.

"You're really funny, Mister," he managed to say before laughter erupted again. "You sure have lots of money in your pocket."

Spectators began snickering. Then everyone was laughing along with Jamal. Preston's face turned beet red and his eyes bulged. Jamal laughed until he rolled off his seat and was sitting on the floor of the box.

Judge Bailey banged his gavel.

"Order," he shouted. "Order in the court."

He had to stand up and look down to see Jamal still sitting on the floor.

"Jamal, get back up on your chair please," Judge Bailey admonished the boy, not unkindly.

Jamal crawled back up on the chair and looked innocently up at the judge.

"I request a short recess," Preston shouted.

Judge Bailey stared in disbelief. *You jerk*, he thought. *What an idiot. You got exactly what your actions deserved. Good job Jamal.* Of course, he didn't say this out loud...

"We just had a recess, counselor. Get on with it."

With some difficulty, Preston gathered his wits. He had never had to question a child this young before. He had assumed it would be the same as an adult; the same scare techniques would work.

"Can you tell the court what the man who entered your apartment looked like, please?"

Jamal stood up and pointed at the defendant.

"He's right there, Mister. See? Right there. You were sittin' next to him. He colored his hair. My new Mom is a hairdresser. She says mostly girls do that. Why'd he do that do ya think? And he's wearin' glasses. It didn't fix his crossed eyes though. He looks not so fat now. Is he sick or somethin'? But that's him all right. Yep. That's him."

Oscar had to tip his head down so that Jamal wouldn't see the expression on his face. This was working out better than Oscar ever expected. A five year old boy was making a defense attorney look incompetent. That had to be one for the books.

Ignoring Jamal's response, Preston pressed on.

"What was the defendant's demeanor when he entered your apartment?"

A look of confusion passed over Jamal's face. He looked at Oscar.

"Uncle Oscar, I don't know that word; 'meanor'."

Judge Bailey intercepted the question.

"It means, how did the person who entered your apartment, act? What did he act like? What were his emotions? Do you know what 'emotions' means?"

"Oh, yes," Jamal answered, shaking his head up and down vigorously. "It means like if you're feeling happy or sad or angry..."

"Yes, that's correct. Now try to answer Atty. Preston's question."

"OK."

Jamal tipped his head back and rolled his eyes to the ceiling, appearing to give the matter much thought.

"Well," Jamal began, "he looked mean when Mommy tried to close the door in his face. He looked really angry when he pushed the door open. My Mommy fell backwards and hit her head on the edge of the coffee table where I was sitting. There was lots of blood. He hollered at her. He said 'get up you stupid bitch.' Sorry Uncle Oscar. I know that's a bad word, but that's what he said."

Atty. Preston feigned patience as he waited for Jamal to continue.

"He started hitting her in the face and yelling. He was sweating a lot and he smelled awful..."

Atty. Preston cut in, hoping to capitalize on the smell; marijuana had a very distinctive smell.

"Can you tell the court what he smelled like?"

Jamal scratched his head and thought for a minute.

"Yep. He smelled like he peed his pants a lot and his mother didn't make him take a bath."

This time even the judge laughed.

Preston turned his back and walked back to the defense table.

"I have no more questions for this witness," he muttered.

Chapter 91

"Atty. Hoffman? Do you have questions on cross?"

"Yes, Your Honor."

Sidney Hoffman stood and straightened her jacket.

"Jamal, she began. "How are you holding up?"

"I'm doing great," he answered with a big grin on his face. "We ate lunch at Andre's and he gave me a great toy. Do ya want to see it?"

Sidney smiled. *This is one darling little boy* she thought. *And he's making my job easy.*

"Maybe later, Jamal," Hoffman responded. "Right now I need you to answer some questions for me. Can you do that?"

"Yep."

"When the man pushed the door open, was this the first time you had ever seen him?"

"Nope. Almost every time me, Keysha and Mom went to the Laundromat, he came in. He tried to get my Mom to talk to him. He would say stuff like, 'I wanna do it with you, Baby.' I don't know what that means... One time he even tried to give her some candy. I wish he woulda gave it to me..."

"Were those the only times you saw him, Jamal?"

"Gosh, no. He would follow us sometimes. All the way back to our apartment. 'Can I carry your laundry for you?' he would say sometimes. Momma always said to just not pay any attention to him and maybe he would go away."

"And did he go away?" Hoffman pressed.

Jamal gave a long exaggerated sigh.

"Nope. He kept right on bothering us."

Atty. Hoffman knew the next series of questions would bother the little boy. She couldn't help it. She needed the jury to hear from his mouth what had happened. The defense had glossed over it. She would not.

"Just a few more questions, okay, Jamal?"

"Okay. Then can I go play with my new airplane?"

"Of course you can. Now, can you tell the court what happened while the man was hitting your mother?"

A scowl wrinkled Jamal's brow.

"It made me real mad! I got up and jumped on his back. I hit him in the head as hard as I could."

A demonstration followed.

"But he was too strong for me. He reached back and grabbed me by my arm. I heard a snap and it hurt somethin' awful. He threw me against the wall by my hurt arm. My eyes got all funny. I could only see black spots for a few seconds."

The little boy swallowed before he continued.

"Keysha came out of the bedroom. That man picked her up and ripped her clothes. She was screaming so loud. I tried my best to stop him, but I couldn't!"

Jamal's voice got louder until he was yelling. He stood up and again pointed at Dennis Lodge.

"He did the bad thing to my sister! Then he threw her on the floor and ran out the door. After she was on the floor she went real quiet. I thought maybe she was dead!"

He dropped back into the chair, buried his face in his crossed arms and sobbed.

Oscar was immediately on his feet. He didn't care about the appropriate protocol at this minute, he raced to the front and gathered Jamal into his arms.

"I want my Daddy Bruce," Jamal wailed.

"We'll take a fifteen minute recess," Judge Bailey said. "Counselor, will that be enough time?"

"Yes, Your Honor. Thank you."

Oscar carried Jamal to the hallway and passed him off to the waiting arms of the people who loved him.

Asia, Bruce and Jamal stood for several minutes in an all-encompassing embrace until Jamal finally calmed down and stopped crying.

Bruce sat down and continued to hold the child on his lap.

"Jamal, I'm so proud of you. You're doing such a fine job in there. It's almost over; just a few more questions and you'll be done and we can go home. Okay, Son?"

Jamal sniffed and hic-cupped.

"Okay. I'll try. It makes me so mad though. To see that man sitting there while my Mommy is dead and Keysha is...almost dead."

Asia wiped his face with a paper towel soaked in cool water she had gotten from the restroom. Then she hugged the little boy.

"Asia so proud too. Your Mommy, she look down, she help you talk more."

By the time the bailiff came out to get him, Jamal had had a juice box and a sugar cookie. He took the hand the bailiff offered and they went back into the courtroom. The bailiff helped him back up onto the chair.

Dennis sat slumped over the defense table picking at his fingernails with a bent paperclip. He looked bored.

Sidney Hoffman's sympathy toward Jamal was obvious.

"Are you feeling better, Jamal?" she asked.

"I guess so," he answered in a quiet little voice.

"Can you tell us what happened after the man 'did the bad thing' to your sister?"

She knew she should ask what "the bad thing" was, but she didn't have the heart for it. Everyone who had heard the prosecution's evidence should know exactly what Jamal was talking about.

"After he ran out, I shook Mommy but she didn't wake up. Keysha was bleeding all over the place. She could hardly stand up. I knew I had to get her out of there in case the man came back, so I carried her to the back stairs and dragged her down. She didn't make a sound."

Jamal wiped his nose across his coat sleeve.

"My arm hurt real bad."

He ground his fists into his eyes to stop the tears that had begun to seep from beneath his lashes.

Pulling himself together one more time, he continued.

"I stuck her in a hole in the side of the hill in the woods where no one could find her 'cept me. I tripped on something and rolled down the hill. It hurt awful, awful bad! I got to the sidewalk and started walking. Then Officer Watson found me and I went to the hospital. He promised me he would find Keysha."

The brave little boy sat up straight and sighed deeply.

"The next thing I know I wake up and my arm is in a red cast. They gave me medicine so it didn't hurt so bad. Officer Watson came and stayed with me for a while. I told him everything I could remember. He said he had a dog that could find Keysha and he left and that's it."

Several of the women in the jury box were dabbing their eyes. The men were stoic but obviously moved by the little boy's rendition of that had happened to him and his family.

"You are excused, Jamal. Bailiff will you take him back to his parents," Atty. Hoffman said.

Jamal looked into Sidney's eyes with the saddest little look on his face that this hardened prosecutor had ever seen.

"I'm really done now?"

Atty. Hoffman turned and gave Atty. Preston a long hard stare. *You'd better not ask for a re-cross you bastard*, she thought. When he looked away, she turned back to Jamal.

"Yes, Honey. You can go home now."

Chapter 92

Oscar had stayed until the bitter end. He wanted to hear the closing statements. He wasn't disappointed. Sidney Hoffman wasn't reelected for her good looks, she knew how to bring a case home.

"The facts in this case are clear," she began. "Dennis Lodge stalked and harassed Emma Williams and her children for months. He made it abundantly clear what he wanted from her and after being rebuffed time and time again, he purposely went to her apartment to forcefully take what she wouldn't give.

She died as a direct result of the defendant's actions. This in itself would be, should be, enough to convict. However, the defendant didn't stop there. Realizing he would never get what he wanted from Emma Williams he turned on her daughter - her three year old daughter."

Pausing, she gave the jury a few seconds to absorb what she had said.

"The defendant, Dennis Lodge, caused the death of Emma Williams and then raped her young daughter, destroying her life and the lives of those around her. He assaulted young Jamal Williams, an innocent boy who was only trying to defend his mother and his sister from the horrors being inflicted on them."

She walked over and stood in front of the jury box.

"These are the facts. The medical evidence is indisputable. The defense will try to tell you that Mr. Lodge was not in his right mind when this incident occurred. The drugs had robbed him of his ability to know what was right or wrong."

Taking a moment to look each juror in the eyes, she continued.

"We know that isn't true. Dennis Lodge knew exactly what he had done when he saw Emma Williams lying on the floor, a pool of blood around her head. He knew what he was doing when he beat her face. He knew what he was doing when he assaulted Jamal Williams. And he knew what he was doing while he was raping a three your old child. He just didn't care."

Being on the edge of losing her self control, she turned away from the jury and gave the defendant a long, hard look of disgust. When she turned back, her face did not reveal the inner struggle that had almost overwhelmed her.

"This man must be held accountable for his actions. Because of the heinous nature of his crimes, I ask you to find him guilty of involuntary man slaughter, rape, sexual abuse, two counts of child endangerment and two counts of aggravated assault and battery. Don't send a message that says it's all right to do these despicable things and never have to take responsibility for them."

Dennis Lodge was found guilty on all counts. Of course an appeal would be filed immediately. He probably wouldn't serve nearly the time he deserved.

Chapter 93

By the time Biggy arrived back at the Peterson Estate it was late evening. Tinker was still snoring away. *Maybe it's a good thing he's still passed out*, Biggy thought as he pulled his jeep into its parking spot behind Luke's barn. He would never voluntarily admit himself to Biggy's brand of rehab.

Leaving Tinker in the front seat, Biggy went to the pasture and whistled for "Buck," his buckskin gelding. The horse trotted over and nuzzled his hand for the cube of sugar he knew would be there.

It didn't take long to saddle up and attach the travois over the big horse's rump. Getting Tinker on board was another matter. The guy was dead weight and awkward to move. By the time he was strapped in, along with the supplies Biggy was taking back to the cabin, it was dark. Fortunately, there was a full moon.

The ride for Tinker was a rough one. Groaning and cursing could be heard from the passenger in the back as Biggy guided the horse along the trail through the thick woods.

"Hey! What the hell, man. Get me off this thing. Where am I?"

Other more colorful expletives were also ignored and the conveyance bounced along.

As he rounded the bend that lead to the little canyon at the foot of the mountains, Biggy could smell the wood smoke. He knew "Flower" had a fire going and she was probably keeping some grub warm for him. "Spaz" came running out to meet him.

Chapter 94

B iggy had never planned to be responsible for anyone but himself. Marriage, all of them, had ended badly. The cabin in the woods, far from other humans, was perfect for him. He was happy to patrol the outer boundaries of the Peterson Estate, for which he was paid a handsome salary.

Now with all this helicopter stuff, he was way busier than he wanted to be. It was an extra incentive to get Tinker back on his feet...or foot, as the case may be.

When the Peterson Clan needed help with something out of the ordinary, like the kidnapping of Ann Peterson, he was called in. He was known around the area as someone who could "get the job done" under any circumstances. His many idiosyncrasies were accepted.

During his patrol early in the winter before the first heavy snow fall, he had noticed black vultures or Coragyps atratus according to his bird book, circling and decided to check it out. What he found caused great concern.

Carcasses of three deer had been left in one of the fields not far from the canyon. Only the best meat had been taken, the rest was left to rot. Natural prey had not been the culprit; they had been shot. Someone was pouching on Peterson land.

A call on his wrist unit alerted Luke and Horace to the situation. Luke's cows would be a tempting, easy target. Getting down from his horse, Biggy took a closer look around. Tracks from at least two other horses were evident as well as tracks from an all-terrain vehicle of some sort.

This is not good. Not good at all, he thought as he continued in a widening circle around the carcasses. The tracks headed up into the mountains. This incident would have to be investigated further, but not without going back to the cabin for supplies, overnight camping equipment and additional fire-power.

He hadn't gone far toward the canyon when Buck reared, nearly unseating him. Something was wrong. The horse sensed it. Biggy dismounted and spoke softly to his nervous mount. It took considerable petting and sweet-talking before the animal calmed down. Biggy tied the reins to a bush and began looking around on foot; rifle in hand.

He heard what sounded like a young, wounded animal coming from under a rock outcropping. Getting down on his hands and knees he peered into the opening. Cautiously, he belly-crawled under the outcropping. When his eyes adjusted to the darkness, he spotted a tiny ball of fur with its back against the far wall.

Biggy pulled on his thick leather gloves and reached into the hole. What he pulled out was a spitting, hissing, biting wolf pup. He was very young, maybe three or four weeks old, and born during the wrong season of the year. He looked around quickly to see if mama wolf or the rest of the pack was close by.

Satisfied the pup had been left alone, Biggy did a thorough examination of the little critter. It was a male and it was apparent that mama wolf hadn't been here for at least several hours. Probing the ribs elicited a sharp yip, there was blood clotted on a head wound and it looked like his front leg was broken.

Biggy stroked the animal until is quieted.

Poor little guy, Biggy thought. *I wonder what happened; how the pup was injured but managed to get back to this hole. My guess is mama tried to get a share of one of those deer.*

I bet, for whatever reason, she was a loner. I don't see any evidence of a pack, even round this hole. I didn't find her body so maybe whoever did this took it for the fur. It's a mystery to me. Well, I can't just leave it here and I can't kill it...

He pulled a handkerchief from his pocket and carefully wrapped it snuggly around the pup's midsection. Ripping a strip of cloth off the bottom of his shirt and finding a couple of short twigs he fashioned a splint for the leg. *There. That will have to do until we get home. And speaking of getting home, how am I going to get this little fellow there safely?*

The heavy winter coat he wore had large, deep pockets. Ripping apart more of his shirt he wrapped it around the pup and carefully laid him at the bottom of one of the pockets. *Buck will just have to get over himself.*

The wolf scent was strong on the approaching man. Buck danced and side-stepped, nostrils flaring, ears laid back. It took several minutes of fiddling around before Biggy could mount.

Chapter 95

Throughout the rest of the winter months Biggy nursed the wolf pup back to health. In the beginning feeding him was a problem. Powdered milk mixed with water, mashed up tiny shreds of dried venison and some finely ground grains made up a watery gruel kind of concoction. The pup was starving so he wasn't finicky about the taste or the consistency. It didn't take him long to learn how to suck up the food, such as it was.

At first the splint on his leg caused him to walk sideways, stagger and fall down. Never dissuaded, he got back up again and again to wobbled around the cabin.

"You're one spastic little pup," Biggy would laugh.

This phrase was repeated so many times the pup began coming to Biggy every time he heard it. Biggy shortened it to Spaz and that became the little canine's name.

Unconsciously, through their daily interaction, the pup was learning. When Biggy realized how Spaz was beginning to respond to what he said, the training began in earnest.

"If you and me are going to team up permanently there are a few rules," Biggy told the pup.

Spaz would cock his head to the side and listen intently. The man and the wolf developed a close bond and by the time spring came they lived and worked together effortlessly.

Because Spaz never lacked for food, he grew fast. He was much larger than any litter mates would have been at the same age. Being eager to please, he learned quickly and was soon house-broken and obedient.

A wolf would never be like a domesticated animal. Taking him to meet the rest of the Peterson family wasn't an option, at least not at this point. The other dogs would see him as a threat and even though Spaz was well trained, he was still a wild animal and he was young. He would attack if threatened by the other dogs.

When the cabin had been built, Bryce had wanted to put in electricity, plumbing; all the comforts. Biggy had declined. He liked rustic. He finally agreed to a generator, just in case. That was his only concession to a modern convenience.

There were two bedrooms and a living room/kitchen. Food was cooked on the huge fireplace that dominated the back wall. A table and a couple of chairs occupied one corner. A couch and easy chair were grouped in front of the fireplace. Clothes were hung on pegs.

Because the cabin was sparsely furnished, didn't mean it was flimsy. Even the coldest winds didn't penetrate the solidly constructed walls and roof. Biggy would have been fine with a dirt floor, but he had to admit the thick, wood floor was warmer and easier to keep clean.

A well with a hand pump provided water. An out-house was enough to take care of other business. During the winter refrigeration wasn't a problem. Some other arrangements might have to be made during the warmer months, but Biggy would worry about that later.

Buck had a small barn with a correl. Horace had helped Biggy fill the mow with hay in case of a longer than usual, hard winter. There was grain in the bin and a trough for water. Now with Spaz for company, Biggy was the happiest he had ever been.

Fresh meat was a necessity and that meant hunting. With another mouth to feed, Biggy had to hunt more often. When Spaz was old enough to bring down prey by himself, it would be easier. Right now, he was a nuisance.

Learning to stay alone at the cabin without tearing it apart was a must. Biggy began leaving him for short periods, gradually lengthening the time to several hours. Eventually, as he got older and could fend for himself, the hope was that he could be left for as long as necessary.

Chapter 96

Thus far, the day's hunt had been unsuccessful. Biggy was ready to head back to the cabin when he heard yelling and commotion coming from a gully a short distance away.

Dismounting, he dropped Buck's reins, knowing the horse would stay put. Finding two horses tied to a line, he took off their tack and let them go. Biggy had an inkling that what he would find up ahead might be his poachers and he didn't want them to escape on horseback.

Making sure his rifle was loaded, he silently crept through the trees and up to the top of the rise. From this vantage point, and using his binoculars, he could see exactly what was happening in the gully.

The two men were so engrossed in their current activity, they didn't hear their horses thundering away. One youngish looking man with long red hair and a scruffy red beard was sitting astride a tall, copper-skinned woman holding her down and pinning her arms to her sides with his knees. She was thrashing and yelling in a language Biggy had never heard before.

An older gray haired man was tending a fire. He poked at it with a stick until sparks were flying lazily into the air. A branding iron was turning red hot as it laid in the coals. He stooped and stuck a large knife blade into the flames until it too was red hot.

For a split second Biggy watched in horror as the older man quickly pulled the iron out of the fire, turned and pressed it to the woman's breast. Her scream split the air.

She must have passed out from shock and pain because she stopped flailing and lay still. The smell of burnt human flesh was overpowering. The younger man laughed uproariously.

The iron was tossed aside. As the woman's mouth was forced open, the knife flashed toward her face and with one quick flick her tongue landed on the dusty ground. Because the knife was red hot, it immediately cauterized the stump.

A bullet sent the man with the knife spinning into the fire. Now his were the screams that echoed through the forest. The other man sprang up from the woman's limp body. The second bullet caught him as he reached for his gun.

If Biggy had wanted him dead...he would be dead. The shot caught him high in the right side of his chest. He would survive to answer the questions that he would be asked later.

Chapter 97

Biggy hauled the injured young man over to a tree and tied him securely to the trunk.

"You're hurting me. You're hurting me," he screamed. "I'm bleeding."

Biggy grunted.

"Do I look like I care? Now shut up."

He called Luke on his wrist unit.

"Luke, you'd better get out here ASAP. I'm about a mile west of the canyon. Bring either Mark or Ann and some medical supplies. I've got a seriously injured woman, a dead guy and another guy with a gunshot wound. I'm sure he'll be more than happy to give us information about what's been going on out there."

"What kind of injuries on the woman?"

"Burns, mutilation...I don't know what else. She's unconscious right now."

"Okay, Big. I know mom's home. I'll get her and dad. Bruce is busy so I'll get a couple of other officers and we'll be there as fast as we can. We'll take the four-wheelers."

"No great rush," Biggy replied. "Nobody's going any place."

The dead man's charred, still smoking body lay about fifty yards from the now smoldering fire. *I have to give the old guy props,* Biggy thought. *He ran a good ways before he fell. Must have been a tough old bird.*

More wood was added to the fire. It would be a signal for Luke plus the woman had to be kept warm. The rags she wore weren't enough to protect her from the spring chill.

A long piercing whistle brought Buck galloping toward him. A stake was driven in the ground and a long line was attached to the horse's bridle. This would insure Buck wouldn't run if he was spooked by the influx of people and the four-wheelers.

The next order of business was to assess the woman's injuries and try to make her as comfortable as possible until help arrived. It was clear this was not the first time she had experienced abuse. There was old bruising around her eyes and nose. There was a partially healed laceration on her scalp where blood had dried in her long black hair.

It was hard to tell her age. Her ravaged body could be that of a young woman or someone older. She was most certainly malnourished by the look of her skinny arms and legs. The letters "SB" were burned into her breast. Blood dripped from her right ear canal. By the look of her ripped and ragged clothes, she had probably been raped.

And her mouth. Biggy was a big, tough, hardened Ex-Marine. He thought surely he had seen it all. But this? It turned his stomach.

Pulling blankets from his pack Biggy covered the woman. A roughly constructed lean-to sheltered her from the harsh wind. She gagged and moaned. Saliva and fluids from her mangled mouth were pooling in the back of her throat.

Biggy stuffed another blanket under her upper back and head to raise her to a semi-reclining position and gently turned her head to the side. Otherwise she would choke to death on her own secretions.

Other than what he did for the woman, he didn't touch anything. He wanted Luke and the other officers to see everything exactly as it was. The evidence clearly told the story of what had happened here. Biggy was looking forward to interrogating the man who was now silent and slumped against the tree.

Chapter 98

"Oh, my God," Ann gasped when she saw the condition of the woman's mouth.

Biggy pointed to the tongue lying in the dirt. Ann photographed it in-situ and then placed it in an evidence bag. The other injuries were photographed and the woman's fingerprints were taken.

Ann closely examined her many injuries.

"Bruce could come and get her in the chopper, but I'm not sure she would survive long enough to get to the hospital. She was in bad shape before this attack happened. And now..."

"I'll throw a travois together. My cabin isn't far. If she makes it then maybe she has a chance. I've got nothin' but time. I'll look after her, just show me what to do."

Biggy didn't know why he felt so protective of this strange, nameless woman. He had always been a sucker for the underdog. She certainly fit into that category.

Somehow he felt she wouldn't want a lot of people looking at her, judging her. At the cabin, if she made it, she would have privacy. No one to scrutinize every little thing about her, question her, expose her secrets... Under these circumstances, it was what he himself would want.

While Luke and his team photographed the area and collected evidence Ann worked to stabilize her patient as best she could. From working with Ann at the clinic, Bryce had become an able assistant. He readily handed her whatever she asked for from her medical bag. Gunner sat close by.

Approaching darkness presented a problem. The decision was made to take everyone back to Biggy's cabin, then transport the prisoner into town in the morning. If the woman lived, it was anybody's guess if she would be able to make any kind of statement to the police. Biggy wasn't even sure she spoke English. He had witnessed the attack and described what had happened to Luke and the other officers. That should be enough.

The woman opened her eyes and moaned for a few seconds when they lifted her to the travois. The pain would be excruciating if and when she was fully awake so it was probably for the best that she remained unconscious during the duration of the trip to the cabin.

As the little party rounded the bend into the canyon, Biggy called a halt. He didn't know exactly how to explain Spaz.

"Let me go in alone first," he called back over his shoulder. "My dog isn't use to strangers."

Upon seeing his master, Spaz ran in circles, jumped and yipped. Buck had become comfortable around the pup and paid his antics no mind. Then Spaz spotted the travois with the woman tied to it.

He cautiously approached; sniffing, jumping back, circling and sniffing some more. He attempted a growl, but he was too young to make it sound fierce and threatening like it would when he was full grown.

Biggy had dismounted and had his arm around the pup's chest to hold him still.

"It's okay, boy. She won't bother you," he explained to the nervous pup. "She's hurt real bad and she's going to be staying with us for a while. I want you to accept her into your pack. Can you do that little guy?"

Spaz seemed to understand. He sniffed the woman again, then licked her neck. And just like that, she was one of the family.

Chapter 99

B iggy waved in Luke and the rest of the group. They proceeded to the cabin. Luke and the other officers along with the prisoner would bunk in the barn. Ann and Bryce would stay in the cabin to be near the woman. There was only one problem. Gunner and Spaz.

Spaz had been sequestered in Biggy's bedroom before Gunner came in with Ann and Bryce. Both animals were aware of the presence of the other. Spaz paced back and forth, back and forth, back and forth within the confines of the bedroom.

Gunner was on high alert, the hair on his back standing up, a low deep growl rumbling through his chest. Bryce sternly commanded him to silence and to stand down. Gunner obeyed...reluctantly. He curled up in a corner of the room, but remained alert.

Water was set to boil in the fireplace, an intravenous line was inserted in the woman's arm so that fluids, antibiotics and pain medication could be administered. She didn't regain consciousness. It was a blessing. Getting her from the travois, to the house and into bed would have been excruciatingly painful for her.

Ann carefully cut the rags that passed for clothes from her battered body, cleaned her up and did a more thorough examination of her injuries. She looked like she'd been used as a punching bag and she had been raped...repeatedly.

What is your story? How did you come to this point in life? I can't imagine what you've been through, Ann breathed as she ministered to the woman's wounds.

"I have to figure out a way to get some nutrition into this poor soul," Ann told Bryce and Biggy. "In the hospital I would insert a tube through her abdominal wall into her stomach with the aid of an endoscope. I hate to put a nasogastric tube down. With so much damage to her face and mouth I really don't want to do that, but I don't see any other choice."

"Can you do the procedure without an...what did you call it? The scope thing?" Biggy questioned.

"We could make this area sterile and I certainly know where the stomach is, generally speaking, unless she has some anomaly. However, without the endoscope I would have no idea if the tube was exactly in the right place. It could prove very dangerous, even fatal."

"Well, she'll starve to death if you don't do it, right, Doc? And the odds are high she won't survive no matter what you do or don't do. I say give it a try."

"I agree, Honey. It looks like her only chance to me," Bryce interjected.

Ann thought for several minutes as she went through the supplies she had brought with her. She had the things she would need, but the risk was enormous. Whatever she decided, she would have to do quickly while the woman was still unconscious because... no anesthesia.

"Okay, guys. Let's do this. I'll need your help; both of you."

Chapter 100

The tube was in place. Ann breathed a sigh of relief. The woman had moaned when the small incision was made, otherwise she hadn't responded in any way. Now the problem was what to feed her. She didn't have a chance of healing if her nutritional status remained non-existent.

Biggy came up with the only logical solution.

"When I first brought Spaz home, I made up a batch of powdered milk, venison and grains. It worked for him. Maybe something similar would work for her."

"Yes. Yes, that might just do it. The meat and the grains will have to be completely mashed otherwise the tube will become clogged and we'll have done all this for nothing. It will have to be more watery... And we can only give her very small amounts at a time. Frequent small feedings will be all she can tolerate."

"I'll get right on it," Biggy responded.

"Bryce, I'm going to need to stay with her at least through the first several days; until she's out of the woods...or she dies." Ann's voice trailed off.

Bryce had anticipated as much as soon as he realized the seriousness of the woman's condition. *This little wife of mine will do whatever is necessary to save this woman*, he thought as he held Ann tight for a few minutes. *I expected nothing less. I'll put in a call to Bobby. He's been up here before. He can bring whatever we need.*

- 235 -

"Make a list of what you need. I'll call Bobby."

Ann let out a deep breath she hadn't realized she was holding.

"Thank you, Sweetheart," she whispered against his throat before pulling her head back and looking into his eyes. "I love you so much."

The usual protocol for use of a gastrostomy tube would be to feed the patient intravenously for twenty-four hours. When bowel sounds were heard, the gut would be able to handle something more substantial. Under the circumstances, this wasn't possible.

When the first batch of Biggy's goop was ready, the gastrostomy tube was flushed with water first, then a teaspoon of it was put down followed by more water. It worked perfectly. Feedings would be given at one teaspoon every half hour. Now all they could do was watch and wait.

There wasn't much Ann could do about the mutilation of the woman's mouth other than clean the wound. If she survived, talking and swallowing... Ann's eyes filled with tears. It would take a miracle.

The burn on the woman's breast would be extremely painful and disfiguring, but it wasn't life threatening. Ann wondered briefly what the "SB" stood for, if anything. Maybe it had been done just for the sake of cruelty.

Luke came in around midnight.

"How's it going?" he asked. "Is she going to make it?"

"We don't know, Son. Your mom has done everything she can. We just have to wait and see. I've called Bobby with a list of supplies. He'll be here sometime in the morning. How are you guys holding up out in the barn?"

"We're fine. Our prisoner is hollering that he needs a doctor; he's in pain blah, blah, blah. If Mom has a few minutes maybe she could take a look at him. He's blathering like a baby about his partners-in-crime. Only interested is saving his own skin. Already told us where the camp is up in the mountains. I've called for backup. The plan is to take the other three men at the camp tomorrow at first light. Then we'll take them all into town."

Luke shook his head.

"I know Biggy wants a crack at the guy in the barn. I don't think that's such a good idea."

"I'll talk to him. Right now he's got his hands full learning how to take care of the woman. Your mom will be along in a few minutes."

When Ann got to the barn the prisoner was in full voice.

"I need a doctor. I need something for this pain. I'll sue your asses, all of you. Police brutality, that's what it is."

The wound wasn't serious. Ann cleaned it and put a dressing in place.

"Have him checked out in the emergency room when you get him back to town, Luke. He should be fine."

"What about something for the pain," he whined.

Ann gave him two Tylenol

"I don't have anything else for you," she replied.

She wasn't giving him any medicine that the woman in the cabin needed. He could wait until he got to the emergency room.

Chapter 101

⌇

T he SWAT team arrived sometime during the middle of the night. They pulled out before it was light. The prisoner gave them explicit directions to his base camp. There were probably three other men there, a four-wheeler and several more horses. All the men had guns and plenty of ammunition.

Ann had made coffee and sandwiches for the men before they left. Biggy didn't ask if he could go; he was going either with the team or by himself. Luke decided with the team was the better option. Bryce and Ann would take care of the woman. Spaz would stay in the barn.

A sniper rifle was in a sling across Biggy's back, his face was painted with black grease, a huge bowie knife was attached to his belt and strapped to his thigh and his camo's were spotless and pressed. Luke wondered how he managed that, but didn't ask.

As they got closer to the camp the prisoner was gagged and tied to a tree. Luke didn't want him alerting the men in the camp. One officer was left behind to guard him. The team had planned to surround the camp, then call for the men to surrender before taking them by force.

Fat chance of that happening, Biggy thought as he inconspicuously separated himself from the group. *These guys are ruthless. They aren't going to surrender just because the cops ask them to.*

By the time the SWAT team had positioned themselves around the camp, Biggy was already inside the camp hidden among the horses. With his night vision goggles on he looked like a monster from a child's worst nightmare.

He silently crept to within a few feet of the sleeping, unsuspecting men. Two steps brought him to the closest man's head. The knife went to the man's throat as his other hand covered his mouth.

"Make a sound and you're dead," he breathed into the man's ear.

One by one he captured each man. When Luke called for the surrender, Biggy answered.

"All clear, fellows. Come on in."

They entered the camp, weapons at the ready. The shocked looks on their faces was the high-point of Biggy's day thus far.

"Well, Biggy," Luke laughed. "Looks like you've been busy."

Three men sat on the ground off to the side, gagged and bound. Biggy spat in the dust.

"You guys take too long to get things done. Too much talkin' and not enough doin'," were his only comments.

Luke signaled the officer waiting with the prisoner to bring the guy into the camp. Luke wanted answers and good old Jerry Brickman had been talking non-stop before they had gagged him.

"We already know who the ringleader is; the guy who calls the shots. Your friend here has filled us in on what you fine gentleman have been doing up here. Now I think my good friend Mr. Bigelow has some questions for you. Biggy? The floor is yours."

Biggy drew his knife and began circling the group of huddled men. In a move so quick even Luke was amazed, the knife was at the throat of one of the terrified men.

"I want to know who the woman is and why you had her," he said with deceptive calm while drawing the knife lightly across the man's throat. "And if you give me some dip-shit story, I'll know, so think carefully before you answer."

The man gulped before blurting out what he knew about the woman, which wasn't much.

"We found her walking along the street alone at night in a town up north. The Boss wanted a woman for his personal needs so we grabbed her. We were drunk and it was dark. We didn't realize she was a filthy squaw until the next morning. Hell, everyone knows those people are nothing but animals. Me and Abe here, we both used her. Figured the boss wouldn't care, her being nothing but a dirty Indian."

Biggy yanked the man's head back by his hair, his knife poise over the Adam's apple. The prick was just enough to draw some blood and cause pain.

"Big. Careful," Luke said quietly.

"What is her name, why was she branded with 'SB' and why cut out her tongue?"

"She was the boss's property. Sam Beardsley. 'SB.' Sam's a mean SOB and he used her hard. She was always blatting in that funny talk shit so Sam wanted her shut up for good, but he wanted her alive. I don't know her name. I swear I don't know anything else about her."

Biggy violently threw the man forward into the dirt and stalked away into the forest. He would let Luke handle everything from here. If he couldn't rip the guy's head off at least he had found out what he wanted to know.

Chapter 102

When the woman was out of danger and tolerating Biggy's food mixture in larger quantities, Ann and Bryce left for home. Against all odds, the woman was on the road to recovery. She squeezed Ann's hand and received a warm hug in return.

"Are you sure you don't want to come back with us and see the plastic surgeon at the hospital in Cedarville? He may be able to help you learn to speak and assist you with the swallowing difficulty."

The woman shook her head "No." She took the paper and pencil Ann offered. This would be the first time any form of communication besides a rudimentary sort of sign language had taken place.

"I want to stay here with the man who rescued me," she wrote. "If he will have me. He is a good, kind, brave man."

Ann could have sworn Biggy blushed.

"Sure you can stay," he answered. "But what's your name? I don't know what to call you."

She wrote, "My name in my language means Morning Flower. I am Mohican and my tribe speaks Algonquian. My ancestors lived in Vermont long, long ago."

"I'll call you Flower. A beautiful name for a beautiful lady."

Ann hid a smile. She had never witnessed Biggy being so solicitous. She had to admit, he had stayed by the woman's side since the day he came back from hunting down the men who had hurt her.

Bryce shook Biggy's hand.

"Bring her for a visit when she's ready. She'll be welcome any time. Better leave Spaz at home though. I don't think he and Gunner will ever be friends."

As they rode away on the four-wheeler, Ann looked back and waved. Biggy was standing with his arm around the woman's shoulders.

Chapter 103

Sam Beardsley had not been at the camp when the poachers were arrested. According to his "friends," he had missed the company of his squaw and had gone into town to find a replacement.

That may very well be true, however Biggy knew he was a coward at heart. Men who beat and abuse women are cowards. Running is what they do best when faced with someone who fights back. His behavior would not change despite what the do-gooders would have you believe. Another woman would eventually suffer at his hands.

The police were looking for him. The investigation into his prior activity and possible current whereabouts was ongoing. Biggy would do his own investigating on the down-low.

Time was not a factor. Let the scumbag think he had gotten away scot-free. Sooner or later, he would get lazy and careless. At some point in the future, he would wake up in the middle of the night and his worst nightmare would be standing over him.

When he found "SB," and he would find him sooner or later, Biggy would let Flower decide what would happen to him. It was only fair.

Chapter 104

❦

Tiny had been tailing Otis for the better part of a month. Otis had promised Vito that he had a plan in place that would net him enough money to pay off the debt plus interest.

"I don't know how a little worm like Otis Williams could possibly come up with a plan involving that much money," Vito had told Tiny. "I want you to watch every move he makes; even in the crapper. If there is such a plan, I want to know about it. Maybe there's a way I can hijack it and turn it into a bigger financial advantage for me."

"You want I should bring him in and work him over? I can make him tell me the plan, save myself a lot of running around."

As fast as a striking rattle snake, Vito cuffed Tiny in the head.

"Did you hear what I just said? Follow him. Now get your lazy ass out of my sight and do what I tell you."

Tiny shrugged.

"Whatever you say, Boss."

Otis wasn't stupid. Every time he looked up, there was Tiny trying to look inconspicuous. *It's hard to miss a giant with a bald head. Looks like Mr. Clean. I'd have to be a blind man not to see him.*

Having never been a dishonest person, at first Otis had a hard time being stealthy. But you tend to learn fast when your life is at stake. He began watching the re-runs of crime shows; Law and Order, Criminal Minds, Bones and the like. He quickly learned what the "bad guys" did to evade capture and what the cops did to catch them.

He became pretty good at losing Tiny when the need arose. Never was a call made on his cell phone; always from a public phone. Not wanting to raise any red flags with Tiny, he stayed with his regular work schedule, ate in the same restaurants and continued at the same gym three times a week.

Slinking around in the shadows and looking over his shoulder all the time while trying to maintain a level of normalcy had brought his stress level to the boiling point. He couldn't sleep, ordered food then didn't eat much of it and bit his fingernails down to the quick. Staying focused at his job was getting harder and harder.

Tiny wasn't the only one following Otis. Detective Billy Stokes and his partner, Trevor Baker, were watching Tiny, watch Otis. Billy was a lot better at tailing a suspect. Tiny was a knee-breaker, not a genius.

Billy knew that Otis had taken all the money out of his savings account and bought a plane ticket to Dixon, Vermont. He knew Otis had put in for vacation time. A plan was in play; to what end, Billy had yet to figure out.

Harold Tweaks got a call from the Las Vegas police department.

"Hey, Tweaks. I've got some information for you. It looks like your man, Otis Williams, is heading your way. He's got a flight booked for October; I'll text you the details. I don't know what he's up to just yet, but I'll keep you informed."

"I think I might be able to help you out with that. Otis has two kids; a boy and a girl. Since the death of their mother they have been in foster care with Asia Kim and Bruce Watson. The foster family wants to adopt them."

Harold paused to check his notes.

"The natural father would have to sign over his parental rights in order for that to happen. The lawyer handling the adoption attempt is Oscar Schwartz. I have it on good authority that Otis has contacted the attorney and he wants his kids. It's caused quite an uproar on this end."

"Well, well, well. That's interesting to be sure. My captain has given me the go-ahead to stay on the case no matter where it leads. Tiny Granger isn't smart enough to come in out of the rain unless somebody tells him to do it. We're pretty sure Vito Petrelli is the one calling the shots. In order for Vito to be interested in this, a lot of money has to be involved. Tweaks, we want him. Bad."

"We'll work it from both ends. You follow Otis. I'll intercept him when he arrives in Dixon. I'll keep the police here updated. Thanks, Stokes. I'm sure I'll be seeing you."

Chapter 105

The hot and humid days of summer were slowly turning into cooler days and chilly nights. The boys would be going back to school in a week; a fact that JB had been lamenting for at least a month.

Keysha's surgery had been done two weeks ago and the family was facing some new challenges. Regaining control of her newly attached bowel and bladder was proving to be more difficult than first anticipated.

Asia pottied her every two hours and Keysha wore pull-ups, but there were frequent accidents. The fact that Keysha was still mostly non-verbal didn't help. The doctor, however, was pleased with her progress.

"Considering what happened to her; what she's been through, I think she's doing amazingly well. The credit goes to you two," he told Bruce and Asia at one of Keysha's follow-up visits. "I hope everything works out so that you can adopt her."

A now well behaved Olyvia was her constant companion. Asia began to notice that Olyvia would whine just before Keysha had an accident. She mentioned it to Bruce one night after the kids were in bed.

"I think Olyvia know when Keysha have to pee. How that possible? She whine. I put Keysha on potty. No accident for many hour."

"Dogs have many different natural abilities. Training them is a matter of tapping into each dog's individual talent, so to speak. People have service dogs for all kinds of health reasons. I knew a guy once who had a dog who could tell when he was going to have a seizure. Another guy had a dog who would wake him up at night when his blood sugar dropped too low."

Bruce stopped to scratch Olyvia's head.

"She must sense something with Keysha. I can't explain it."

"Whatever reason, I happy. I think Keysha more happy too."

Every single day, Bruce thanked God for Asia Kim. After the disaster with Tonya, his first wife, he didn't think there were any good women on the planet. His grandma had died and she was the last of them. Then he had met the Petersons and subsequently Asia.

It's funny how things work out, he thought one day as he drove home from work. She gave his life new meaning. The kids were icing on the cake. If something happened...he couldn't even think about it.

Chapter 106

Oscar asked Bruce to come to his office. Bruce had a knot in the pit of his stomach. He had a feeling it wasn't good news. When Oscar told him that Otis Williams had been in contact and he wanted his children, the world began to collapse for Bruce. He could hardly breath.

"Oscar. Can't you do something? Stop it somehow? He can't just march in here after all this time and take them, can he?"

"There are still a lot of family court judges who feel children are better off with their natural parents. If the parent has corrected whatever behavior caused the children to be removed in the first place, most of the time the kids go back. That correction is, all too often, temporary and the kids are pulled again."

Oscar pushed his chair away from his desk in disgust. He paced back and forth in front of his office window, his back to Bruce.

"I personally think it's a crime to put children through it, especially when they are in a stable foster home with people who love them. They just get straightened out, start doing better in school... then things go in the toilet when they have to go back to the natural parent. I don't want you and Asia to get your hopes up."

Bruce had never been so transparent with his feelings. He prided himself on being tough; able to handle any situation. Now he was groveling like a girl. It felt like he was fighting for his life.

"We can't lose them, Oscar. We just can't," Bruce said. "It tears me up inside just to... And Asia. I don't know how I would ever be able to console her if the worst happened. I think, in time, Jamal would adjust. But Keysha? She would never survive being torn away from us. She's just beginning to trust us!"

"I know, Bruce. I know. I'm doing everything I can."

Chapter 107

F lower and Biggy had built a sweat lodge some distance from the cabin. Biggy had half carried, half dragged his friend into the small round structure. Tinker Parker screamed, cursed, vomited, sweated and felt generally miserable as the alcohol was leached from his system.

The fire burned, the hot rocks sizzled when water was poured over them and the steam rose. The scent of the herbs Flower had put in the water gagged Tinker.

"Get me the hell out of here," he ranted. "I need a drink. Damn you, Biggy. The first chance I get, I'm going to kill you."

"Well, that may be so," Biggy drawled. "But you have to be able to stand up first. Right now you wouldn't get an inch on your own. So why don't you just calm down and let the process work. Flower says it will do wonders..."

He was interrupted by another string of curses. Flower poured more water over the rocks...

Over the ensuing weeks, Tinker underwent this torture several times. Usually Biggy had to hold him down to keep him from escaping. With all the sweating, Flower was careful to keep him hydrated with fresh water. This also helped to flush the poison from his body. Food was offered frequently, and refused. The poor man hallucinated, thrashed around in the bed, screamed, swore, called out for his mother and nearly died.

Finally he slept peacefully.

Upon awaking, he was ravenous. Flower tried to get him to eat smaller portions, slowly and more often.

"So first you try to parboil me and now you're trying to starve me? Is that it? Well it won't work. I'll go hunt for myself. Make my own damn food."

Flower just shook her head. She knew he wouldn't make it ten feet on his own. He could barely make it to the outhouse by himself.

The next order of business was to get Tinker back into "fighting condition." It wouldn't be easy because the man was lazy as a pet raccoon. Biggy was hard pressed to know how to motivate him into action. He finally hit upon a technique that worked strictly by accident.

Tinker was sitting on the porch with his leg up on the railing. He was gazing off into space and puffing on a hand-rolled cigarette. Where he had gotten the tobacco and papers, Biggy didn't know. They must have been stashed in the ratty back pack he kept in his room.

Out of frustration, Biggy yelled.

"So what, man. You lost your guts along with your leg? You're content now to sit around and live off other people like an old woman?"

Biggy was taken completely by surprise when Tinker launched himself off the porch and landed on top of him. Flower heard the commotion and came outside to find two grown men rolling around in the dirt. Each trying to gain the upper hand.

The fight was short lived only because Tinker didn't have any stamina.

"That's more like it you son of a gun," Biggy panted. "Your training begins today. If you want the job I'm offering, you have to be in shape."

"What job..."

"Training dogs, doing search and rescue, working security. A lot of the same stuff we did in the military. You interested or what?"

Because he only had one leg, it was hard for Tinker to follow the program Biggy had put together. He could do push-ups, life weights; anything that didn't require two good legs.

Biggy called Ann. Being a man of few word, he got right to the point.

"Ya know that contraption John uses when he wants to stand up? Well I've got a friend up here who needs a leg."

Ann was surprised at the request. In all the time she had known him, Biggy had never needed anything from anybody. She was also extremely curious. Who was this mystery man and where did he come from?

Chapter 108

The next time Biggy went for supplies, he was gone longer than usual. Flower was beginning to worry. She had been left to baby-sit Tinker and the task quickly got tiresome. The man was impossible. He talked incessantly and he seemed to think he was an authority on everything.

She was relieved when Spaz began...spazzing. Someone was coming, however her relief was short lived. From the cloud of dust she could see rising in the distance, it was more than just Biggy returning. Flower was nervous.

Grabbing the rifle that was always by the door, she checked to make sure it was loaded and the safety was off. Tinker had been snoozing on the porch when she made a dash for the corner of the cabin and took up a firing position.

"What the..." he stammered as he jerked awake.

He shaded his eyes with his hand and looked in the direction Flower pointed. Sure enough. They were getting company.

Two men were approaching on horseback. As they got closer Flower gasped as she recognized one of them. Her hands shook as she attempted to raise the heavy gun to her shoulder.

Sam Beardsley sat relaxed in his saddle, a rifle resting casually across his lap. He and two friends had been watching the comings and goings at the cabin from a ridge above the canyon. With Biggy gone, it was time to extract his revenge. The woman would pay. The one-legged guy would die. And he would wait for the return of the man responsible for the loss of his property.

He swung his right over the saddle horn and dropped lightly to the ground. The rifle Flower had pointed in his direction didn't seem to bother him at all as he sauntered toward her.

Tinker made a clumsy move to intercept and a bullet landed in the dirt just in front of him.

"Joe's a pretty good shot. I wouldn't try that again if I was you. And what were you going to do anyway? Hit me with your crutch?" Sam mocked.

In two long strides Sam reached Flower and easily snatched the rifle out of her hands and tossed it aside. He grabbed her by the back of her neck and forced her face to within inches of his own.

"Is that any way to welcome and old friend?"

He kissed her long and hard. She struggled.

"I see you got your fight back. I like that. Now let's go in that there cabin of yours and have ourselves a reunion. Joe will keep an eye on gimpy. Oh. I've got another man waiting down the trail to intercept anyone who might come along. We'll have a nice, long, uninterrupted afternoon," Sam said as he gave her a shove toward the cabin door.

Tinker had never felt so helpless in his life. He was effectively pinned down by some loser while Flower was about to be assaulted. Biggy had been right. He really did need to get back in shape.

He had participated in the exercise program Biggy had put together for him only half-heartedly. Feeling sorry for himself had gotten him into this awkward position and he didn't like feeling emasculated.

What happened in the next few minutes was a blur. Tinker could only watch; paralyzed. Spaz flew out from behind the cabin. Sam never saw him coming. Before he had time to raise his gun he was on his back with his throat being torn open by the huge wolf. A scream erupted, then gurgled to a stop.

Joe raised his gun, but never got off a shot. Biggy leapt from his position behind the chimney on the cabin roof knocking the man from his saddle. After a short scuffle the man was lying face down in the dirt with his hands behind his back.

The "look out" man was tied to a tree down the trail. The message was clear. Don't mess with Biggy or anyone who belongs to him.

From that day on Tinker applied himself with great determination to the program Biggy insisted he follow. Every day he got a little stronger; a little quicker. Even with only one leg he was surprised at what he could accomplish if he tried hard enough.

Chapter 109

The family had gathered for their usual Wednesday meeting. Luke was in the middle of his report on the progress being made with the training of Angel's puppies.

"JB has done a fantastic job teaching them the basic commands. It's time to bump them up to more intensive work. We've already got a waiting list of agencies and individual property owners who want to buy one of the pups. I'll talk to Biggy. We'll need his help."

As if on cue, the door opened and in walked Biggy followed by his little entourage: Flower, Spaz and Tinker.

Around the table, conversation stopped for a millisecond before chaos erupted as everyone rose and began moving forward to meet Biggy's friends. They all stopped short when Spaz placed himself between the approaching group of people and Flower.

With teeth bared in a menacing snarl and a growl rumbling in his throat, the wolf stopped everyone dead in their tracks. Ann and Bryce had met Spaz at the cabin so they were prepared. It would be interesting to see how everyone else reacted to this newest addition to the group.

Gunner had taken up the same stance in front of Ann. However, Gunner was a seasoned professional guard dog, he knew everyone in the family and he was comfortable with crowds of people. Spaz was not.

Flower put her hand on the huge wolf's head and made a soft grunting noise in the back of her throat. The wolf stood at ease, more or less, but no one dared to approach...or move at all. For a wild animal, he was amazingly well controlled just by the touch of Flower's hand.

Biggy felt it was time to make some introductions.

"This here wolf is Spaz. As you can see, he's pretty protective of Flower, which brings me to the reason for our visit. I've got a couple of presents for you, Luke. One's dead. The other two have got some damage, but they'll survive. They're tied up in your barn. Didn't see the need to drag their sorry asses down here. The dead one's Sam Beardsley. You remember him, right? Spaz got him when he tried to assault Flower."

Biggy took several minutes to recreate the early morning drama for the rest of the family. It was the most anyone had ever heard he talk.

Ann smiled up at Bryce.

"It seems all it took to bring Biggy out of his shell was a good woman," she whispered.

Bryce squeezed her hand.

"Bobby. Victor. Why don't you two bring another table over here so Biggy and his friends can sit and have some refreshments."

Biggy smiled as he helped Victor and Bobby wrestle the table into place.

"That'd be great. Oh, yeah. This is my lady, Flower, and my good friend, Justice 'Tinker' Parker. Luke, he's the guy I was telling you about who could help us with the dogs."

He stopped for a minute and looked at each familiar face.

"Flower. Tinker. This is...my family," he finished looking a little embarrassed.

Mama Rosa disappeared into the kitchen. She brought back plates and coffee mugs. The platter of cookies was passed around and coffee was poured. Ann noticed that Flower made no move to take either.

Maybe she's ready to see a speech and swallowing specialist, Ann mused as she glanced at Flower and smiled. *And Tinker, poor guy. I guess he's the one who needs the leg!*

Mama's next trip to the kitchen produced two dog food bowls. She put one of the bowls on the floor well away from Gunner. She motioned the wolf forward.

"Come on, Spaz. Over here. Come on," she commanded.

Spaz cocked his head to the side. He listened to the tone of Mama's voice. He didn't understand the words, but he recognized the authority in the posture that spoke alpha female.

To everyone's surprise, especially Biggy's, Spaz obeyed and was soon lapping up whatever was in the bowl.

"Gunner. Over here," Mama said as she placed the second bowl down close to Ann.

Georgio chuckled at the looks on the faces of their new guests.

"My Rosa, she has a way with dogs," he stated by way of explanation.

Everyone breathed a sigh of relief when the two big canines were distracted and relaxed.

Bryce was a little concerned about the wolf. He was, after all, a wild animal no matter how much training had been put into him. Biggy answered his questions before he had to ask.

"Spaz is just for Flower's protection. He won't be coming around unless he's with her. He ain't very social as you can imagine. With him around, I don't have to worry about Flower when I'm away from the cabin. I just wanted you all to meet him and be aware of his place."

Bobby laughed and broke the tension in the room.

"We appreciate that, Big. I don't have any desire to be his lunch."

Biggy continued to munch on his cookie. He paused with crumbs falling to the front of his shirt.

"He wouldn't bother you much, Bobby. Not enough meat on your bones."

Chapter 110

$\sim\!\!\sim\!\!\sim$

Otis Williams would be arriving at the end of October to pick up his children. Asia and Bruce were out of their minds with grief and worry. Jamal and Keysha were not stupid children. They realized something was terribly wrong. Bruce decided it was time to discuss the situation with them. It was only fair that they be prepared for what was going to happen. He didn't even know how to begin.

"Keysha. Jamal," he began, choking back the sob that threatened to escape his trembling lip.

Jamal immediately tensed as if he were bracing to be slapped. Keysha stared wide-eyed and sucked fiercely on her thumb.

"I'm afraid I have some news that will be very hard for you both to hear and accept. Please know that Asia and I have done everything we can possibly do legally to stop it from happening. Uncle Oscar has worked hard..." his voice trailed off and he dropped his face into his hands before continuing.

When he lifted his head there were tears in his eyes. Now Jamal was terrified. His big, tough Daddy Bruce never cried!

"Jamal, do you remember your father; your real father?"

"Yes! He left us all alone. We had to move out of our house and into a nasty apartment. He made my mommy cry. I hate him!" was the little boys instant response.

"Keysha. Baby. You were too little to remember," Bruce continued as he pulled the child onto his lap. "But your real father wants you back; both of you."

Jamal flew out of his chair and stood defiantly in front of Bruce.

"Well, I'm not going! And Keysha doesn't want to go either. We don't have to go...do we?"

With a deep sigh, Bruce took the little boy's hand. He shook his head.

"I'm afraid we don't have any choice. Uncle Oscar is trying to get us in to see the family court judge, but it doesn't look good for us. I'm so sorry, Jamal."

Jamal pulled his hand away and screamed, "If you really loved us, you wouldn't let us go!"

He turned and ran to his room, slamming the door. Bruce and Asia could hear him crying and throwing his toys.

Keysha slipped off Bruce's lap and quietly left the room, dragging her chi chi.

Bruce collapsed in Asia's arms. They held each other and wept.

Chapter 111

W hat was going on with Bruce and Asia affected the whole family. The mood was somber and contemplative. No one knew what to say or do to make things better.

Harold and Oscar had called for a meeting with the men of the Peterson clan. Oscar began by telling them that the judge had declined to meet with Bruce and Asia stating that there wasn't anything to discuss. It wasn't as if two parents were fighting over custody of their children. Bruce and Asia had no standing.

According to the family court judge, children belonged with their biological parents. Otis Williams had a clean record, a job, an apartment; there was no reason he couldn't take care of his kids. End of story.

Bruce fumed and cursed.

"What kind of idiot is the damn judge? He doesn't even know us; or the kids. He's making a decision based on...what? I can't believe this is happening."

Harold spoke up from his place at the table.

"I might have some interesting information to add to this whole mess. This is Billy Stokes from the Las Vegas Police Department."

Everyone had been so focused on Bruce they hadn't noticed the man sitting quietly next to Harold.

"I'll let him fill you in on the investigation into one Otis Williams."

All eyes turned to the detective. He cleared his throat before he began to speak.

"I don't think fatherly love is what's prompting Williams to come after his kids. As we speak, and for the last month or so, a thug named Alvin 'Tiny' Granger has been tailing Williams. Not sure whether or not Williams is aware. If he is, he's a cool character because he's going about his business as usual. Granger works for a mobster named Vito Petrelli. We're pretty sure a large sum of money is involved and ties directly, or indirectly, to these children."

Bruce was again on his feet.

"My kids might be in danger! Is that what you're saying?"

"Yes. If our speculations are accurate, they could very likely be put in danger. Vito doesn't care about anyone but himself. He wouldn't think twice about the welfare of these kids. My partner and I have been following Granger. He has a seat booked to Dixon on the same flight as Williams. They will be here at the end of October so we have time to put a game-plan together."

The change in Bruce was instantaneous. His grief and anger were reined in and compartmentalized. He focused on the task at hand.

"Okay. What do we do?"

Chapter 112

 ✦

A
nn had made arrangements for Tinker to be seen by a friend of hers at Boston General. His specialty was prosthetic limbs. Tinker had been a willing participant in this endeavor as the veteran's administration didn't seem to be in any hurry to address his plight.

They would be staying in Boston for a while as Tinker was getting measurements and fittings, and starting physical therapy. It felt good to get away by themselves. Ann loved her family dearly, but she and Bryce hadn't been able to get away for some quality time together since the uproar started over Jamal and Keysha.

Bryce knew Ann was worried sick for Bruce, Asia and the kids. She was passionate when it came to the welfare of children. With her painful childhood, it was understandable. *Well that's not ALL she's passionate about,* he thought smiling to himself. He was determined to take her mind away from the problems at home if only for a short time.

They strolled hand-in-hand through the streets of Boston. Ann had seen these streets many times as a homeless teenager, but these memories had long lost their power to control her.

She showed Bryce the alley where she and Gert had lived under a pile of trash and the spot where Richard had frozen to death...it all seemed like yesterday. This walk was cathartic for Ann. With

Bryce by her side she could think about these events without the overwhelming fear that had once been associated with remembering.

Bryce had helped to heal all those painful memories. He took her in his arms right there in the middle of the sidewalk. He took her face in his hands, he kissed her tenderly. "Those kisses" always made her stomach flutter with anticipation of what was to come later that night.

People walked around them, some giving them angry looks and curses for blocking the way, others smiled with remembered intimacies of their own and some just ignored them. They didn't care.

They got back to the hotel and decided to take a "nap" before going out for the evening to one of their favorite dining and dancing restaurants.

"Tinker must still be at the hospital," Ann said as she was slipping out of her clothes. "Should we ask him if he wants to go out to eat with us? I wonder if he brought dress clothes to wear? He probably doesn't even own dress clothes. The restaurant won't let him in wearing jeans and a tee-shirt. He really needs a haircut too. Do you think he would be offended if I suggested it?"

Bryce interrupted her dialogue with a passionate kiss.

"At the moment, I don't really care."

The afternoon passed pleasantly.

Chapter 113

While Ann and Bryce were spending quality time together, Tinker was having his last visit with the doctor and physical therapist at the hospital.

Holding onto the parallel bars, Tinker took the first steps on his new leg. The doctor had told him it would be painful until his stump became accustomed to the pressure and the fit of the prosthetic limb.

"You can use crutches or a cane at first if you want to," the doctor said. "You'll have to come back in a couple of weeks to have adjustments made, but so far things look good."

Dr. Benton watched him carefully as he traversed the bars back and forth several times.

"The benefit of getting the leg so long after the injury is that we don't have to deal with postoperative healing and swelling," he continued. "If you have any questions or problems before your next appointment, don't hesitate to give me a call."

Tinker laughed and shook his head.

"Thanks for everything Doc. I'll call if I need to, but I'm sure Dr. Peterson will keep a close eye on me."

It seemed strange to Tinker to be standing on two legs again. *I'm going to be all right,* he thought. A big smile spread slowly across his face. The doctor clapped him on the shoulder.

"Try not to over-do. Take the leg off at night and massage the stump. Watch for any skin breakdown...I think you'll do fine!"

The nurse went over a whole list of instructions regarding the care of his stump and the maintenance of the prosthetic limb. He had no idea it was so involved. He had thought you just stuck the thing on and you were good to go.

She also gave him everything in writing so he could go over it again at home. She knew he wouldn't remember everything she had said.

"Do you have any questions?"

"Nope. I think I can manage everything," was his excited response.

He opted for a cane. *I'm not going to use this thing for long,* he promised himself.

It felt so good to be more or less "whole" again. His first stop was the barber shop in the hotel, then to the men's clothing store. Since Biggy had taken him in he had saved his meager government pension checks so he had money to buy clothes.

By the time he got back to his room, his stump was throbbing! He carefully took the prosthesis off, downed some Ibuprofen and stretched out of the bed. He had refused the stronger pain medication the doctor had offered for fear it would trigger his addiction to alcohol.

After an hour or so the pain dulled enough for him to hop into the shower. As the hot water ran down his body and the steam rose, he felt like a new man. *Screw the VA,* he thought. *I'll do fine without them.*

Chapter 114

B ryce had called Tinker asking if he would like to go out to dinner with them.

"The food is excellent. The service is superb. We have a great table...we would love for you to join us if you feel up to it. How about seven o'clock?"

"That would be great, Bryce. I'll meet you in the lobby."

Won't they be surprised, he thought as he pulled on his tux jacket.

He tried walking around the room without the cane, however, his stump was still too sore and he found he walked with a pronounced limp. *I guess it's the cane for now. Don't want to embarrass myself by falling flat on my face!*

When Ann and Bryce got off the elevator, a very handsome man using a cane walked toward them. For a few seconds neither of them recognized him. The shave and the military haircut completely changed his appearance. The tux fit him perfectly.

"Oh, my gosh! Tinker!" Ann gasped when the realization clicked in her brain. "You look absolutely wonderful!"

He was soon lost in her tight embrace, followed by a "man hug" from Bryce. There were a few awkward moments when nobody knew what to say next.

"I thought you two were taking me out for dinner! Well...I'm starving."

Bryce regained his composure first.

"Right this way. We have a car and driver waiting."

Tinker was the recipient of many covert glances from ladies present in the dining room. He pretended not to notice, but he couldn't stop smiling.

Chapter 115

Oscar had called a planning session with everyone he thought would have something to offer as they prepared for Otis to take his children. Luke, Harold, Biggy, Tinker and of course Bruce were all anxious to get started.

Detective Morrow from the Cedarville Police Department would coordinate things with Billy Stokes and the Los Vegas Police Department.

Bryce, Ann and Gunner came as an accepted threesome. If a large sum of money was needed, Bryce, as owner of Peterson Enterprise, was the man who could get it quickly.

Ann offered her medical expertise as to the health and well-being of Jamal and Keysha. This was going to be difficult, especially with Keysha. No one really knew how much she understood about what was happening around her. The emotional trauma to the child would likely be significant. Ann was unsure how to prevent or prepare for it.

Gunner...just offered his reassuring presence. Butch would be brought in if there was a part for him to play. He was extremely protective of all the children in the family and Luke wanted the option of using him if it became necessary. Rex was progressing in his training, but wasn't ready to be put into a real life situation.

Brainstorming provided several viable options. They had to plan for every possible contingency since they didn't know what the end game would entail. The possibility for violence was on everyone's mind. The kids would be in danger; that was a given. Every possible precaution would be taken to keep them safe.

Jamal would be given a small wrist unit similar to the ones worn by every man in the Peterson family. To all appearances, it was just a watch; a good-bye gift from Bruce and Asia to Jamal. It actually contained a GPS, extra long-life battery, long range receiver and transmitter with a two-way radio and a panic button.

Instructions as to its use would be given to Jamal a few days before Otis came to pick them up. He would have a chance to practice with the unit and ask any questions that might pop up. He was a smart, brave little boy, even so, this would be expecting a lot of him.

It was debated just how much to tell Keysha. Bruce and Asia had explained as best they could to both kids what was going to happen and why. So far, Jamal was angry and Keysha was silent...as usual.

Bruce hoped that by including Jamal in the plan to expose Otis and the people controlling him, that some of his anger would be channeled toward keeping himself and his sister safe.

As soon as the children were in his possession, Otis would be followed. The transmitter/receiver on Jamal's wrist unit would be open at all times, allowing the team to hear everything that was going on around the kids. They could also speak to Jamal through the unit. This would only be done as a last resort. If Jamal could hear them, so could anyone else who was close by.

Jamal and Keysha had never seen Biggy or Tinker so they would be the ones responsible for the close tail. This didn't set well with Bruce. He wanted to be the person nearby in case something happened.

Luke tried to explain his reasons for this strategy.

"Hey, man, if the kids see you they will likely do something that will give our plan away. We can't afford to let that happen. You know how this stuff works, Bruce. We want to keep the element of surprise."

Biggy spoke up.

"You can trust us to keep the kids safe. Tinker and I have a lot of experience doing surveillance and recon. Nothing's going to get past us. We'll be armed. If things go hair-wire, we'll break cover and move in. It'll be fine."

Luke, Bruce and Butch would follow further back. The other members of the team, including police officers in plain clothes from Cedarville and Los Vegas, would be intermittent observers passing in and out randomly where ever Otis went.

Detectives Stokes and Morrow would keep track of Tiny and be on the lookout for Vito in case he showed up. Stokes had altered his appearance until Harold hardly recognized him. Stokes had brought Tiny in for questioning more than once. Tiny would "make" him in a heartbeat if he looked like the same old Billy.

"Good job, Stokes. You look like an idiot with the buck teeth and the mustache," Harold taunted. "The wig and glasses are a nice touch too."

Harold walked away laughing. Billy grunted.

"What does he know anyway. I look fantastic," he muttered to no one in particular.

Ann and Bryce would monitor everything from the home base and keep the rest of the family updated. Ann would be ready with medical advice as necessary.

The plan was in place and everyone knew their role. Now all they had to do was wait.

Chapter 116

I t was the night before Otis would fly to Vermont. He sat in his apartment holding an ice bag to his eye.

The last thing he remembered was sitting at the juice bar at his gym asking a tall, lanky, blonde girl why Joyce wasn't working. He was told she had called in sick. The next thing he knew he was tied to a chair in Vito Petrelli's office with Tiny standing over him.

"Wake up you little pussy," Tiny snarled, jerking Otis's head up by his hair. "We want to know your plan for getting the money and we want to know now!"

"What plan?" Otis mumbled, trying to buy himself some time so he could think.

Tiny punched him in the face. His head snapped back.

"We know you're going to Vermont tomorrow. What's in Vermont besides snow and bears? If you don't spit it out, you'll be walking with a permanent limp and using a white cane."

Having been worked over by Tiny once before, Otis complied.

"My kids! My kids are in Vermont!" he yelled. "Don't hit me again. I'll tell you everything."

Tiny circled the chair flexing his biceps and pounding his ham sized fist into his other palm.

"Well now. That's more like it. So your kids are in Vermont. So what?"

Otis began to sob out his fear and frustration.

"Their mother died. I have to take them, I'm the only living relative."

"And..." Tiny prompted impatiently.

"There's a family who wants to adopt them. I'm going to take them and then offer to sell them back for the amount of money I supposedly owe Mr. Petrelli."

Vito drummed his fingers on his desk.

"Otis. Otis. Otis. You're not very creative are you? I see the potential for a lot more money than what you owe me. Millions, I think. Yes. Several million."

"These are just plain, ordinary people. They don't have that kind of money," Otis whined.

"I guess they'll have to take out a loan or something won't they?" Vito countered. "If they want your kids bad enough, they'll figure out a way. Tiny will be right behind you every step of the way to make sure you don't screw us over. If you try to alert the police you and the kids will get to experience a slow, painful death. They go first. You can watch."

Otis dropped his head to his chest. *Why is this happening to me?* he asked himself. *I don't bother anybody. I'm a peace loving guy. All I want to do is go to work, have a few beers with my friends on Friday night and get laid every once in a while! Is that asking too much?*

His hands were untied. He was hauled to his feet and shoved toward the door.

"See you on the plane, shithead," were Tiny's parting words.

The next morning when Otis boarded his plane, true to his word, there was Tiny a few rows back.

Chapter 117

As soon as Otis stepped off the plane in Dixon a flagman radioed Stokes.

"Our man is on the ground. The shadow is just behind him."

Upon entering the terminal, a waiting "passenger" folded his newspaper and followed a few feet behind Tiny.

When Otis proceeded to the carousel to get his bag, the baggage handler was there to monitor his progress.

Otis stood there for a few minutes looking around at the signage, then headed toward the car rental counter.

A young graduate from the police academy stepped forward.

"Can I help you, Sir," he asked politely.

"I need to rent a car going one way to Las Vegas."

"We can help you with that. I have a nice mid-sized sedan cleaned and gassed up. Would that be satisfactory?"

Several different cars, a mini-van and a SUV had been made ready with tracking devices attached in the wheel wells in case Otis didn't want the sedan.

"Whatever's the cheapest. The sedan is fine."

Otis signed the appropriate papers and accepted the keys.

"One of my associates will have the car waiting for you right out front. And have a safe trip."

As Otis stepped away from the counter, another young officer was alerted to bring the car around.

Tiny had been watching from a distance. As soon as Otis was out the door, Tiny moved forward. Yellow cab number nineteen was waiting in line at the curb driven by a seasoned plain clothed officer.

He threw himself into the rear passenger side seat and slammed the door.

"Where to, buddy," the driver asked as he chewed on the end of an unlit cigar.

"Follow that blue Toyota," Tiny barked. "Don't let the driver see us and don't lose the car. There's an extra fifty in it for you."

The driver glanced in the rearview mirror.

"Yes, SIR," he said with exaggerated politeness, pulling out into traffic several car lengths behind Otis.

A stylishly dressed young woman standing on the sidewalk spoke into her wrist as she ran her fingers through her hair.

"The birds have flown."

"Roger that," Detective Morrow responded from an unmarked car in the parking lot.

He pulled out several cars behind cab number nineteen. The tail would be picked up outside town by another officer. Morrow would take a short cut and meet up with Stokes at a road side rest area about half way to Cedarville.

Luke would be waiting in the garage across the street from the restaurant ready to alert Bruce when Otis arrived. Stokes and Morrow would continue to follow Tiny.

Biggy and Tinker were nowhere to be found, at least not with the naked eye. Luke and Bruce were well aware of the talent these two men had for "disappearing in plain sight" and popping up whenever the situation required.

Chapter 118

Georgio and Mama Rosa, Ann, Bryce and Gunner were the only ones waiting with Bruce, Asia Kim and the children. The other family members had approached the kids at different times during the day to say their goodbyes.

There were boxes of toys and clothes packed and ready to go with Jamal and Keysha. Asia had packed each child a backpack. Jamal had books, paper, crayons, pencils and his new Nintendo 3DS game system. He had a change of clothes, PJ's and his toothbrush. There were juice boxes, a peanut butter and jelly sandwich and several cookies in case he got hungry during the trip.

His wrist unit was in place and operating properly. There was a charger in his backpack, but Bruce told him it shouldn't need charging for several days. He was hopeful that by the time the unit needed charging, he would have the kids back. He went over the panic button on the back of the unit one more time.

"Jamal, this is really important. If something really serious is happening press the red button. I'll come immediately."

"You mean if I see a gun or something? Of if he's going to hit me or Keysha?"

"Yes! Something like that. Be careful, Jamal," Bruce cautioned. "Even if something happens that you think is strange or scary, press the button, take your sister and hide. Uncle Luke and I will be able to hear everything and I'll come and get you."

Luke had checked the receiver to make sure they could follow the kids without any hang-ups. Everything was working perfectly.

"I know it's a lot to remember, Buddy. Do you understand everything?"

Jamal shook his head yes. Tears were gathering in his eyes. Bruce pulled the boy into a tight embrace and held him for several minutes before letting him go.

"Things will work out, Jamal. I promise."

Keysha's pack contained similar items. In addition, she also had clothes for her favorite doll, some of her picture books, dog treats and several pull-ups. Olyvia had her leash on and was waiting patiently for whatever came next.

Keysha hardly looked up when Bruce embraced her. It was as if she were detaching herself from him already. It broke his heart.

"Baby, everything is going to be okay," Bruce whispered against her curls. "Let your...father... know if you have to go to the potty. Can you do that, Keysha?"

The little girl just stared off into space, never blinking. Bruce knew she was incapable of telling anybody anything.

Unless Otis paid attention to Olyvia's cues, Keysha would be wet all the time. This was a major concern of Ann's. It would be a long trip by car to Las Vegas. There would eventually be diaper rash and skin breakdown if she wasn't changed regularly. Not to mention the smell. Somehow she didn't think Otis was the kind of person to care about any of this.

Asia had packed a bag for Olyvia containing her pull toys, dog food and the towel she had come to love.

Mama Rosa was stoic. Georgio was constantly wiping his eyes with his big white handkerchief. There was coffee made, but no one wanted any. Bruce's stomach was in such a knot he didn't think he could ever eat again. Asia had picked at her food for the last several weeks.

Bruce chided himself. *Get a grip! It's almost show time. I WILL get my babies back unharmed. I WILL get them back. I WILL get them back...*

His wrist unit beeped pulling him back to the here and now.

"He's parking the car," Luke whispered. "It's a blue Toyota Corolla. The tracking device in the wheel well is functioning properly and I've got it on the receiver. Nothing unusual so far. Hang tight, Bruce. We've got this under control."

Harold and Billy checked in.

"Tiny is still in the cab parked out of sight up the road a ways. It looks like he's just waiting for things to go down."

"Okay, everyone. Be alert," Luke responded.

Chapter 119

Otis sat in his car for a long time; forehead resting on the steering wheel. He didn't really want to do this! When he met with Atty. Schwartz he had been made aware of Keysha's problems. There was no way he could deal with all that. But what choice did he have? Tiny was out there watching every move he made. If he didn't take the kids, they were all dead.

His plan had been to travel by car for a day. Stay in a motel over night and make the ransom call in the morning. With any luck, the kids would be back with their adoptive parents by tomorrow night. He would collect the money, fly back to Vegas and turn the cash over to Vito. Then he would disappear somewhere far away.

Unfortunately, Vito had other plans. He wanted the kids brought all the way to Vegas where HE would then make the calls and set up the ransom. Otis was to pick Tiny up at a gas station at the outskirts of Cedarville, thus guarantying compliance with Vito's requirements.

What am I going to do? I know Vito has no intentions of returning the kids! And if I go through with this, I'm as guilty as he is and he will own me. The demands will never stop! Either that or he'll just kill me too.

Otis felt sick to his stomach as he slowly got out of the car and headed across the road. This thing had spiraled out of control. There was no going back. The thought of exposing the plan to the police briefly crossed his mind.

When he opened the door to the restaurant, the animosity rolled over him like fog on a damp morning. It almost drove him back to his car...almost.

He recognized Jamal. The kid was holding tight to the hand of a huge, scar-faced black man. A little girl, Keysha he presumed, had one arm wrapped around the neck of a dog and the other was clutching a tattered blanket and an equally tattered rag doll.

Otis took a few tentative steps into the room. No one stepped forward to greet him. In fact, no one said a word. Keysha started to whimper like a wounded animal. The big man picked her up and began patting her back. The struggle and the pain on his face was obvious.

"Why are you doing this?" Bruce asked. "The kids are happy and loved here. Keysha doesn't even know you. She has special needs that we are only now beginning to be able to address. Taking her from us will significantly traumatize her to the point she may never recover. Do you even care?"

Otis gulped and tried to bring his pounding heart and rapid breathing under control.

"Of course I care. This is something I have to do. I left them. As a result, their mother is dead. If I had stayed things would have been different. They're my children; my responsibility."

Even as he said those words, Otis knew they were a lie. He was doing this to save his own skin. He justified his actions by telling himself he would do everything in his power to see that the kids were returned.

"Come on kids, it's time to go. We have a long drive..."

He didn't get to finish his sentence before Jamal began to scream.

"Noooo, noooo. I hate you. You're not my father any more. I don't want to go. Please, Daddy Bruce. Don't make us go!"

Olyvia, who generally loved everyone, was immediately barking. Gunner pulled himself up off the floor and took several steps toward Otis.

Bruce looked stricken. He would rather face down middle eastern terrorists in the desert than hand these children over to a stranger.

Bryce stepped in.

"Let's everybody calm down,"

He turned and looked at Otis.

"Are you absolutely sure this is what you want to do, Mr. Williams? Look at these children. They're terrified."

"Yes. Yes, sir," Otis stammered. "I have to do it. I'm sorry."

"Why, Otis? Why do you have to do this? Is there someone threatening you?"

This was the perfect opening for Otis to come clean. Let the police handle it. But visions of a terrible, painful death flashed before his eyes. He didn't dare take the chance. Tiny was waiting...

"I'm not taking all that stuff," Otis said, pointing to the boxes and ignoring Bryce's question. "I don't have room. And I hope you don't think the dog is coming with us. I live in a high-rise. I can't have dogs. I'll take the suitcases and the backpacks. That's it."

He looked at Jamal.

"Jamal. Come on. Right now, Boy."

Otis stepped forward and reached for Keysha. She clung tighter to Bruce's neck. The sound that emitted from the little girl was like nothing human. Bruce pried her arms off and handed her, kicking and screaming, to Otis.

"Daaaaaddy!," she wailed, her arms reaching out to him.

Bruce choked back a sob. This was the first time she had ever called him that. It was one of the only times he had ever heard her say anything at all.

Otis headed for the door, hardly able to control the flailing child.

"Jamal! Now!" he called over his shoulder.

Olyvia jumped forward. Bryce caught her leash. Even though she was not full grown, he could barely hold her back. Ann put a hand on Gunner's head or he would have been on Otis in a flash.

Weeping hysterically, Asia fell into Mama Rosa's arms.

As they went through the door, Jamal glanced back. The look on his face was one of pathetic resignation. Bruce dropped to his knees and fell forward until his forehead was on the floor. His broad shoulders heaved with gasping sobs.

Georgio picked up the suitcases and headed for the door, tears streaming unchecked down his face.

Chapter 120

They had been in the car for, what seemed like, hours. Keysha had not stopped whimpering since she had been stripped from her family and buckled into the car seat Bruce had provided.

"You better stop, Otis," Jamal said from the back seat, refusing to call his father anything but his name. "She probably should be put on the pot. Otherwise, she'll pee...or worse and it will smell really, really bad..."

Tiny leaned over the seat and stuck his finger in Jamal's face.

"Shut the fuck up. We'll stop when I say so and not before."

Jamal wisely decided not to comment further even though he knew what was going to happen. And sure enough...

"What the hell is that smell," Tiny thundered. "Take the next exit, Williams. The sign back a ways said there's a Motel 6. Oh, God. It smells like she shit herself. Ooohhh, damn."

Upon hearing this plan to take the exit, Biggy and Tinker sped ahead arriving at the motel several minutes before Otis.

As soon as Otis pulled into the parking lot of the motel, Tiny threw himself out the door. He headed for the office yelling back over his shoulder to Otis.

"That is fucking horrible. Geeezzzz. I'll get a room. We'll stay here tonight. Williams, get her cleaned up and I mean now!"

By the time Tiny entered the office, Tinker was in the motel's small lobby perusing the maps and pamphlets for nearby tourist attractions. Biggy was out of sight and waiting.

When Tiny came back to the car he threw a keycard at Otis.

"That room had better smell like rosebuds when I get back," he yelled as he stomped off down the street toward Gilly's Bar & Grille.

Tinker alerted Biggy as to which room was being used. In a matter of minutes, Biggy had gained entrance into the room and was looking for a place to conceal himself.

Otis sat paralyzed while a mushroom cloud of odor filled the car. Jamal finally took action. He unbuckled his sister from the car seat and gingerly helped her out to stand on the sidewalk leading to their room. Stool and urine ran down her legs and into her shoes. A puddle formed on the sidewalk. Keysha continued to cry.

"Come on, Otis! You got to wash her up before that man comes back. Didn't ya hear him? She's got clean stuff in her back pack. I told you this would happen!"

Chapter 121

B ruce and Luke were about a mile up the road. The receiver was picking up the conversation clearly. Bruce slammed his fist on the dashboard.

"Move in around the motel," Luke directed. "Stokes? You hearing this? How is Tiny likely to react if things don't go his way?"

"Stokes, here. Yeah, I can hear everything. He's volatile, he's impatient, he's dumb as a brick and he's probably in that sports bar tossing back a few. Bad combination, Luke. No telling what he'll do if he comes back and the girl hasn't been cleaned up. Morrow will pose as a customer and head into the bar. He'll let us know when Tiny's on his way out."

Chapter 122

Finally, Otis pulled himself together enough to, at least, exit the car. He had absolutely no idea how to deal with the situation. After several seconds of fumbling with the keycard, he finally got the motel room door open. It opened directly off the sidewalk; a plus for the police officers who were quietly getting into position.

As soon as Tiny was safely seated in the bar, a plain clothed officer entered the motel office to explain to the desk clerk what was happening. Guests who were in close proximity to the room Otis and the kids occupied, were quietly evacuated to the other side of the motel.

No one knew exactly what would happen upon Tiny's return, but they were planning for the worst possible scenario.

If Bruce simply took the children, he would be the one arrested for kidnapping! The court had made it crystal clear. He was not to interfere in any way with Otis taking custody of his children. Otis Williams was their biological father. He had his rights. To the family court judge, nothing else mattered.

For Bruce, the frustration and anger he was feeling was almost incapacitating. He could have easily strangled the judge. That's what he wanted to do; fantasized about doing. However, that line of thinking wouldn't help in this current crisis. He had to keep a level head if he was going to get the kids back safe and sound.

And when he got them back, would he ever be able to explain to them why this happened in the first place? Why he had let them go? Would they ever understand and forgive him? Jamal? Maybe. Keysha? Probably not.

Chapter 123

Otis was terrified. Keysha stood in the middle of the room dripping all over the carpet. She had been crying for so long her breathing was coming in short gasps between sobs.

Jamal was close to panicking.

"Do something," he yelled. "Put her in the tub or something. Throw the clothes away. They're ruined anyway. Why are you just standing there? That man could come back any minute!"

It was almost an hour before Tiny stumbled back to the motel. The door flew open and banged against the wall. His huge frame blocked the sunlight. For a minute, no one moved. Tiny took in the scene in front of him through blurry eyes and a mind-altering buzz.

"What. The. Hell! I told you to take care of this, Williams."

Keysha's constant mewing like a sick kitten had given Tiny an enormous migraine headache and his patience was at the breaking point. He had thrown back shot after shot in the bar; enough to dull the migraine and make him surly.

"I'm fucking done with your constant crying and carrying on," he yelled in Keysha's face. "Shut the fuck up, girl."

Tiny drew a gun from under his jacket and pulled back the hammer. He put the barrel against Keysha's temple. He wasn't planning on really shooting one of his little money-makers, he was just hoping the threat would insure some peace and quiet.

Biggy heard this exchange from his hiding place behind a large chest of drawers, which he had muscled away from the wall and placed in front of him across the corner of the room. If he held his head at just the right angle, he could see Tiny and Keysha through the crack between the dresser and the wall. Jamal was out of his line of sight.

It had been a gamble, but he didn't think the occupants of the room would notice the indentation on the rug where the chest had been. They would be too caught up in the drama that was unfolding to pay any attention to the rug.

Biggy also instinctively knew that Tiny wasn't going to do anything that would jeopardize the plan for collecting the money by shooting the little girl. He was stupid and drunk, but not <u>that</u> stupid and drunk!

Tiny's mind was racing. He wasn't going to miss out on a fortune; Vito had promised him ten percent of the take. If he didn't bring the boss two healthy cash-cows, Vito would end life, as he knew it, in an exceedingly painful and permanent way.

For a moment, all action was suspended in time. No one had counted on Otis.

Otis watched Tiny put a gun to his daughter's head. A daughter he had left when she was an infant. A little girl, his own flesh and blood, who had already suffered so much because of his negligence.

How did I get there? he wondered, not for the first time in recent months. *I always thought I was a good person.* In the space of a heartbeat he realized it was his own stupid choices and selfishness that had brought him and his children to this place.

He glanced at Jamal. The poor kid was petrified. They had had a relationship once; years ago. Otis quickly looked back over at Tiny and Keysha. Two words flashed into his mind: *no more!*

"You take that damn gun away from my baby girl," he said, hoping Tiny was too drunk to notice the quiver in his voice.

"Or what?" Tiny challenged. "You gonna do som..." the words died in his throat as Otis threw himself at the much bigger man.

The momentum carried them into the bedside table. The lamp burst against the wall and the table collapsed. They thrashed around on the floor amid broken wood and glass with Otis struggling desperately for control of the gun.

Jamal hit the panic button on his wrist unit. Then everything seemed to happen in a blur of slow-motion images.

Chapter 124

Biggy sprang from his hiding place, grabbed Jamal and Keysha and shielded them with his own body.

CRACK!

The gunshot was deafening. When Jamal opened his eyes and peered out from behind Biggy's shoulder, Tiny was standing there, the gun still in his hand, with a look of confusion on his big, dumb face. Otis was on the floor, blood blossoming on his chest.

"Shit!" Tiny exclaimed, looking wild-eyed around the room. "SHIT!"

At that moment, Bruce burst through the door like a freight train, tackling Tiny and dropping him like a sack of potatoes. The gun skittered under the bed. Tinker and several of the other officers flooded into the room.

Bruce had Tiny on the floor and was pummeling his face. It took Luke and two other officers to pull him off.

"You son of a bitch," Bruce bellowed, struggling against the hands that held him.

"Bruce, calm down. We've got him," Luke spoke quietly in his ear. "It's okay, man. We've got him. The kids need you."

With enormous effort, Bruce slowly regained control.

"Get off me," he growled, shaking himself like a wet dog.

Luke nodded to the other officers and they let the big man go. He dragged a blanket off one of the beds and immediately went to the children, scooping Keysha out of Biggy's arms.

Bruce's eyes met Biggy's.

"Thanks, man."

"No problem, Bruce," Biggy mumbled before he and Tinker disappeared.

"It's okay, Baby. It's okay. Daddy's got you now," Bruce murmured as he tenderly wrapped the blanket around the little girl and pressed her to his chest. "Jamal. Son. You all right?"

With his other arm he reached for the little boy.

"I'm all right. But you sure took your time getting in here," Jamal said as he flung himself at Bruce and held on tight.

Stokes and Morrow wrestled Tiny to a waiting patrol car and, none too gently, slammed him in the back seat. His head bounced against the door frame. Blood ran down the side of his face.

"Police brutality," he screamed. "I'll sue your fucking asses."

"I didn't see anything. Did you, Stokes?" Detective Morrow commented nonchalantly.

Detective Stokes shrugged.

"He's drunk. He tripped. Clumsy turd, ain't he?"

Chapter 125

Paramedics had been called. Bruce knew they wouldn't arrive in time to do anything for Otis.

"Jamal," Otis croaked.

The little boy broke away from Bruce and knelt beside his father.

"I'm...sorry, Jamal," he whispered, blood bubbling from his lips. "I never wanted any of this to happen. I...I love you."

It was a struggle for Otis to say these last few words. His eyes slowly went blank and he was gone.

Jamal stood over his dead father. No one could have predicted what happened next.

"You liar!" he shrieked, the stress of the last few weeks finally pushing him over the edge.

He began wildly kicking Otis in the ribs. "Liar! Liar! Liar! You left us!"

Luke grabbed the now sobbing, hysterical child and held him tight.

"It's over, Jamal. Let's go home, Buddy."

Keysha and Jamal were both checked over at the hospital to make sure they were uninjured; physically anyway. Keysha was cleaned up and wrapped in a hospital blanket. Realizing the tattered rag and the doll held special meaning for the little girl, the nurse put those items in a plastic bag and tucked the bag under Keysha's arm.

Chapter 126

B ruce and Luke bundled the children into the car and headed back to Cedarville. Exhaustion finally won out, and lulled by the safety and movement of the car, they were soon asleep in the back seat.

Not so for Bruce. The adrenaline was still pumping through his veins. In his sleep deprived mind, he relived the aftermath of the shooting over and over as he drove. The thought of what could have happened sent his stomach churning and the acid burning his throat.

His hands clutched the steering wheel as if it was Tiny's throat. But by the time they crossed the border into Vermont, the high was slipping away and he felt like he had been hit by a bus. He pulled the car onto the berm.

"Luke. Wake up, man. You're going to have to drive. I'm completely done in."

Awakened from a sweet dream about holding his twins, Luke took over for the last leg of their journey. Now that he was awake, he mind traveled to the upcoming delivery of his son and daughter.

Tess had been on complete bed rest for the last month. The C-section would be performed between Thanksgiving and Christmas, four weeks before her January due date. The doctor had been monitoring the twins throughout the pregnancy and he didn't want the babies, especially Galva Grace, to go through the trauma of birth. So far, Charley was doing fine; developing normally.

Gracie, the smaller of the two, had a heart problem not uncommon in Down Syndrome children. She would need surgery soon after birth. As the time approached, Luke and Tess would be flown to Boston for the delivery. There was a children's hospital there that was one of the best in the country. Pediatric surgeons would be standing by to address the heart issue as soon as she was born.

With Bruce practically comatose and slumped in the passenger seat, Luke's mind ran rampant. He thought of every possible complication to the delivery and subsequent surgery. By the time the sun was peeking over the horizon, he had conjured up the worst possible outcomes for his wife and children.

Chapter 127

Luke radioed ahead to Bryce.

"Dad, we're almost home. Be there in about fifteen."

Bruce jerked awake as soon as the car stopped. Asia Kim had been watching out the window and as soon as the car pulled in she was out the door. She met Bruce as he was gently lifting a still sleeping Keysha out of her car seat. He laid her in Asia's waiting arms. Bruce reached back into the car and picked up Jamal. The little boy was rubbing sleep out of his eyes.

"Are we home, Dad?" he asked.

"Yes, Son. We're home. And you never have to leave us again. I promise," he said, knowing he would keep that promise even if it meant moving to Canada or to a far off cabin in the mountains...

Olyvia went nuts as soon as she heard the car. The dog hadn't eaten or drank anything since Keysha was taken. No matter how much coaxing and cajoling Mama Rosa had done, nothing had gotten Olyvia to leave her spot on Keysha's bed.

The barking immediately woke Keysha up. She struggled to get down. With reluctance, Asia let her go. The child threw her arms around the dog's neck and buried her face in the red fur.

Jamal replaced Keysha in Asia's arms.

"Oh, Jamal. You my strong, brave boy. You take care of sister. Bring her back. This humble woman love you."

"I love you too...Mom. Is there anything to eat? I'm starved."

Mama Rosa wiped the tears from her face and smiled for the first time in, what felt like, weeks.

"Of course there's something to eat. Your favorite. Cinnamon buns."

Jamal wolfed down two big buns and a glass of milk. Keysha nibbled her bun, giving every other bite to Olyvia.

With the edge off their appetites, Asia managed to propel them toward the apartment where she got them cleaned up and dressed for the day. It was the first time Asia had felt normal since this whole ordeal began. The simple act of washing Keysha's hair was a soothing balm to the young woman who loved both children so much.

Jamal seemed to spring back quickly, all things considered. He returned to his usual routine of school and helping John in the office for a few hours on Saturday morning.

He and JB picked up right where they had left off, arguing over video games and doing their homework together sitting at Grandma Rosa's kitchen table after the school bus dropped them off.

Not so with Keysha. She ate only if she sat with Olyvia on the floor under the table. She slept clutching Olyvia, her Chi-Chi and her doll. No one could entice her to play or read a book, not even Bobby with his crazy antics.

Back to sitting under the table or behind a chair Keysha withdrew from everyone into a world of her own. She looked at people with a blank expression on her face as if she had never seen them before. No one knew how to reach her.

Bruce blamed the family court judge. He ranted about it to anyone who would listen. The rest of the family understood his anger and tried to be patient, however, it was getting on everyone's nerves. Asia had finally had enough.

"Bruce. It over. Nothing to do. This not help Keysha. Not help our family. It make me not want to be around you! You must stop to dwell on this. We have back. Make most of it."

To hear this from his soft-spoken, always accepting and patient little wife was a wakeup call for Bruce.

"I know, Asia. And I'm sorry. You're right. My main goal must be to keep our family together and help Keysha and Jamal in any way I can."

He hugged Asia tight.

"What would I ever do without you? I love you, Asia. Don't ever doubt that."

"This woman love you too," Asia replied, with a sigh of contentment.

It was going to be a good night; a very good night.

Chapter 128

Tess and Luke were flown via the Peterson Enterprise corporate jet to Boston. They were both nervous, anxious, tired, afraid; you name it. Emotions were flying in every direction.

Bryce, Ann and Gunner accompanied them; Ann being the better one to understand the medical lingo. Luke just felt better with his mother there to ask the questions he would never think to ask.

The C-section went off without incident. Tess had insisted on a spinal anesthetic so she could be awake through the births. Luke was right beside her, holding her hand and trying not to throw up, pass out or both.

As a police officer, he had seen more than his share of blood and gore. Seeing his wife's blood was an entirely different matter. The sweat poured into his eyes. His stomach heaved. Swallowing hard helped to keep the gorge down.

"You okay there, Luke?" the nurse asked. "You're looking a little pale."

She got him a stool and put it close by Tess's head. Luke gratefully sat down. *I have to get control of myself,* he thought. *Guess I shouldn't have had that bacon for breakfast. The worst is probably yet to come and I can't have my head hanging over a bucket!*

Charley was born first. He cried immediately upon leaving his comfortable temporary home in his mother's womb. He was taken to an incubator where he would be examined by a pediatrician, weighed, measured; all the things that happened with a newborn.

"Luke," Tess said. "Go be with Charley. I'm fine."

Reluctantly Luke complied. One of the nurses made room for him. Happy tears came to his eyes as he looked at his son for the first time. Charley's arms were flailing, his legs were kicking and he was wailing for all he was worth.

Luke touched the baby's tiny fist and four perfect fingers and a thumb responded by closing around his finger. The bond was instantaneous.

When Gracie was brought into this world, she was eerily silent. She was hustled over to her incubator where the doctors and nurses began a frantic effort to save her life.

There wasn't room for Luke to even get close enough to see what was going on. His heart pounded. He was enveloped by a fear, the likes of which he had never felt before.

"She can't die. Please, God. Don't let my baby girl die," he whispered to an unseen God that he hoped was listening.

In answer to his prayer, Gracie emitted a gasping, bleating sound. The tension level around the incubator lessened ever so slightly.

"Okay people. Let's get her to the neonatal intensive care ASAP," the doctor in charge directed, and off they went.

Charley was wrapped snuggly in a striped blanket, a tiny blue hat was slipped over his head and he was handed to his father. Luke could barely breath. He gazed down into his son's face with amazement.

He slowly and carefully brought the baby to Tess. Luke slipped into the bed beside his wife and cradled them both in his arms. The joy in their son was somewhat tempered by the worry for their daughter.

The surgery on Gracie took almost all day. Luke was exhausted. He tried to split his time between Tess and Charley and the surgical waiting room. A nurse came out every hour to update him, which helped somewhat.

Ann and Bryce were quietly supportive, bringing coffee and food, taking turns in the waiting room and with Tess. They had both held Charley and already loved him. Ann thought he looked like his father. His eyes were a dark blue, but that could change as he got older. Since he didn't have any hair, it was hard to tell if he would have the thick auburn hair like his father or carrot red like his mother. Either way, they had another redhead in the family.

And Gracie...no one had really had a chance to look her over before she was whisked away to the neonatal nursery and then to surgery. They had been told she had all her fingers and toes at least. Her features were slightly Down Syndrome; it was hard to tell at this stage. There may also be a problem with her vision, but so far, her hearing seemed to be intact. Any other issues would be addressed after her surgery.

Except for some problems with stabilizing Gracie's blood pressure at the beginning of the surgery, things went as expected. The plan was to fly her to the hospital in Cedarville as soon as she could be released in Boston.

In the meantime, home for Tess, Luke and Charley would be a hotel room close to the hospital. Ann, Bryce and Gunner also had a room and would stay for as long as they were needed.

Chapter 129

I t had been two months since Otis Williams had been killed. His body was ready to be released to his family, except the only family he had was Keysha and Jamal.

Detective Stokes called Bruce.

"Hey, Bruce. Billy Stokes here. How's it going? How are the kids?"

"Billy! Good to hear from you. Jamal is doing okay. Keysha...she won't even look at us. It's as if she blames us all. And it didn't have to happen. Asia and I are talking with Oscar about bringing charges against the judge. He should be strung up for what he allowed to happen!"

Billy sighed. He certainly sympathized with his friend. But he had seen things like this happen too many times to count. The family court system was screwed up and the outcome was damaged children.

"I wish you luck with that. If you need anything from me, all you have to do is ask."

"Thanks, Billy. Appreciate it. I know you didn't call just to pass the time of day, so what's up?"

"Well... I didn't know who else to call about this. Otis Williams' body is ready to be released to the family for burial. He doesn't have any living relatives except for the kids. What do you want me to do?"

"Let me talk to Jamal. He's one tough little kid, and smart as a whip. He's also mature beyond his years. I'll talk to him and get back to you within a couple of days. Oh, by the way. What's going on with the trial of Petrelli and Tiny?"

"You know how it goes," an exasperated Billy answered. "Motions back and forth, waiting for this and that...It's ridiculous. They won't go to trial for months...maybe not even until next year."

Bruce snorted in disgust.

"Please tell me they won't walk on this. They're both guilty as sin."

"We've got evidence up the wazoo. Tiny couldn't wait to try for a deal by implicating Petrelli. It was like a rat fleeing a sinking ship. I don't think either of them will get off, but you never know."

"Yeah. Unfortunately, I do know," Bruce replied. "Well, nice talking with you, Billy, and I'll get back about Williams."

Chapter 130

Jamal was playing a video game in his room after supper. His homework and his chores were done and the half hour game time was his reward. He would spend all day and all night playing with his game system if Bruce and Asia would allow it.

Bruce knocked before entering the room with Keysha in his arms. He didn't know if she was even listening to what was being said around her, but he wanted to include her in this conversation anyway.

"Hey, Buddy," Bruce began. "I've got something important I need to discuss with you."

Jamal looked up from his game with concern in his eyes.

"What, Dad?"

Bruce sat down on the bed. He cuddled Keysha close and kissed her forehead.

"Well, Detective Stokes called me this morning and they need to release your father's body so it can be buried. I was wondering what your thoughts are; what do you want to do?"

Jamal just stared at Bruce. He was silent for several minutes, then went back to playing his game.

"I don't care what happens to it," he stated, matter-of-factly.

Bruce knew he could never fully understand how Jamal felt so he didn't try to persuade the boy that he did. Thinking about the situation over the last couple of hours had brought him to a conclusion he hoped Jamal would consider.

"In the end he did man-up and try to save you both from Tiny. That should count for something, don't you think?"

Jamal came over and plopped down on the bed next to Bruce. His shoulders slumped.

"I guess it counts. But I'm only a kid. What can I do?"

"Well, I was thinking maybe Grandpa Bryce would let you bury your father in the cemetery on the Peterson Estate. What do you think?"

The little boy dropped his head into his hands. For a few minutes, his shoulders shook with silent sobs. Much to Bruce's surprise, Keysha reached over and touched her brother's head. Olyvia whined her sympathy as she pushed her nose under Jamal's arm. Bruce hugged all three. That's the way Asia found them a half hour later.

"Do you want me to talk to Grandpa Bryce, Jamal?" Bruce finally asked.

The boy raised his head and wiped his eyes.

"Nope. It's my 'sponsibility. I'll do it."

The next day, Jamal approached Bryce.

"Can I talk to ya man to man?" he began.

Bryce covered his smile with, what he hoped was, a serious expression.

"Of course, Jamal. What's up?"

Jamal sighed before he looked up at Bryce.

"Can I bury Otis in your cemetery?" he asked without preliminaries.

Bryce was taken aback by the boys forthrightness. He managed to keep the surprise from showing on his face.

"Well, I guess that could be arranged. Do you know how soon you would like this to happen?"

"As soon as we can. I just want to get it over with."

The body was flown in the following week. Bryce and Ann asked Father Madigan to say a few words over the grave. The whole family attended the somber, brief graveside service. JB stood beside his friend.

When it was over Jamal breathed a sigh of relief. He punched his friend in the arm.

"Come on, JB. Race you to the bottom of the hill."

The end. And off they went.

The tomb stone was engraved with just Otis's name, the date of his birth and his death. Now, finally, maybe Jamal and Keysha could get on with the rest of their lives without a shadow hanging over their heads.

Chapter 131

～∾～

Peterson Search and Rescue was extremely busy. Bruce and Luke couldn't keep up with the demand. Even with Biggy taking a turn piloting the big chopper, there weren't enough hours in a day.

Every time the chopper went up on a medical transport, they had to have a paramedic on board. This meant using someone from the Cedarville Ambulance service. So far there hadn't been a problem. However, it was bound to happen sooner or later. Then they had a big problem!

Tess was qualified, but with the twins she already had her hands full. If Ann went, that meant Bryce and Gunner went and that just wasn't practical. Besides, there wasn't room in the chopper for the three of them plus the causalities or people needing transport.

Luke brought it up at the weekly family meeting.

He gave his report including the status of the puppies that were being trained and the number of transports they had done in the previous week.

"JB is a big help with the dogs, even if it's only on the weekends," Luke assured John and Carla. "The boy's got a real knack for the work. Now that the puppies are older, Biggy and Tinker will be taking over more of the training. We will still need JB and the rest of you guys with the socialization part."

"Do we have buyers for the dogs? was Bobby's question. "We're in this to make money, you know."

"I'm happy to say all the puppies are spoken for and deposits have been made," Luke responded. "We aren't letting any of them go until they are at least a year old and have completed some work in the field. Our reputation is on the line here and I don't want to send out a dog that isn't well trained. These buyers are paying big money for a Peterson dog. I want to make sure they get their money's worth. I'm afraid it will be a while before we see a profit from this venture."

Luke shuffled some papers.

"Moving on. Last week we were called in to look for a lost child over in Fremont. Butch picked up the scent right away and we found the kid unharmed. We transported a victim from a car accident to the hospital in Dixon. Fortunately, there was a paramedic available who was able to go with us for that one. Plus we had two runs in the private sector transporting some big-wigs to a conferences and another guy to a speaking engagement out of state."

Georgio spoke up.

"Do you have suggestions as to what we can do to help alleviate the situation?"

"Yes, as a matter a fact, I do," Luke smiled. We need to get Tinker recertified so he can fly the chopper and we need to hire our own paramedic. A secretary or someone to keep track of the jobs, the dogs, the buyers...all that office stuff, would also be helpful."

"Oh, well, that's simple enough," Bobby laughed. "I'm sure qualified paramedics are a dime a dozen and it shouldn't be too hard to find a secretary. Seriously though, I can put out some feelers, see what I can find."

"Okay," Bryce said. "Let's get Tinker the classes he needs and Bobby, start your search for a secretary and a paramedic."

Bryce continued.

"Victor. Anika. What's coming up in the world of dance competition for us? Helena how are dance classes going? Does anyone need anything along those lines?"

"We're good," Victor responded. "Lots of students. Mama is very busy with lessons. Seems like everyone want to take ballroom dance all of a sudden."

He passed around a competition schedule and a schedule for practices to everyone.

Bobby groaned and winked at his wife.

"Oh, come on, dude. Maria and I have other things to do besides practice the Salsa."

"You keep practice or not win," Victor stated, glaring at Bobby.

"Carla. Any problems with the kitchen or the wait staff? How about housekeeping?" Bryce asked.

"No. Everything's running smoothly."

"John. Financials for this month?"

His full report was done on a monthly basis. If problems arose, he brought them up at the weekly meetings. Copies of the monthly statement were passed around.

"As you can see, we're making money, that's for sure," he said with a big smile. "I don't have anything of consequence to report this week. Our biggest expenditure presently is the chopper. If things continue to go the way Luke and Bruce report, it should pay for itself sooner than we anticipated."

"How about you, Mama?" Georgio said, pinching Rosa's cheek. "You have any problems my little pumpkin?"

She swatted his hand away, but a blush rose in her cheeks.

"You old fool," she grumbled good naturedly.

Georgio chuckled as she stomped away to get more coffee.

"Anything else we need to discuss this week?" he asked before he officially closed the meeting. "Okay, Mama. We'll have those donuts and more coffee now."

Chapter 132

Everyone was talking and laughing as they chowed down Mama's glazed donuts when the door opened. Much excitement followed as Tess walked in hauling a carrier with Gracie tucked inside. Molly Reidy followed carrying Charley, who was sleeping peacefully.

Gracie was crying her little bleating gasps which, according to Luke and Tess, never stopped. Tess had dark circles under her eyes and she looked completely exhausted. The strain was starting to show.

The baby had been home for several weeks, going back to the hospital every week for a progress check. The doctor expressed his concerns to Luke and Tess.

"She seems to be holding steady, but she needs to be gaining a little weight every week. I would hate to have to put her back in the hospital. For whatever reason, she's not thriving on breast milk. It may be a digestion problem or she's not latching on to the nipple properly. I know you've been in contact with the lactation specialist, but I think you need to consider bottle-feedings."

At this point, Tess was willing to try anything. Unfortunately, bottle feedings didn't prove to be the fix she expected. The first formula they tried gave Gracie horrible colic and diarrhea, as did the next.

It was trial and error until Molly suggested goat's milk. She had a tried and true recipe that would preserve the healthy benefits of live enzymes and good bacteria closely resembling breast milk. Of course, this meant getting a couple more goats, milking them, preparing the formula; it was time-consuming. That's just what Tess needed. More to do.

Ann hurried over and took Charley so Molly could get something to eat. Mama Rosa carefully lifted Gracie out of her carrier, sat down and began rocking her gently back and forth.

Tess flopped down next to Luke. His arm immediately went around her shoulders. He felt bad that she had taken the brunt of caring for the twins. Thank God for Molly! Biggy, Tinker and Bruce had picked up his work since the birth of the twins. He had needed to get back to doing his share, leaving Tess to deal with the babies.

"I've done everything I can think of to get her to stop crying," Tess moaned with tears threatening. "Nothing works! I'm at the end of my rope. I don't know what to do!"

She turned her face into Luke's shoulder and sobbed. Luke looked stricken. Everyone was at a loss. Luke had confided to Ann and Bryce that he and Tess were both at their wit's end and they needed help.

Help came from a surprising source.

Keysha had been sitting in her usual spot under the table, sucking her thumb. When she heard Gracie her thumb popped out and she came over to Mama Rosa and stared at the baby.

Everyone held their collective breath.

Ever so slowly, Keysha reached out and began caressing the baby's cheek; light as a feather's touch. In a high, sweet voice, Keysha began singing a song she seemed to be making up as she went along.

Gracie opened her eyes. It was obvious she was trying to focus on the little girl standing close to her. The bleating stopped. A wisp of a smile passed over Keysha's face.

From that moment on, Keysha had found a purpose. She dropped her rag doll and her chi-chi as she moved closer to Gracie. Rosa tentatively put her free arm around the little girl's waist. Keysha didn't pull away.

"Keysha, would you like to hold Gracie?" Rosa whispered. Keysha looked directly into Rosa's eyes. She shook her head, yes. Bobby hopped up and brought a big stuffed chair over beside Mama. He lifted Keysha up and deposited her in the chair. Mama carefully laid the now quiet infant in the little girl's arms.

Gracie drifted off to sleep as Keysha rocked her. It was as if Keysha had been born to do this very thing. She tenderly tucked the blanket around the sleeping baby and kissed her nose.

It was a quiet, spiritual moment. No one spoke, not wanting to interrupt the peace and tranquility that had descended. Each person present knew they were witness to something very special.

Chapter 133

More and more, Keysha stayed with Tess and the babies during the day. Tess assured Bruce and Asia that she was a huge help, especially with Gracie.

Over the next days and weeks Tess began to teach Keysha how to milk the goats and how the baby formula was made. She let Keysha help feed the chickens and gather the eggs. Mostly, she talked to the child about everything and anything always hoping Keysha would respond.

Keysha paid close attention to what Tess said. She was a smart little girl and learned quickly. With supervision, it wasn't long before she could do a passable job with changing wet diapers and dressing the babies. Almost all the eggs made it to the house and the chickens didn't suffer from lack of food.

The only small problem was Keysha's bladder and bowel control issue. Olyvia was always there to alert Tess when a potty break was necessary, however, it was just one more thing for Tess to do. The only solution was to teach Keysha how to deal with the situation herself.

Tess felt that Asia and Bruce babied the child more than was necessary. And she understood; yes, Keysha had been through a lot in her young life. She was four years old, going on five. The trauma was over. It was time to move on. With Olyvia's help, potty training began in earnest.

When Olyvia gave the signal, Tess showed Keysha how to get her panties down and scoot up on the toilet. When they heard the tinkle, Tess clapped her hands and did a happy dance. Keysha almost laughed.

Tess showed her how to use the toilet paper and get her pants back up. Washing her hands was the most fun part for Keysha. Tess had to admonish her not to splash in the water, but dry her hands and hang up the towel.

After each successful experience Keysha's confidence grew. As time went on, Keysha became proficient enough to take care of business all by herself. Tess breathed a sigh of relief.

Gracie was thriving under Keysha's watchful eye. She didn't quite smile yet, but she flapped her hands and made little grunting noises, much to Keysha's delight. Once she got the hang of drinking from a bottle, she started gaining weight and didn't look so much like a baby alien; all head and eyes.

The Peterson household had finally turned the corner and things had smoothed out. Not so in the Watson household. Bruce was not happy about his daughter spending so much time away from home. He needed someone to blame so he blamed Luke.

"It's like she doesn't want to live here anymore," he raged. "Why doesn't Luke put his foot down and just send her home. He's supposed to be the man of the house..." and on and on.

The tension became a tangible thing between Luke and Bruce. It soon escalated and spilled over onto the rest of the family. All laughter and casual conversation stopped as soon as Bruce stomped into a family meeting. Nobody knew exactly what to say. Even Bobby was at a loss for words.

Mama Rosa was worried. Oh, there had been disagreements and arguing over small things over the years, but nothing like this. She knew this situation couldn't continue; it was eating Bruce alive. And as a result, the rest of the family was suffering from the fall-out.

It was after midnight one night after a particularly difficult family meeting and Rosa was flopping and turning in bed. After she had punched her pillow a few times, Georgio finally pulled her close as he made his shushing, clucking noises in her ear.

"Okay, Mama. What's bothering you? Your pillow will never survive another beating."

"Georgio, what are we going to do about all this? It breaks my heart that our family is in all this turmoil. I know Bruce is upset and not coping very well and I'm sorry for him. But this behavior is so unlike him!"

She cuddled close and put her head on her husband's shoulder.

"It kind of scares me," she admitted so softly Georgio almost missed what she said.

And that statement scared Georgio more than Bruce did. His Rosa wasn't afraid of anything!

"How about we ask Ann and Bryce to go out with us somewhere; a picnic or something where we won't be interrupted. We can put our heads together and see if we can come up with a way to handle this diplomatically."

Rosa propped herself up on her elbow so she could look into Georgio's face. She kissed him tenderly.

"I love you, old man. I think that's a wonderful idea. Don't know why I didn't think of it myself," she responded with a twinkle in her eyes that could only mean one thing to Georgio.

He relaxed and thoroughly enjoyed the rest of the night.

Chapter 134

After their get-together with Georgio and Rosa, Ann and Bryce had discussed the situation. Ann thought she knew what might help. When she explained her intentions to Bryce, he had some reservations.

"Are you sure you want to do this?" he asked as he took her in his arms. "I know how hard it will be for you. And it could back-fire and only make things worse."

Ann cupped his face in her hands and looked into his eyes. His concern for her was evident. But how could she stand by and watch Bruce and Asia suffer without trying to help them find the path to peace.

"I know, my love. But I have to try."

They invited Bruce for breakfast. The grave-yard shift was a long, hard one and Bruce was always famished by the time he was done. Ann had spoken with Asia Kim about what she was doing so that the young woman wouldn't feel left out.

"If it will help husband, Asia will be very grateful," was her heartfelt response.

Breakfast was at eight o'clock and since nothing of consequence had happened during the night requiring a lot of paperwork, Bruce was right on time. Ann had outdone herself with the preparations. Steak and home fried potatoes with onions, fresh fruit, homemade bread with strawberry jam, and of course, plenty of hot coffee using her own secret blend of beans.

Bruce pushed back his chair and rubbed his belly.

"Ann, that was spectacular. Asia has me on a 'healthy diet.' I know she's doing it because she loves me, but man! I sure appreciate this real food. I can only go so long on twigs and sprouts."

Ann laughed as she began clearing the table.

"Oh, Bruce, it can't be that bad. I know Asia is a good cook. Asian food is different than good old meat and potatoes though."

Bryce and Bruce chatted about Peterson Search and Rescue, the progress of the puppy-training; anything except Jamal and Keysha. They stayed on safe ground while they finished a second cup of coffee.

When Ann was finished in the kitchen, she turned to Bruce.

"Bruce, do you have a few minutes? I want to show you something."

Bryce knew what was coming. He had promised to wait on the patio, no matter how nervous it made him to have her out of his sight. Gunner would follow along, just in case.

Bruce got up from the table and took his empty coffee cup to the sink.

"Sure. Lead the way."

He was surprised when their walk ended in the Peterson Cemetery. Ann led him off to the right away from the other graves into a secluded area with one small stone. It was a beautiful spot filled with a plethora of wild flowers growing around a koi pond. A small, round, wrought-iron table and a couple of chairs sat off to the side under a grape arbor. Only a very few people knew about this private place.

Bruce was curious. Ann laid a small bouquet of wild flowers she had picked along the way at the base of the small grave stone. When she finally looked up at Bruce there were tears in her eyes.

"I know you were made aware of some of my background so that you could help provide security. The abuse, the trials...but what most people don't know is that I had a baby; a son. I was only a teenager and I wanted the baby with all my heart. It was the only good thing to come out of that horrible marriage. I somehow knew I was carrying a boy. I named him Lucas. When I went into labor, it was too early. He only survived a short time and died in my arms."

Ann looked away for several minutes as she struggled to control her emotions. Bruce shifted from one foot to the other feeling very uncomfortable with this conversation. He had no idea where it was headed.

"I was devastated," Ann finally continued. "I had planned the rest of my life around this baby. Without him, all my dreams were shattered. I never even knew what happened to his body. Was it just thrown in the trash somewhere? Was he buried? When the doctor told me I couldn't have any more children, I wanted to die."

After a few more painful moments, she lovingly touched the headstone.

"I wanted to blame somebody. I needed to blame somebody. But my husband, whose continual beatings had probably caused the early delivery, was already dead. I harbored hatred and bitterness in my heart over my situation for a long time."

Bruce was acutely aware of how hard this was for Ann to talk about. He was still confused as to why she was confiding this obviously painful time in her life, to him.

"I didn't know until Mark and I reconnected that he had taken my baby, buried him and tended his grave for all these years. Bryce made arrangements to bring Baby Lucas home."

A sad smile spread across Ann's face. She laid her hand gently on Bruce's arm.

"Sometimes we have to accept the fact that what our heart desires most is just not going to happen no matter how bad we want it. We have to stop focusing all our time and energy on what we want, but will never have. It only makes us, and everyone around us, miserable. In the beginning, I had to force my mind away from the negative feelings and thoughts and actively concentrate on the good things in my life. It gets easier with time."

Bruce began to realize what Ann was trying to tell him. He wasn't sure if he was angry with her intrusion or not. Before he had time to dwell on it, Ann went on.

"You can't change Keysha. You have done everything humanly possible. I know how much you love her, but you have to let this go. She seems happy. She has people around her who love her. You can still see her every day. You know where she is and what she's doing. Take comfort in that, Bruce. I think you might be surprised at what will happen."

Bruce saw the serenity on Ann's face. Then he looked down at the headstone. The inscription read: *Baby Lucas. Beloved by his mother.* He didn't know when Ann left, he was too lost in his own thoughts. *I've got some fences to mend,* he decided as he finally turned and walked away.

Chapter 135

Tess was making progress on another front in the Watson family. Keysha was beginning to talk to her; albeit only to ask a question or get clarification about something she didn't understand. It was a start.

One afternoon they were milking the goats.

"You're doing a wonderful job, Keysha. You're a natural with the goats."

Keysha kept gently pulling milk from her favorite brown and white goat with a small smile on her face.

The milk squirted into the pail at regular intervals.

"You know, Keysha, Gracie loves you so much. She trusts you so she isn't afraid when you're nearby."

Now a huge smile spread over the child's face.

"I love her a lot, a lot, a lot," she said quietly.

Tess kept milking her all-white goat.

"Let's play pretend for a minute, okay? Tess said. "Let's pretend you had to go back into the hospital for something; say... to have your tonsils out. You didn't want to go, but your throat hurt so bad you had to go. The doctor ordered it, so it was out of your control. Do you think Gracie would miss you?"

Keysha faltered in her milking rhythm.

"I think she would."

"Do you think she would still love you? Even though you left her behind? She's too little to understand, you know."

The milking stopped altogether as Keysha's brow furrowed into a scowl. Then tears came to her eyes.

"I hope she would. I would still love her a lot, a lot, a lot even if I was gone away. Do you think she would still love me?" she asked Tess, her face serious. Her eyes frantically searching Tess's face.

"If you thought she didn't love you any more, would you be sad about it?"

"I would be so sad I would cry and cry and cry," Keysha answered, her chin on her chest, her lips trembling.

"You know, your daddy loves you a lot, a lot, a lot and he didn't want to give you to Otis. If he hadn't, he would have been arrested and possibly put in jail. Then he wouldn't have been able to come after you."

Tess moved on to the next goat giving Keysha a few minutes to think about what she said.

"He was so upset, he cried and cried. So did your mommy. Your daddy, Uncle Luke, Mr. Biggy and Mr. Tinker had a plan from the minute Otis took you and Jamal how they were going to get you back. And they did get you back."

The goat forgotten, Keysha stared off into the distance with unseeing eyes as she mulled over this new information. She had learned to trust Tess. She knew Tess wouldn't lie to her.

She didn't really understand the "arrest and jail" part, but that her big, strong daddy had cried and cried; that, she understood. It's what she would do if she had to leave Gracie. Maybe her daddy really did love her a lot, a lot, a lot!

Keysha was quiet for the rest of the afternoon. When Gracie went down for her nap, Keysha sat in her little rocking chair, and for the first time in a long while, she held her chi-chi and her old doll to her chest.

She buried her face in the soft, clean fabric. The doll's face was almost worn off and there was a hole in the blanket, but they had a distinctive smell. They smelled like home; the home she loved. The mommy and daddy she loved.

Chapter 136

Bruce pulled the car into the Peterson driveway. With the ignition off, he just sat there. His big shoulders sagged and he rested his forehead against the steering wheel. It ripped his heart out every time he came to pick Keysha up and she didn't want to go home with him.

She would turn her back to him and cross her arms over her chest, her body rigid. Usually he had to pick her up and carry her to the car. Getting her stiff little body into the car seat without hurting her was a challenge. He had no reason to think today would be any different.

Tess had seen him drive up and opened the door before he could knock. Charley was in her arms kicking and waving his hands, drool running down his chin as he smiled and giggled.

Bruce tickled the baby under his fat little chin.

"Hey, little man. How you doin'? You sure are a happy little guy."

He couldn't use the baby as a distraction forever. Finally, he dragged his eyes away from Charley and looked at Tess. He sighed heavily and shook his head.

"Tess, I need to talk to Luke. Is he around? I've been acting like an ass and I don't even have a good reason for it. I'm really sorry."

"He's not home right now. Horace needed his help with something in the upper pasture," she replied. "He should be home for supper though. Give him a call later. I'm sure he'll want to talk to you. He's missed the 'old Bruce.' We all have."

Being preoccupied with the baby and then Tess, Bruce didn't notice Keysha as she came up and stood next to Tess.

When he did finally see her, he was shocked when her eyes met his. She walked over to him and grabbed his hand.

"Come on, Dad. Let's go home," was all she said; like nothing had ever happened!

So overwhelmed with emotion he could hardly speak, Bruce swept the little girl up in his arms and hugged her close. Her arms went around him, as far as she could reach and she buried her face in the curve of his neck.

When Bruce finally looked up, tears were streaming down his cheek.

"Thank you," he silently mouthed to Tess.

Chapter 137

This wasn't the only surprise in the Watson family. Asia Kim had not been feeling well. Just looking at food made her stomach queasy. On most days, by mid-afternoon she was so tired she could hardly hold her head up. *What wrong with me?* she wondered.

Finally, she made an appointment with the doctor who had treated her after her rescue from Hong Cho's prostitution ring.

She had experienced malnutrition, beatings and one pelvic infection after another without medical attention as she was dragged across China, finally ending up as one of Mr. Cho's girls in the United States. It had taken a very long course of powerful antibiotics to rid her body of the infection that lurked there, ready to flare up at any time.

The doctor had told her that there was scar tissue from the infections, not to mention the abuse, and getting pregnant was very unlikely. She had given up any hope of having children of her own.

When she had met Bruce Watson, everything changed. All her love and attention was lavished on him. Later on, she opened her heart to include Jamal and Keysha. She had been happy with her little family.

With Keysha off in her own world, Jamal always busy and Bruce morose and short tempered, she felt very alone. She could have shared her concerns with Mama Rosa or Ann, even Anika or Maria, but she was an extremely shy, introspective young lady. Baring her soul wasn't something she had ever felt comfortable doing. So...she suffered in silence.

Now she was sick. And afraid. The thought of being examined by the doctor petrified her. She felt too embarrassed to ask anyone to go with her. And she certainly couldn't ask her husband. He was too consumed with the whole Keysha situation to bother with her.

During the examination, Asia kept her eyes closed to stop the tears from spilling down her face. She turned her head toward the wall and gritted her teeth to keep from crying out in pain. Humiliation stained her cheeks.

"Mrs. Watson, the nurse is going to take you to the x-ray department for an abdominal ultrasound."

He patted her shoulder.

"Don't worry. It'll be over before you know it and it won't hurt. I'll talk to you after it's done."

It seemed to take forever. Asia sat in a wheelchair waiting her turn, feeling exposed and wishing she had never come. *Maybe it better for Asia to die in sleep,* she thought.

Finally, she was lying on the hard table, the cold, gel-coated transducer gliding over her bare belly.

"Oh, look!" the technician exclaimed excitedly. "You're having a girl! Look right here. No little 'hooper' sticking up. And here. That's the heart beating. This is her head. Down here are her feet. It looks like you're about four months along."

Asia gasped. The technician's head snapped around. She stared at Asia.

"You...you didn't know you were pregnant?"

Asia Kim shook her head no before bursting into tears. She was still sup-supping when the nurse delivered her back to the doctor's office. He wasn't too concerned by her crying, after all, pregnant women were sometimes emotional over nothing.

"Hey, now. What's the matter?" he asked, taking her hands in his. "The baby looks healthy. Are you upset because you're not having a boy?"

"I not know there was baby at all," Asia sobbed.

"You mean you didn't do a home pregnancy test? I'm so sorry. I thought you already knew and that's why you were here."

"You told me never have baby. I give up wanting. Do not know about home test. Never think to try."

Dr. Montgomery was at a loss. He had told her conception was highly unlikely. He never said it was impossible.

"I'm going to have the nurse call your husband. I don't want you driving home right now."

Bruce and Keysha were almost home when his cell phone rang. He pulled the car over to answer.

"Mr. Watson? This is Dr. Montgomery's office. Your wife is here and she's very upset. Our office is on the first floor, D wing of the hospital. Could you possibly come and pick her up? The doctor doesn't think she should be driving..."

"What! What do you mean she's at the doctor's office? Is she okay? Is she sick? Hurt? Oh, my God. I'll be right there."

Bruce disconnected before the nurse could finish. He threw the car into drive and made a "U" turn. He wished he had driven his cruiser home, then he could have used the siren!

"Keysha, honey. Mommy must be sick. We have to go to the hospital!"

Chapter 138

B ruce was several steps away from the car before he remembered Keysha was in the back seat. He turned around to see Keysha waving at him through the window. *What am I thinking*, he mumbled to himself as he raced back to the car.

He threw the door open and began unbuckling the straps of her car seat feeling like there were only thumbs on his hands.

"Come on, Keysha. There you go. Let's go see what's going on with Mommy."

Heads turned as a huge, scar-faced, black man charged through the hospital lobby carrying a little girl desperately clinging to his neck. With each step, her curls bounced up and down as her head bobbed.

"Which way is the D wing," he yelled as he ran past the girl behind the information desk.

She pointed in the general direction he needed to go. He never even slowed down.

Meanwhile, the nurse had helped Asia calm down and get dressed. She was sitting in the waiting room with her emotions controlled and tucked away when Bruce came thundering through the door.

Bruce skidded to a stop in front of his wife and dropped to his knees. His heart was thudding in his chest so hard he could feel his pulse in his ears. He couldn't speak. Keysha squirmed out of his grasp and leaned against Asia.

"What's wrong, Mommy?" she asked, concern on her face.

The look of surprise, giving way to pure joy, on Asia's face was priceless.

Asia wrapped her arms around the little girl and kissed her cheek. When she looked up at Bruce, all tears were gone, replaced with a huge smile.

"Asia have baby in five month."

"What? Baby? How?" was all Bruce could manage to say.

All the other ladies in the waiting room began clapping and cheering. Bruce couldn't do anything but sit on the floor with a big, lopsided grin on this face.

Keysha got into the spirit of the whole celebration and began jumping up and down excitedly.

"We're going to have a baby! We're going to have a baby!"

Then she stopped and turned very serious.

"Mommy? How are we going to have a baby?"

Laughter erupted in the waiting room. Bruce picked himself up off the floor and gathered his wife and his daughter in his arms.

"I think I'll take my girls and go home," he announced to his audience of well-wishers.

Chapter 139

Ann stood in front of the floor to ceiling windows in the living room gazing out over the perfectly manicured lawn that stretched all the way to the woods beyond. The home she and Bryce had built together satisfied her in a way she couldn't easily explain.

She absent-mindedly rubbed her chest where a dull ache persisted. *Maybe I should have Mark run an EKG. I don't have any pain down my arm or running into my jaw. I don't have any other symptoms of a heart attack. I think I might have pulled a muscle or something.*

Bryce came up behind her and curled his arms around her waist. His lips nuzzled her neck. Slowly he turned her to face him.

"What's wrong, Honey? You tossed and turned all night. Nightmares?"

"No. No nightmares anymore. Not since you, my love. You drove all the bad dreams away," she said with a smile. "I just haven't felt myself the last few days. I don't know what it is. I have this little ache in my chest and I've felt more tired than usual."

Bryce's forehead knotted in concern.

"Maybe we've been practicing too hard. Victor is certainly getting us whipped into shape for the next competition. Why don't we take a few days off and drive to the coast. We could stay in a B & B, eat some fresh seafood... How does that sound? We have to dance tonight at the restaurant, but we could leave first thing in the morning."

Ann sighed as she relaxed in his arms.

"That sounds wonderful. I'll pack a bag for us this afternoon and maybe we'll also have time for a little nap. In the meantime, let's drive into town for a light lunch."

Bryce held her tight for a few seconds.

"Okay, let's go. Come on, Gunner."

Arm in arm they headed for the garage. Gunner trotted along behind, eager for an outing.

Ann picked at her salad during lunch even though it was one of her favorites. Bryce was worried. He chastised himself for not paying closer attention. He had noticed she was a little pale and she did tire quickly. Chalking it up to long, hard practice sessions he hadn't given it much thought. *What if there's something really wrong?* Panic seized his mind. *I'll talk to Mark tonight. Ask him to give her a check up before we leave town.*

The nap seemed to revive Ann. When Bryce asked her about the ache in her chest, she assured him it was gone. Her eyes sparkled and her cheeks were pink. The white, floor-length dress fit her womanly curves like a glove. Diamond tear-drop earrings matched the necklace Bryce had given her on their last anniversary.

"You look drop dead gorgeous. Makes me want to just stay in for the night," Bryce whispered in her ear.

Ann cuffed him lightly on the arm as she smiled into his eyes.

"And you, Sir, look especially handsome tonight."

Bryce was wearing one of his white tuxedos. They made a very striking couple. Being the featured dancers before the dance floor was opened for the guests, they had dressed for the occasion.

Chapter 140

It was Friday night, no school in the morning, so the older children were allowed to come to the restaurant for dinner. Jamal and JB looked like miniature adults in their black tuxedos. Keysha looked like a princess in a pale pink, tea length party dress that complimented her skin and glossy black ringlets.

The Peterson's were firm believers in helping children grow into adulthood learning how to behave properly. How to be respectful. How to be kind and helpful. How to speak to people intelligently. They were taught to take pride in their appearance and in their accomplishments and how to be good losers as well.

It was not done through yelling threats, "time out," spanking or any other punitive measures. The children were led by example. This is not to say there weren't times when discipline was required for some major infraction, but those times were few and far between. The kids soon learned a reward for a job well done was preferable to losing certain privileges or a favorite video game.

The most important ingredient in the Peterson child rearing recipe was unconditional love. Each child knew without reservation that every adult in their family circle loved them no matter what. Each adult carried him or herself in such a way that they inspired confidence and healthy self esteem. The kids looked up to the adults; wanted to be like them.

Friday and Saturday nights were formal dining and dancing nights and everyone was expected to appear in formal attire; even the kids. Wednesday and Thursday nights were less formal, but still dressy.

The boys sometimes complained about the "dressing up code," as they called it.

"It's always good to look your best, like me and Mama," Georgio admonished with a twinkle in his eyes. "You can dress like a rag-a-muffin when you play or when you're picking up dog poop."

The last comment always brought laughter from the boys. They loved the dogs, but hated cleaning up after them. They were, however, made very aware of how crucial it was to keep things clean and sanitary.

Each child was pared with an adult who would be a "life teacher." The children could become familiar with the responsibilities of each adult. They would learn that every single person was important; that every job from the cleaning crew to Grandpa Georgio, the family patriarch, was vital to the success of the family as a whole.

Tonight, Jamal was standing with John, observing what he was doing as he greeted people, checked off the reservations and directed guests to their tables. As Jamal learned what this job entailed, he was allowed to greet the guests and mark off their reservation.

John explained the necessity of making sure they didn't accept more guests than there were tables to seat them. The fire codes and safety regulations had to be followed exactly based on the seating capacity of the room, otherwise the restaurant/ballroom could be closed down by the authorities.

In case of an emergency evacuation, it was important to know the names of the guests so that all could be accounted for outside the building. Jamal had no idea there was so much to greeting people! It was an important job.

JB was with Bruce and Butch at the main door acting as a "junior security officer." Bruce explained the need for maintaining orderly behavior so that all the guests would be safe and their experience at Vincenzo's would be enjoyable. It was rare that someone had to be "muscled" out of the building, but it had happened a few times.

"We want our guests to feel safe when they come here and know they won't have to put up with any bullsh.... er, obnoxious behavior from other diners," Bruce told JB. "We want everyone to have a good time. That way, they'll want to come back again."

Both boys took their training seriously and understood the reasoning behind it. They were also equipped with a smaller version of the wrist units worn by all the men in the family. Jamal had some experience using one, but it was all new to JB. Luke had given them some basic instructions on the appropriate use of the units. They weren't for chatting with each other. Misuse would result in the loss of the unit.

As had been the habit from the reopening of the restaurant, each couple on the dance team would visit each table after the guests were seated. It was a personal connection that was essential to Georgio and Rosa's "guest relations philosophy." They wanted every customer to feel like a personal friend.

JB and Jamal were busy with their assignments, but Keysha didn't really have a "job" other than being cute. Ann decided now that Keysha was functioning in the real world again, walking among the guest tables would help build her social skills and confidence. She learned to talk politely to strangers in a controlled environment, always holding Ann's hand. Soon she was the darling of Friday nights.

"Don't let the attention go to your head, Keysha," Ann kindly cautioned the little girl. "Nobody likes a bratty, self-centered child."

Huge, brown eyes fastened on Ann's face.

"Oh, Grandma. I would never be like that. I promise." Keysha replied, shaking her head until her curls danced.

Chapter 141

The evening had progressed without incident so far. Bryce watched Ann like a hawk. A thread of fear wrapped itself around his heart and pulled a little tighter every time she pushed another bit of food around on her plate without taking a bite.

Ann knew something wasn't quite right; she just couldn't put her finger on what it was. Pain high in her back and through to her chest kept nagging at her. A flutter in her upper abdomen took her by surprise and she felt a little breathless. *I'm just tired*, she decided. *Bryce is right. A few days away is what I need.*

Precisely at nine o'clock Luke introduced all the members of the dance team.

He concluded by announcing, "Now please enjoy a short dance presentation by your favorite King and Queen of Romance, Ann and Bryce Peterson."

Much applause followed as Ann and Bryce took positions for their signature waltz. As the music swelled Bryce swept Ann away in the first flowing, graceful steps of the dance.

Without warning, Ann faltered; something that had never happened before. Her eyes locked onto Bryce's face before she took two more steps and collapsed. Bryce lowered her to the floor, his heart in his mouth, his mind suddenly numb.

A few seconds of absolute silence followed. It took that long for people to realize what had just happened. Then chaos erupted. Mark was immediately at Ann's side. It only took a quick assessment for him to determine that something serious had happened.

"Bryce, we need to get her to the emergency room ASAP!"

Bruce had rushed forward as soon as Ann fell. Upon hearing those words, he went into action. He was definitely the man in charge and everyone scurried to follow his commands.

He was immediately on his radio calling for one of his men to bring the cruiser to the main entrance.

"If we transport her ourselves, we can get her to the hospital before an ambulance even has time to respond," he said to Mark"

Gunner, upon seeing the crowd of people pressing forward, took up a stand next to Ann, a deep growl rumbling through his massive chest.

"JB, get a leash on Gunner. We can't have him attacking someone because he perceives their actions as a threat to Ann. I don't think he'll be allowed in the emergency room anyway. Keep control of him."

Always prepared, JB pulled a thin, leather leash out of his pocket. He pulled Gunner aside, talking quietly to him. He began walking the big dog back and forth between those kneeling around Ann and the nervous guests. JB didn't realize it at the time, but he was instinctively providing crowd control.

John, with Jamal following him, got on the PA system. His voice was one of calm reassurance.

"Please. Everyone. Return to your seats and try to remain calm. We need to give Dr. Goodwin space. Mrs. Peterson is being taken care of. If you wish to leave, please find you way quickly and quietly to the reception area. Jamal will escort you to the coat room and call for your car to be brought around."

Many people stood and began flocking toward the door. Victor and Bobby hurried forward to assist Jamal in calling for cars.

Maria and Anika took charge of a very upset little girl. Keysha was already sobbing and terrified.

"Keysha. Honey. Look at me," Maria said. "Uncle Mark will help Grandma. You don't have to worry."

"Should we take her back to her Mama?" a shaken Anika whispered to Maria.

"Do you want to go home, Keysha? Aunt Anika will take you to your mom if you want to go."

"NO!" Keysha stated emphatically. "I want to go with Grandma Ann!"

Maria held the child tight and patted her back.

"Anika, why don't you go get Asia. I know she's not feeling well tonight, but I'm sure she will want to be here."

"Yes. Yes. I go now."

Georgio and Rosa were immediately on their feet and hurrying toward where Bryce was hunched over Ann's lifeless body. All they could do was give Bryce moral support and be there in case something else was needed.

Bryce was frantic. He held Ann's hand while Mark worked furiously to get her almost non-existent vital signs.

"Ann! Wake up, Ann. Can you open your eyes? Mark! What's going on?" he sobbed.

Ann felt herself sliding down a dark tunnel. The pain in her chest was excruciating and she couldn't breathe. She was vaguely aware that Mark was doing something to her. The only thing she was sure of was Bryce's voice in her ear. She clung to that sound.

Bruce reappeared at Mark's side.

"Mark, the cruiser is waiting. Bryce, can you carry her?"

Floating. That's what the sensation felt like to Ann. The only sound she could hear now was the voice urging her to hang on. Everything else had gotten strangely quiet.

Mark knew she was going into shock. Her pulse had become weak and rapid. Her breathing was shallow. He touched her arm. It was cool and clammy. From somewhere, Helena had gotten a blanket. As Bryce lifted her, Mark tucked the blanket in place.

Bruce trotted in front of Bryce carrying Ann. JB followed with Gunner. Jamal held the door open. Luke was waiting to help his father into the back seat of the cruiser, then slid in beside him. Bruce slid behind the wheel. JB and Gunner climbed into the front seat beside Bruce.

Lights flashing, siren blaring, gravel flying, Bruce took off toward the hospital in Cedarville. Rosa and Georgio pulled out right behind Bruce with Mark and Helena in the back seat. As soon as the door closed, Mark was on his phone to his colleagues in the ER. They needed all the information he had gathered thus far in order to treat Ann as soon as humanly possible. He knew her problem was heart related and he was very worried.

It was normally a fifteen minute drive from Vincenzo's to Cedarville. The cruiser pulled up in front of the emergency room in seven minutes. A team was waiting at the door.

A car had been brought around to take the rest of the family to the hospital. Asia had come and taken a tearful Keysha home. John, Victor and Jamal would stay behind to handle the rest of the evening for those people who remained at their tables. They would be encouraged to go home. A refund for their expenses would be offered. If they wanted to stay, the band would continue playing. After all, they had paid for dinner and dancing.

"Some people will demand we stay open so they can continue their evening," John explained to Jamal.

"But why, Uncle John?" Jamal wailed, tears already welling in his eyes no matter how hard he tried to be grown up.

John sighed and shook his head.

"People are...just people. Some are selfish. Thoughtless. Uncaring. But we have a job to do and a reputation of excellence to maintain. Grandpa Bryce and Grandpa Georgio would expect nothing less from us and they are counting on us."

Jamal scrubbed away his tears on the sleeve of his jacket. John hugged the little boy.

"So let's get busy, Champ. We'll have some people who will want their coats and cars now that the excitement is over. The rest we'll just have to put up with."

Chapter 142

T he emergency team was waiting at the entrance when Bruce screeched to a stop. Several hands reached into the car and gently lifted Ann from Bryce's arms. As soon as she was on the gurney, EKG electrodes were slapped in place and her heart rhythm was up on the portable monitor. Orders were being yelled out by the doctors as nurses and techs scrambled to carry out those orders even as they were transporting her through the emergency room doors.

Bryce wouldn't let go of Ann's hand even when a nurse not so politely told him to back off and give them room to work. Dr. Bartholomew, cardiac surgeon, was putting on his gown and head covering when the team came through the door. Dr. Tipton, a small-statured, arrogant, cocky, little man from cardiology was right behind him.

"What have we got?" Dr. Bartholomew demanded.

Mark repeated the vital signs he had given over the phone when Ann collapsed. He also related the brief history Bryce had given him earlier in the evening.

"I've been her physician for a number of years and she's never had any kind of heart problem, but I think this event is cardiac related. That's why I requested you and Tipton. You guys are the best 'heart men' I know."

Ann was heading toward a light at the end of the tunnel. She wanted to go. It looked peaceful there. But a familiar voice kept calling her name; a voice full of agony and fear.

"Ann. Ann. Please don't leave me! Hang on just a little longer. Stay with me. Please!"

"Mr. Peterson. You cannot come in here," the pushy nurse stated firmly as she shoved him back and shut the door to the treatment area in his face.

The voice became muffled. The hand that had been clutching hers was gone. She was alone and wondering in the darkness; then spiraling down faster and faster. A great sadness engulfed her.

The EKG displayed an erratic heart rhythm.

"Call the code," Dr. Tipton yelled.

"Code Blue, Emergency Room. Code Blue."

People who responded to all Code Blue situations began to flood into the emergency room.

"We're losing her! Start CPR. Let's get her intubated. Get a central line in and hang a unit of blood. She's bleeding from somewhere. Call the OR. We need to get her up there immediately."

When the code was announced, Bryce fell to his knees outside the treatment room.

"AAAANNNNN!" he yelled over and over.

Gunner howled.

Ann's heart jumped. The voice! There it was again. In her mind, she clung to that voice. Her heart rhythm evened out ever so slightly.

Dr. Bartholomew connected the husband's voice to Ann's response. He had heard stories about how close the two were. *Maybe those stories are true after all,* he thought. *I'll take any advantage I can get!*

"Get her husband in here," he ordered Nurse 'Pushy.' "He's what's keeping her going. Do it now!"

With a scowl on her face, the nurse ran out to get Bryce.

"Mr. Peterson. Stand up here by your wife's head. Just keep talking to her. It's making a difference."

Bryce didn't have to be told twice. With one hand cupping her cheek and his other hand on her shoulder, he began whispering in Ann's ear. Her head turned just a wee bit into his hand. It was enough to give him a measure of hope.

She could feel his breath on her face and his lips moving against her ear. The voice pleaded with her again and again to hang on.

The team of nurses and doctors pushed the gurney rapidly down the hall to the operating room. Bryce tripped once, regained his footing and raced along with the stretcher.

Ann was transferred to the operating table. The anesthesiologist began the task of putting her under anesthesia. He glanced at Bryce; then at Dr. Bartholomew.

"He stays. Get him gowned up. I want him sitting behind a drape at her head. I don't think she'll make it without him. Get her on by-pass. Let's be quick!" he instructed. "Mr. Peterson. You doing okay? Somebody get him a stool; it's going to be a long night."

When all the wires and tubes were connected, the team held a collective breath as the machine whirred on. Ann stabilized.

"Good job everyone. Let's all take a minute. Mr. Peterson. Your wife's breathing and circulation are now being maintained by a machine. We're going to open her up and see what's going on. Please keep your hands behind the drape and don't touch anything except your wife's face. Just keep doing what you've been doing. If you feel ill or need a break, let us know."

Bryce gulped.

"Ye...yes. Yes," he replied, his voice already raspy. "I'll be fine. Just help her!"

"Okay, boys and girls. Let's see what we've got," Dr. Bartholomew said to his team as he picked up a scalpel.

Chapter 143

~~~
⚬⚬
~~~

D r. Bartholomew briefly explained to Bryce what was happening as they went along. Ann's aortic valve could not be repaired and had to be replaced. Apparently, unbeknownst to Ann and Dr. Goodwin, it had been leaking for some time. It finally ruptured. The leak became a gusher.

There were a few touch-an-go moments when Ann was taken off by-pass and before her own heart took over. Bryce continued to encourage her.

"Come on, Ann. You can do it. Your heart is all fixed. Come on. Stay with me. I need you!"

A cheer went up from the team when the EKG showed those first few blips, which became a steady rhythm. The trip to the ICU was a slow one. Every member of the team had a wire or tube to maintain in the correct position. Bags of blood, IV fluids and IV medications were swinging from their respective poles. Monitors were beeping. The respirator was pumping away.

Surgery had taken several hours. Ann looked like death warmed over. Bryce didn't look much better. He walked along beside Ann's bed, holding her hand and talking to her like they were taking a walk in the park.

An exhausted Dr. Bartholomew made his way to the waiting room to talk to Ann's family. He wasn't at all surprised to see this large group, including two dogs, waiting for news. The huge German Shepherd met him at the door.

Gunner was certainly no stranger to anyone in Cedarville. After he rescued Mrs. Peterson from her kidnapper, Tony Marco, every kid in town wanted their picture taken with the big, mean-looking dog. It was a well known and accepted fact that where ever the Petersons went, Gunner went.

Olyvia had also become a fixture around Cedarville, accompanying Keysha everywhere. Rumor had it that the child couldn't function without the dog.

Dr. Bartholomew had never actually met the individual members of this prominent family, but he had eaten at Vincenzo's enough times to, at least, recognize most of them. He knew Ann, of course, as she was a colleague. Over the last several hours he had become acquainted with Bryce.

A little girl sat on the floor clutching a very official-looking, red dog wearing a service dog vest. Two young boys instantly looked up from their video games. In matching infant car seats, two babies slept peacefully. A toddler was asleep leaning on the shoulder of a man in a wheelchair. A petite, pregnant woman was sitting with her head hanging over a wastebasket. A big man with a scar on his face, who Dr. Bartholomew knew was Officer Watson, was gently rubbing her back.

Two middle aged men, dressed for combat in camos and face paint, were leaning casually against the far wall. Mr. and Mrs. Vincenzo sat on the sofa holding hands. The two young couples from the dance team were squeezed in around them.

The only absent family members were Flower and Spaz. No one in town knew them. Flower usually refused to come into town and Spaz probably wouldn't be welcome.

There seemed to be all colors and nationalities represented in this diverse group; Ann Peterson's family.

Dr. Goodwin had been pacing back and forth, worry furrowing his brow. He came to an abrupt stop as soon as he saw Dr. Bartholomew. Luke and Bruce immediately stepped forward. Soon the whole family surrounded the doctor, concern etched on every face.

"Please. Let's all sit down," he began calmly.

Everyone found a seat and waited expectantly for him to continue.

"Ann is stable, but in critical condition," he began. "At this point she is not responding. Over the next several hours we expect her to begin to wake up and hopefully begin breathing on her own. Right now a machine is helping her breath. She is getting medication to control her blood pressure and heart rate. Her pain is being addressed as well. Her condition is being monitored continuously."

Luke spoke up.

"What happened to my mom?" What did you have to do?"

Dr. Bartholomew ran his fingers through his hair.

"The easiest way to describe it is that her heart sprung a leak. One of the valves in her heart ruptured. We replaced it with an artificial one. Baring any complications, she should be fine."

Luke sagged back into his chair. The tears he had stoically held in check all night finally made rivulets down his cheeks. He wasn't the only one trying to deal with emotions that had been stretched to the breaking point.

"How's my dad doing?" he finally asked.

Dr. Bartholomew just shook his head.

"I don't understand how or why, but your father saved her as much as the surgery did. The bond they have is...quite amazing. I've never seen anything like it. He has permission to stay with her; it's in the orders on her chart. I understand the dog is also extremely important to her well-being. He can stay as well. The hospital administrator will probably pop a gusset over that one. He'll just have to get over it. All of you might as well go home and get some rest. She won't be able to have any visitors for a while. Luke, if you want to go in and check on your father for just a minute, I'll have the nurse take you."

Chapter 144

While Dr. Bartholomew was speaking with the family, Ann and her entourage were making their way slowly to the ICU. Upon arrival, Dr. Tipton instantly began giving orders. He set up the parameters for Ann's blood pressure and heart rate. He checked and rechecked a myriad of little things that were essential for Ann to improve. The next twenty-four to forty-eight hours were critical.

He gave verbal orders to the nurse; a nurse he had clashed with before. She seemed to be more interested in the rules than she was in the well-being of the patients. He was the doctor. How dare she ever question him?

"Under no circumstances do I want her vital signs to fall outside these parameters. If that happens, page me immediately. I don't care what the rules and regulations say. Mr. Peterson is allowed to stay with his wife 24/7 for as long as necessary. And if the big dog waiting in the hall wants to come in, let him in. He's a service dog; he's clean and well mannered. He won't be a problem."

A horrified look spread across the nurse's face as she began to object.

"This is highly unusual. Appropriate hospital policies must be followed..."

"I don't give a rat's ass about the policies!" he yelled in her face. "You have your orders and I expect them to be followed or I will have your job. Do I make myself perfectly clear?"

"Perfectly," she hissed.

"I'll be back in two hours to check on her," he replied before he turned on his heel and marched away, leaving the nurse angry and red-faced.

A formal complaint against him was probably in the making. It wouldn't be the first time. When you put what was good for the patient's above all else, sometimes the rules got in the way. Oh well...

Dr. Tipton headed for the doctor's lounge and a long hot shower. *The old bitty might be a pain in the ass when it comes to the rules and policies, but she's a damn fine nurse,*" he muttered. Her job was safe and he knew, she knew it. He smiled to himself. *I do love doing battle with her though. She's a worthy opponent. Maybe I should ask her out. Her head would probably explode if I did.* He was whistling by the time he got to the showers.

Chapter 145

I n exactly two hours, when Dr. Tipton came back, Ann was still
unresponsive. He checked the chart and read the nurse's notes.
Then he came into her cubicle and began to check the IV's,
the dials and knobs on the equipment that whirred and hummed,
making sure everything was working properly. With his stethoscope
to her chest, he listened carefully to her heart. When he was satisfied
he turned to Bryce.

Someone had gotten Bryce a stool and he was sitting beside the
bed. The man looked like he was ready to collapse himself. He was
still wearing a white tuxedo; the one he had been wearing when Ann
was brought to the hospital. He now sported a shadow of a beard on
his face. His eyes were bloodshot and his voice was so hoarse it was
hard to understand what he said.

A big dog was curled up in the corner. He raised his head and
stared at the doctor. *Even the dog looks sad,* Dr. Tipton thought as
he turned back to Bryce.

"Mr. Peterson. You should go get some rest. She may be out for
some time yet. I can have someone call you if there are any changes.
Or I can make arrangements for you to lie down in the doctor's
lounge if that would be more convenient for you."

"Thanks, doctor. I appreciate the offer, but I can't leave her!
What if she wakes up and I'm not here? She'll be terrified. I'll be
fine. Really. I'll be fine."

"How long since you've slept?"

Bryce stared into the doctor's eyes.

"I honestly don't know."

Neither Dr. Tipton or Bryce realized Ann was swimming slowly back to the surface. The nurse, a respiratory therapist and a phlebotomist were in and out doing their various tasks. Ann was aware there were other people in the room.

Most important to her, "the voice" was still with her. The hand still held hers. She was afraid, but the voice kept complete panic at bay. Every other voice except his seemed to be muffled or coming from far away.

Where am I? What happened? I can't remember anything! Who am I? On the edge of terror, she clung to the voice. It was her lifeline.

Chapter 146

It had been three days and Ann had yet to open her eyes. She was taking intermittent breaths on her own, but the ventilator was still initiating most of her breathing. Dr. Bartholomew and Dr. Tipton were worried.

"Mr. Peterson, if she doesn't start responding and breathing on her own we will have to do a tracheostomy, which means we will have to cut a hole in her windpipe, and insert a more permanent tube for her to breath. We really don't want to have to do that. Keep asking her to open her eyes; respond in some way," Dr. Bartholomew said in a low, calm voice.

Ann had been hovering just below the surface of consciousness. The other voices had become clearer. She knew her name was Ann. She also knew the voice, the hand, belonged to Bryce Peterson. Now he was begging her to break through the haze; open her eyes.

It was so hard. Her eyelids felt like they were made of cement. So heavy. The cloud was still so thick. She didn't want to wake up; she was afraid to wake up. But the voice had taken on a note of desperation.

"Ann. Please. Sweetheart. You have to open your eyes. I have to know you're all right. Please, please..."

She had to try. For him, she had to try. It took all her willpower. Her eyelids fluttered. It was all she could manage for the moment. *I'll rest for a few minutes* she told herself. *Just a few minutes.*

Both doctors were watching the monitors. She was initiating more and more of her own breathing. The ventilator only kicked in every few minutes. This was a very good sign. They were cautiously hopeful.

Bryce had bent over her still body, his lips against her fingers. She could feel the tears on her hand. Her heart ached for this man, whoever he was. He apparently loved her very much. She heard a dog whine.

When Bryce looked up, tears streaming down his face, Ann opened her eyes. Dark blue eyes, glazed with uncertainty, stared into red-rimmed hazel eyes filled with pain.

Bryce jerked.

"Doctor," he gasped. "She's awake!"

He leaned over all the tubes and wires to tenderly kiss her cheek. He rubbed her arm.

"She's awake," he breathed, relief sweeping over his face.

Both doctors were busily checking the monitors. Dr. Bartholomew put his stethoscope over her heart, her lungs. He listened carefully for several minutes while Bryce held his breath.

When he finally looked up, a wide smile spread over his tired features. He nodded to Bryce.

"Okay! Everything sounds good. She's finally making progress!"

Ann shifted nervous eyes to the doctor's face, then around the room at all the equipment, returning to Bryce; her anchor. Her free hand went to the tube attached to the corner of her mouth by adhesive tape. The doctor carefully pushed her hand away.

"Mrs. Peterson, as soon as you're breathing completely on your own, I'll take the tube out. If you understand, nod your head."

Both physicians were watching Ann closely for an appropriate response. Her brain had been functioning on insufficient blood flow for longer than they would have liked. They were worried about brain damage, which could include memory loss, confusion, lack of coordination, hearing loss, blindness even paralysis. Any or all of it was possible.

It took all the effort Ann could muster to tip her head. Then her eyes closed again. She was exhausted by this little bit of wakefulness.

Bryce looked anxiously at the doctors. Dr. Bartholomew patted Ann's shoulder.

"Very good, Ann. You're doing great."

He looked back at Bryce.

"Now she needs to rest. I'll be back later this afternoon. If she has been breathing on her own all that time, we'll take the tube out. I think your son is waiting in the hall. I'll tell him to come in."

Doctors Tipton and Bartholomew walked out of ICU feeling relieved and thankful. Luke was waiting.

"Luke, your mom has been awake and responded. Why don't you go on in and sit with her for a few minutes; give your dad some time to change his clothes and shave. The tuxedo is looking a little, how shall I say this, a little less than fresh."

Dr. Bartholomew clapped Luke on the back before walking away.

Bryce looked up when Luke entered.

"She woke up, Luke!"

"I know, Dad, the doctor told me. That's great! We've all been so worried."

Luke wiped his eyes on his forearm. He handed his father a small duffle bag and sat a covered glass bowl of something that smelled delicious on the bedside table.

"I'll sit with mom. Here's a change of clothes and your razor. Why don't you take a shower and change? You look like hell. Mama Rosa fixed your favorite stew. She figured you hadn't eaten much since you brought mom to the hospital."

Bryce took the cover off the bowl and inhaled deeply. He picked up the spoon.

"If you don't mind, I think I'll eat first. I'm suddenly starving!"

Luke chuckled.

"That's fine, Dad. Why don't you go sit at the little table over there? I'll sit with mom."

Ann still had her eyes closed, but she had awakened the minute the cover was removed from the steaming bowl of stew. Her stomach gurgled. *Bryce Peterson is my husband. Luke is my son!* The thought made her feel safe. She drifted back to sleep.

Chapter 147

❧

Ann continued to improve throughout the afternoon. Dr. Tipton couldn't be more pleased. He removed the tube and her hand immediately went to her throat.

"Water," she whispered.

Bryce looked different without a three-day growth of whiskers, but his voice was unchanged and his touch was tender. Both familiar to her. The look in his eyes held love beyond belief. Ann gave him a tentative smile. He held a straw to her lips.

"Here you go, Honey. Not too much at first," he cautioned.

Dr. Tipton did his usual exam and proclaimed that, barring any unforeseen events during the night, Ann could be moved to a private room in the morning. She would still be connected to the heart monitor, which would alert the nurse's station if something went awry.

"You can start eating and drinking whatever sounds good to you, within reason that is. Don't be surprised if it takes some time to get your appetite back. The nurse will come in later this evening and start getting you up. You can walk from the bed to the door and back, see how that goes and tomorrow you can walk to the bathroom; with stand-by assist of course. It's been four days from the time you arrived here, you'll be weak as a kitten for a while. I'll arrange for cardiac rehab starting tomorrow and continuing after you're discharged. Slow and steady, Ann. That's how we'll play this."

After the doctor left Bryce began to tell Ann how many people had called and sent cards.

"You can't have the flowers that keep pouring in because of being in the ICU. Tomorrow when you get to your room, it will probably look like a florist shop."

Ann didn't recognize any of the names of the people Bryce mentioned. *What am I going to do,* she wondered. *Should I tell Bryce I can't remember anything? Will he be hurt? Angry? Or will he understand and be patient with me?*

"I told Bruce he could bring Keysha by tonight. She has cried every day for her Grandma Ann. When you collapsed, it scared her to death, poor kid. She's very attached to you." Bryce said with a smile. "I'm pretty attached to you myself," he added.

He leaned over and tenderly kissed her lips.

"I was terrified, Ann. I couldn't bear the thought of going through the rest of my life without you."

Tears filled his eyes. He shook his head.

"But you're going to be fine. I'm so thankful."

He brought her hands to his lips and kissed her fingers.

"You don't have to worry about a thing," he continued. "I swear, Mama has already got meals planned for a month. The girls want to come over and do all the housework. JB will take Gunner for a walk every day. Jamal wants to help you...with something. I'm not sure what."

Ann didn't say anything. Her throat was so sore! It gave her an excuse not to have to say anything. Bryce spooned ice chips into her mouth and kept talking about their home and family. She listened carefully, hoping things would start sounding familiar. So far nothing did.

She could tell by the look on his face how important their family was to him. How he loved each one. How they all loved her. Her heart was warmed even if she had no memory of any of these people. One thing was for sure. She loved his voice and the touch of his hand. Those two things were very familiar to her.

Chapter 148

When Bruce appeared holding Keysha in his arms, Ann could hardly keep the shock off her face. He was a huge man. And he was a very black man. On one side of his face was a scar that ran from the corner of his eye to the side of his mouth. If it hadn't been for the big smile across that not-so-handsome face, she would have been terrified.

Keysha held her little arms out to Ann. She was a beautiful child. Ann immediately felt a connection to her. Bruce placed her carefully on the bed next to Ann.

"Now, Keysha," he admonished. "Grandma has a very big boo-boo on her chest so you have to be careful."

"Okay, Daddy," Keysha answered before turning big brown eyes to Ann.

"My Daddy told me you had a operation. I had a operation too. 'Member, Grandma?"

Fortunately, she didn't wait for Ann to respond before she continued to chatter away.

"I'm all better now. I can even go potty by myself. Olyvia helps me and Aunt Tess showed me how. And my Mommy is going to have a baby. Isn't that so cool? If it's a sister, I can pick out the name. If it's a brother, Jamal gets to pick. I hope it's a sister. Boys are loud and they run a lot...

Bruce cut in.

"Keysha. Take a breath, Baby. We don't want to tire Grandma out on our first visit."

Ann stroked the little girl's soft cheek and kissed her forehead. Keysha beamed and snuggled close to Ann's side.

Bryce asked Bruce how Asia Kim was feeling.

"I've been out of the loop for these past few days," he said, squeezing Ann's hand. "How's Asia Kim feeling? Ann and I couldn't be happier for you guys."

"She still gets sick in the morning and she's really tired. But we are SO excited about this baby. Asia never thought in a million years this would happen..."

The nurse interrupted.

"Time's up, guys. Mrs. Peterson needs her rest."

At the look of disappointment on Keysha's face, the nurse added, "Your Grandma will be in her own room tomorrow and you can visit again, okay, Honey?"

Keysha nodded her head and hopped off the bed, not before giving Ann a big sloppy kiss on the cheek.

"See ya tomorrow, Grandma," Keysha said as she and Bruce headed out the door.

Chapter 149

The following afternoon, Ann was moved to a private room with her own bathroom. It did look like a florist shop. Bryce pulled off all the cards so she could go through them. She did her best to make comments and express appreciation. It was hard considering the names meant nothing to her at all.

Later that evening Bobby and Maria stopped by with a plate of Mama Rosa's chocolate peanut butter brownies.

"Mama sent your favorite brownies. It was all I could do to keep from eating them myself," Bobby said as he put the dish on Ann's over-bed tray table and kissed her cheek.

Maria nudged Bobby aside so she could give Ann a gentle hug and a kiss.

"Yes. It was all I could do on the way over here to keep him from scarfing them all down. He did manage to steal one of them."

"And for that, she hit me!" Bobby laughed.

The conversation went on for about an hour with Bobby and Bryce using the time to discuss some Peterson Enterprise business. After all Bryce had been preoccupied for several days. Bobby gave him a brief synopsis. Fortunately, it had been an uneventful week with the exception of Ann's health crisis. Ann listened carefully.

Since they sometimes referred to her as "Mom" she assumed they were her natural children. But they both had a little darker complexion, dark hair and brown eyes. She didn't know how they fit in with Luke and Bryce. It was all so confusing!

Mark had told the rest of the family to space their visits out, coming two at a time. Ann needed to rest as much as possible and he was afraid if everyone descended on her at once she would be overwhelmed.

Over the next several days they all came for short visits, always bringing some tidbit from Mama Rosa, whoever she was. Ann had yet to actually see the woman.

Victor and Anika also called her something that sounded like "Mama," however with their accents, it was hard to tell. Ann knew they couldn't be her natural children. They sounded like they were Russian or something and they also called Helena, Mark's wife, "Mama."

Dancing seemed to be their passion.

"We withdraw from the next couple dance competitions. Without you and Bryce, it not same. Everyone we see from dance circuit ask about you. Want to know if coming back soon," Victor told her. "When you ready, we take slow. Not to worry."

Must be I dance, Ann thought. *I'm glad. I wonder if I'm any good?*

The day Georgio and Rosa finally came to visit was an emotional one. They had been devastated when Ann collapsed. It brought back painful memories of their own daughter's illness and subsequent demise. They had waited to visit for fear of what they would find.

Ann knew immediately she must have a special relationship with these two older people. Georgio had tears in his eyes when he hugged her.

"We think we lose you! Me and Mama, we pray for you every day, that you would get better. And look at you! Beautiful as ever. How do you feel. Really. You can tell your Papa."

Oh, gosh. Now I really am confused! Am I Italian? Are these people my parents?

"Don't worry. I'm feeling much better," Ann responded, patting his hand.

Rosa smoothed Ann's hair back from her forehead and caressed her cheek.

"What are they feeding you in here?" she said lovingly. "You can eat now, right? Do you have any restrictions on what you can eat? I'll start sending in meals for you. We don't want you wasting away!"

Ann smiled. If the treats everyone kept bringing her were any indication of Mama's cooking, she would look forward to an actual meal!

"Yes, I can eat anything. And I'm really hungry!" was all she could think of to say and it was the truth.

They didn't seem to expect her to say much, for which she was very thankful. Bryce did most of the talking, still holding her hand and glancing at her frequently.

Their visit was interrupted by the nurse who came to take Ann to her first visit with cardiac rehab.

Bruce brought Jamal and JB for a brief visit. Jamal called Bruce, "Dad." JB called him, "Uncle Bruce."

Gunner seemed attached to both boys, but especially to JB.

"My mom would come, but my sister is growing teeth and she cries all the time. Mom said to tell you 'Hi' and she will come when Dad can baby-sit," JB stated matter-of-factly as he scratched Gunner behind his ears.

It gave Ann a headache trying to piece together the fabric of her life and the people in her family. There was mention of someone named Andre. Where he fit in she wasn't sure. Biggy, Flower and Tinker all seemed to be people she should know...but didn't. Spaz must be some sort of pet...

Tess, her daughter-in-law and Molly somebody-or-other had brought in Gracie and Charley, her grandchildren, but then, all the kids called her Grandma... *I must be old enough to be a grandma.*

Chapter 150

A sia Kim was having a good day. The oatmeal she had for breakfast had tasted good and had stayed down. She decided to go visit Ann.

She knocked softly and peeked her head around the door. Ann and Bryce both looked up.

"Asia. Come in. How are you feeling?" Bryce said as he pulled up a chair so she could sit next to Ann's bed.

"I feel pretty good today. I bring this quilt for you. Mama Rosa, she send all food so I decide to give different."

She laid the quilt across Ann's lap. Ann was astounded by the intricate stitching and patterns. It was beautiful and it must have taken a lot of time to make.

"Asia, this is so thoughtful. Thank you so much. It's absolutely gorgeous and I love the colors."

Asia smiled shyly.

"I know favorite colors. Not take too long. Family so nice to help with children and housework, I need something to do with hands when not throwing up!"

Suddenly, Asia's stomach rebelled. She didn't catch Ann's question as she made a bee-line for the bathroom. Bryce, however, didn't miss it.

"Were you this ill with your other two pregnancies?"

Bryce looked up sharply. A thought that had lurked in the back of his mind came rushing to the forefront.

She can't remember! That's why some of the things she has said seemed vague and non-committal. Sometimes her comments didn't make sense. I thought it was the medication she was taking. But it's more serious than that! Does she remember me? Us? What will I do if she doesn't want me?

By the look of panic and fear on Bryce's face, Ann knew she had said something wrong. For several seconds, neither one spoke. Bryce withdrew his hand.

"Bryce. I..."

Tears welled up in Ann's eyes. Her heart ached. This man had never left her side through this whole horrible ordeal. She never meant to hurt him, but somehow, she had.

Bryce turned away. He walked unsteadily to the window and gazed out at nothing.

"Were you ever going to tell me?" he said barely above a whisper. "Or just take advantage of me."

When a nurse came rushing into the room, Bryce turned around in time to see Ann's eyelids flutter as her hand went to her chest.

Dr. Tipton had been sitting at the desk in the nurse's station when Ann's monitor registered a problem. He raced to her bedside. The nurse already had the head of the bed lowered and an oxygen mask in place.

"Page Dr. Bartholomew, respiratory therapy and the lab. And get her vital signs," Dr. Tipton told the nurse as he began his own examination. "What happened, Bryce? Her heart rate has increased and she's throwing some irregular beats."

When Dr. Bartholomew arrived, he did his own quick evaluation.

"Let's get her back down to ICU. Move it!"

Chapter 151

Within minutes, Ann was back in ICU. IV Therapy was inserting a central line so that medications could be delivered quickly and effectively. The lab girl drew several tubes of blood. Respiratory therapy was standing by in case intubation was necessary. Bryce looked on feeling helpless.

He's not here! Ann was floundering in a sea of terror. She could hear the activity going on around her, but his voice was silent. Her heart rate increased. Medication was delivered.

Dr. Tipton looked around finally spotting Bryce standing on the periphery of the group surrounding Ann's bed.

"Bryce! Get in here. She needs you. Come on people. We've got to get her stabilized. There's too much pressure on the new valve. If we don't get her heart rate and blood pressure down she could be in real trouble."

That statement broke the spell that had held Bryce in its grip. *Do I love her less because she can't remember?*

In an instant Bryce knew his answer. He stepped to the head of Ann's bed, gently took her hand and whispered in her ear.

"Everything will be fine. I'll help you remember. It'll be okay. Come back to me, Ann."

Ann's heart rate and blood pressure gradually dropped to an acceptable range. The rhythm evened out. She opened her eyes.

"I'm sorry..."

Bryce put his finger to her lips.

"No, Honey. I'm the one who's sorry. I reacted badly, selfishly. I love you. It's not your fault that your memory is gone. We'll take this one day at a time. When all else fails, our relationship is all that matters to me."

Ann recovered quickly from her set-back. She was so relieved that she didn't have to pretend to remember any more. Without that added stress she was able to relax.

Once she was back in her room, they discussed the current situation.

"Do you want to tell the doctors about this? Maybe there's medication, therapy, something that could help bring back your memories."

"No, I don't think so. I don't want these people who love me so much to know I don't even know their names; especially Luke. How would he feel if his own mother didn't remember giving birth to him?"

"I would like to, at least, discuss it with Mark. Maybe there's further damage that could be done if I just told you everything. I don't know enough about it. Why don't we ask him to come and talk with us on the condition he doesn't tell the rest of the family. How would that be?"

Ann gave Bryce one of those big, eye-popping, breath-taking smiles that never failed to make his heart race and other areas of his body react.

"That sounds good to me."

Mark wasn't as surprised by this development as Bryce expected. Her body had undergone severe trauma. Her brain had been without optimal blood flow for too long. It was amazing she hadn't suffered anything worse than memory loss.

He agreed to keep their secret and promised to help as much as possible. From then on, each day, both men began to give her back pieces of her life. Some things sounded vaguely familiar; as if they were hanging on the edges of her memory not willing to fully come back. Other things...it was like listening to someone else's life story.

The men didn't hold anything back. Both felt that if she was going to function normally she had to know everything. There were going to be questions she would ask if they were not forthcoming about even the abuse she had suffered. Why did she have a hideous scar on her back? Why did she need witness protection?

Mark started with what he knew about her parents and the accident that took their lives, the foster care travesty, Harriet, her life on the street, her disastrous first marriage, the abuse, the trials... She was visibly shaken by these revelations, but she insisted they keep going.

Over several days Bryce would lie next to her on her hospital bed and explain the events of their life together. He told her how they had met when his first wife died of cancer. How they had fallen in love. Ann's eyes never left his face.

The way he spoke to her, caressed her, held her tenderly in his arms; she began to understand how deep his feelings were for her. At times, there was a certain look that passed over his face. It spoke of longing, desire, vulnerability and unconditional love. She realized she could crush him with her words; destroy him. She began to fall in love with her husband all over again.

She was surprised to learn she was a doctor who operated a clinic and had privileges in this very hospital. The doctors who were treating her were her colleagues! The whole medical thing might not be possible now, but they would cross that bridge when they came to it.

"Do we need the money?" she asked in all seriousness. "There must be other jobs I could do..."

"Sweetheart," Bryce laughed. "We have plenty of money. That's one thing you never have to worry about."

Chapter 152

⌒♦⌒

The doctors kept Ann in the hospital a full two weeks after her successful surgery even though she could have been discharged much sooner. If the insurance didn't cover the cost of the extended stay, Bryce was more than willing to pay for it. He wanted to be absolutely sure she would be all right when he finally took her home.

If truth be told, the doctors, nurses, aids, ancillary people all loved her and weren't anxious to let her go. Her quiet nature and positive attitude was infectious. Everything they asked her to do she did willingly and without complaint.

Grudgingly, Dr. Bartholomew discharged her. She would be coming back on a regular basis for cardiac rehab and for check-ups, but he had to admit he would miss her. In his specialty, there were only a handful of success stories; especially in a hospital this size. She was certainly one of them.

Several staff members had gathered in the lobby to give her a proper send-off.

"Thank you all for everything you did for me," Ann said with a big smile.

"Yes," Bryce interjected. "You'll have a seat at Vincenzo's any time you want to come."

Bryce had told the rest of the family when Ann would be discharged.

"She's anxious to have you all visit, but please give her a couple of days to adjust."

He wanted to introduce her to their home privately. Let her get comfortable with everything before the family descended.

Mama Rosa had hugged Bryce tight.

"Of course. Just let us know when you're ready. Papa and I went in yesterday and stocked your fridge, but if you need anything, you know where we are."

Chapter 153

B
ryce stopped the white Mercedes at the bottom of the driveway so Ann could get a good look at the outside of the house.

"Oh, Bryce. It's so beautiful. This is really our home?"

"Yes," Bryce responded with a crooked smile. "It's small, but it's cozy. We like it."

He hit a button on the dash and the garage door went up. Opening her door and helping her out of the car had always been his habit. He lifted her in his arms and headed for the door.

In the short hallway between the house and the garage, he sat her down. Cupping her face in his hands, he kissed her gently.

"Welcome to your new, old home, my love."

The fluttering she felt in her chest had nothing to do with her surgery. Her arms went around him as she buried her face in his chest. She loved the feel of him, the smell of him. It felt familiar. It felt safe.

When she finally raised her head there were unshed tears glistening on her long lashes.

"I think I'm falling in love with you, Mr. Peterson."

"How fortunate for me, Mrs. Peterson."

They stood like this for a few more minutes enjoying the comfortable closeness.

"Come on," Bryce finally said, breaking the spell. "Let me show you the house. We designed it and built it together with the help of our friend, Doug Hagan. I think you're going to love it. Actually, I know you love it."

From the end of the hallway Ann could see into the kitchen. There was a huge bouquet of red roses sitting in the middle of a marble topped island. She cupped one of the blooms in her hands and breathed in the delicate aroma. Then she looked around. There were different colored roses everywhere!

"I think I like roses and I must like to cook," she murmured. "Do I like to cook, Bryce? Am I any good at it?"

Bruce chuckled.

"You are a marvelous cook. Between you and Mama Rosa it's a wonder I don't weigh two ton."

When she looked back at the kitchen island, she spotted something she hadn't noticed initially. I was a heart shaped locket.

"Bryce, what's this," she said as she poked it around on the counter with her index finger.

"It's yours. Go ahead. Have a look. I got it for you as a wedding present."

Slowly Ann picked up the locket. Engraved on the front were the words, "With love." Turning it over in her hand she found the words "Always and forever, Bryce."

For several seconds, Ann stared at the locket. As her fingers curled around the delicate necklace, she brought it to her lips. Tears spilled from under her lashes and ran down her cheeks. A memory came rushing through her mind of another day when she opened a velvet box...

Of their own accord her fingers sought out the tiny clasp and the locket popped open. Smiling back at her were Luke and Bryce. The other picture was an old black and white photo. The woman was gazing up at a tall handsome man.

Mom and Daddy, Ann breathed. Her arms crept around her husband's neck. She pressed her body to his as if she wanted to crawl inside his skin. He held her tight and stroked her hair.

"Bryce. It's my mom and daddy," she sobbed.

Bryce took the locket from her clenched fist and slipped it around her neck.

"It's your favorite piece of jewelry. They took if off in the emergency room and gave it to me for safe keeping. Now it's back where it belongs."

Ann dried her tears and smiled up at Bryce.

"I think I'm probably the luckiest woman alive."

They continued the tour, hand in hand. From the wide open kitchen they stepped into the high-ceilinged great room. The floor to ceiling windows, the natural stone fire place; it was stunning. The view out the windows along the back of the house looked out over undulating, well-tended lawns.

Bryce was watching her closely. He loved the expressions that played over her features as she discovered each new thing. As she looked out over the lawns to the mountains beyond, her lips parted and a contented sigh escaped.

She stepped into his arms.

"Oh, Bryce," was all she could manage to say.

The opposite wall was nothing but bookshelves surrounding a sound system that Ann suddenly realized had been playing from the minute they had entered the house. In the corner in front of another large, floor to ceiling window sat a cream-colored, baby grand piano.

Bryce sat down on the bench and pulled her down beside him. Her head dropped to his shoulder as he began to play. As his fingers glided effortlessly over the keys, she closed her eyes. This was familiar.

Chapter 154

"Come on, Sweetheart. There's still more to see," Bryce said as he helped her to stand.

When they entered the master bedroom, the memories were so close, yet slightly out of focus. It was like trying to see herself in the mirror in a steamy bathroom. She just knew if she could wipe away the condensation, she would be able to see clearly; she would remember.

Frustration was evident on her face.

"Don't try so hard. We don't have any time limits on this. Relax. Take a deep breath."

Bryce took her hand and gently pulled her into the room. Her eyes traveled over the king sized bed with the bright handmade quilt, the pictures on the walls and the matching lamps on the bedside tables.

They continued through the room, along the huge walk-in clothes closet and into the bathroom with a large, double shower.

Bryce nuzzled her neck.

"We could put the shower to good use later if you want."

"Mmmmm," Ann sighed. "The lukewarm water in the hospital shower wasn't very appealing. It certainly didn't encourage spending any length of time in there."

"I can assure you our water is as hot as you want it and we have spent a lot of quality time in there."

Ann could hear the desire in his voice. She instinctively knew he would wait until she was ready to make any passionate advances.

Past the bathroom was a small room that took her breath away. She knew immediately it was her room; her own private space. It was decorated in shades of pink. In front of a bow window was a huge, claw-foot, white bathtub. Along the windowsill were pink and white roses and pink and white candles just waiting to be lit.

In the corner was a makeup table with a huge, three-sided mirror. Pulling out the little drawers she found brushes, combs, lipstick in every conceivable color along with eye shadow, mascara...everything a woman would ever need to make herself look pretty.

There were several expensive looking perfume bottles lining the area under the mirror. Ann picked up one, and putting the stopper to her nose, she breathed deeply. The fragrance was intoxicating.

Bryce took the bottle from her hands and dabbed a little of the scent at the base of her throat.

"This is one of my personal favorites," he said with a smile curving his lips.

Sitting off to the side was a beautifully carved jewelry box. Ann lifted the lid and gasped at what she saw. Diamonds. She picked up a bracelet and laid it across her wrist.

"Are these really all mine?" she breathed. "I must have a really generous husband who has excellent taste in fine jewelry!"

Bryce laughed.

"Indeed you do. I love buying you pretty things. And diamonds... are a girl's best friend, you know."

Putting the bracelet back inside the box, Ann continued around the room. A white, antique writing desk sat along one wall. She pulled out the padded chair and sat down. Next to the desk sat a small, white book case.

She pulled out one of the leather bound books. It was a book of poetry that included poems and writings by several different authors. She opened it to the page marked with a slip of paper.

Bryce took the book from her hands and read aloud from the bookmarked passage.

"We are one

In your eyes
I see my own reflection
One heart, one soul, one mind
It comes from somewhere
Deep down within
Where I end, you begin
It's a magic so few ever find"
By R. McKown

"I know that poem," Ann whispered. "I know it."

Bryce dropped to his knees in front of his wife. He took her hands in his.

"How do you know it, Ann? Please tell me."

A solitary tear made its way down Ann's cheek.

"I remember reading this poem. It so touched my heart that I put the paper in the book to mark the page. I remember thinking how much I wanted someone to love me like that. I was sitting by your bed. You were sleeping; recovering from something. It was in a different room...not here in this house..."

Bryce knew she was trying hard to remember more, but it just wouldn't come.

"That's wonderful, Honey! And it's a valid memory. It was several months after Monica died. I came to the emergency room with a horrible pain in my side. Lucky for me, I got you for my doctor. It was appendicitis. You took out my appendix, then looked after me for a week to make sure I recovered. After you had gone home I found the book with this page marked lying on the chair next to my bed. I've always kept it."

He squeezed her hands.

"At the time, I wondered if any woman could ever love me that way. It's exactly how I feel about you, Ann; it's the way we came to feel about each other."

Bryce was still kneeling on the floor, looking up at her, his heart in his eyes. Ann slid off the chair and onto his lap. He cradled her against his chest and rocked her slowly back and forth. She fell asleep in his arms. He kissed the top of her head.

He knew this whole experience of coming home had been an emotional roller-coaster for her. The stress of trying to remember, the partial memories, the frustration over not being able to remember had drained her. No power on earth could have moved him from this spot until she woke up.

It was approaching four o'clock in the afternoon when she finally began to stir. Ann lifted her head and her eyes met his. What a wonderful connection they had. Whether she remembered anything more or not, of one thing she was very sure. He loved her. And she loved him.

He kissed her tenderly; a kiss full of promise for things to come... when she was ready.

Chapter 155

Ann had been discharged from cardiac rehabilitation with a clean bill of health. Dr. Bartholomew and Dr. Tipton were very pleased with her progress, most of that progress they attributed to Bryce. He was her biggest fan and guardian angel.

"Ann," Dr. Bartholomew said. "I don't think you need us anymore. Bryce, you can pick up the pace of your dancing when you feel she's ready. I want to see you in my office in six months."

Bryce shook hands with both doctors.

"I can't thank you guys enough. You both did something amazing when you saved my wife. I am ever in your debt."

After Ann's appointment, they headed for Vincenzo's. Ann wanted to see how Asia was doing and Bryce needed to talk with Georgio. They hadn't been to the regular family meetings since Ann's collapse and subsequent surgery. It was time to get back in the swing of things.

Ann and Bryce had been dancing for about three weeks. Even if Ann's mind didn't remember the steps of the dances, her body did. Muscle memory kicked in and she followed Bryce through the patterns of steps as if nothing had happened. Of course her stamina wasn't as good, but that wasn't an insurmountable problem. With regular practice she would be back to her "pre-collapse status," as Bobby called it, in no time.

This Friday night would be her re-entry into the public eye. She and Bryce would open the evening's dancing. The Channel Nine news team would be at their reserved table. Bobby had been the one to suggest they have a table always available to them.

"Good publicity can't hurt, and it's free," Bobby had stated to get his agenda approved.

Claire had created a spectacular new gown for the occasion. It was white with tiny, black sequins dotting the bodice and the hemline. Unlike her other form-hugging gowns, this creation flared out from her tiny waist into layer upon layer of lacy ruffles all the way to the floor. The back of the dress was cut low with appropriate placing of crisscross straps to cover her scar.

Keeping to the black and white theme of the dance team, Bryce had a new white, cut-away tuxedo. A black tie, black handkerchief with black onyx cufflinks completing his "look." Together, they were stunning.

The story of her collapse and hospitalization had spread like wildfire. One headline even stated "husband brings wife back from the dead." The mystique that surrounded their King and Queen of Romance status had grown to outlandish proportions. Bobby loved it.

When Bryce expressed his displeasure with all the hype, Bobby had a ready answer.

"Are you kidding, Bryce. We'll have to add on room to accommodate all the people who want reservations just to get a look at you guys!"

Next thing you know we'll be on the front of the tabloids because we're having an alien baby or something, Bryce muttered to himself.

They arrived at the ballroom well before the restaurant opened for the evenings dinner and dancing. As expected, the family was ecstatic to have Ann and Bryce back at the family table.

At promptly nine o'clock Luke took center stage with his microphone.

"Ladies and gentleman. Welcome to Vincenzo's Restaurant and Ballroom. I'm Luke Peterson."

With a huge smile across his face, Luke waited for the applause to die down.

"It is my pleasure to introduce our state-wide champion ballroom dance team. Victor and Anika Petrov, Bobby and Maria Rodriguez, Rosa and Georgio Vincenzo..."

He was interrupted by applause before he even introduced Ann and Bryce. They were the ones the huge crowd had come to see.

"Ann and Bryce Peterson," he finally shouted over the cheers of the guests.

Ann couldn't remember the interest they generated so she was totally unprepared for the over-the-top response to their debut performance even though Bryce had tried to warn her.

As they walked hand in hand to the middle of the dance floor, Bryce thought she had never looked more beautiful. He hadn't realized until now how pale she had been before. *How did I miss that? How did we all miss it?* he wondered. *She must have been sick for a long time, but she never complained!*

Tonight her eyes sparkled with excitement, her cheeks were pink as a blush slowly made its way up her face. Bryce drew her into his arms for the first steps of their dance. The smile she gave him, tugged at his heart. Oh, how he loved her.

When the last notes of the music faded away and their dance was over, Bryce kissed her. The crowd went wild; clapping, whistling, cheering... Ann looked around in amazement, then back at Bryce.

"I told you, my love," he whispered in her ear.

When the evening was over and they were finally cuddled up in their bed, nature took its course. It was slow and sweet. Whether she remembered anything more or not, Ann was finally at peace.

Chapter 156

I t was March and the winter had been mild by Vermont standards. Asia had given birth to a beautiful baby girl, much to Keysha's delight. She wanted to name the baby Emma after her mother. Jamal was in agreement and pleased that his sister had thought of it all on her own. Little Emma Kim was joyously welcomed into the Peterson Clan as its youngest member.

Bruce had never been so happy. His new little daughter had dark complexion like his. Her eyes were more almond shaped and her hair was black and straight as a pin. Keysha and Jamal loved her to death.

Snow was in the forecast. When the flakes began to fall on a Sunday night it wasn't expected to amount to much, but by Monday mid-afternoon the wind had picked up and the snowfall had become heavy. Now the weatherman on Channel Nine was predicting twelve inches.

Conditions worsened through Monday night and into Tuesday. The roads were starting to get really nasty. Visibility dropped to zero due to the blowing, drifting snow. The plows couldn't keep up. They no sooner got a road open and it was blown shut again.

A state of emergency was declared by the Cedarville city officials and the road all the way to Dixon was shut down to everything except for emergency vehicles.

Georgio and Bryce had advised everyone to stay at home where they would be safe and comfortable. Dance practice could wait until conditions improved. The restaurant wasn't open on Monday or Tuesday anyway so there was no need for anyone to take chances on the road.

Each house had a generator in case the electric went off; something Georgio fully expected to happen. He and Rosa had lived through many Vermont winters and they knew how fast things could get bad.

Peterson Search and Rescue was busy, however. It always amazed Bruce that people insisted on going out in bad weather, putting not only themselves at risk, but also the emergency response people who had to come and get them when they got in trouble.

He had just gotten home after pulling an old lady out of a ditch and getting her to the pharmacy to get her medicine when another call came in. He groaned. What he really wanted was something to eat.

Bruce pulled his soggy coat and wet boots back on. He hated the thought of leaving his snug apartment and his family to go out and rescue some idiot who was stuck out beyond Cedarville.

He grumbled as he kissed Asia goodbye. She handed him a thermos of coffee, and a paper bag, which held three peanut butter and jelly sandwiches; his supper.

"The chopper certainly can't fly in this weather. That means Luke and I will have to go get this guy on a dog sled or something..."

"You use snowmobile, yes?" Asia asked as she handed Bruce a dry pair of gloves. "Asia not think Butch big enough to pull you."

Bruce laughed. Sometimes Asia didn't understand English sarcasm.

"We use snowmobile, yes," he teased her.

Before he headed out, he knocked on Victor and Anika's door.

"Hey, Victor. Luke and I've got to go out on a rescue run. Could you please keep an eye on Asia and the kids for me. I don't know how long this is going to take."

"No problem, Bruce. We happy to help," Victor assured him. "Don't worry, Anika and I, we take care. Be safe."

The minute Bruce stepped outside, he knew this was no ordinary winter storm. The wind practically ripped his hat off, the blowing snow stung his exposed face. He stepped back inside and pulled a ski mask down over his face, flipped his hood up over his hat and tied everything down with his scarf.

Geez. This sucks, he thought as he made his way across the street to the Peterson maintenance garage. He was just checking the gas and oil in the fully equipped emergency rescue snowmobiles they would use when Luke came through the side door.

He stomped the excess snow off his boots.

"This is just great. The dispatcher said a guy and his girlfriend slid off the road out on Route 209. They're banged up and cold, but didn't report any serious injuries. They should be able to ride behind us okay don't you think?"

"Yeah, probably," Bruce replied right before he fired up his ride. "Let's go."

The automatic door rolled up and Luke and Bruce headed out into the storm.

Chapter 157

Ann and Bryce were curled up on the couch in front of a roaring fire. The outside lights were on making the view through the big windows spectacular. The swirling snow was piling up making them glad they were home; safe and sound.

They hadn't been completely content until they had checked in with everyone. Horace and Molly were staying with Tess and the children while Luke and Bruce were working.

Bobby and Maria were happily about to try and make a baby, as Bobby so eloquently put it.

"TMI (too much information)," Bryce laughed.

"Are you kidding? We would make great parents," he told Bryce. "Can't you just imagine a miniature Bobby Rodriguez running around?"

"I'm not quite sure I can imagine that, Bobby. Good luck though," he said right before disconnecting.

John, Carla, JB and Melissa-Ann were in for the duration. Carla had gotten to the store right before the roads were closed so they had plenty of milk, diapers and snacks. John and JB were planning a bowling tournament on the Wii system.

Biggy and Flower were staying put in their cabin at the foot of the mountain. Tinker was making his way to Vincenzo's. He had been told Luke and Bruce were on a call and that Victor and Anika were watching out for Asia and the kids.

He was worried about Rosa and Georgio. They were older and he wanted to make sure that if they needed something, someone would be there. He knew the restaurant still maintained a couple of guest rooms from back in the day when it was a restaurant and small motel. He could stay in one of them.

When Bryce spoke with Georgio and Rosa, he let them know Tinker was on his way.

"He's worried about you and Mama," Bryce said. "Let us know when he arrives so we don't have to think about him being up-side-down in a snow bank somewhere."

Georgio chuckled.

"That Tinker. He's such a good boy. But me and Mama are fine. We've got a nice fire in our fireplace, lots of wood by the back door and a good bottle of wine. Really, Bryce. We'll be fine. Don't you two worry. We'll probably go to bed early. I'll give you a ring when Tinker gets here."

Chapter 158

Luke and Bruce were making slow progress toward Route 209. The blowing, drifting snow was making it very difficult to stay on track. They kept as close together as they safely could so as not to lose each other in the almost total whiteout.

The snowmobiles were equipped with compasses, radios, on-board computer tracking systems, not to mention advanced first-aid kits and rescue gear. Luke just hoped they could make it to the car before the passengers froze to death or died of carbon monoxide from keeping the car running with the exhaust plugged with drifted snow.

Before they left they had been given the general location of Neal Munson's red Ford Fusion by the police dispatcher. Fortunately, Mr. Munson's phone had a GPS, which would make finding him and his friend much easier as long as the phone's battery lasted. The biggest problem was getting through the snow.

When Tinker finally got to Vincenzo's it was after midnight. He was exhausted, cold to the bone, wet and starving. His stump throbbed. For a while during the trip he wondered if he had been foolish to make the attempt. He had a compass and that's the only reason he made it. Landmarks were obliterated by the flying snow.

Georgio and Mama were very concerned when he didn't show up in a reasonable length of time. When they finally heard him at the back door, relief flooded through Mama.

"Tinker's finally here. What is the matter with that boy, coming in this kind of weather? He could've gotten lost and we wouldn't have found him until the snow melted!"

Georgio opened the door and there stood Tinker. Encased in snow.

"Come in and get out of those wet clothes before you freeze to death," Mama chided him. "What on earth possessed you to come here on a night like this?"

Mama sometimes used gruffness to cover up how she really felt. It touched her heart that Tinker was worried enough about them to come all this way in a horrible storm just to be there in case they needed something.

He was soon sitting by the fire sipping a hot toddy and eating a thick roast beef sandwich and a bowl of hot soup.

Georgio called Bryce.

"I know you were probably asleep, but Tinker just arrived. He's cold and wet, but okay. Mama's feeding him...you know Mama. Food is the answer to every problem. He said Victor and Anika are watching over Asia and the kids so they have their hands full already. He didn't want us to be alone."

"Thanks for calling, Georgio. Ann and I feel better knowing he's with you and Mama just in case. Tinker's a good man. I'm glad he decided to join us. Sleep well, my friend, and we'll talk in the morning."

Tinker stretched and yawned.

"Man! I'm tired. Guess I'll hit the sack."

Georgio showed him to one of the guest rooms on the other side of the restaurant's huge kitchen. Mama gave him extra blankets and a hot brick for the foot of his bed. She patted his cheek.

"Thank you, Tinker, for coming. You're a good boy. Sleep well. I'll fix you a special breakfast in the morning."

Georgio banked the fire in the fireplace and they hustled off to bed. The wind howled. The snow continued to fall and the temperature continued to drop. It wasn't long before the electricity went off and the generator kicked in.

Chapter 159

Bruce spotted something red through the blowing snow. He spoke to Luke through his head set.

"Luke. Over there. I think that's the car."

Sure enough. There was a red car stuck in the ditch. The snow had piled up until only the roof was visible. Leaving the snowmobiles idling, they plowed through the drifts to get to the car. They would have to do a fair amount of shoveling before they could get the door open.

Bruce wiped the snow off the window with his forearm and cupping his hands around his eyes, he peered inside. The couple had moved to the back seat and were huddled together. He banged on the window and hollered. No response.

"This doesn't look good, Luke. They aren't responding. Here. Take a look," he said as he stepped aside so Luke could see through the small opening where he had cleared off the snow.

Luke hit the window several times and hollered. Still nothing.

"You're right. They aren't moving. We've got to get them out right now. Let's get the shovels. We don't have much time and who knows, maybe we're too late already."

The shoveling was hard work and soon both men were dripping wet with sweat. As soon as they got a space cleared a gust of wind would fill it back in.

"Let's bring the snowmobiles in close. Maybe we can block some of the wind. I don't think putting up a shield will work. The wind is just too strong."

With the snowmobile runners right up against the car, Bruce and Luke resumed shoveling. When Luke tried the door, it was either locked or frozen shut.

"Shit! We're going to have to either break the window or pry the door off."

Breaking the window wasn't really an option. Glass would fly everywhere. In a small car, the shards could easily hit the people trapped inside. Bruce got the crowbars and they went to work on the back door.

The door popped open easier than they expected. Luke crawled across the seat and over to the young couple. He felt for a pulse. Neither had one. But then, he wasn't a doctor. He had heard of people being submerged in icy water who had been warmed up and lived. It made the need for speed all the more important in this case.

While Luke was examining the victims, Bruce looked around in the front seat. The cell phone was on the dashboard. The battery was dead. It's a good thing the police station was able to get the coordinates before that happened. They wouldn't have been found until the weather warmed up enough to melt the snow. The ignition was in the on position and the gas gage showed empty suggesting they had run the car heater until the gas was gone.

"What do you think, Luke. Do they have a chance?"

"I don't know. Maybe if we can get them to the hospital fast enough..."

"They aren't going to be able to ride behind us, that's for sure. The snow is too deep for a travois to work. We need a sled of some kind that we can pull behind one of the snowmobiles," Bruce said as he looked around for something suitable.

Luke backed out of the car.

"It has to be big enough for the both of them. I wouldn't dare to try and pry them apart. They seem to be frozen together. What about the hood of the car. We could take it off the car and I could pull it behind me."

"Great idea. I think it just might work."

They wrangled the hood off the car, not without great difficulty. Yes, it would act as a sled, but it also acted like a kite. More than once the wind took it, resulting in Bruce and Luke being dragged through the snow as they fought to hold on.

When the hood was finally attached and secure, the next problem was getting the two frozen people out of the back seat. Bruce got in and wrapped his arms under their knees and behind their shoulders.

He had to really tug to get them loose from the seat. Backing out slowly, he pulled the young couple with him. When they were finally on the "sled" they were covered with all the blankets from the emergency packs.

Bruce shook his head.

"I'm not sure this will be enough."

Finally they were ready to head to the hospital. From where they were, the hospital wasn't that far. Getting there was the big problem. Bruce would lead the way, finding the best route. Luke would follow hauling their precious cargo. It would be slow going.

Fortunately, the wind had abated somewhat and visibility was better. Bruce was able to pick his way through leaving a trail for Luke to follow. They never got so far apart that Luke lost sight of Bruce's wide back and bright blue scarf.

It took them an hour to travel a distance that normally would take fifteen minutes. Bruce radioed ahead to the hospital. He told them the status of the people they were bringing in.

When they finally pulled up in front of the emergency room, the staff was ready. Instead of trying to get the passengers off the hood outside, the hood was detached and the whole thing was dragged through the sliding doors and into the lobby. Now it was up to the doctors and nurses...and God.

Bruce and Luke were exhausted and cold to the bone. One of the aides shoved hot cups of coffee into their hands.

Before they could get out of their wet coats, a police officer came rushing over to them.

"Guys! Vincenzo's is on fire!"

Bruce jerked, spilling his coffee on the floor.

"What! What did you say?"

"It came over the scanner. A tree fell, ruptured a propane tank... the building is on fire..."

Before the officer could finish Luke and Bruce were barreling for the door.

Chapter 160

Tinker had been asleep for only a short time when he was jolted out of bed and onto the floor by something that felt like an earthquake. The noise was thunderous. Falling plaster and sheetrock pinned him to the floor. The soft glow of the night light powered by the generator was off.

"What the hell!" he yelled, as he pulled himself from under the rubble.

His arms and legs seemed to work. Blood gushed from a good sized laceration on the side of his head where a lump was already forming. Mama had given him a flashlight, which he had put on his bedside table. The first order of business was to find that flashlight and his clothes.

Combing through the rubble with his bare hands he found the flashlight, his boots and his prosthetic leg. His clothes had been in the closet across from the bed. If he didn't get dressed soon, he would freeze to death.

Shining the flashlight around what had been his room, he was shocked to find a huge tree branch had fallen through the roof. His Marine training kicked in as he evaluated his situation.

Managing to wiggle himself between the smaller branches and fallen debris, he got to what was left of the closet. He dragged on his cargo pants, sweatshirt and jacket. Thankfully, his hat, scarf and gloves were still stuffed in the pocket of his heavy coat.

His wrist unit beeped. It was Victor. He was totally panicked.

"Tinker! You there? What the hell going on?"

At that moment, there was a loud explosion.

"Tinker!" he screamed.

Tinker could smell gas fumes. In just seconds, downed electrical wires sparked a fire that quickly ignited curtains and rugs. The Vincenzo's apartment was part of the oldest section of the restaurant/ballroom. The wood was dry.

"Shit! I think the tree behind the building came down. It must have hit the propane tank and probably took down the electrical wires. You and Anika get Asia and the kids across the road to the maintenance building. Hurry! Then get back here and help me get Georgio and Rosa out!"

Tinker immediately dialed 911 from his wrist unit.

"Vincenzo's is on fire. A good portion of the building has collapsed. Send help! Hurry!"

He had pushed the button on his unit which also alerted all the Peterson Clan households.

Bryce bolted out of bed and began pulling on his clothes.

"Ann! Come on! We have to get to Mama and Georgio."

Bobby and Maria had never really gotten to sleep. They had been "busy" most of the night. When the call came through they had just fixed hot chocolate and were getting ready to go back to bed.

"Holy crap!" Bobby yelled. "Maria. Get dressed. I'll get the snowmobile started."

Carla had been up with Melissa when the call came. She knew by the look on John's face that he wanted to go help. But a man in a wheelchair...he wouldn't be able to do much even if the roads were passable.

"Carla, why don't you get some coffee going and start getting some food ready. Everyone will be hungry. We have extra room. We can take in maybe Bruce, Asia and the kids. Oh my gosh. I can't believe this is happening..."

All Biggy and Flower could do was agonize and pray. There was no way they could get out and travel the distance to the main road.

Luke spoke briefly to Tess.

"Stay put with the children. I'll keep you posted. Luv you."

He also spoke with Horace.

"Could you and Molly please stay with Tess and the children? I'd feel better knowing you were with them. Don't know when I'll get home."

Chapter 161

Fortunately, the tree, weighed down by the heavy snow and pushed by the high wind gusts, had fallen on the ballroom/dining room section of the building and not directly on Georgio and Rosa's apartment.

The side wall of their apartment caved in. The roof didn't collapse completely because the fireplace was propping it up. It wouldn't hold for long. Their bedroom was on the other side of the living room on an outside wall just beyond their private entrance from the back parking lot.

Georgio ended up on the floor, unconscious. Rosa was pinned to the bed by a large branch.

"Georgio!" Rosa screamed. "Georgio!"

The Watson and Petrov apartments were on the other side of the ballroom in the new addition, farthest away from where the tree was now embedded in the floor. They were uninjured and had a few extra minutes to get out.

Asia was already in the hall between the apartments when Victor came busting out of his door.

"Get kids! Come to door. I take to maintenance building where safe. HURRY!"

Jamal was right behind Asia. His eyes as big as saucers.

"Mom! What's going on?"

"Get Keysha. No time explain. Get dressed. Throw some clothes in you backpacks. Hurry! We must get out. Victor will help us!"

It took only minutes for Asia, Jamal, Keysha and baby Emma to get to the back door leading out of the building. Victor knew there was no way all of them would fit on one snowmobile. Walking was out of the question. The snow was too deep.

Just when he was trying to decide who to take first, headlights popped up out of the blowing snow. It was Bobby and Maria, followed closely by Bryce and Ann.

Bryce immediately took charge.

"Asia, you and the baby get between Ann and me. Jamal. You're with Bobby and Maria. Keysha. Hop up there between Victor and Anika."

In no time, the small group was standing in the office of the maintenance building. Bryce flipped on the lights and turned up the heat.

"Ladies. Stay here. Victor. Bobby. You're with me. Let's go help Tinker."

Chapter 162

⁓⁓

The men left the snowmobiles a distance from the building and out of danger. They couldn't afford to lose the only transportation available. They slugged through the snow to what had been the back door of Rosa and Georgio's apartment. The way was blocked by tree limbs.

As they were assessing the situation, Bruce and Luke pulled in beside them.

"Asia and the kids are safe across the street," Bryce said before Bruce could ask. "We need chain saws. We won't be able to get in without cutting out these big branches. Bobby. You and Victor go get them. We have a couple in the storage room at the back of the building across the street. Bruce. Luke. Let's see if we can wiggle in somewhere."

Bryce, being the smaller of the three men, managed to wedge his way forward. He spotted the beam of Tinker's flashlight at the same time Tinker saw him.

"Tinker," he yelled, his voice mostly evaporating in the wind, the sounds of falling timber and the crackling of the fire. "I don't think we can depend on the fire department getting here in time to help us. It's up to us to find Georgio and Rosa. Everyone else is safe."

Bruce and Luke began furiously digging out around the branches that blocked the door. When Bobby and Victor arrived with the chain saws, they immediately went to work clearing away the huge tree limbs.

Inside, Bryce and Tinker made their way toward the bedroom in the back of the apartment, being careful not to dislodge anything that was providing temporary support to the remaining roof.

The smoke was thick. The fire was popping and snapping, devouring everything in its path. Time was short.

"Georgio. Rosa." Bryce yelled, knowing it was probably impossible for them to hear him.

There was a lull in the wind just long enough for Bryce to hear Rosa calling Georgio.

"That way," Bryce pointed.

The two men pushed their way through the remaining few yards to the bedroom. Bryce went immediately to Georgio. Tinker began prying the branches apart so that Mama could slip out.

Tinker pulled a blanket off the bed and wrapped it around Mama. She was almost out of her mind with fear. When she saw her husband face down on the floor, a pool of blood already freezing around his head, she ran to his side.

"Oh, my God! Georgio," she cried.

Bryce tried to reassure her.

"He's got a pulse, Rosa. He's alive. The boys are coming. We'll get him out. Tinker. See if you can get another blanket over here."

Outside, Bruce and Luke carved away the limbs blocking the door. Bobby and Victor pulled them back and out of the way as best they could. Due to the damage done by the tree, the foundation of the building was off-kilter just enough to jam the door shut.

Finding a crack just big enough to accommodate his fingers, Bruce proceeded to rip the door completely off the hinges.

From that point on, Bruce was giving the orders.

"Luke. Find a plank or something, maybe we can use the door, so we can carry Georgio out of here without moving him too much. Possible head injury. Victor. Get Rosa across the road."

Rosa started to object. Bruce shook his head. He took her shoulders and turned her so that she had to look him in the eyes.

She had to know he meant business. There was no time for arguing about it.

"No, Rosa. I know what you're thinking. You would just be in the way. We need to concentrate on getting Georgio out of here without having to worry about you."

She saw the wisdom of his words. Bending over Georgio, she kissed his cheek and whispered in his ear.

"Don't you dare die on me, old man! I'll never be able to forgive you if you do."

Victor helped her through the rubble toward the door. On the way, Rosa stooped to pick up a picture that had fallen to the floor. The glass was shattered. She clutched it to her chest under the blanket.

The door to the office flew open. Snow and cold air rushed in along with Rosa and Victor. It took all Victor could do to push the door shut against the wind. Mama was freezing, wearing only her nightgown and the blanket from her bed. No shoes. No coat...

Ann didn't think. She acted. She may not remember being a doctor, but reflexes took over. Mama was soon sitting close to the heater, her fingers around a steaming mug of hot coffee. Ann found wool blankets in the office closet and tucked them snugly around the older woman's shoulders.

From under her blankets, Rosa withdrew the picture of her daughter that she had picked up when she left the only home she had known for most of her adult life. She began to sob.

Victor quietly took his leave, hoping there was something he could do to help his friends get Georgio back to the family alive.

Chapter 163

A path had been cleared to the back door. Luke and Bruce carefully lifted Georgio and placed him on the door Tinker and Bryce had dragged in. They wrapped him in the comforter from the bed.

Now the problem was transporting him through the storm, across the road to the maintenance building. They had to get away quickly before the whole structure collapsed.

Bobby came up with the only plausible solution.

"Victor and I can go a few steps ahead and clear the way as much as we can. The four of you can carry Georgio. It'll be slow going, but I think it will work."

Bruce looked around at each man; his friends, his family. He was proud of every one of them.

"Okay. Let's do this."

Bruce and Luke picked up the ends of the door. Bryce and Tinker lifted on either side in the middle. Slowly and painstakingly, they made their way to the road. Victor and Bobby could only do so much removing the snow in front of them. They slipped and slid, forcing their feet through the snow that re-accumulated almost as fast as Bobby and Victor could shovel it away.

They were almost to the road when the remainder of the building came down sending sparks and debris flying into the air. The sound was deafening. Bryce and Tinker leaned over Georgio to protect him. Sparks landed on the blanket where they were quickly extinguished.

Bruce was hit in the back of his leg by a piece of timber. His leg gave out. As he struggled to regain his footing, the door tipped precariously and Georgio was almost thrown into the snow. Tinker lifted higher on his side and the door came level again.

The women were watching from across the street. Every once in a while they could catch a glimpse of the men carrying Georgio through the churning, whirling snow. When the building finally succumbed to the flames, they gasped in unison.

Maria and Ann pushed the door open as soon as the rescue party approached. A blast of frigid wind and snow accompanied them inside.

The door carrying Georgio was gently placed on the floor. Bruce turned to help the girls get the outside door shut, then he slumped down onto the floor. His leg was throbbing. His hat and coat showed singe spots where sparks had landed. Being in the back, he had taken the brunt of the damage.

The other men had not escaped unscathed. Tinker's head laceration had clotted, but needed attention. Bryce had a burn on the side of his face. Luke had twisted his wrist badly as he had righted the door when Bruce stumbled.

Victor and Bobby were hardly able to move. Their arms and legs felt like they were made of lead. Shoveling the heavy snow and slogging through the drifts as they had plowed a path had taken a toll.

Chapter 164

A nn immediately knelt beside Georgio. Her years of training overrode her lack of memory. Assessing for back or neck injuries, broken bones, other cuts or bruises took several minutes.

"Can someone help me roll him over?"

Luke and Bryce crawled forward and helped Ann carefully turn Georgio face-up."

Rosa was trying to be brave, but she couldn't control the sob that escaped when she saw Georgio's bruised and bleeding face. Keysha climbed up on her lap and hugged her.

"It'll be all right. Grandma Ann will fix him good as new. She's the best fixer-upper, you know."

Ann saw the burn on her husband's cheek. Her first instinct was to go to him, however Georgio was the most seriously hurt. Ann looked around at the other men.

"Any of you have injuries I need to look at right now?" she asked.

"Take care of Georgio first," Tinker responded. "I think the rest of us can wait."

Ann began giving orders in a calm, quiet voice.

"Bobby, I think there are cots in the storage room. Could you please get one so we can get Georgio up off the floor. It will be warmer and also make it easier for me to do what I have to do."

Bobby hurried off, returning in just a few minutes, dragging a cart carrying several cots.

"I thought maybe others might like to lie down and try to get some sleep, plus if we are stuck here for a while, we will all need to get some rest."

The men gently lifted Georgio onto the cot Bobby sat up near the heater.

"I need my medical bag..." she hesitated. "Bryce do I have my bag?" she asked.

Why did I say that? she wondered. *I think I've said it before! Will I know what to do with it?*

"I grabbed it on the way out of the house and stuck it in the storage compartment on the snowmobile. I'll go get it."

Ann didn't remember ever having a medical bag, but when it was in her hands, she knew exactly what to do. Georgio's head laceration was cleaned and sutured. He probably had a concussion. Only an x-ray could verify that, so Ann decided to treat him as if he did have one. When she was finished, she moved aside so Rosa could take her place beside him.

His eyes opened when Rosa took his hand.

"Rosa! What has happened?" Georgio gasped, struggling to sit up.

"You old fool," she replied lovingly. "You're hurt. Just be still."

His hand went to the bandage on his forehead above this eyebrow.

"Ouch. That really hurts," he moaned as he slumped back on the cot. "And I've got a wicked headache!"

When he was quiet and somewhat comfortable again, Rosa explained their current situation.

"The oak tree fell, the building caught fire. Georgio, we've lost everything; our home, the restaurant, everything. I almost lost you! If it hadn't been for Tinker..."

Mama Rosa, always the stoic one, dropped her head to her husband's chest and sobbed out her heartache. She only allowed herself a few minutes to grieve over what she had lost before she pulled herself together and wiped the tears from her face.

"We are all safe. That's the important thing."

Georgio gently touched her cheek.

"That's my girl. We can rebuild. We have our family. We'll be fine."

Chapter 165

Each man's injuries were then treated. Thankfully, none of them were serious enough to be life threatening. No doubt, they would all be very uncomfortable for a few days.

Maria called Biggy and Flower, John and Carla to let them know what was happening. Both families were very relieved to know everyone had gotten to safety. They were worried about Georgio though.

Maria glanced over at Georgio, already talking to Bryce about starting the clean-up as soon as the storm abated.

"He's fine," she said. "He'll bounce back."

Luke checked in with Tess. Horace had brought the animals into the barn and he was checking on them periodically. Molly was busy baking something that smelled delicious. The babies were still asleep.

"Don't worry about us," Tess said. "Just take care of yourself and come home soon."

Anika passed out mugs of hot coffee. The coffee maker in the office hadn't been used this much since it was installed. The next pot would be hot water for the tea and hot chocolate drinkers.

Fortunately for Butch and Gunner, the dog kennels were behind the maintenance building. Luke had battled the elements and retrieved a bag of dog food so the big dogs wouldn't go hungry. No so for the humans.

There was a bathroom equipped with a shower in the building. The generator would keep the pump running and the lights on. Food was the problem. They didn't have any.

How long they would be stuck where they were was anybody's guess. Bobby checked his phone for the weather.

"The snow and wind is supposed to begin to slow down by tomorrow morning, according to Channel Nine," he reported. "So we're going to be here for a while; maybe a few days."

They discussed all of them making the short trek to the Peterson house, which was the closest. However, Georgio's condition was still fragile. It could be dangerous to move him even if they could manage it.

"We could take you ladies and the kids to the house. You can all ride behind one of us and we could bring back food," Tinker offered. "Ann, you and Bryce would probably need to stay with Georgio..."

"Oh, no," Maria and Anika interjected at once.

"We all go or we all stay," Maria stated emphatically.

Everyone shook their heads in agreement.

"Asia, what about you and the baby? Will you be okay if we all stay together here?"

"We fine. Emma good baby. I nurse so food not a problem for her," Asia replied as she stroked the baby's soft cheek. "We warm. We safe. All good."

Just then, John called.

"Carla made up extra food as soon as the weather got bad. We've got lots. If someone can come and get it..."

A cheer went up from the rest of the family.

Bobby jumped up and began gathering his outdoor gear.

"Well, okay then. Victor, you and I can go round up that food and bring it back."

"Oh, to be young again," Bryce sighed with a smile tugging at the corners of his mouth.

Bruce instantly put a plan together. His leg was so painful, he didn't think he would be much help, and more likely, a hindrance. It grated on him that he wasn't the best person for the mission.

"We've got a couple of carts on runners. They're not very big, but better than nothing. We can attach them to the snowmobiles. That way you would only have to make one trip. We may only need food for a couple of days. You two," he said looking sternly at Bobby and Victor. "Stay together. No cowboy stuff out there, understand? Don't take any chances."

"We got it. We got it, Dad," Bobby retorted.

He punched Bruce in the arm.

"Don't worry. The dangerous duo to the rescue. We will save you all from starvation! You can thank us later."

Bruce rolled his eyes heavenward. *Oh, great*, he thought. *I'll have to live with this for the rest of my life.*

Jamal tugged on Bobby's sleeve.

"Can you bring cake?"

Bobby laughed.

"Sure, little man. Cake it is."

Chapter 166

Bobby and Victor made the trip to John and Carla's and back without mishap. The storm was already lessening. By midmorning the snow had stopped. The wind was still howling so the family decided to stay put in the maintenance office another day.

Georgio was feeling better. The headache had settled down to a dull roar and he was able to eat some soup. When he looked out the window for the first time at the smoldering heap that was once his home, he could only shake his head.

"We were very lucky, Mama. If it hadn't been for Tinker and the other boys..."

He pulled Rosa close and kissed her forehead before enveloping her in a big hug.

"We have our family. Everyone's okay. We haven't lost anything that can't be replaced."

Rosa buried her face in Georgio's chest. She had been terrified that she would lose him. He had been the center of her life since she was a young girl. How would she have been able to go on without him?

When she looked up, there were tears in his eyes.

"We're gonna be fine, Mama. We're gonna be fine," he whispered in her ear.

As soon as the wind died down, Bruce and Luke got the big plows fired up. They managed to get paths through the snow big enough for everyone to leave the office.

The fire department had tried to get to Vincenzo's when the call came in. Even with a snow plow leading the way, it had been impossible. The fire chief felt terrible. He had known Georgio and Rosa for years and had eaten at their table many times. No one blamed him or his men. It had been a monster of a storm and the circumstances could not have been predicted.

Victor and Anika moved in with Bobby and Maria. When the house had been built, it was with a future family in mind so there was plenty of room. The basement housed a family room with a pool table and a big-screen TV. The arrangement would work for the short term.

Georgio and Rosa would stay with Ann and Bryce. Bryce offered the apartment over the garage as a permanent solution to their living arrangements.

"Oh, Bryce, my boy. I don't know," Georgio said, stroking his mustache. "Would you want me and Mama right on top of you all the time? Mama can be a handful, you know."

Mama slapped his arm.

"Georgio! For heaven's sake. If anyone's a handful, it's you."

Georgio couldn't help but laugh at the fire in Rosa's eyes. It was good to see that spark again.

"We will certainly consider your generous offer, Bryce," Georgio replied as he slipped his arm around his disgruntled wife.

The Watson's, all five of them, squeezed in with John and Carla. JB and Jamal were ecstatic. Jamal had stayed over with JB on numerous occasions and JB had bunk beds so no problem there.

Keysha would share Melissa's room. Bruce, Asia and baby Emma would take the guest room. The house was a large, one-story ranch. The guest suite was on the opposite end from John and Carla's master bedroom, so both couples were afforded some privacy.

Ann and Bryce were glad to be home. As they snuggled together in bed their first night back in their own house, they were both extremely thankful that things had turned out the way they did. It had been a harrowing experience for everyone and the outcome could have been so much worse.

Chapter 167

T he clean-up of Vincenzo's began as soon as the roads were open. Bulldozer, backhoes and dump trucks made quick work of clearing the site. Rebuilding would begin immediately, weather permitting.

In the old building, upgrades had been made within the confines of the existing structure. As a result, some areas were cramped and inconvenient. At a family meeting held soon after the storm, everyone was asked to think about changes that would improve the functionality of the new building.

The new Vincenzo's would be reconstructed very similar to the old building. However, it would be bigger and without the apartments attached. It would sit further back from the road and include a large lobby, coat room and hostess station.

Bruce and Luke had some ideas for the security office. They wanted a little bit more office space and they wanted a bedroom and bath attached in case it became necessary for someone to be in the building overnight. All the monitors and other equipment would be state-of-the-art as it had been in the old building.

Asia's hair salon would stay. Added to that would be a sewing room, closets for costumes and supplies as well as dressing rooms for each couple on the dance team. In the past, all the dancers had to keep their clothes at home, bringing them to the ballroom for every event. This would make things more convenient for everyone.

There would be three individual dance studios in the back of the building for dance lessons and practice sessions. Victor suggested a fully equipped exercise room.

Bobby had moaned and groaned for a week, complaining to Victor.

"Oh, man. Don't we get enough exercise just with your outrageous practice sessions?"

"Dancers are athletes. Must be in excellent physical condition. It help to prevent injuries and help us win. You want continue win, don't you?"

"I guess," Bobby muttered.

Carla was thrilled to be involved in the designing of a new kitchen and dining room. Doug spent considerable time with her putting a plan together. With a larger dining room to accommodate more patrons, three large buffet tables were added instead of one to avoid wait time for guests to get their food. The menu items would remain, but preparing them and serving them would be so much easier.

Everyone agreed that the enormous fireplace would be reconstructed at one end of the restaurant. Hopefully, many of the original stones that Georgio and Rosa had so lovingly gathered many years ago could be salvaged and used again.

There was insurance money to cover most of the cost for the restaurant and ballroom. Even building the Petrov and Watson homes would be covered as they had lived in apartments attached to the original building. Both families had carried separate insurance on the contents of their apartments so replacing things like furniture and appliances would be covered.

Victor and Anika wanted to live in Peterson Village. It would be separate from, but close to, the ballroom making it ideal for them.

Asia and Bruce wanted privacy, peace and quiet so they had opted for a home built on the Peterson Estate on the opposite side of the estate from Luke and Tess. A road was put in along the restaurant's parking lot, chopper pad, dog kennels and the maintenance building. The Watson family home would be at the end of that road.

Georgio and Rosa decided to stay in the apartment over Bryce and Ann's garage. Rosa would redecorate and renovate as the space was decidedly masculine thanks to Luke's tastes before he was married. A beautiful deck would be added to the back.

"We can sit out there in our old age, sip good wine and enjoy nature," Georgio had mused with a dreamy, faraway look in his eyes. "We can have the grandkids over..."

Doug Hagan's construction company would have an extremely busy year! Thanks to Peterson Enterprise using his company exclusively for all their building projects, his reputation had grown. His company was now the largest in the whole state.

With several crews operating simultaneously, one crew for each building, everything would be finished around the same time.

Toward the end of completion, the excitement was at a fever pitch. Reservations had been pouring in for the grand opening of the restaurant and ballroom in September. Of course, those guests who had lost their spot due to the storm and the rebuilding were taken first.

Toward the end of August, it was decided they needed to do a "dry-run" for the new kitchen and the staff. They invited all the people who worked for Hagan Construction for an evening of dinner and dancing...on the house. It was a way to say thank you for all the hard work and dedication it had taken to get Vincenzo's back to its former glory so quickly.

There were a few glitches making some changes necessary, but all in all, it was a spectacular success. The grand opening was scheduled for Saturday night, September fifteenth.

The big night finally arrived.

"Ladies and gentleman. Welcome to Vincenzo's Restaurant and Ballroom. I'm Luke Peterson."

Epilogue

nn and Bryce sat together on their leather couch in front of a roaring fire. In their seventies, they were still as in love as they were on the day they were married. Bryce folded Ann into his arms and kissed her passionately.

"We've been so fortunate, haven't we, Sweetheart?" he murmured against her hair. "We've come through some hard times, but the family has always stood together."

"Yes, my love. And I wouldn't have had things any other way," Ann responded. "You are the love of my life and I know we will be together for all time, even into the next life."

"Hey! Don't be talking about the after-life quite yet. I still have some loving and dancing to do," Bryce laughed.

They walked hand in hand toward their bedroom. There was plenty of time. The love-making was slow and easy. When they were both satisfied, they fell asleep wrapped in each other's arms.

They slept peacefully knowing that Peterson Enterprise and the Peterson family were in good hands with the next generation of leadership.

Charley Peterson and JB Benson had brought the Search and Rescue team to national attention with their dangerous and daring rescues. The Peterson K-9 and service dogs were in demand across the country. Gunner, Butch, Rex, Angel, Olyvia and Spaz had provided a firm foundation for the dogs that followed.

Dimitri Petrov had fallen in love and married Maribel Rodriquez and they were in charge of all the dancing activities at the ballroom.

They continued the winning legacy of the first team to dance for Vincenzo's.

Jamal Williams-Watson attended Georgetown University for his undergraduate studies, then on to Harvard Law School. He took over the Schwartz Law Firm upon passing the bar exam. With Oscar as his mentor, the practice grew. Jamal's goal had always been to affect the lives of children in a positive way by becoming a family court judge. His friends and colleagues called him "King Solomon" because of his wise, yet often controversial, decisions.

Even in his eighties, Oscar took on a case once in a while; especially if it involved children. Jamal was always happy for his help and expertise. After the death of his wife, Mildred, Oscar and his long time friend, Harold Tweaks, could be found involved in a highly competitive game of chess. The Vincenzo Restaurant would always have places for both men at the family table.

Dr. Mark Goodwin developed serious health problems associated with his years of alcoholism. He valiantly battled liver disease before he finally died at age seventy-one. Ann was devastated. She lost a little piece of her heart that day. Helena went to live with Anika and Victor and continued to teach ballroom dancing. She and Ann remained close friends for many years.

Galva Grace passed away at age eighteen. The heart problem with which she was born re-surfaced and took her life. She was buried in the Peterson Cemetery.

Keysha Williams-Watson was devastated by the loss of her friend. It took some time for her to regain her footing and move forward. Fingering the necklace she always wore, left to her by her grandmother Page, gave her a measure of comfort. Never leaving the safety of her family circle, she had been home schooled. She was extremely well educated and well read. She was interested in every facet of Peterson Enterprise and was soon learning from Bobby how to run the business.

Clifford Benson, JB's younger brother, followed in his father's footsteps and attended MIT for his Master's in Business Administration. He and Keysha took over leadership of Peterson Enterprise.

Melissa Ann Benson learned to cook at her mother's apron strings. Upon her graduation from culinary school, she ran the Vincenzo Restaurant. All of Mama's secret recipes continued to bring in diners from all over the country.

Bridgette Peterson, one of Tess and Luke's daughters, went to medical school and became the person in charge of the Goodwin-Schwartz Free Clinic.

Sally Peterson fell in love with the handsome and charming Stone Watson. Asia Kim and Bruce were pleased that one of their children loved the land and the farming as much as Bruce had come to appreciate it in his later years. Fresh meat and vegetables would continue to be served in the Vincenzo dining room.

Flower and Biggy never left their cabin in the mountains. They had four boys who followed their father's example and entered the Marine Corp. If truth be known, they were little soldiers from birth, camo diapers and all. After their military service, they came back home to jobs with Peterson Search and Rescue.

Tinker never married, but was never at a loss for women vying for the position as Mrs. Justice Parker. He built a cabin of his own not far from his friends, Flower and Biggy. He made frequent trips home to visit his aging parents. After a rough start, he had made them very proud. The rest of his time was spent helping to raise his four "nephews."

Georgio and Rosa lived into their nineties, satisfied that their legacy would continue. In their later years, Keysha moved into the second bedroom of the apartment above the Peterson garage and lovingly cared for them. They died three months apart.

The family expanded and Wednesday family meetings continued. All the older members of the Peterson Clan were encouraged to be as active as they wanted to be. Their wisdom and experience were drawn upon and they were loved and cared for to the end of their lives.

Dr. Lauren Ann Reynolds-Peterson and M. Bryce Peterson also lived long healthy lives. Ann never regained all of her memory, but it really didn't matter. They loved each other deeply until the very end and beyond. They will forever be the King and Queen of Romance.

Printed in the United States
By Bookmasters